"For Peelo

The Great Right Hope

by
Mark Jackman
(Book One of the Sid Tillsley Chronicles)

ISBN: 978-1-905091-42-3
Paperback version

© 2009
Published by LL-Publications, Scotland, UK
www.ll-publications.com

Cover by Helen E. H. Madden www.pixelarcana.com
© 2008 LL-Publications

The Great Right Hope is a work of fiction. The names, characters, and incidents are entirely the work of the author's imagination. Any resemblance to actual persons, living or dead, or events, is entirely coincidental.

All rights reserved. No part of this publication may be copied, transmitted, or recorded by any means whatsoever, including printing, photocopying, file transfer, or any form of data storage, mechanical or electronic, without the express written consent of the publisher. In addition, no part of this publication may be lent, re-sold, hired, or otherwise circulated or distributed, in any form whatsoever, without the express written consent of the publisher.

Acknowledgments

We would like to acknowledge several trademarks used with fair use within the "The Great Right Hope";

Esso
Esso Tiger
Esso Tiger Tokens
Dooley's
Warninks
Baileys
Ford cars
Ford Capri
Austin cars
Montego Estate

1

Ben Edric was in over his head. He breathed slowly and deeply, trying not to let on that he was verging on a panic attack. He consciously tried to slow his beating heart. He was convinced that the members of this council, sat around this vast table would hear his heartbeat thundering from his chest. A glowing orb, suspended high above, directed light to the edge of the group leaving all else engulfed in darkness, and it made him claustrophobic. He was a madman. Revenge was not worth this.

He forgot the danger at hand when a beautiful, slender woman stood up and took the floor. Flowing raven-black hair spilled over the shoulders of her black suit. She was immaculately dressed, although it was difficult to notice anything apart from her face. Unblemished pale skin encompassed high cheekbones, a small, perfect nose and luscious red lips. She appeared to be in her thirties, until he fell into her eyes. They were a vivid emerald green; stunning, yet there was something more to them. Looking into them, he could see something more sinister hidden beneath, like the thorns lurking beneath the petals of a rose. Deep into that unblinking stare he fell until everything else around him was...He snapped back into the room. That's how they got you.

"Last year, the total crop was twenty thousand and ninety-seven. That is twelve per cent over the quota we set the previous year." Her well-spoken English accent made her complete perfection. Her voice was as enchanting as her face, and he longed to hear her talk again. "This is slightly unexpected, but it did not prove to be a problem for—"

"I admit that the farming has been well calculated and the clean-up, as ever, has been carried out efficiently and professionally," said a hoarse voice from next to Ben, snapping him out of his trance. His heart was now racing for a different reason and he was glad that Charles Durrant interrupted the siren and brought him back to normality.

Charles was a portly man in his fifties, with thinning grey hair combed desperately over his balding scalp to give the impression of substance. Ben hated the way that he stared over the top of his small half-moon glasses. The fat pompous toad continued, "But, Lucia, twelve per cent over quota is the worst year we have had since records began. This, I think you will agree, is a problem or at least a cause for concern?"

Ben looked around at the other councillors nodding in agreement. His fear returned when he cast his eyes on a monster. But Lucia, the beautiful Lucia brought him back with her magical tones. He knew it was camouflage, but he didn't care. "What do you want us to do about it? Are we not doing enough?"

"The fact remains that over two thousand were taken unnecessarily," said Charles. "This puts a huge strain on our resources and incurs a huge cost, which eventually comes out of your pockets. It is in both our interests to deal with this now."

Lucia sighed. "There is no need to make a mountain out of a molehill. I have seen these events many times before."

"Because we have not seen these events in person, please do not think that we do not know of their occurrence. Our place on this group is well earned," said Caroline.

Ben could feel the tension mount, and it felt good. It felt like the attention was turned from him. Caroline was involved now and she was one hard-nosed bitch. She never wanted him on this council to start with. Now, a year later, he wished she had her way. She didn't look like she would say boo to a goose. The cream suit she wore contrasted starkly with her dark black skin. She looked almost motherly, yet he knew the truth. Surely, she struggled sleeping at night, with the decisions she made.

"No disrespect was intended, Caroline," said Lucia, "but this council should not blow matters out of proportion. The two sides have been at peace for hundreds of years. As a group, we have the expertise to deal with anything that is thrown at us."

"I would agree with you, Lucia," said Charles. "But that isn't all, is it?"

* * * *

That smell. That scent. It washes over him and engulfs him. Every sense shuts down in order to amplify that enchanting odour. Everything else is meaningless. He needs it. He wants it. He will kill for it. He hates to lose control, but he has no choice. These were the instincts he was born with. He cannot deny what he is.

* * * *

"No, Charles, you're right," said Lucia. "Augustus?" She looked over to where Augustus sat, lounging in one of the great chairs surrounding the table. "Now would be a good time to present the details of our population."

"Thank you, Lucia." Augustus sat up straight and yawned.

Ben felt jealousy rip his heart in two. *I fucking hate you*, he screamed from inside. His heart banged against his ribcage again. This meeting was an emotional roller coaster: fear, lust, hate, all in a minute. He slowly reached into his pocket for a pill that would take away his anxiety. He drew it out and popped it in his mouth. He was only thirty-two, but he needed them, especially now. He felt it take instant effect, but was he drawing attention to himself? He looked around, as far as the monster, but daren't look up to see if he held his gaze. Ben's shirt was saturated with sweat. They knew...they had to.

Ben tried to concentrate on Augustus. His shirt was open to half-way down his chest revealing bulging pectoral muscles, on which a large gold crucifix sat. He wore it to laugh in the face of every man and woman here. His blonde hair hung roughly in a ponytail down his back. He didn't even have to try to look good. Those sapphire blue eyes...Was that what she saw in him? *Was that why she did it?* Ben thought. *You are going to pay, you bastard!*

"One thousand, nine hundred and eighty-two was the registered count at the end of April. Our numbers have increased by 3.8 per cent over the last decade. The following figures are only an estimate, as we are not kept on a leash as some may wish. About a third of us are permanently based here in London, whilst half reside in the cities: Glasgow, Manchester, Belfast, Birmingham and Bristol.

"The remainder work in our industrial services such as Dover, for import/export, and Seal Sands, Middlesbrough, in our chemical sector. Two per cent of our permanent residents are either abroad or living the peaceful, nomadic life that nature intended us. How quaint," he mocked. "The nomads among us populate the Highlands and the North Yorkshire Moors. I hope that is sufficient information for you all." He slouched back into his chair. His arrogance was sickening.

"Thank you, Augustus," said Charles. "Can I please ask how the population densities match up with the farming statistics?"

"I can deal with this one, sir,"

Jeremy Pervis, you snivelling, arse-kissing snake. Ben hated Pervis. They were both raised to councillors at the same time, and Pervis had seen it as his duty to outdo him at every opportunity.

Pervis's clothes were expensive, yet they did not suit him. He looked awkward and nothing he did was natural. He was tall and gangly and struggled to control his limbs. Ben would have put his house on Pervis still living with his mother. His ginger hair was gelled back over his head. Strands broke free and he swept them back over his head in between nervously pushing his glasses up the bridge of his nose. For all his brains, he had no place here.

"Do not call me 'sir' at these meetings, Jeremy." Charles sighed. "We all stand equal here."

Ben pressed his lips together. *Stand fucking equal? Who are you trying to kid?*

"Yes, sir," Pervis said before turning to the others. "Good evening, ladies and gentlemen. I'll get straight to business, shall I? I have statistically analysed the data by combining the regional farming and the population density of the corresponding districts. Except one, each region is well within the acceptable limit, if I take into account the standard deviation of similar cultured societies across Europe." He smiled as he briefed the report from memory, but no-one smiled back. Ben smirked.

Loser.

"However, the farming rate for the northeast of England, Tyne and Wear, is abnormally high. It is still excessive, even if I combine data that—"

Caroline interrupted him. "Jeremy, could you please just give us the facts, dear boy?"

"But these are the facts, ma'am. I am merely—"

"Simplify the best you can."

Ben noticed the annoyance in her voice, and for the first time in weeks, he actually smiled.

"As you wish," Pervis managed dejectedly.

"Overall, where was the farming carried out?"

"Nationally, five per cent of all crops were harvested through the Prison Justice Programme."

Ben loved that one. Sure, a few criminals were wiped out, but how many innocent victims were killed when the executioners became a little too enthusiastic?

"As for the Judicial Programme recently introduced, it has accounted for approximately forty-two per cent of the harvest this year. Known rapists, paedophiles, drug dealers, pimps and prostitutes were taken from the streets. Some key figures in organised crime have met an untimely and also rather grizzly end.

"Thirty per cent were harvested in the Euthanasia Project, which incidentally saved the National Health Service thirty-four million pounds. Our contacts in Parliament were delighted. The discreteness of the clean-up operations carried out by Sanderson has meant that no untoward questions were asked. Another fantastic job, sir."

Sanderson ignored him entirely. He was a soldier who hated the little office-jockey as much as Ben did.

"Twenty-three per cent were unplanned, unsanctioned murders. Although this figure is high, it remains within the confidence limits considering the economic and demographic factors. However, this is where the northeast of England raises alarm bells." Jeremy offered the floor. "Sanderson?"

Sanderson stood up. A tall man in his forties, grey streaked the sides of his short brown hair. He was a handsome man who was casually well dressed, but his face did not suit his relaxed appearance. Ben could see the lines of worry were heavily etched on his forehead, and you could understand why. The horror that this man witnessed, every day...

Ben felt safe when Sanderson was around, but a thousand Sandersons would not help him here, not if they knew.

"I've been in the team for twenty-five years and this is the most stretched we have ever been. It's not just the number of incidents that we have had to deal with; the ferocity of the attacks which have happened, regular as clockwork in the Northeast, have been sickening. I have had to move my office to Newcastle to help and I have been doing jobs that new recruits should be doing. That thirty-four mill saved on health care has not even scratched the surface of the extra finances that we have had to call upon." He did not share his colleague's well-spoken accent as he was raised in a rougher part of town.

"More officers have been recruited, and that is a task which is never easy. Kids have got no balls any more, and if they have, then they've got no fucking brains. If it keeps going like this then we're fucked!" Sanderson wore his heart on his sleeve and didn't even try to put an act on in front of his fellow councillors.

"In an attempt to cover up the savagery, we've had to make most of the victims look like goddamn burn victims. Some of the things I have seen over the last year…"

Ben tried not to think of the Hell that Sanderson witnessed every single day.

* * * *

Others resisted. Others were stronger willed. Others looked down on him for his urges. He could rip them all apart without breaking into a sweat. How dare they judge him? This was what he was. This hunger. It would be the end of him. That smell. The beautiful scent that she produced. It was her fault. He was powerless. He must destroy and then he must devour.

* * * *

"Is there a pattern to all this?" asked Lucia.

"None," barked Sanderson. "None that we could determine, anyway. The only pattern is that everyone is ripped apart. I have seen men, women, children and even the goddamn family dog ripped to shreds." The tension was getting to him and the veins of his neck protruded with the pressure. Ben hoped he didn't look the same. "It's a fucking war zone up there."

"Have the hunters been involved with the Northeast at all?" asked Charles. "Augustus, I believe you have a report on their activity?"

"Yes, Charles. The number of hunters is at an all-time low, which is good news, depending on your point of view."

Ben's blood boiled as Augustus chuckled to his own joke. *We'll see how fucking funny you find it!*

"We believe that we have had seven losses this year. Three were almost certainly killed by the hunters."

"Three?" asked Charles. "Is that all? Have they given up?"

"It is still a tragedy," piped up a feminine voice.

Once again, Ben was lost in the eyes of a female. Veronique Aimee, her blonde curls...

"If a lamia is too weak or too foolish that they allow themselves to be killed by a mortal, then they have no place on the Earth. They deserve to die."

The interruption came from the monster, a giant with heaving shoulders and a neck as thick as a man's leg. His elbows were on the table, with his chin resting on his giant fists. Tribal tattoos ran up the back of his neck to the top of his completely shaven skull. Ben didn't dare to look into his eyes. Looking into his eyes was not like looking into the eyes of his brethren. Michael Vitrago was a lion amongst wolves. He was a vampire who would put the fear into God himself.

Ben was sent from Heaven to Hell, just by the sound of his voice. The world dropped from under him. He wanted to empty his stomach. He wanted to lose consciousness and never wake. Why did he come here? Why didn't he run? Revenge wasn't worth this.

* * * *

He was close. He tracked her down with ease. From a mile away he could have pointed to her with his eyes closed. He walked past others, but he was already captivated. He already had his target. He let the warm summer's night breeze wash over him, giving him pulses of the captivating essence that drove him wild. He had to feed.

* * * *

"Who was lost?" asked Charles.

"Viktor Kretzig was taken, in London, by Jonathan Russle, who died performing the task. Elizabeth Gray, from Whitby. She was taken in her sleep by Donald McSteel, who…" Augustus let out a small laugh. "Died earlier in the year, ironically from skin cancer."

Keep laughing. Ben grimaced. *We'll see how long you fucking laugh for.*

"Finally, Steven Windmar, killed in Newcastle, whilst working in the chemical sector. We believe Reece Chambers was responsible for this. He is someone we would like to get hold of."

Don't worry, you'll see him soon enough, Augustus. Ben suppressed a smile.

"We believe he is currently residing in the northeast of England. It cannot be coincidence that takes him there. We know very little of this man. There are no records of him even existing until he graduated from Oxford. He is nothing compared to the hunters of yesteryear, but he has operated for well over a decade and has eluded us at every step."

"I think that we should make every effort to get rid of this man," ventured Charles. "Every year brings thousands of extra surveillance cameras into the country. We have enough to conceal without having some bloody idiot running around on a personal vendetta."

"Let the man get on with it, is what I say," spat Sanderson.

"And please tell us why you think he should continue murdering us?" hissed Lucia.

Ben regained his composure. He had cowered like a rabbit in the headlights when he heard Vitrago's deep voice. Sanderson would hopefully take the heat off him.

"Perhaps Chambers may have a fucking go at finding out what's causing the atrocities up there? Maybe he'll have a go at ending the merciless mutilation of whole fucking families, of children, of babies, of fucking pregnant mothers!"

"That's enough, Sanderson!" Caroline shouted. "We have had enough profanities from you for one evening, thank you. This is a place for impartiality, and you should know that more than anyone."

Sanderson continued unabashed. "Whatever's out there isn't normal. We haven't seen anything like this before. What I have seen in the last two years..." He paused before turning his gaze on Vitrago. "What is out there?"

Ben couldn't believe his eyes. This man had balls of steel, yet Michael ignored him.

"What the fuck is out there!" he screamed, before standing up and smashing his fist into the table.

"Sanderson!" yelled Caroline. "Control yourself!"

Sanderson fell into his seat shaking. He had punched the table so hard that he had cut his knuckles.

"Go and sort yourself out," she growled under her breath.

He staggered to the edge of the hall with the weight of the world upon him. A slit of light appeared on the wall and then expanded, revealing the dark stone corridor beyond. Sanderson walked through the light and darkness immediately closed in on him. How Ben wished he could have gone with him.

* * * *

He knocked pedestrians aside as he went. The quickest way was a straight line, and he paid no heed to the bodies that stood in his path. No-one dared say a word. They could sense the hunger that fuelled the beast inside and it terrified them. A beauty waited for him, and he couldn't get there quick enough. She had no idea what was going to hit her. There was no way she could prepare for him. His dominance would be absolute.

* * * *

"I must apologise, members of the council," Caroline began. "I did not realise that the stress of the situation had affected Sanderson so greatly. I apologise, Michael. He will beg for forgiveness as soon as he is of sound mind."

Michael smiled. "Caroline, you need not apologise. I forgive our colleague, entirely. He blames me because I am the easiest person to blame. I am the one with the history, which will never be forgotten. However, that was a different age, a savage age. We should not dwell on the past. There is business to attend."

Ben stared into the table, praying that he didn't mean him.

"The Northeast needs investigating," said Caroline, "There is no doubt that something is happening in the area that is out of our immediate control. I suggest that we set up teams from both parties to research the situation."

"Agreed," finalised Michael.

"Sanderson would be my first choice, but I believe the dear fellow could use a holiday. Pervis, you will assist in the matter."

"I would be honoured to take on the assignment, ma'am." Pervis smiled smugly at Ben, who, for once, didn't care.

"Good. Which vampire will reciprocate?"

Michael answered without a pause. "I'll inform Franco Stoloni of his new role."

"Very well, I believe we have dealt with everything on the agenda. Is there any other business?" Caroline waited for a shake of the head from each councillor. Ben tried to look as confident as possible when it came to his turn. "Meeting adjourned."

Ben breathed a sigh of relief. One more meeting, one dangerous meeting, and then one-way tickets to Tahiti were the order of the day.

* * * *

In front of him is the object of his desire. His nose is saturated with the smell, but now other senses compete with the overpowering scent. He can't take his eyes away. Everything he expected from that heavenly fragrance fills his vision. Not an ounce of disappointment enters his mind. He wishes to touch, to feel the delicate shape in his strong, powerful fingers. He wants to taste. He wants to completely annihilate. It is too much. He cannot control the animal inside him.

* * * *

Ben gathered as many of his possessions as he dared. Time was of the essence. Once he was out of this damned building, he at least had a chance. He filled his briefcase with papers, vital papers that, if he did find himself in a sticky situation, would be good material for negotiation. He was done. The only personal item he left was the photo of a beautiful woman. She smiled back at him, as if butter would not melt in her mouth.

"You fucking whore!"

He threw the picture with all his might at the wall, resulting in the satisfying breaking of glass.

"Temper, temper."

Ben's life flashed before his eyes.

* * * *

She turns. She is startled, not expecting him. He smiles. There would be nothing left. There would be nothing to find once he had finished. He would decimate, and she knew it. She knew what he was. She had heard the legends. She knew his hunger could not be satisfied.

"W-w-what do you want?"

As if she didn't know.

* * * *

"Michael, what brings you here?" asked Ben, trying to stay calm when his basic instincts screamed at him to run and hide.

"Going somewhere?"

"No, just taking a few things back home with me, that's all."

Michael didn't say a word. He walked over to the broken photo frame and picked out the picture of Ben's ex-girlfriend. "She's very pretty. I can see why you're...upset."

Ben couldn't deny his rage, not after Michael had witnessed his outburst. He tried to bluff instead. "With my best friend, who wouldn't be?"

"I didn't realise that you and Augustus were so close."

Ben's knees buckled beneath him, but he kept his feet.

The massive vampire walked around Ben's desk and took a seat on his comfortable desk chair and poured himself a whisky from a crystal decanter.

"I know why I am not trusted; I am Michael Vitrago, or as I was named, 'The Bloodlord.' That's why people suspect me of the massacres that are causing the upheaval in the Northeast. Three-hundred years ago, it would have been me causing the destruction. Three-hundred years ago, rivers of blood flowed and the carnage was wondrous. How things have changed. Even the wildest animals can be tamed and now I am a simple bureaucrat, a politician." He takes a sip before continuing.

"It is a common saying: move with the times. It affects humans in their business, fashion, and everyday life. For us, who are here for millennia, this saying is life or death. If we do not adapt then we bring attention to ourselves. If we bring attention to ourselves then we die. You are our food and that will not change. We cannot survive without you, but you can survive without us. If a war broke out between the species, I could foresee no other alternative but mankind's victory. Your numbers are too great and modern-day weaponry is too advanced, although nothing compares to the power daylight gives you."

Finishing his whisky, Michael poured himself another.

"Can you imagine the losses? Can you imagine the firepower needed to bring a lamia like myself down? However, the human loss of life would be insignificant compared to the scientific and cultural demise that you would suffer. Where would the human race be now if vampires did not walk among you? Would humans have walked on the moon? Would humans have discovered that the Earth revolves around the sun? Can you imagine facing the next millennium alone, without thousands of years of knowledge to guide you?

"The Agreement that was made between vampires and humans, two hundred and eighty-four years ago must be upheld. If it is not, then the consequences will be catastrophic. Do you think that I would imprison the animal inside me for three-hundred years just because I wanted to save your pitiful lives? Do you think I would deny my instincts and sit on this council, the so-called *Coalition*, with you monkeys, as equals, because of my love of mankind? The only reason I uphold the Agreement is because the vampire needs it to survive." The whisky tumbler shattered in Michael's hand. All Ben could hope for now was a quick death.

"Whatever is causing this upheaval in the Northeast must be reigned in immediately. It has the potential to destroy everything. The sole purpose of the Coalition is to vigilantly uphold the Agreement. The vampire has disappeared into the shadows. Our kills are sanctioned, arranged. We were born to kill you and now we are on the end of a leash, and that leash keeps us alive. Do you really think that I will let you try and break it because of a filthy wench who lusted after a vampire, a God compared to your worthless flesh?"

Michael got to his feet and advanced towards the terrified human.

"I...I...wasn't going to..."

"What insults me is that you even tried. Did you not think that we would know? We know everything about you. You are our puppet. You are my puppet, but the strings are now broken. We know you were going to tell Reece Chambers all he needed to know about Augustus's movements so that he could kill him. He fucked your wife and she begged him for it. You were willing to destroy us all because of it. You have allowed your personal feelings to come in the way of your job. You are the first human councillor to make this mistake since the Agreement was formed. It is lucky that we intercepted the information you tried to send. It is lucky that the information in your briefcase did not reach the public eye. If it did, your end would have been...more interesting. Still, it would be wrong not to set an example."

With one hand, Michael grabbed Ben by the collar and lifted him off his feet. Ben had avoided staring into the eyes of the monster for the entire meeting, but now he had no choice and stared into the eyes of Death, itself.

"Please, please make it quick!" Ben sunk to his knees. A merciful death was all he could wish for.

Michael laughed. The wish would not be granted.

* * * *

It was time to take what he desired.

"What do you want?"

"Donner kebab, please, flower. Make it extra, extra large too."

"Extra, extra large?" The girl set about her wares to fulfil his desire. "I knew you were hungry, like. I could hear your belly rumbling from half way down road. You want chilli sauce, our Sid?"

"Aye, pet, lots of it. Hold the salad."

2

He kicked open the door and stood in the doorway, silhouetted against the moonlight. A howling wind whipped snow into the log cabin. A child playing in front of the fire screamed when she saw him and a middle-aged man ran through from an adjoining room to check on his daughter. The father yelled, but his cries fell on deaf ears. Bloodlust had devoured the senses.

In a moment he crossed the room and picked the man up by the throat so that his feet dangled six inches from the floor. He sunk his teeth deep into the neck of the struggling victim. Blood sprayed onto his face and gushed down his throat, satisfying his thirst; the pure pleasure of it, every molecule of his body emanated life. These mortals could never experience such a feeling. Sex? Love? This was everything.

He let the limp body drop to the floor, and the senses returned with the wailing of the young girl who sat hugging her dead father. Her cries ceased the instant he snapped her neck. She wouldn't have felt a thing. Not that he cared. He was simply tired of the noise.

* * * *

He held the human's throat in a vice-like grip. Eyes looked back at him with the utmost calm. No fear. No panic. No hatred.

"You bastard. Your mother should never have dropped you from her putrid womb. Look what you are. You are nothing, and you have taken everything from me. I hate you." His voice matched the human's gaze, utter calm. Rage had subsided. Nothing that he could do to this man could possibly match the debt that the man owed him.

He tore the human's throat out and watched as his eyes glazed over. The human's pain was a moment. This pain, however, would burn for centuries. This would hurt until the very end.

Gunnar awoke in a cold sweat. Those two events had haunted his dreams often of late. That log cabin had saved his life. He had been trapped in an avalanche in Canada, starved of blood for weeks on end. A tragedy if he had died that way—Gunnar Ivansey, killed by a snowball. He laughed at the absurdity of it all. It had taken weeks to tunnel out of that drift, and then it had seemed like an eternity as he wandered around in a daze. Stumbling across that cabin had been pure luck. Blood had never tasted so good. The other dream…it was hard to put aside such utter despair.

He got out of the gigantic bed where he had slept. The room was pitch black but he could see perfectly. There was only one door to this secret room and he closed it behind him when he exited, climbing the stairs into a massive hallway that was grand and extravagant. Gunnar noted the time on the grandfather clock that stood next to the huge oak front doors: quarter past eleven. He really was bad at keeping time.

In the equally grand bathroom he ran water in the sink so hot that it was almost boiling. He lathered soap between his hands and applied it across his face before shaving with a cut-throat razor. Satisfied that not a trace of stubble remained on his face or head, he entered the shower cubicle that occupied a corner of the room. Gold water jets were aligned at every possible angle and water exploded from every corner. He spent thirty minutes meticulously cleaning himself before turning off the taps and drying naturally.

He left the bathroom and walked through to the next room. An entire wall was a mirror. To each side of the room stood open wardrobes that contained suits and shirts of every fabric and hue. He picked out an outfit with no hesitancy and dressed quickly, but impeccably.

Gunnar admired himself in the mirror for several minutes before turning on his heels and heading for his enormous underground garage, which contained dozens of different cars. He looked longingly at a black Porsche GT3. He should really drive a more inconspicuous vehicle to tonight's destination.

"Fuck it."

The garage opened automatically and Gunnar raced the Porsche up the ramp and out onto the driveway.

It was a significant distance to the front gates, which opened automatically. He didn't have to slow down to pass onto the country road. Once on it, he raced through the twisting roads like a rally driver. Driving was a love of his, and speed was the only thing in this modern age that held his attention.

He was ten miles from Newcastle City Centre and it was time to meet an old friend. Ricard was the complete opposite to Gunnar. He was one of the major contributors to the formation of the Agreement and he was certainly not a vampire of modern technology. Gunnar had taken him out in his Aston Martin DB5 in the 1960s and even that amazing machine didn't impress the old fool. *"We have an eternity to travel the corners of the world and we have an infinite number of things to observe and behold. If we travel at one hundred miles an hour we will miss everything."*

They say opposites attract, and that was the only explanation for their close friendship. Ricard was at least three thousand years old and had been a keen politician and an influential thinker from a young age. He was a true gentleman, and a scholar of unprecedented intellect. However, the two fervently disagreed on the status of mankind. He treated humans with respect and with a kindness that disgusted Gunnar.

Ricard was a wiser vampire than he, and certainly a better creature. Nevertheless, this would certainly lead to his eventual downfall. Respect humans? If they knew of us, would they show us the same courtesy? Gunnar reached the city centre. Tonight he would meet with others of his kind. He would relax, unwind and talk to his heart's content throughout the night and safely through the day if the need presented itself.

He arrived at his destination, Rapunzel's Nightclub. It was full of human vermin who entertained themselves by drinking, fucking and fighting; seemingly all that they could manage with their brief spell on this Earth. How could Ricard hold any feelings for this race as a whole?

The door to the club's underground garage opened as he drew near. He drove through the dimly lit parking lot, full of vintage and high-priced motor vehicles. Was one of them Ricard's? Had he finally invested an insignificant portion of his immense wealth in a car? He laughed again at Ricard's disdain for speed, although on some occasions the old goat was right. Gunnar could remember, all too well, the look on the paramedic's face before his death. It was not in their basic training to deal with car crash victims that could walk and talk with half a windscreen protruding from their heart.

Gunnar parked the car and climbed the stairs situated in the centre of the garage. At the top of the stairs was an imposing black door. There was no visible handle, but it opened slowly as Gunnar approached it. Music poured through as the door opened and heavy bass boomed off the lilac coloured walls beyond.

A giant of a doorman stood on the other side of the entrance, approximately six-foot ten and twenty-five stone of muscle. His hair had receded due to steroid abuse and a large scar tracked its way from his left ear, down his face and across his throat. He stood in front of a short staircase that led to a similar door to the one Gunnar had just passed.

Further down the hallway, Gunnar could see humans dancing, drinking and making utter fools of themselves; taking for granted what little time they had on the Earth and intoxicating themselves into an early grave. They deserved to die. He paid the doorman no heed and started to climb the stairs. A huge arm barred his path.

"Where do you think you are going, son?"

Gunnar halted but didn't look at the giant. "Move your arm and never bother me again." He spoke to the bouncer as if he was the lowest form of life on the planet. To Gunnar Ivansey, he was just that.

"Who the fuck do you think you are, you little prick?" yelled the doorman as steroid-induced rage raced through his bloodstream. "Do you know who the fuck I am?"

Some partygoers from further up the hall had noticed the commotion and the added attention fuelled the giant's anger.

"Has Richmond not told you that all guests who enter through the garage door can use the facilities at their leisure?" Gunnar didn't give the bouncer as much as a glance.

The bouncer made to grab Gunnar by the coat, but curled up into a ball instead. Gunnar had struck him, like lightning, in the solar plexus. The doorman struggled for breath on the floor and turned a shade of blue through lack of oxygen. If it wasn't for a night club full of people in the next room, Gunnar would have tortured the imbecile.

He continued up the stairs and, again, the door at the top opened automatically. A fire roared inside, radiating a tremendous amount of heat. It was the only source of light, but lit the room beautifully. Strewn around the room were tapestries, paintings and sculptures from the last two millennia. A bar was set up on the far wall containing whiskies and brandies, centuries old. The decorator of this room certainly appreciated the finer things in life; massive, comfortable armchairs were placed around the room and a small table accompanied each chair, which held a selection of fine cigars. In an armchair nearest the fire sat Ricard.

"Ricard!"

Ricard turned from the fire. "Good evening, Gunnar," he said affectionately. Ricard showed a very slight receding of his hairline, and his thick black hair was streaked with grey at the wings. His face was lined and he would appear to be a man in his fifties if it was not for his ageless green eyes. Although he looked aged for a vampire, he was still incredibly handsome. He was of medium build, and Gunnar's hand completely encompassed his as he shook it warmly.

"Was one of the motor vehicles in the car park yours?" Gunnar asked with a grin as he poured himself a brandy.

"It may surprise you to know that one of them was mine. I purchased a hybrid motor-vehicle that is economical, and thus the least polluting of your favoured smog-wagons."

Gunnar laughed. "Smog-wagons? I have never heard them called that before. But, at least you have realised that they are a necessity in this modern age. Who knows, you may even enjoy driving one day?"

"I will have a suntan first."

"How are you feeling, Ricard? Three thousand years must be taking its toll by now? Surely those knees can't take more than a brisk walk?"

Ricard laughed at the jest. "I feel the same as I did two thousand years ago, but as you know I have never been the most athletic of our kind. I was born to use my head, dear boy, and if the need arises, rent muscle-for-hire like you. How about you? How are your knees?"

"I feel like my body gets stronger every day, I really do, but…" He rubbed his hands awkwardly over his shaven scalp, "my head does not hold the same strength, no matter how hard I try." Gunnar trembled with emotion as he finished the sentence.

"What's bothering you?"

"Dreams," said Gunnar as he stared wistfully into his brandy.

"Dreams of your mother?"

Gunnar looked up from the glass.

"That obvious?"

Ricard smiled sympathetically.

"Bah! Five hundred years ago. What is the point of hating yourself over the death of a low-life whore!" spat Gunnar through gritted teeth. "She deserved everything that happened to her, Ricard, everything."

Gunnar's mother was executed in 1503, beheaded after a trial by the Lamian Consilium. Her crime was to fall in love and have sexual relations with a human, punishable by death at that time. A powerful vampire-hunter had slain his father a century previous so his mother's death left Gunnar an orphan.

"She left me for him, a mortal. How can I forgive her? And how can I forgive them?" Five hundred years. When would the guilt end? He remembered looking into the human's eyes, remembered his fingers tightening around his throat and slowly, so slowly, tearing out his windpipe. The thrill of killing was not present that day. He was just doing what had to be done.

"Love, Gunnar. Love is a more powerful entity than our entire race combined," Ricard said as he remembered his own pains and his own suffering.

"Fuck you, Ricard! What love do we have that is not taken from us? How many years of happiness can be ruined in one night? How can you sit there so calm and so fucking righteous?" Gunnar punched the wall, shaking the room, and leaving three knuckle marks in the solid concrete.

"We are all different, Gunnar. Your heart has ruled you since the day I met you. I, however, have always been ruled by this." Ricard tapped his head. "I admire your fire and I admire your spirit, but Gunnar, you are in danger of burning yourself out. There is not room in your life for the pain that you desperately hold on to. You punish yourself and the humans for the death of your mother."

Gunnar sank to his knees with tears streaming down his face. "It's over five hundred years since I took my mother in for trial. Five hundred years of utter guilt. Humans killed my father, and then my mother took one into her arms, into her bed! I hate her! She was all I had."

Ricard had been through this on numerous occasions. So much rage controlled this young vampire's life. Nevertheless, that was what made him so powerful. He was a good ally to have fighting in your corner and no politics ruled his head. Ricard poured another brandy and placed it next to Gunnar's armchair. The vampire stopped his sobbing in an instant, picked up the brandy, and drained the significant measure.

"Thank you, Ricard. You have been a father figure to me for nearly half a millennium. I am sorry I spoke out of turn."

"Don't be silly, dear boy. I have heard far worse profanities in my three thousand years, and from people for whom I felt a lot less love."

Gunnar snapped back from his sorrow. He had tried for the past five hundred years to shake his rage and to rid himself of his hate and guilt, but he couldn't. Instead, he pushed it to the back of his consciousness where it gnawed away at his soul.

"So, my learned companion, what news do you have from our great species and our dealings with your beloved humans?" The question was asked with no outward sign of the breakdown he had suffered.

"Gunnar Ivansey, concerned with the dealings of the Coalition? That surely is a first," said the older vampire, genuinely surprised.

"I probably should keep up to date on council matters. I do not want to get hit by any more bolts from the blue, such as the extortionate tax on killing our own food."

"That is an absolute necessity. It may be expensive and an inconvenience, but with modern day surveillance it has become an absolute must. Especially with predators out there like your good self."

The comment was not greeted with a smile and the subject was left alone. "Any other notes of interest then?" Gunnar asked brusquely.

"Not particularly," said Ricard, ignoring the younger vampire's tone. "There has been a sharp rise in the number of humans killed in this region over the last year, and they were killed in a rather gruesome manner." He paused.

Gunnar sensed what the older vampire was getting at and raised his hands in defence. "It has nothing, whatsoever, to do with me. I can't believe you would suspect me of such a foul deed in the first place!" he proclaimed with mock innocence. "And what of you? What does our great and wise Lamian Consilium have for you to occupy your time with of late?"

"Oh, this and that. I am too old for political games, especially with those that affect mankind and not just our own conduct. I am there to offer my advice when it is needed. I do not lust for power for myself or for our people. I wish for harmony between the species, although I accept that this harmony cannot be absolute. Michael still rules the Coalition and the Lamian Consilium with an iron fist. I do not think that he could do it any other way."

"Michael Vitrago," Gunnar mused. "Now that is someone that would put fear into the Creator himself. Gabriel and I followed him for decades, possibly the best decades of my life. Let's hope he regains his senses one day."

"It will be a dark day for the world if he does," said Ricard, forebodingly.

The door to the study opened and Richmond entered the room with a beaming smile for his guests. As always, he was elaborately dressed, and wore an immense, white fur coat, which covered his broad muscular shoulders. A matching white fur top hat held in his long dreadlocks.

"Hey there, boys!"

No-one could dislike the massive African. The first impression that Richmond gave was that he was the epitome of happiness. That first impression was the right one. Moods were eased wherever he went, by the presence he possessed.

The two vampires stood up to greet their host with warm embraces. Nightclubs: the perfect business for Richmond. He didn't need to work as, like most vampires, he had amassed great wealth over the centuries. In this room alone, he had enough priceless historical artefacts to live a life of luxury. Richmond was in the business purely for the enjoyment of it all. He owned nightclubs, all over the world, and each club had a room similar to the one where they now sat. In each country, he would entertain his guests with the utmost hospitality.

It was possible that he didn't have an enemy in the vampire world. If he were human, things would be different as some would hate him because of his African origin. Vampires were different and there was no sexism, racism or any discrimination at all. The main divide was due to human-vampire relations and, with all species, the lust for power.

"My friends, how has it been, apart from the terrible weather?" Richmond complained about the weather whenever he travelled outside of the West Indies, the place he adopted as home.

"Where to start, Richmond, where to start?" posed Ricard. "It has certainly been lacking a certain something without you around for the past twenty years. I'm sure you are up-to-date with the Coalition's dealings?" Ricard considered his question. "Or perhaps the marijuana and Jamaican rum have created adequate diversions?"

Richmond let out a deep bellowing laugh. "I think you know me a little too well."

"It has been a strange twenty years," said Ricard. "The technological advancement of the age means that life has changed considerably, in the blinking of the eye. The rate of change also increases. I cannot predict where we will be in twenty years' time. Nevertheless, I am still me. I watch with interest as events unfold, but I still look further into the past in an attempt to answer questions of the future."

"I've driven some fucking fast cars," laughed Gunnar.

"And I've ridden some fucking fast women," bellowed Richmond.

Richmond loved women and whether it was a lamia, or a human, it mattered not. If a woman was beautiful then he would pursue her.

Sex was a strange thing in the vampire world, and a large proportion of the race was asexual. Most would never have sex of any kind throughout their entire existence because reproduction was not a straightforward affair. The oldest living vampire was five thousand years old and had the appearance of an eighty-year old man. There was no biological urge to procreate.

Procreation did take place, but it was not as simple as in humans. A male seed was required for the female egg, but what made it different was that huge amounts of the male's blood had to be ingested by the female. Throughout history, this had often led to the male's demise and was a natural deterrent. The process kept the vampire population to a relatively low number when compared to their prey.

Sleeping with a human was once punishable by death, which was the crime Gunnar's mother committed. In this modern age, there were no constrictions as conception had been proven impossible. However, if a vampire of either sex forced intercourse on a man, woman or child, then it was best practice to kill whatever was wronged. Vampire DNA samples would create interesting problems down the line. This was another reason why the Agreement couldn't stand without the efforts of Sanderson's team.

"So then, although the world changes around us," continued Richmond, "the three dinosaurs in this room do not." He raised his glass and his companions followed suit.

The night continued into the morning and well into the daylight hours. Ricard and Gunnar would enjoy the hospitality of their host until the safety of night time returned. That would bring a reunion of a different sort. For Gunnar would be reunited with his closest friend and, for mankind, his most dangerous ally.

3

"You see, Sid," said Brian, "if you flash your headlights at another car five times, it means you want to go over and take a look at the action—" He was cut off as nearly half a pint of best bitter hit him in the face.

Sid wiped his chin and attempted to regain his senses. "If you want a shag, why the Hell would you want to watch some other bugger doing it?"

Brian, who considered himself a man of the world, sighed and mopped the beer from his face with a handkerchief. "Sid, my old pal, everyone has different tastes. Some people out there love others watching them, whilst some just want to watch other people doing it. It's a funny old world out there, mate. Just think about what some of them Germans get up to!"

Sid took a moment to consider this. He had absolutely no idea at all what the Germans might get up to, apart from invading places. No German was invading Sid Tillsley!

"My uncle was a Dambuster, Brian, and I ain't having one of *them lot* watching me!" Suspicion dawned on big Sid Tillsley. "Have you been up there watching *them lot*."

Sid was the most homophobic man in the North, which technically made him the most homophobic man in the universe. Sid's homophobia didn't extend any further than the male half of the species. Lesbians were OK with Sid; he didn't really know what they did. He just assumed that they watched a lot of soaps together and had double the cleaning power of most households. Male homosexuals, however, were a different story entirely. It was a genuine fear that affected his every move.

Sid had never flown in his life and not for fear of flying. Sid was scared of very little, but was petrified of air stewards. He had heard rumours of these *men*. Men who wore make-up, paraded around in aprons and talked in strange lady ways. This alone was enough to keep him out of the air and stop Sid Tillsley from ever going *international*.

Sid was worried that Brian may have applied for a vacancy as an air steward. He was worried that his friend of many years may have well been watching *them lot* or worse. He could have been doing German stuff!

Brian Garforth was an intelligent man. He was considered by many to be the most educated man on the Smithson Estate, home of the fine drinking establishment, The Miner's Arms, where the two friends now sat. After all, he was the only man on the Smithson Estate who worked in *the city*, and managed a small team of cleaners in Middlesbrough Hospital. Brian, being the academic that he was, had sensed Sid's fear.

"No, Sid," said Brian with caution. "No, Sid, I haven't." Brian paused to allow the words to sink into his friend's large but slow brain. "You know that Janice who works in chippy up on Charleston Street?"

Sid nodded, still sporting a suspicious glint in his eye.

"Well her hubby, Charlie, has been getting into it apparently."

Sid's gay defence system roared into action.

"Charlie? He's been up there with them—them Germans?" The activation of Sid's gay defence caused other bodily functions to shut down, especially thinking. It was similar to when Captain Kirk diverted all of the Starship Enterprise's power to the front shields and weakened other parts of the ship (although Sid always kept rear shields at maximum power).

"No, Sid," reassured Brian, ignoring the comments about the Germans. He knew what his friend was like when he was on Pink Alert. "I heard that he goes up there on Wednesdays and Fridays to meet ladies, which I confirmed at a later date."

"How?"

"Well, after hearing he was out Wednesdays and Fridays, I started going round and servicing Janice."

Suspicion finally drained from Sid's face. Mastery of the spoken word enabled Brian to reassure his homophobic friend that he was batting for the correct side by recounting a story of a heterosexual encounter with a woman, not a man. He was indeed the smartest man on the Smithson Estate, and also one of its biggest lady-killers.

Brian breathed a sigh of relief. He was glad that the big man had believed him about Janice. It was a true story, but Sid was not a man to upset. Six-foot five with shoulders that were still out of proportion to his height, he was built like a silverback gorilla, albeit an obese one, whose days of tree-swinging were well and truly behind him. On top of the shoulders sat his big, bald head where not a single hair had survived the storm of male pattern baldness. A five o'clock shadow covered Sid's face and ran down his neck to join the thick black curly hair that carpeted his chest. A nose that appeared to have been broken at least a dozen times split two dark, beady eyes. His thin lips covered a set of yellow teeth that could only be obtained by years of hard smoking. Technically he owned a neck, but only taking an x-ray would prove it. Thick rolls of fat sat on the tops of his shoulders and rose to just under his ears, the type that doormen collected over the years. In doormen this indicates rank; the more rolls of fat at the back of their necks, the higher the rank. This was not the case with Sid. Sid was a fat bastard.

Sid's attire for the evening consisted of a black leather jacket that was made from at least four cows, accompanied with a pair of skin-tight blue denim jeans. Under the jacket, Sid was wearing a faded Esso Tiger Token T-shirt. In his younger days, he wore the combination to try to look like the Fonz. Alas,

The Great Right Hope

Father Time had not been kind, and Mother Nature was a bit of a bitch in the first place.

In the top pocket of Sid's jacket was a packet of "El Sphinxo" Egyptian cigarettes. Four hundred he now owned, and all he had to do was help local Egyptian entrepreneur, Anhur Jahari, move a tonne of sand from Seal Sands beach to his warehouse in Stockton for the get-rich-quick venture of selling genuine Sphinx rubble. Sid loved smoking. He both metaphorically and literally died for it. He was the definition of a chain-smoker. His brand: anything cheap. In the last decade, he had paid zero tax to the government for cigarette duty. Every cigarette that had passed through his lungs had been ripped off or smuggled in from abroad.

"So," started Sid, all fear of Brian's homosexuality having subsided. "Are you thinking of going to get some action from some of those dirty lasses then?"

Brian shook his head. "Nah, I'm seeing Janice two nights a week, and then there's Maureen from deli at Morrisons. Oh yeah, I've just started seeing that Karen who works in The Duke's Head, as well."

"Karen?"

"You know...that bottle-blonde lass with the limp who works behind bar. Works with her tits out on weekends," said Brian matter-of-factly. "Anyway, I can't be doing with any more ladies at the moment. Too many names to remember."

"Bloody hell, mon! Three on the go!" said Sid flabbergasted. "So this doggin' lark, then, you just go out, pick a lass and start a shaggin'?"

"Well it ain't quite that simple, like. Dogging has been all over the news lately, but you still have to make sure you are in the right place, at the right time. You can't just whip out the old man in Tesco's car park. It normally takes place in nature reserve car-parks and lay-bys. Oh, and the coppers are trying to knock it on the head. You can get banged up for it, like."

"Sound complicated, mon. So, why are you telling me about this doggin' lark then?"

Brian hesitated. It had finally come to the crunch and it was time to tell his good friend the real reason he had brought up this particularly sordid topic of conversation. He didn't want to upset the big fella, and not just because of his fearsome reputation of handing out swift, right-hand justice; Sid was his best friend. "Well, Sid, you haven't been doing too well with the ladies of late, have you?"

"What do you mean? I split up from that lass not too long ago," he said defensively.

"That was over a year ago now, fella, and Gladys, well, she wasn't exactly Middlesbrough's finest now, was she?"

Brian could see the big man reminiscing over Gladys and her feminine wiles…and it didn't bear thinking about. He couldn't comprehend how a man could become physically or emotionally attached to a sixty-two year-old retired prison guard whose party trick was extinguishing cigarettes on her nipples.

Sid grinned. "Any port in a storm, you know that." Although everybody knew that he would rather die than risk docking in Greece.

"Well anyway, I thought that maybe a good-looking, young go-getter like you may not have time in his busy schedule for meeting ladies. I thought that a bit of no-strings fun would be right up your alley. What do you say?"

Brian was one of Middlesbrough's finest and most successful ladies' men. He had lost his virginity at the age of thirteen to a thirty-five year-old lap-dancer. He was now forty-five and had not stopped shagging since. Short and fat-skinny (an unappealing combination of skinny limbs and a pot-belly), he was not an attractive man to look at. Even his impeccably-kept thin moustache and little pointy beard couldn't rescue his looks. He was not a well-endowed man either, although he certainly knew how to use the tool that God gave him.

Brian dyed his hair jet black on a weekly basis so that the world would never know about the grey lurking beneath. All other evidence of grey he destroyed with a razor; something that he had always done as the ladies preferred it anyway. His hair was slicked back over his skull, but a slightly balding patch could be seen under the brightest of spotlights (a subject that had caused the spilling of much blood). Brian was always suited and booted. Tonight, he sported a red woollen suit with a matching thin red woollen tie. A black Italian shirt, without a crease in sight, matched his shoes that were polished into mirrors.

Brian knew he was not the sexiest man in Middlesbrough, but he knew he could do well with what he had. The reason for his success with the fairer sex was because he was a silver-tongued fox. He could talk his way into any job or any pair of knickers. It was his gift, and he used it. He left school with no qualifications, and only a few pregnancy scares proved that he ever attended Middlesbrough High.

"I'll think about it, Brian," said Sid unconvincingly. "Now then, mate, I do believe it's your round."

"Sid, I've already bought you two beers tonight and it is most definitely your round." Both men knew whose round it was. Brian knew what was coming next.

"Brian, me ol' mate, I don't pick me sickness benefit up for another couple of days." Sid coughed for dramatic effect. It was a well rehearsed and magnificent performance. "Don't suppose you could lend a good man a ten pound note, or possibly buy him an ale?"

Unfortunately, the audience had seen this particular performance before, one that had been repeated more times than *The Man with the Golden Gun* on a rainy Bank Holiday Monday. "I've already bought you two beers and there is as much chance of me seeing that tenner again as you not taking the lift."

The Great Right Hope

Sid's second mortal fear was stairs. His head dropped. Surely this couldn't be the end of tonight's drinking?

Brian sighed. "Tell you what, mate."

Sid's head rose.

"You can earn that tenner."

Sid's head dropped again.

"If you pick me up some stuff from shops next week. How 'bout it?"

Sid knew that Brian was not a lazy man. "What stuff? Why can't you get it yourself?"

"It's just that I'm busy next week and I need to pick up a few things from Abdul," said Brian looking sheepish.

"Abdul? Ain't he the guy who owns that mucky shop down in Birch Street?"

"Err…yeah," admitted Brian.

"What are you buying from a mucky store?"

This was a delicate situation, for he was Brian Garforth, Middlesbrough's finest swordsman. He had gone through every feasible possibility as to why he would have the need to go into a mucky store. He was proud of his rightful reputation as a swordsman, and entering this sort of establishment could ruin it all. Unfortunately, the most intelligent man on the Smithson Estate couldn't think of a single good excuse to be seen entering the Store of Shame.

Excuse number 1:	To buy dirty mags/films. Brian Garforth didn't need to take matters, literally, into his own hands.
Excuse number 2:	Marital aids. Brian Garforth didn't need the help of a plastic abomination to take a lady to heaven and back.
Excuse Number 3:	Leather/bondage gear. Brian Garforth was a meat and potatoes man, thank you very much.

But Abdul Zafar, purveyor of gentlemen's' interest magazines, did have something that Brian wanted to try. Brian's art of seducing ladies had developed with age, like the swordsmanship of a wizened Samurai master. However, this Samurai master's sword was not as sharp as it had been in recent years, despite getting a lot of use. The old Samurai master knew that he had the goods to deal with any particular adversary on any particular day. Nevertheless, to face an opponent more than once was now proving difficult, or in all honesty, nigh on bloody impossible. Brian needed a little help. He needed a little blue pill of help, having recently come to terms with needing Viagra for occasional use, just in case, probably won't need it at all, definitely wouldn't…just as a safety net.

Abdul had the cheapest stock in town, but Brian had to find a way to obtain the goods without anyone knowing. He had decided to ask Sid, his most trusted friend.

"Sid, I want you to buy me some Viagra from Abdul. I am asking you to perform this task in utmost confidence." He needed his friend to understand that the confidentiality of the subject was life or death to a swordsman.

"What's up with your pecker, Brian?" smirked Sid.

"You bastard!" The Middlesbrough Casanova's face turned crimson. How could anyone see a funny side in this? This was like Maradonna losing his football Beethoven losing his piano, Cliff Richard losing his virginity.

"Calm down, mon, I'm only pulling your leg," reassured Sid. "Of course I'll pick up your stuff and I won't mention it t'anyone," said the modern day saint.

"Thank you, Sid." said Brian relieved. "You truly are a good—"

"Sixty quid for me troubles."

"Bastard!"

"Brian, I am putting my reputation on the line entering this seedy back-street shop," said Sid Tillsley, Pillar of the Community.

"Very well," conceded Brian. "But if word gets out, to anyone about me experimenting with sexual enhancers, then I will let a few secrets out about you!"

"No problems, Brian. May I have the cash in advance, please?"

"Half now and half on the delivery of the merchandise. I'll give you the money you need for the stuff later in the week." Brian reached into the top pocket of his jacket and pulled out his imitation crocodile skin wallet. He took out thirty pounds and handed it to Sid who took the money graciously, got up, and moved his massive frame to the bar so that he could purchase fresh ale.

"Same again, Sid?" enquired the Miner's Arms' landlord.

"Yes please, Kev."

Kevin Ackroyd pulled two pints of Bolton Bitter; two exact pints. He made sure never to pull a small measure for Sid, but no one ever received a pint over the limit. The best way to describe Kevin would involve taking Sid and making him into a Russian doll. Then you would have to take the top off Sid, then the top off the mini-Sid, then the top off the mini-mini Sid and then add a grey scraggily moustache. Behold: a pretty-accurate representation of Kevin Ackroyd. He was about five and a half feet in both directions, and where Sid's shoulders were out of proportion to his body, Kevin's belly was out of proportion to his. The nose was not broken as was Sid's, but was incredibly red with all the years of alcohol abuse.

Sid lit his eightieth Egyptian of the day. "How's the extension going round back?"

The Landlord's face dropped. "Don't get me started, Sid. The bleedin' missus nags all day long about getting a new bedroom in. She wants to move her bleedin' mother in, doesn't she? As if my life couldn't get any bleedin' worse!"

"Sorry for askin', Kev, didn't realise. How much do I owe yer?"

"£3.92 please."

Sid passed over a ten-pound note and waited for his change.

"I'm sorry, Sid. I didn't mean to snap there. It's just, you know how our Marie gets about bleedin' home improvements and bleedin' decorating."

Sid asked the million-dollar question. "You ain't changing the inside of the Miner's?"

Kev looked genuinely offended. "God no. I let her have her own way in everything, Sid. I am a good husband, but she will never alter the inside of this fine public house."

The Miner's Arms had not changed since Kevin took over from his old man in '67. Not even the breweries had managed to convince the stubborn landlord to decorate, and even Kev's own failed arson attempts had not warranted a lick of paint.

It was a small pub. A pub for locals. Only one student had ever ventured into the public house, but that was only because he had been thrown in through the window. Tonight it was relatively empty, being a weeknight. Weekends weren't much livelier. Apart from Sid and Brian, there were only the lads in. They sat round a small black and white telly near the bar watching *Who wants to be a Millionaire?* They were silent apart from the odd shout of: "Tarrant, you 'miscellaneous four-letter word.'"

As you walked in from the street, the first thing that hit you was the smell of stale beer and cigarettes (unless you were a student, and then the first thing to hit you would be one of the locals). The smoking ban was paid no heed in these parts. Most patrons thought it was make-believe, like Father Christmas, paying taxes, or safe sex.

No pictures adorned the nicotine-stained wallpaper. Three flying ducks and a postcard from Great Yarmouth were the only decoration inside. The only other feature was the dart board. The Miner's had a wicked team that inspired fear in the opposition, and not just because of their good *arras*. As you walked to the bar, the next thing you noticed was that your feet stuck to the carpet. It was terribly worn, and the pattern was indistinguishable from the cigarette burns, chewing gum, beer spillages and other stains of bodily origin.

There was a mismatch of furniture on the way to the bar. There wasn't a single chair or table alike in the entire pub. The bar, however, was a beautiful immaculate oak of which Kevin Ackroyd was very proud. Bar stools were placed equidistantly along its length, which occupied the entire left wall up to the toilet door.

Only one toilet was originally built in the Miner's: the gents. It comprised of two urinals and a flushable toilet (unless Sid was caught short, in which case the flushable toilet would become a non-flushable toilet). The pub did have one small alteration since Kevin took over from his Dad. The new landlord had designed the Miner's only refurbishment himself. In what was deemed at the time to be a crazy venture, he had installed a ladies' toilet.

The venture only took an afternoon. He merely wrote "Ladies" on the Gents cubicle door in a permanent marker and put a mirror over the washbasin so the fairer sex could apply their war paint. It was still acceptable for gentlemen to use the ladies loo. After all, it was not an uncommon sight to see the ladies using the urinals, and this was the age of equal rights. A regular Ladies' Night of variable vigour had been held periodically since the refurbishment; an event that has proven itself hugely popular with the locals.

On the wall to the right of the bar were the remains of the Miner's Arms' jukebox. Kevin was once extremely proud of his music collection and had updated the jukebox's collection of *Manrock* monthly, until that ill-fated Christmas Eve…

Kevin had organised a karaoke night, the first-ever for the Miner's Arms and for the Smithson Estate. He was feeling particularly festive that year and saw it as a Christmas present for the locals. Karaoke LPs purchased from a car boot sale along with a lyric list made up the playlist, and Kevin had even bought a microphone he could plug into a speaker borrowed from one of the lads. Everything was going swimmingly. The singers would pick their songs from the list and tell Kevin. He would then write the lyrics on a blackboard and hold them up. It worked a treat until Sid Tillsley finished his five minutes of fame.

Sid had performed the most beautiful rendition of Wham's "Last Christmas." No one had expected the big man could sing, let alone sing in tune. Even Sid himself was a little emotional after the song. "I love it. It's me favourite song of all time. I really feel for him, mon."

It was the last song of the evening and it was the perfect end to a perfect night. Or that would have been the case if Keith Hargreaves, a nineteen year-old trainee mechanic, hadn't asked, "Ain't he a bummer, Sid?"

It had broken Kevin Ackroyd's heart and six of Keith Hargreaves teeth when the young mechanic was thrown through the jukebox. Sid never sang again, Kev never bought *Manrock* again, and Keith Hargreaves never ate solid food again. Kev couldn't bring himself to remove the shell of the jukebox and it stood broken, a sad reminder of the day the music died.

Sid took the beers and returned to sit next to his friend.

"Cheers, Sid," said Brian, taking down a large draft of ale. "Now then, what do you say about giving this doggin' a go?"

Sid shook his head. "I don't know, Brian. It's a lot of hassle and you never know who's going to be there, like. If I'm that desperate I can always go and see that prossy, Lizzie, who lives down road."

"No, Sid. I won't let you pay for it again. Anyway, Lizzie has weathered since you last saw her and she was never exactly a looker in the first place. I heard that you can get *the lot* for a four-pack of Skol."

The Great Right Hope

Sid looked around. Not a single female in sight. "Guess I could give it a go, like."

"That's the spirit," said Brian beaming. "Tomorrow night up at Middlesbrough Memorial Park they are having one of their regular meetings. Don't worry. It's a one hundred per cent heterosexual spot. After Charlie told me about it I looked it all up on Internet." More proof that Brian was the brainiest man on the Smithson Estate: he had used a computer.

"Shit the bed!" said Sid slightly in awe. He respected Brian for his worldly ways and extensive knowledge of modern-day technology. "If it was on that computer thing then it's got to be reet. OK, tell me how I go about getting some ladies."

Brian explained to Sid what he had found out on the World Wide Web and about the etiquette of the dogger. The two friends smoked, supped ale, and chatted into the night until Kevin Ackroyd kicked them into the street because he wanted to go to bed. The walk home was exciting for Sid as tomorrow, after two years of waiting, he was going to get lucky.

"Howay, the lads!"

4

It was the following evening, and a beautiful, bright summer's evening at that. Sid had shaken off his hangover by mid afternoon and was now bright as a button in anticipation of a night of adult entertainment. He was parked in Middlesbrough Memorial Park in his 1987 maroon Montego Estate. Sid was applying the finishing touches to a look that said, "Suck me off, love."

Sid pinned on his uncle's Dambuster medal as he knew the ladies could never turn down a war-hero. He got out of the Montego and applied a final splash of Male aftershave, which Brian had lent him especially for the occasion, giving a quick sweep with the accompanying body-spray (with special attention taking place around the crotch). Now he was officially irresistible.

Reaching inside the car he took out a dog lead he had picked up (stolen) off a guide dog so that he could look the part. There were a few other cars in the car park and they were empty. Obviously, the desperate, nubile young ladies had left their cars to seek rough, masculine loving out in the wilderness.

"They are gonna be gaggin' for it." Sid rubbed his hands at the prospect and pushed on.

Middlesbrough Memorial park was a beautiful place. It was mostly set on a hillside with views of the surrounding valleys and the sea in the distance, but this was all wasted on Sid as the hill was rapidly taking the fire out of his loins. After trekking fifty yards up a shallow incline, the Male Body Spray had given up the ghost. Sid's personal hygiene was now in a bad-place, or, rather, a worse place.

Luckily, Sid's leather jacket hid the sweat rings that were growing at an alarming rate. Like the Germans (who he now feared as much as air stewards), the sweat rings from his armpits were invading the surrounding territory with ruthless efficiency. The tiger on his Esso Tiger Token T-shirt was now in danger of drowning. Even a heavy leather jacket wouldn't disguise the smell that these sweat rings would start making in the next ten minutes. Snorting bleach wouldn't disguise the smell they were going to make.

He continued along the path, huffing and puffing, and smoking "Al Arabo" Iranian cigarettes. He had picked up four hundred of these full-tar, no-filter, and carcinogentastic bad-boys as reward for finding Middlesbrough's only Iranian tobacconist, Isha Majeera's, dog.

The tree-lined car park had been left behind and Sid was walking around the hill on one of the nature trails. The first park bench he came across was structurally tested as his considerable backside hit it with force. Sweat poured off him. He must have walked at least—he surveyed the trek—three hundred yards.

"Shit the bed!"

Who would have thought this doggin' malarkey would be so strenuous, and he had not even started yet! It would all be worth it though, in the long run. Sid was hoping for at least two ladies tonight. He had come to the conclusion that he would have to kill two birds with one stone (metaphorically speaking of course; he didn't have AIDS, or only one functioning gonad) as his heart couldn't manage it twice. Maybe he could manage two if the first lass were on the receiving end of a quickie, although the chances were high that the second lass would be on the receiving end of a quickie too.

He regained his breath after going through an Iranian per minute. From where he sat, he had a beautiful view of the surrounding countryside and woodland, marred only by the presence of Seal Sands' Chemical site in the distance. Sid's lust began to wane. He couldn't see any ladies anywhere and the Male Body Spray had been beaten into complete submission. It was about time to depart, and the factor encouraging Sid to leave, most of all, was that he could still get a gallon of ale in before the Miner's closed. However, a little voice in his pants said: "Keep trying, please! Not another cosy night in, just the two of us!"

The out of shape Casanova got to his feet. Another three hundred yard stint around the hill and if nothing came of it, the Miner's was calling. Sid psyched himself up, and set off around the hill of hidden passion. He took two steps and then stopped.

Hang on! He could hear something up ahead. His mind raced. Unfortunately, he wasn't very imaginative when it came to the bedroom department, or any other department for that matter, and he could only imagine his old school teacher Miss Stevens reading *Razzle*. But, that was enough for Sid's sex drive to pump some blood towards an underused appendage. He strode forward, reached the brow of the hill, and...

This wasn't part of the plan. This wasn't part of the plan at all. Sid had gone through every possible scenario he could think of—except this one. In front of him was a well-dressed, middle-aged gentleman with a Scottish Highland Terrier.

The colour drained from the big man's face, which took a significant amount of time considering how red it was to start with. His mouth dropped open, and the power of speech evaded him. Blind panic consumed him. He didn't know that this was a gay hill. He didn't even know what a gay hill was! There was meant to be women up here, not men.

What if he was German?

"Good evening, squire," greeted the English gentleman.

Worse! Southern! The man was Southern, possibly from London. Sid assumed every single living breathing man born in London was a homosexual.

"Are you alright there, old boy?"

Sid's eyes widened. The man had mentioned his tackle!

The gentleman noticed Sid's empty lead. "Lost your dog, I see?"

Sid thought fast—thirty seconds later—"No."

"O…kay….," replied the gentleman. "Well, good day to you, sir." He nodded his head and walked on.

Sid waited until the man was well out of sight before heaving a sigh of relief. That was close, too close. He was going to have serious words with Brian. A cold clammy sweat covered him, the type only raw fear can induce, and the ordeal that he had just gone through persuaded him to call it a day. If this was dogging area for *them lot*, he was getting the fook out of Dodge. He smoked some more Iranians and prepared for the 300-yard marathon ahead.

His only saving grace was that the journey was downhill, and as he approached the car park, he spied a blonde figure up ahead. He prayed for a female and not one of them transeck…transet…*thingies*. The blonde hair quickened his pace and soon it became apparent that it was indeed a she, and a forty-ish-year-old beauty, at that!

"Fooking 'ell! Right, Sid, it is time, my son," he murmured to himself as all memories of the gay hill floated away, literally, with the fairies.

The peroxide blonde was wearing blue jeans that appeared painted on. How she got the waistline of the jeans over her massive buttocks could only explained by forty-ish peroxide blondes who refuse to accept they are getting old. She wore a vest, which didn't do much to conceal her impressive cleavage (although some do consider hippos fighting as impressive), or the tattoos on top of each breast.

Titty tattoos!

Contact.

"Good evening, young lady." Sid Tillsley had transformed into a fat, Northern, Nigel Havers.

"Y'alllllrrrrriiigggght?" It took a good two seconds for the word to be completed. The strong Leeds accent went from his ears to his loins at the speed of light. She was from Leeds, she was blonde, she was forty, and she had tattoos on her titties. Sid Tillsley knew that he would be getting down to it in a matter of minutes, possibly seconds.

"I am very well, thank you, my dear. What is the reason that I come across you this fine summers evening?" Oh yes, Sid had upped his smoothness from Nigel Havers to…was it possible? Had he reached the level of smoothness of the one and only Roger Moore?

"Walkin' dog, mate," she replied, then bellowed, "C'MON, ENRIQUE!" at which a red setter bounded from a cluster of trees. "Catch ya later," said the Northern rose, and began to walk past Sid.

"…Err, hang on there, love." Smoothness levels dropped down to that of Mike Reid. He didn't know what to say to initiate sexual contact and his earlier innuendo had clearly failed. Sid looked down at his lead. He'd have to make a more obvious innuendo to entice the Jewel of the North into letting him give her one. Roger Moore returned.

"It is such a beautiful evening, and my dog is out…shagging."

Unfortunately, Bernard Manning finished the sentence.

The lady looked at Sid blankly. "Oh, that's grand," she said, slightly bewildered. "I think I'll be on my way." She turned to follow the red setter that had disappeared from view.

Sid didn't know what to do. She hadn't taken the bait, but he was so close. Shit or bust, he decided. "My dog's off…shagging and I was thinking…maybe…erm…I could give you one behind the hedge over there?"

The real Roger Moore would have his kecks round his ankles by now. However, Northern Roger Moore was kicked in the knackers.

After ten minutes of gentle massaging later, a dejected Sid got up, lit up an Iranian, and headed for the Miner's.

5

It was all so different now. A planned kill. What was the point in that? "The Golden Age," they called it. At least Michael, for all his hypocrisy, did. He was responsible for the massacre of tens of thousands of humans, all unnecessary and all for the pure fun of it. Michael was the most powerful vampire of the last two millennia. He was a force to be reckoned with and a beast of a lamia. Who could predict his fall from grace?

Gabriel was his second in command during the true Golden Age, the tenth century. It was a time when humans lived their lives in righteous fear of the vampire. It was not hunting, it was feasting. Lords, Ladies, there was no-one powerful enough to avoid their fangs.

And now: an organised hunt in Middlesbrough. They hunted local criminals who didn't deserve to die of leprosy, let alone be taken by a vampire. Nevertheless, if you didn't move with the times then you died and that was the way of the world.

Gabriel was to meet Gunnar in a local public house after his old acquaintance had met up with Ricard and Richmond. Three completely different characters, each of whom was dear to his heart, but Gunnar was his kindred spirit. Born thousands of miles and hundreds of years apart, yet the same desires drove them. They were predators born to hunt and rejoice in the kill. This modern age was for the Ricard's of the world: artists, philosophers, musicians. But the good times would return. Everything travels in cycles and the balance would be restored one day. How he lusted for war.

Gabriel watched the locals pour out of the pubs and clubs. Witnessing it made him nauseous. They drunkenly shouted at each other and threw punches, whilst others simply vomited on their own streets. The men were just as bad as the women. If vampires had sunk in stature, then humans had surely plummeted. He surveyed his surroundings. It would be almost worth his death, slaughtering the whole godforsaken town, he thought before turning down the dark alleyway leading to the back of the Wolf's Head free house.

Gunnar stood outside waiting.

"I thought we were meeting inside the pub?"

"We were," said Gunnar, "but I cannot waste time with you by drinking and reminiscing. After fifty years, we can hunt together once more."

Gabriel embraced his closest friend. "Then let us hunt."

* * * *

Pete took a large drag of the marijuana spliff and lounged back into the comfortable seat of the car. He took one more puff before passing it to Steve sitting next to him. Steve took a deep draw and lounged back into his chair, copying Pete. He stared at the burning embers of the illegal cigarette. "Want any, Darren?"

"Nah mon, you know I ain't into that shit."

They all sat in Steve's wreck of a Ford Escort Cosworth. Like so many other seventeen year olds, Steve had attempted to customise his car with a detrimental effect. They had been parked for an hour in an empty car park behind Middlesbrough's town hall smoking cannabis and drinking copious amounts of vodka.

"There!" Pete pointed at a girl staggering around on the other side of the car park. "I think we have our lucky lady for the evening."

"Stupid bitch can't even stand up. She ain't fooking bad, either." Steve wound down the window and stuck his head out. "Wanna lift home, love?"

Steve started the car up on the second attempt and drove slowly towards the girl, who appeared not to notice the lads driving behind her. She had peroxide blonde hair and wore virtually nothing except her make-up. Even though she had tried to create the illusion of an adult, she still didn't appear old enough to drink. However, she had certainly been served her fair share.

"How 'bout a lift home, love?" Darren got out of the car and walked up to her. He was tall, gangly and riddled with acne. Only fifteen years old and just a child, yet his intentions didn't contain child-like innocence. He put his arm around her and beckoned her towards the car. She offered no resistance, as she was virtually comatose from alcohol. "Where are ya mates, ey? Where have all your mates got to?"

The girl mumbled something inaudible and the boys knew they were in luck. Steve reached out of the car and grabbed her hand. "You want to go home don't ya, babe? We'll take you back home. You'll be nice and safe with us."

The girl nodded at them. She didn't know what she was doing, but she did want to be home, tucked up in bed. Darren helped her into the car and got in after her. Steve put his foot down, causing a massive wheel spin and the screeching of bald tyres.

"'Ere lads, she's fooking passed out," squeaked Darren excitedly. "This is gonna be fookin' it"

"It's going to be your first time isn't it, you little boy virgin?" mocked Pete.

"Is it fook!" yelled Darren defensively. "I've had loads of birds, me!"

"Yeah, right!" Pete was about twenty-five and had no friends of his own age so he hung round with teenage lads. He liked it because they looked up to him, just because he was twenty-five. He didn't even have a car, let alone know how to drive. It was the only respect he had ever been given and he thrived on being a big fish in a very small pond.

The car roared on as Steve drove dangerously through Middlesbrough town centre. Every corner resulted in a squeal of rubber as Steve attempted to impress his older friend. Normally, huge levels of bass blared out of the car because Steve had filled the boot with various subwoofers. However, now the music was turned off because they didn't want to wake the girl, although she was so drunk a foghorn to her ear wouldn't wake her from her alcohol induced slumber.

Steve had been up here before with Pete and he knew what was going to happen. He hated it, but it impressed Pete so he did it anyway. He was glad Darren was here. At least someone else would feel worse than he would tomorrow morning.

They reached the east car park of Middlesbrough's Memorial Park. Steve drove slowly down the gravel track because he didn't want to chip his already battered paintwork. Once in the car park he drove around the perimeter to make sure there was no one else around. Certain they were alone, he braked slowly to a standstill and turned off the engine. It was almost pitch black outside and only a feint orange glow could be seen over the trees from where the town was. He didn't like it when it was pitch black outside. Nothing outside the car made what happened inside feel so much more real.

"Darren, you can have the honours as it is your first time," announced Pete.

There was no defiance with respect to his virginity now. The talk was talked and it was now time to walk the walk. Pete switched on the interior light. "Go on! What are you fooking waiting for?" he asked aggressively. "Are you fooking queer or summat?"

Darren reached out gingerly until his hand touched her leg. The girl didn't move at all. She was not aware of the abuse she was about to suffer. It was probably for the best. Slowly, he put his hand up her skirt, and his hand trembled all the way until he reached her underwear. He froze. Finally here, he found he didn't want to be.

"What are you fooking waiting for?" spat Pete. "Don't you fooking want her?" He reached back over the seat and ripped down her top, revealing the girl's breasts. "You ever seen a pair in real life before, you little fooking faggot?" He slapped Darren hard on the face causing him to recoil back into his seat and as far away from the girl as he could.

"What good are you? You call yourself a man?" Pete got out of the car and slammed the door. He walked around to the side where the girl sat, yanked the door open, reached inside and grabbed her roughly, angry at his young protégé's weakness.

The girl miraculously awoke with the sudden movement of being heaved from the car. Even in such an inebriated state, she still managed to comprehend the intense danger she was in and the shock of finding herself half-naked and surrounded by strangers sent her fight or flight instinct into overdrive. She erupted into a rage, clawing and yelling at Pete as he tried to grab her flailing arms and legs. He slapped her hard but she still kept fighting, fighting for what she thought was her life. She kicked him hard and he flew back from the car door to land fully twenty feet away.

Steve and Darren stared agog at the girl who had performed a seemingly superhuman feat of strength. A face appeared at the door, which caused the girl to jump back in shock.

"Are you OK, girl?"

She nodded but couldn't speak. It was not because of the alcohol but because of the beauty of the man that had saved her life. Dark hair blew across his perfect face and she couldn't escape from his transfixing brown eyes. He took off his coat to reveal powerful, broad shoulders and gave it to her. Suddenly aware of her nakedness she quickly wrapped herself in it. The ordeal was sobering her up, fast.

"My friend and I have to deal with these young gentlemen, so please, shut your eyes. Whatever you hear, do not open them. You are safe now."

She struggled to shut her eyes and stop looking at perfection, but she had to obey this angel. There was the sound of car doors opening and closing, and then nothing.

* * * *

Steve was dragged to where Pete still lay motionless. By the dim light of the moon he could see Pete was still breathing, but Steve couldn't make up his mind if that was a good thing. He watched as a bald man pulled Darren out of the car and dragged him over, with remarkably little effort, to where they sat.

Both men were tall and heavily built. They had to be the police. This was all that Steve needed. He already had two cautions and this was serious stuff, probably a jail sentence.

The dark haired copper touched Pete's neck and suddenly, as if he had a cold bucket of water thrown over him, he came to, coughing and wheezing.

"You were going to force yourself on that young lady," said the copper. It was not a question because the pig knew what was going on.

Pete couldn't speak as he couldn't get enough air into his lungs to muster a response.

Steve broke in. "We weren't, copper! She wanted to come out here with us. We met her tonight and she was well up for it."

The dark haired policeman smiled. "What makes you think I am an officer of the law?" He picked up Pete by the throat and lifted him a foot above the ground. Steve's eyes widened.

"My acquaintance is the great Gunnar Ivansey and I am Gabriel. I was born in Hungary centuries ago. Do you know what we did to rapists in Hungary, my friends?" He paused as if waiting for an answer. "No? The education system today…" He sighed and shook his head mockingly. "We ripped off their genitals until they bled to death." He reached down and grabbed Pete's crotch. "Dear boy, you are going to relive the past. Have you anything worthwhile to say?"

Only terror filled Pete and then pain, intense, excruciating pain. Steve vomited. Pete began to scream but Gabriel pushed Pete's tongue to the top of his jaw to quench his cries and his mouth distorted as he unleashed a silent scream upon the world. His eyes began to close as the pain tried to take away his consciousness. However, Gabriel massaged another part of his neck causing Pete's eyes to bolt open once more.

"Do you not want to witness your last few minutes on this earth?" The torturer lifted his hand so he could show Pete his dismembered, blood-dripping genitals. "You value these tiny little things so much, don't you?" He shook his head at the dying man. "It is true what they say, 'Those who live by the sword, die by the sword!'" He gave out a guffaw that held no mirth and threw Pete to the ground, who screamed for a second before the pain took him. Gabriel threw Pete's genitals at Darren who didn't dare move for the terror that bound him. "And you…"

Darren lost control of his bladder. He couldn't take his eyes off Pete whose breathing was getting slower and slower.

"Were you going to rape that poor defenceless girl? Do you wish to share the same fate as your friend? Were you more twisted than your friend? Maybe your punishment should be more severe?"

Darren's gaze was ripped from Pete's dying body at the mention of a more severe punishment. "Mister, I…I…"

"Perhaps, you were just going to watch then? You do not look the sort who could force himself on a woman, but you would have sat there and watched wouldn't you? For that, I will take your eyes."

"Wha…No! AAARRRHGGHH!"

Gabriel picked Darren up and thrust a forefinger into his eye-socket, hooked the finger once inside, and deftly plucked out his left eye. Darren screamed and Gabriel kindly allowed him to vent his emotions. Darren writhed in pain while clutching at his empty eye socket.

Gabriel turned to Steve. "And then there's you."

Steve was pale with fright. He shut his eyes tight, hoping it was all a nightmare.

"Now then, young man, if it wasn't for you, that poor girl would be tucked up in bed right now. If it wasn't for you, your chum over there would be able to see and your chum over there would be able to fuck. Are you the cause of all of this?"

"No! No! NO!" sobbed Steve. "It was Pete! It was Pete, I swear it!"

"I like a man who sticks by his friends, very loyal, young man." He laughed at the nature of mankind. "I'm going to give you a chance, young sir. You can walk away, a free man and with everything intact. Aren't you the lucky one?"

Steve nodded nervously trying to go along with the situation, to do his best to survive.

"There are two things you have to do to walk away. Number one." Gabriel held the dripping eye and rubbed his stomach mockingly. "Dinner time!"

Steve's face had looked pale before, but now it was practically translucent in the moonlight. "Wh-wh-what?"

Gabriel threw the detached eye to Steve and it hit him in the chest leaving a blood stain over his white T-shirt. It bounced to the ground in front of his knees and stared right back at him. The oozing blood from the optic nerve and the limp extraocular muscles were enough to make Steve empty his stomach again.

"Oh, poor show, poor show." Gabriel looked away in disgust.

Gunnar, who had been standing by the now-dead Peter, looked on and shook his head. He had always had a reputation for cruelty amongst the vampire community, but Gabriel was in a league of his own.

"Now pick it up, there's a good chap," Gabriel instructed.

Steve reached down slowly towards the eye, his hand shaking unrelentingly. He paused millimetres from the sickening object.

"I…I can't," he whimpered in between tears.

The complete annihilation of the young man's soul was obviously not enough for the warped vampire. "Do you have your wallet with you, young man? Do not answer, just listen. If you have, then I have your address. If you do not do as I ask, then I can play these games with your mother and father. Perhaps your little brother would like to eat parts of your little sister? What do you think?"

Steve picked up the eye and placed it in his mouth. He bit down on the soft tissue and liquid exploded inside his mouth, and poured down his throat.

"Good boy! Now just one more thing to eat. What was it again that I took from Pete?"

* * * *

"Have you finished playing judge, jury and executioner?" asked Gunnar.

Gabriel smirked. "Well, I do like to teach the cattle the error of their ways before sending them on their journey to the afterlife." He stood over the dead bodies of the three young lads.

"The boy, Steve. Has a human ever gone that far before?"

"Oh, yes. He was a coward compared to some. I can't believe what some of them will do to protect their kin."

"Have you ever let one live?"

Gabriel laughed. "What do you think?"

"Can we eat now?"

Gabriel gestured at the car where the girl still sat with her eyes tightly shut. "Dinner is served."

Gunnar strode purposefully towards the car, opened the door, grabbed the girl, and yanked her out of the vehicle. A shuddering crack indicated a dislocated shoulder. She screamed as the vampire picked her up by her useless arm. "What do you have to say for this wench, Gabriel?"

His companion didn't speak, but rushed over and gorged himself on the girl's neck. Gunnar joined him and savaged the other side. The girl went into spasms and blood gushed from her mouth as her arteries and veins were ripped to pieces. She died in seconds as the two vampires continued to feed. As one, they stepped back with their faces covered in blood that glistened in the moonlight. Gunnar held his hands aloft and roared.

"To be alive! Only death can take this away from us!"

Gabriel laughed and fell backwards onto the ground. "Indeed my friend, indeed. Nothing matters when you feed. It is the moment after the rapture that we realise we live in dark times, and life returns to normal."

Gunnar spat on the ground and pulled out his mobile phone. "Four to clean up as expected." He hung up without waiting for a reply, shaking his head. "Poor Sanderson. It must destroy him knowing that he has to come and clean up his own kind. Shall we leave the place in a state?" he chuckled as he ripped off the girls dislocated arm.

"No, let us not play games. Let us hunt, for the night is young. Let us hunt, Gunnar, for old time's sake." He tore off the girl's other arm and held it up as if making a toast. "To old times."

"To old times."

* * * *

They ran through the night. They jumped from tree to tree and leapt over hedges as if they were not there. This was what their lives used to be. Every vampire's life had been about running; either running to catch food, or running away from a lot of food. These two however, never backed down, and always fought, no matter what the odds.

They had not been together since World War II where they travelled across France. They had killed at will and to them it was the greatest time in the past century. Now was a time to taste blood and remember a better life. Neither cared what trouble they would get into for the crimes they were about to commit. Nothing could come close to the sixty years of boredom since the war.

Up ahead was the north car park of the Memorial Park and human activity was unusually high. The two ran at pace until they reached the outskirts of the clearing.

"Like old times, Gunnar?"

Gunnar smiled. "Not quite the same. There are no arrows or bullets flying past our ears." He vaulted a small tree. "Same old man in the moon smiling down on us, though."

"Better that than the sun."

They both stopped on a sixpence and were unrecognisable in the shadows. From where they lay, they could see three cars.

"There is a young couple in that Astra, early twenties," said Gunnar. "They are intimately entangled and she is a very friendly young lady." He laughed. "In the Land Rover are a couple in their early thirties; two attractive young women enjoying each other's company."

Gabriel grinned. "Perhaps this is the 'Golden age,' after all?"

"Yin and Yang. There's a fifty year old man being intimate with himself in that Volkswagen Beetle."

Gabriel's grin turned to a look of utter disdain. "Humans, bah! What is the plan?"

Gunnar raised an eyebrow, "My plan? This is a turn-up for the books." The younger vampire turned to survey the car park and looked at the Beetle. "I want that man dead."

"As you wish." Gabriel saluted and disappeared into the night. A moment later Gunnar saw the door of the Beetle open and the man's head fall forwards. Gabriel was back by his side in a matter of seconds.

"Very good, assassin."

Gabriel flourished the black blade. "It didn't deserve me to touch it. That leaves us with a choice of two. The females...or the more conventional couple?"

Gunnar considered his actions. "We'll kill the boy and the girl and we'll have our fun with the lesbians," he decided. "Then let's move on. I don't want to spend all night killing sexual deviants. Killing innocents is so much more fun."

After two relatively quick murders, Gunnar nodded back towards the land-rover and he and Gabriel surrounded the car. Gunnar opened the passenger's door whilst his companion opened the driver's door. They were rewarded with the sight of two very attractive women, kissing and touching each other passionately. The two vampires grinned at each other. The girls didn't look up, and they became increasingly intimate, turned on by their audience.

"Do you just want to watch? Or do you want to join in?" asked the more dominant of the girls without even pausing to look at her captive crowd.

"What do you think?" asked Gabriel.

Gunnar smiled. "I think I am hungry." He climbed into the car and shut the door behind him. Gabriel followed suit. Gunnar bit the first warm piece of flesh that he reached. He ripped into an arm and blood sprayed onto the windshield. The victim screamed and clutched at her wrist. She thrashed about but couldn't make the vampire release his bite.

Gabriel went straight for his victim's neck and the girl died in an instant.

However, Gunnar was not finished. His hunger was satisfied and it was time for fun once more. He grabbed her wrist with a vice like grip in order to quell the blood loss. He wanted his game to last as long as possible

"Ask me to kill you," he said. The girl thrashed harder, kicking and screaming. "Ask me to kill you and it will be over. You can then join your friend." He grabbed the girl's dark black hair and pushed her face into that of her lover's. Lifeless eyes stared back and she stopped kicking and screaming as she realised her soul mate was dead.

Gunnar persisted. "Ask me to kill you, and it will be all over." He pulled back her head and kissed her, smearing her own blood across her face, but suddenly her eyes deadened and she fell limp. He looked up to see Gabriel spit out a giant hunk of the girl's neck.

"Why did you do that?" Gunnar asked with calm annoyance.

"That car flashed us." Gabriel he nodded at the car on the opposite side of the car park. "There is no time for games if there are witnesses. You can have your fun with them."

Gunnar frowned. The occupant would pay more than anyone had, this night. The two left the Land Rover and crossed the park until they drew near to the car. A fat human jumped out and shouted obscenities at them in an inaudible language. He was a horrible wreck, even by human standards. They could sense his diseased veins from metres away and the smell of the man's unwashed body was overpowering.

Gabriel circled the man leaving Gunnar to attack the front. The man was petrified and fear oozed from every pore of his clammy skin. Gabriel could sense his pulse racing through clogged veins. He would have taken his time if it wasn't for the foul nature of this being. With a nod towards his comrade, Gabriel leapt.

And then there was nothing.

6

The Miner's was empty except for a few lads that were watching Tarrant. Brian was entertaining a thirty-ish year old redhead and it appeared that he was "in the zone," as he normally described it. Seeing the master was at work, Sid bought himself a pint of Bolton Bitter, and took a seat by the former jukebox, lighting up an Iranian. It had been a terrible day but a few ales would sort him out. A few ales sorted everything out.

Brian noticed that Sid was in the pub and he excused himself from his date, walking over to see if his sexual-experimenting friend was psyched up for the evening.

"What are you doing here, Sid? You should be getting ready for a night of shaggin', you ol' stud, you."

"I've been, Brian," said Sid dejectedly. "It went pissing terrible." Rubbing his swollen genitals to emphasise the point, she had managed to connect with both of them.

"What do you mean: you've been? It's only quarter past ten. It's only just got dark for fook's sake. The only people up there in daytime are bird-watchers and dog-walkers!"

Many things fell into place. "Shit the bed, it all makes sense."

Brian looked over his shoulder at the redhead who was playing with her hair in, what some would consider, a seductive way. "Look, mate, I'm on for one here. She's a dead cert, and she's fooking gagging for it, like."

"Who is she? I thought you were servicing Charlie's missus tonight?"

"Charlie's done his knee in. He won't be going out for a few weeks so I canna go round," said Brian with a look of disappointment on his face. "That there, is a new cleaner from work. And Sid, I am going to give her something to clean up!"

"She's a bit young for one of your cleaners, ain't she?"

"Yeah, but she just got out of the nick, and they set her up with a job. She don't speak much English, like." He looked over again. "I've got to go, mate. I don't want to lose this one. Give the car park thing a go tonight. I told you: it don't start 'til 'bout midnight. Remember, keep your interior light on and flash your headlights twice because that means you're a man…and a straight man at that," he added wisely.

"But," began the unconvinced Sid Tillsley before Brian cut him off.

"You obviously want some. Otherwise, you wouldn't have gone there this evening. Get your arse over there, Sid! Go get your end away. You deserve it." He turned and walked back to the redhead. Within seconds, she was laughing at one of his jokes. He was indeed "in the zone," and he was indeed a swordsman.

Sid finished his pint, and downed another for good measure whilst enjoying his ninety-first, second, third, and fourth Iranians of the day. He watched his friend work his magic: the master gracefully moved in for a kiss, and a less graceful tweak of the breast. Brian Garforth was a swordsman of the finest quality.

That blonde lovely had fired Sid up enough to warrant another visit. Also, it was not fair that Brian got all the luck.

"Fook it!" Sid stood up and left the pub.

* * * *

Sid Tillsley, forty-six, GSOH. Likes: tits. Dislikes: cocks; sat in his maroon Montego Estate. The back seats were down and the radio was turned up. Status Quo bashed out riff after riff of unadulterated *Manrock*.

His Montego was a well-known vehicle around the streets of Middlesbrough. Local legend has it that the maroon estate was the first one of its kind. Mr. David Montego was the mastermind behind the ultimate human-transportation-device, an idea had come to him after he was struck by lightning one afternoon whilst playing golf. He said that God himself had told him to build a machine worthy of the almighty. David took fifteen years to design the Montego and helped build the very first with his own hands. He put his very heart and soul into his creation. When he finished, he passed away mysteriously. Some say that he had sacrificed his very own life-essence in creating the car. Others say that God punished him because the car was utter shite.

Sid's Montego did, however, exhibit some very strange attributes. It always passed its MOT and never obtained speeding tickets, or parking fines either. This was most likely because the majority of the people in Middlesbrough knew of Sid and of Sid's devastating right hand. Therefore, rumours of David Montego haunting the car to ensure that no ill befalls his beloved creation were probably bollocks.

There were three other cars in the Middlesbrough Memorial car park. No artificial lighting meant that Sid could only see by the moonlight. The other cars consisted of a Land Rover, a clapped out Astra and a new Volkswagen Beetle. Sid had his eye on the VW Beetle. After all, it just had to be lady driving it, and if it wasn't, then it was best he kept an eye on it. He assumed that the Astra was a young lad with his girlfriend, and that the Land Rover was probably a businessman looking for some action, just like him. He didn't consider that the driver could be one of *them lot*. They could never drive such a big car. They drove the new kind of minis with buttons in them that helped you park.

The Great Right Hope

The Beetle's interior light had not been set to "Howay the lads!" The Land Rover and the Astra were both unlit and motionless too. Sid had been here for fifteen minutes now, nervous yet excited. His nerves had the upper hand at the moment and he had not plucked up the courage to turn on his own light.

How things had changed since his heyday. Sex was such a private thing when he was growing up; so private that he did it on his own until he was twenty-five. He remembered the days of wining and dining girls, not meeting them in car parks. Brian had changed with the times. Sid hadn't, he was an old romantic at heart.

Sid flicked through the copy of *Tits* he had bought at the local newsagent. All he wanted was a gigantic set of breasts in his face. Was that too much to ask? He looked up.

Movement! Near the Land Rover. Maybe a lady had gone over to the lad in the 4x4. Sid's heart rate increased. He could see a couple of shadows each side of the car.

"Where have these horny sluts come from?"

Both front doors of the Land Rover opened simultaneously, and the two shadows entered the car, which instantly began to rock up and down.

"Fookin' Hell! Dirty bitches!" Sid rubbed his hands together and looked down at his crotch. "Tonight, son, you end the biggest drought of your life!"

The rocking of the car stopped when the big man flashed his lights over-enthusiastically at the Land Rover. The doors opened and the two ladies jumped out of the car, turning to face the Montego and edging slowly towards the erect Sid. The moon was shining behind the two girls that kept them covered in shadows but he had decided on the way down here that it didn't matter what they looked like. In fact, he had decided when he was fifteen that it didn't matter what women looked like. They continued slowly towards the car.

"Jackpot!"

It dawned on Sid that the two girls were a little bit on the large side, not fat, more…Amazonian, but that was O.K. Sid had slept with big women before, some unbelievably big women, but he had certainly never slept with any women as tall or as broad as these two.

"They've got their titties out!" said Sid with glee, although he was not very happy about how small the ladies' breasts were. As the two young, nympho sluts walked in front of the headlights, a horrible realisation dawned on Sid. The young nympho sluts were actually tall, athletic, bare-chested men.

"*Them lot!*"

The two men were now ten feet from the car and the only way Sid could get away was through them (in a heterosexual way). He went for the keys in the ignition, but the sheer terror of having two gay men ten feet from his Montego Estate caused him to drop them. Fight took over from flight, and he jumped out of the car.

"Right, yous twos. I'm a fanny man, so fook off!" He clenched his fists, the equivalent to taking the safety off a gun.

The threat didn't affect the men and both snarled back at him.

"What the fook have you done to your teeth, you pissin' weirdoes? I didna realise you fookers had different teeth as well!"

Slowly the two began to circle Sid. They were sly fookers which meant he could only see one of them in his field of vision. They both entered striking distance.

"You ain't getting any, ya bastards!"

Suddenly, the man outside of Sid's vision leapt at him, but Sid was aware. His Gay Defence System gave him eyes in the back of his head *and* his arse. Spinning around with a speed that defied his size, he unfurled the right arm and connected fully and firmly with the airborne attacker. He continued his spin until he faced the other fairy. Sid knew the first one was out cold. When he dealt his right hook they always were.

"Now then, Maureen, your turn."

Sid's attacker was not looking at him. He was staring behind him to where his fallen comrade was lying. Sid knew it was a trick because they never came round until morning. The young man turned his gaze to Sid. Pure terror filled his piercing blue eyes. He somersaulted backwards and twisted in mid-air to run at full speed upon landing, sprinting across the car park and out of sight.

Sid looked down at his right and smiled. "Won't be trying that again will you, Shirley?" He turned around to look at the fallen fairy.

But he had gone.

* * * *

Gunnar ran like the wind, not caring who saw him. No care of life. No care of death. What he just witnessed added more pain, more suffering, and more anguish to a soul already saturated with hatred and vengeance. He stopped dead on the edge of the cliff tops, having covered thirty miles in what seemed like a moment. The North Sea crashed below, unrelenting as his woe. The moonlight shone beautifully on the water.

He leapt.

The wind whistled past his ears, and he plunged deep into the icy water. His foot shattered against a rock. It would heal in an hour, not that he cared. He floated to the surface and gazed at the moon. That same beauty he had looked upon when he lost his mother. Why must something so beautiful signify something so terrible?

7

"Pint of Bolton, please, Kevin." Sid lit up a Turk. He had acquired four hundred "El Kebabo" for delivering a case of dodgy meat to Jock the Turk's Kebabateria. This was the closest Sid had ever been to "delivering meat around the back."

Kevin poured a perfect pint. "You alright there, our Sid? You look a little peaky."

Sid was a little pale; more of a bright pink rather than his normal heart-attack red.

"Oh, aye, just great." Sid guzzled half the beer in one manly draught and then finished the rest with a mighty second. "Same again, like."

Kevin didn't look surprised. This was the usual ritual for Sid's first three pints. Sid took his fourth pint to an empty table. They were all empty except for a few lads in the corner watching a re-run of Tarrant.

Sid lit up another Turk. It was eight o'clock, the day after his confrontation. Yesterday had not been a good day for Sid Tillsley: a shot to the stones, a gay confrontation, and a bizarre fight that ended with someone actually getting up.

Brian entered the pub. He sauntered to the bar and bought a single pint of Bolton bitter. Seeing Sid, he sat down at the table and gave him a concerned look. "Alright there? You look a bit peaky."

"Aye, I'll be reet, like. How did you get on with that piece last night?"

"Nailed her, like. Easy really. She's been inside with all them lasses so she was just gaggin' for some Middlesbrough meat, the dirty bitch!"

"Class! What did you get out of her?"

"Well, not quite as much as she got out of me."

Sid gave his friend a puzzled look. "What do ya mean?"

"Well, the bitch was inside for burglary. She nicked me stereo on the way out," chuckled Brian.

"What you so happy about? Go round there and get the bastard thing back. Surprised you stood for that, like."

Brian smiled. "You see, Sid, I work closely with her parole officer. She is now in me debt and anytime I fancy a bit, she can help me out or I'll tell her parole guy."

"That's brilliant, mon!" said Sid in awe. Brian Garforth was truly the most intelligent man on the Smithson Estate. He bet Poirot didn't get sucked off as much as Brian did.

"Give it a few weeks and I'll grass her up anyway. They've got to learn that crime does not pay," said the righteous scholar.

Both men sat for a while in silence. Both were content that justice had, or rather would, be done.

"Well, Sid, what happened last night, then?"

"*Them lot*, Brian," said Sid in deadly seriousness. "*Them lot.*"

"Are you sure, mate? I know you can be a little over-cautious when it comes to the gays." Brian flinched and hoped that Sid wouldn't think he was gay because he used the word.

"I swear on my uncle's Dambuster medal that it was definitely *them lot*. That's not what I'm worried about though. *Them lot* are always after a bit of me. I realise that I am a bit of a catch, and in some ways I canna blame them. It's just…the one that I hit…he got up."

Brian dropped his pint and glass smashed all over the floor. Beer sprayed up his burgundy suit but he appeared not to notice. Kevin Ackroyd noticed.

"What are you fooking doing, Garforth? They cost bleeding money you know?"

"Shut up, Ackroyd, I spend enough in here," said Brian dismissively. He turned back to Sid, and whispered in disbelief, "He got up? Are you sure?"

"I turned around and he was gone."

"I guess…I-I don't know, Sid, you are forty-six, now, perhaps you have lost a bit of the power you used to have." Brian didn't sound convinced though.

"That's what I thought, so I tested it out, like. Stopped off by a bunch of cows on the drive back. Put some big, bastard bull out with a fooking right jab. It's still there." He kissed his right fist.

"I'll get the beers in." Brian made his way to the bar to order more beverages from the seething landlord. At the same time, a scruffy character walked into the Miner's. Everyone turned to look at the stranger. Strangers always received funny looks in the Miner's Arms.

The stranger had long grey hair tied into a rough pony-tail, which instantly inspired distrust in the locals. Long hair was for hippies and *them lot*. His attire didn't help his cause, either. A long wax jacket and filthy hiking boots gave him the look of an outdoorsy type. Pub goers don't trust the outdoorsy type for they are normally health-conscious and not man enough to drive home after fifteen pints. Scum. He took a seat at the bar and waited to be served.

The arrival of the stranger took the heat off Brian for breaking one of Kevin Ackroyd's beloved glasses. Brian took the purchased beers back to Sid who sat calmly smoking a Turk. "Busy tonight," he said nodding towards the traveller. "Haven't seen him before, have you?"

"No, and the fooker keeps looking over here at me."

"Nah, mon, you're just being paranoid after what happened last night. Forget about it. More importantly, what do you think happened with that fella up at the park? Perhaps you caught him wrong or summat?"

Sid could tell that Brian was grasping at straws. They both knew that when he hit people they went down. Always had, always will. Sid put an end to the speculation.

"Caught him perfect. Awesome connection." Sid noticed Kevin look over in his direction as he spoke to the stranger. "He's talking about me, Brian, I know he is."

Brian could see his chum was on edge. He was himself. Someone getting up from Sid's right hand was unheard of. Sid could knock out a camel, which he proved at Blackpool beach during Miner's Arms' Summer Excursion, '84. "Give us a fiver and I'll go get another round in and check it out." When Sid handed over the note without question, Brian knew that he wasn't feeling right.

Brian sauntered over to the bar. "Two pints of Bolton, please, Kevin." He nodded at the stranger. "Evening, mate." The stranger ignored him. Brian noticed that his pint of beer was untouched. "Not a fan of the beer?"

"Just here for the atmosphere." The voice was deep and it wasn't a Middlesbrough accent.

"Not from round here, then? What brings you to the great town of 'boro?"

"Just passing through." The stranger still had not made eye contact and Brian was aggravated by the man's rudeness. This wasn't even his local pub.

"Don't say much do ya?"

"Who's your friend?"

"Why?"

"Just wondered."

"Well stop fooking wondering? Who the fook do you think you are? Stepping into a pub you've never been to, thinking you're fooking Clint fooking Eastwood?" Brian's temper got the better of him. It wasn't something he lost often (compared to the average Northerner) as he didn't need to. He was an educated man and besides, Sid normally lost his temper for him.

At the sound of Brian's raised voice, Sid got up to assist. "You OK, Brian?"

Kevin ran over as Sid rolled his sleeves up. "Sid! Pack it in! Leave the man alone. I'm not having my pub smashed up again." Kevin was doing his best to calm the situation, but Brian jumping up and down whilst screaming didn't help.

"Knock his fooking head off, Sid!"

Sid went to grab the stranger by the coat.

"Where were you in the early hours of this morning?" His voice, calm and steady, knocked Sid for six.

"Wh-wh-what?"

"I was merely enquiring to your whereabouts last night. I just thought that I could answer a few questions that may have been troubling you since."

Various scenarios raced through Sid's mind. Was he a copper looking for doggers? Was he one of *them lot* thinking he could try it on? Was he a benefit officer who saw him deliver the meat to the kebab house? Every single option ended up with Sid in shit. It was best to get out of here, and fast. He headed for the door.

"Wait!" Desperation crept into the deep voice. "I am not looking for trouble. Hear my story and I'll buy you a beer!"

Sid turned a neat one-hundred and eighty degree pirouette at the offer. Fraud squad or not, there was no way they could get a free beer back unless he pissed on them.

"Kevin," called Sid, "a pint of your finest ale!"

Kevin pulled a pint of Bolton Bitter and handed it to Sid, who drained it in a single gulp.

"Better make it one more, you know, to keep my concentration."

The stranger nodded at the landlord who set about pouring Sid another ale. "May we talk in private?" The stranger looked at Brian, and then at Sid.

"Can I have a quick word please, mate?" Brian took Sid to one side and whispered so no one could overhear. "Look, Sid, this bastard could be anyone, fooking anyone. He could be with the benefit office for all you know. I don't like it one bit."

"Brian, this is my second free ale. I canna turn down free booze. Please, don't kick up a fuss as I could be on for a five-pinter."

Brian sighed, "Very well, Sid. I shall sit at the bar and talk with Kevin. Good luck."

Brian grudgingly took his place at the bar, giving the mystery man filthy scowls. The stranger took a seat opposite Sid near the broken Jukebox. "What's your name?"

"If you want to keep me talking then keep these beers flowing, OK?" If he was getting arrested for anything then he was going down drunk.

"OK. What's your name?"

"Sid."

"Sid who?"

"Me glass is empty."

"Landlord," the stranger called, "keep this man's glass full." He looked at Sid. "If you stop talking you'll stop drinking."

"Tillsley. Sid Tillsley."

"What do you do?"

Here it comes, Sid thought. The benefit office thought they could get him this easy? No chance. He coughed a couple of times for effect. "Me? I canna work cos of me angina and me back. Oh, what cruel fate cursed me with these dreadful diseases…'nother beer, please."

The stranger didn't look impressed. It wasn't Sid's best performance as the ale had started to kick in.

"I'll level with you, Sid. I was tracking two men last night, and you bumped into both of them in Middlesbrough Park in the early hours of this morning. I saw you fighting, and I want you to tell me what happened."

Sid didn't think the guy was one of *them lot*. That left benefit officer or copper. "You a copper?"

He grinned, "Not the sort that you'd know of."

"You with benefit office?"

The stranger laughed. "God, no, you couldn't be further from the truth. I was after those two men last night. They have a violent history and are wanted by the authorities. It is an extremely delicate matter. However, normal constabularies are not involved and are not informed about these individuals."

"Shit the bed!" interrupted Sid.

The stranger continued. "Sid, you are not in any trouble whatsoever. You will not need to give any statements or have any connection with the law, I promise you." He paused to let the comments sink in. "I just want to know what happened during the fight," the stranger almost pleaded.

"What's your name? Where were you?"

"I was in a tree in front of your car. I knew those men you fought were going to be at the park. I was waiting for them." He offered his hand to Sid. "My name is Reece Chambers and I'm one of the good guys. Tell me about the fight, Sid, please."

Kevin walked over with a fresh pint. "You better be paying for these bastards," he threatened.

Reece reached into his pocket and pulled out a plump money clip. A stunned silence would have filled the room if there were enough people to make the effect work. Reece flicked off a twenty-pound note and gave it to Kevin. It was the first ever twenty-pound note seen in the Miner's Arms. "Keep them coming."

"Yes, sir, right away, sir." It was the first time anyone had been called "sir" in the Miner's Arms.

"Twenty quid! Flash bastard! Who the fook does he think he is coming in here with his fooking twenty quids?"

Reece ignored the background ranting of the angry Brian Garforth. "Please continue, Sid. All information is useful to me."

"Are they criminals?" Sid asked Reece. He knew lots of criminals. All of his mates were criminals. "What they done wrong?"

Brian, however, wouldn't let up and put on a voice of mock aristocracy. "Look at me, look at me! I can pay for things with my mighty twenty-pound note! Am I not the biggest wanker in the land?"

"Shut up, Garforth!" said the landlord. "He had more money in his hand than you earn in a year!"

Reece ignored the commotion. "Murder. Mass murder. They are animals. Just tell me what happened and I'll be on my way."

"How dare you?" Brian yelled. "How fooking dare you? I spend hundreds of pounds a month on this shit beer, Ackroyd, and you have the nerve to treat me like this? You, sir, are a penis and a twat!"

It was the second time that the word "sir" had been used in the Miner's Arms.

Sid contemplated what harm it could do telling this stranger what happened, but as always, it was best to say nothing.

"Penis?" replied an outraged Keith. "Twat? You are barred, Brian Garforth! You are barred!"

"Please, Sid?" begged Reece. "Just tell me what happened."

"Barred? You can't bar me, you bastard!"

None of the patrons even turned to look after hearing the sound of breaking glass. They were used to it.

Sid gave in to the begging as it made him uncomfortable. "*Them lot* surrounded me. The dark-haired one circled behind, which was his first mistake. He jumped at me so I hit him. I turned to face the other one, but he legged it. The first one must have done a runner as well 'cos he was gone when I turned round.

"I will not be threatened in my own home!" Kevin reached below the bar and picked up an antique musket, of all things. "Have at thee, sir!"

Reece waited. "That's it?"

"Yeah." Sid shrugged.

"Make your move, sir!" Kevin held the antique rifle out, bayonet pointed at the heart of Brian Garforth.

"That thing don't work. You got that when you were an extra in *Sharpe*, ya fat bastard. You know as well I do that gun is a fake! If I make it past that bayonet then you are a dead man!" Brian flourished the broken bottle.

"Got up again?" asked Reece.

"Yeah, well he weren't there when I turned round."

"What did you hit him with?"

Sid was amazed that Reece didn't understand the simple story. He clearly was not from these parts or he'd have heard of Sid's infamous right so he held it up. "This."

"Make your choice, you worthless dog! You're dead or barred!"

"But surely you were holding something? Were you wearing any rings?" Reece seemed desperate for an answer.

"*AAAAAAAARRRRRRGGGGGHH!*" Brian Garforth let out a deafening war cry.

"Nope, only need this." Sid kissed the right.

"*For King and Country!*" Kevin Ackroyd let out the battle cry that he had to shout when he was an extra in *Sharpe*.

"This can't be!" Reece reached for Sid's right hand.

BANG!

Several things happened at once: Brian Garforth made a courageous charge at Kevin Ackroyd, and Kevin Ackroyd fired his antique musket whilst Reece Chambers grabbed at Sid's hand to see what secrets it held. This bothered Sid considerably since he doesn't believe in holding hands with any man. The bang from the gun coincided with Sid's left fist landing squarely on Reece's jaw. Smoke filled the air…and then silence.

When the smoke cleared, both Brian and Kevin were lying unconscious on the floor. The musket had exploded and the resulting force had knocked out both duellists. Reece Chambers lay unconscious on the table. Sid stood above him wondering if he was OK. After all, he still had seven or eight potential pints to drink before he passed out. The remaining patrons of the Miner's still sat round watching the end of Tarrant.

"What a fookin' mess," said Sid shaking his head. He walked behind the bar and pulled himself a pint of Bolton. "What a mess." After lighting up a Turk he helped himself to a brandy, three brandies in fact. "What a mess, indeed." He switched to a treble whisky. "Bastards. What's the world…coming to?"

Sid Tillsley was putting the world to rights. "Problem with…with…fooking kids." He poured and swallowed a large Baileys, belched loudly, and then helped himself to quadruple rum before urinating underneath the cash register.

"Fooking mess! Them fookin Jap…Jap…Japan…Frogs! It's the bastard Frogs!" Pleased with this revelation, he got halfway through a celebratory pint of Bolton and promptly collapsed into a heap next to his fallen comrades.

* * * *

Sid awoke on his back, turned and vomited into the face of Kevin Ackroyd.

Kevin jumped up with a start before grabbing his head. "Jesus wept!" he moaned.

"Nnnnnggghhh." Brian acknowledged that he was alive.

Reece still lay unconscious on the bar table. It was approximately eight o'clock the following morning. The lads watching Tarrant had passed out in front of the telly. Empty pint glasses and whisky tumblers were strewn where they lay. They had gone the same way as the big man.

Kevin staggered to his feet. "You…bastards." He tried to shout but his pounding head permitted him from raising his voice so instead he surveyed the surroundings. Gunpowder blackened everything within a ten-foot radius. Sid lay in a heap with a string of sick connecting his mouth to the mess that was spreading towards the box of Seabrook crisps on the floor. "You bastard!"

Kevin turned to look at the lads who had been watching Tarrant, and at the empty bottle of malt whisky in the optic. "You bastards!"

Brian Garforth lay spread-eagled on the floor, his face blackened, his tie burnt off up to the knot, and his little beard completely missing. "You bastard!"

Kevin remembered the musket Sean Bean had autographed personally that now lay on the floor, blown into two. "You bastard!"

Sid slowly got to his feet. He was sixty-three per cent certain that he had shit himself, but then worse things happen at sea. "You alright there, Kev?"

"You bastard!"

"What do you mean, mon? I was knocked out when the gun went off! I could have been killed!" Sid argued, unconvincingly.

Kevin pulled regurgitated pork scratching from his cheek. It actually looked more appetising than usual. "You bastard!"

"Concussion, it makes you sick!" Sid pretended to go dizzy for effect.

"Who's shit 'emselves?" Brian had got to his feet.

"You bastard!"

"Kevin we need to talk about this," Brian began. "Some events took place last night that are best forgotten. Everyone drunk a little too much, like." He watched as Kevin surveyed the damage. "You did try to shoot me, for fook's sake!"

"WHAT THE FOOK IS GOING ON HERE!" A high-pitched shriek tore through the men's abused bodies to shred at their nerves. "Get out, you arseholes! Kevin, what have you done!"

Kevin's better half had arrived home from her mother's. Things had gone from bad to worse for Kevin Ackroyd. She laid a less than ladylike boot into the nearest lad who had been watching Tarrant.

"Fook off, you worthless pieces of shit!"

The landlady of the Miner's Arms was feared all over the Smithson Estate and the lads were making remarkable recoveries and exiting before she could really get to work. She confronted her husband.

"I believe you have some explaining to do, dear," she said calmly. She noticed Reece unconscious on the table and poked him with her umbrella.

"Erm…excuse me, ma'am," ventured Sid guiltily. "I think he is a little bit knocked out."

"Oh, Sidney," she said disappointingly, but with a sign of affection. "Could you and Brian be so good to escort him off the premises, please?" She smiled at the two as they picked up Reece, Sid taking the arms and Brian taking the legs.

"And Sidney…?"

"Yes ma'am?"

"Go change your kecks, son. It is not right for a grown man to shat himself."

"Yes, ma'am."

"Now, Kevin dear…"

Sid and Brian, with the comatose Reece suspended between them, made it through the door before it was slammed behind them. Fresh cries of pain and anguish echoed from the closed door. No man would want to witness the beating that Kevin Ackroyd was now taking from his wife.

Reece was taken down a passage and into an alleyway that ran down the back of the Miner's where he was dumped in a skip outside one of the adjoining houses.

"When will he come around, Sid?"

"About midday I reckon, mate." Sid could judge his punches to perfection.

"What did he want then? He was a reet wanker when I spoke to him."

Sid looked at the stranger curiously. "He saw what happened with them fairies the other night. He was amazed that I used me bare fist to smack one of 'em. Strange lad. But there are more important things to attend to." Sid set off at a brisk pace down the alley. It was the closest he had been to a run for years.

Brian called after him. "What is it, mate? What's so important?"

"Hangover dump!" Sid yelled in mid-stride.

Sid Tillsley stopped his sprint at the end of the alleyway. Too late.

"Shit the bed!"

* * * *

Reece Chambers opened his eyes. They burned with the bright midday sun that shone down on him. The smell of rotting vegetables and dog excrement filled his nose. His jaw ached and his head throbbed.

What the hell happened? He thought, realising he was in a skip. He recounted the evening, the monster of a man who had done the unthinkable, the annoying weasel, the greedy barman, and the tip of a pub. He had tried to conduct himself with all the composure he could muster. He needed to see if the oaf was wearing any rings, or amulets.

Ah…the punch.

He didn't even see it coming, and he was a black belt in five martial arts. It was certainly a mighty blow, more powerful than anything he had been hit with before. Nevertheless, surely it couldn't do what he thought it had done?

Impossible! He didn't even know what he was fighting.

Reece pulled himself groggily out of the skip. One thing was certain: he needed to find Sid Tillsley again. But that wouldn't prove difficult.

8

Ricard opened the door of his cottage and witnessed a sight he thought he would never see. Gunnar Ivansey stood before him, but not the vain, self-obsessed vampire that Ricard had grown to know and love. Instead, he saw a dishevelled character, unshaven, and soaking from head to toe, slumped pathetically against the door. The once beautiful and noble predator had been replaced with what looked like a drunk that had fallen asleep on the beach.

"Come inside, dear boy," Ricard helped him inside and sat him down by the fire that blazed in the hearth. "Have you fed recently?" Ricard didn't wait for the answer, but hurried from the living room and returned a minute later with a tankard of blood. "Drink!"

Gunnar took the tankard and put it to his lips. He took an insignificant draught before sobbing uncontrollably. It was if the blood had brought forth all the emotion from his troubled soul. Ricard knelt beside him.

"What is it? Tell me what ails you?"

Through the pain of the tears Gunnar managed, "He's gone."

Ricard knew who he meant instantly. Gabriel. The fall of Gabriel was the only thing that could turn Gunnar into this shadow of his former self.

Ricard took the young vampire's head in his hands. "How?"

"At the hands of a mortal," Gunnar spoke as if he didn't believe it himself.

Ricard spoke slowly and meticulously. "Gunnar, how? Was he taken in his sleep?"

Gunnar shook his head before pulling away from Ricard's gaze. Ricard left him and paced the floor in front of the fire. This was an unexpected event, indeed. Gabriel was one of the most physically dominant vampires of the age and had been for the last two millennia. A human couldn't take an animal like him.

Gunnar continued to weep. Centuries old and still unable to control his emotions, and that was what made him so dangerous. He was a threat to everything around him, vampire, human and the Agreement. Ricard feared what the younger vampire might do.

The fire roared as Ricard refuelled it with more wood. It had taken an hour for Gunnar to regain his senses and now he sat expressionless in the armchair. "We were hunting. It was the first time in decades we had run together and it was as if I was alive again. We stumbled across a car park where human scum go for sexual gratification. We killed all there, all unsanctioned." He held up a hand, wearily. "Do not lecture me on that, not now!"

Ricard remained silent. Gunnar continued.

"One car was left. A single human male, tall and broad, but fat and grotesque. He was a hideous mess, even for a human. I could sense his clogged arteries, his damaged lungs, and failing liver and kidneys. He was the bottom of the barrel, even by their standards." Gunnar shook his head. The loss of his friend had sunk in, but the loss of his friend to that "thing" had not.

"Gabriel," he winced with pain at the mention of the name, "circled to the rear and I stayed in front. The human muttered something, but his accent was so strong and his voice so slurred that I couldn't understand him. Gabriel moved first and leapt at the human. The man turned with speed I was not expecting. He punched Gabriel square in the jaw and that was it."

"What do you mean, 'that was it?'" asked Ricard. "What was it?"

"That was it. He was gone." Emptiness refilled Gunnar's voice.

Ricard's mind raced. How could a punch kill a vampire? Surely, it was not possible? Decapitation would kill, but that was it. A bullet would only kill a vampire if it took the head clean off. So what killed Gabriel? Perhaps he was struck with a force so great the spinal column severed. He doubted a vampire could release the kinetic energy needed to create such power. "Gunnar, whom have you told of this?"

"Nobody. Who is there to tell? Who is worthy enough to hear of Gabriel's demise…to a *human*." The last word he spat with pure hatred. The embarrassment and humiliation of being killed by a mortal!

"I will find him, Ricard." Gunnar's tears were done and it was time for vengeance. "I will make his death last his lifetime," he said through gritted teeth. "I will make every nerve in his body experience pain. I will torture his family and his friends. Everyone close to him will pay."

Ricard gripped Gunnar and looked him in the eye. "You are not to tell anyone about this, do you understand? Gunnar, listen to me and listen to me carefully. You are not to pursue this man."

"Do not get in my way, old man," threatened Gunnar.

Ricard did his best to calm him. "A vampire has been killed by a human's bare hands. Not any vampire, but Gabriel. This matter is more important than your revenge! I warn you not to be foolish. You cannot jeopardise the Agreement!"

"Revenge will be mine, Ricard. I will break the world for it. Fuck the Agreement. For centuries, the world has been spared my wrath, and now it will tremble once more." He leapt up, breaking Ricard's grip on his arm and bolted out of the door and into the night.

"So be it." Ricard shut the door to the warm summer night breeze and poured himself a whisky from the drinks cabinet. Whisky, a human invention, and one of their finest. The future was going to be interesting.

Ricard knew Gunnar wouldn't tell another soul of all that had befallen. He couldn't cope with a human killing Gabriel. Rage would cloud his judgement for a while, and this would give Ricard time to work.

Ricard raised his glass in toast to Gabriel. He was one of the greatest vampires of all time. It was best that he was gone. It would make Ricard's work a lot easier.

* * * *

Sid looked in the mirror of the Miner's Arms' toilet and adjusted his *Question of Sport* tie. Tied around his massive neck, it would have almost passed for smart if he wore a proper shirt with it. His *Jaws* T-shirt was in pristine condition and his leather jacket always made him look dapper.

He took out a comb to tend to his scalp, but paused and took another look at himself.

"Aaaaayyyy." The comb went back in his pocket.

Sid went back into the bar hoping that some ladies may have stopped by. He was looking his Sunday-best and they wouldn't be able to resist. Seeing that there was no one to impress, a quick pint was the only option. "Pint of Bolton, Kev."

Kevin pulled the pint of best bitter. He had a shining black eye and his eyebrows were singed. "You're lucky you ain't barred, too, Tillsley. That's £1.98."

It was like a dagger to Sid's heart.

"£1.98? Shit the bed! 2p on a pint? That's highway fooking robbery you, little, fat, Dick Turpin bastard, you!"

"Now then, Tillsley!" he winced as he lifted his arm to point threateningly at Sid. The musket blast was not as damaging as the beating his wife gave him. "A lot of damage was caused last night, and a lot of booze has gone missing. I cannot prove it's you, but I *know* it's you. That will be £1.98. And you can tell that scrawny little bastard, Garforth, that he is barred—for life!"

Sid paid up with a scowl, and Kevin went to sit at the other end of the bar. It was not a day for conversation, not until his losses were covered.

Arthur Peasley entered the pub. "Hey, man, I heard there was a little bit of a hoedown in here last night, everything cool?"

Sid shook his good friend's hand. "Aye, mon. I had to knock one client out, but that was n'owt. Kevin and Brian had a bit of a scrap, like. They're both sulking at the moment. Kevin has barred Brian, again, but it'll blow over in a few days…in time for Ladies' Night."

"Oh yeah, man, Ladies' Night!" Arthur slicked back his perfect hair. He, like Brian, was a devil with the fairer sex.

Kevin walked over and banged a pint of Bolton in front of Arthur, spilling it over the sides, "£1.98."

"Hey man," Arthur started. "Don't you take your grievances out wit—" Then it hit home. "£1.98? That's daylight robbery! You little, fat, Dick Turpin, bast—"

"Now, now! You can blame Garforth for it!" Kevin went back to the other end of the bar, and back to his sulk.

Sid lit up a Nigerian "El Deserto." He had picked up eight-hundred by helping Areed Nafal, a local Nigerian market trader, transport a load of fake designer wear to Doncaster Market. "Aye, Ladies' Night," he said. "You definitely coming then?"

"You better believe it, man. I wouldn't miss it for the world. You know me, baby!" Arthur threw out a catalogue pose. "Sorry I didn't mention it earlier, Sid, but you're looking mighty fine today."

Sid could never take anything that Arthur Peasley said in a homosexual context due to his unparalleled skill with women-folk.

Sid straightened his tie and smiled. "Cheers, pal. It's time for the benefit office interview, again."

"That's a tough break, man, a tough break. I hope they don't catch you. You've been dodging them son of a bitches for so long now."

"Aye, but old Wally Harwood is interviewing me."

Arthur smiled. "Shucks, man, why didn't you say?" Arthur raised his glass to Sid and gave him a knowing wink over the top of his seventies' sunglasses.

Wally Harwood was a man of the people. Born on the Smithson Estate, raised on the Smithson Estate, due to retire in a year's time on the Smithson Estate, and will almost certainly die on the Smithson Estate. He was also the most racist man in the North, which by default made him the most racist man in the universe. He blamed the government for all the non-white people living in his hometown.

Wally wasn't really a man of the people. It just so happened that virtually every single member of the Smithson Estate was white…except all the men over forty, who were generally a deep, red-purple colour. And the fairer sex who were more of an orange colour. And a fair few patrons of the Miner's Arms, and similar pubs, who were a sickly yellow from their poisoned livers.

The reason Wally was loved by the people was because Wally was the most crooked benefit officer in the whole of Teesside. Wally was the main reason that Sid had worked for the last thirty years whilst claiming benefit. He had set Sid up with work since he was a young nipper, including jobs that were a little less savoury. Sid had done his share of debt collecting, bare knuckle fighting, and a one-night-only role as a Donkey in a pantomime, which resulted in Sid's only ever kicking. Meeting with Wally was the only reason that Sid wasn't shitting himself over the Job Centre visit.

* * * *

The Job Centre was just outside the Smithson Estate boundaries. It was a modern building; accidental firebombing had burnt down the last one. Sid had to psych himself up before going in because the place burned his soul, not to mention there were quite a few stairs. He walked through the main doors and Hell enveloped. Despite that, he felt a cold shiver as all the employees turned to stare at him. Everyone in there knew who Sid was. He was infamous for fraudulently claiming benefit…but there was no proof.

Sid gave a nod to all and sundry before joining the nearest queue. There were five queues to five desks where five Job Centre employees sat. They had the illustrious task of processing Middlesbrough's finest unemployed into Middlesbrough's finest employed—a difficult task, indeed. There were about thirty or so seats, half were full of people waiting to see their assigned "work-seeking co-ordinator." On the other side of the room were boards with job vacancies pinned up. Sid felt sorry for the lost souls who searched them for the agony of work.

There were two people in front of Sid. The lad in front was only a bairn. Sid tapped him on the shoulder.

"How old are you, lad?"

The young man turned around and looked Sid up and down. "Why do you want to know?" He hadn't heard of Sid Tillsley…yet.

Sid was rather taken aback by the lad's reaction. "I'm just asking. How old are ya?"

"Nineteen."

Sid shook his head. It was terrible that the bastards got their claws into kids so early. "I'm sorry there, mon. Trying to get you working at your age, the evil bastards."

"I want a job. I'm studying History of Art at York University and require a summer job to fund my studies," said the student pompously.

Sid was confused. He'd never spoken to a student before. "Where you from?"

"Well, I am here in front of you, aren't I?" he said patronisingly. "Therefore, the chances are quite high that I am from Middlesbrough." He gave Sid a look that one reserves for imbeciles.

"Are ye fook!"

The young student gave an annoyed sigh. "I *am* from Middlesbrough, but that does not mean that I have to talk like an uneducated ox." He turned his back on Sid and tapped his foot impatiently.

"History of art? What's that about?"

The student faced Sid again. "I'll give you three guesses at what it's about."

Sid scratched his head. The action caused a considerable amount of armpit odour to diffuse into the student's spotty face and he recoiled as if struck. "Well lad, I reckon you learn about the history of pictures and stuff."

This infuriated the bespectacled student further. "The history of art is far deeper than learning the 'history of a few pictures.' It studies our creative side across the ages. You *townies* do not understand that university is not just about learning a subject. It is about learning people skills and about interacting with your fellow man."

"Why are you such a wanker, then?" asked Sid innocently.

The student wasn't used to this sort of behaviour. "How dare—"

"Next!" yelled the Job Centre employee.

The student gave Sid an evil stare, turned on his heel and sat down at the table.

Sid chuckled. Students! The legends were true. Wankers.

"Name?"

"Gareth Wigglesworth."

Sid's ears pricked up. Wigglesworth? "Ain't your ma'am Sharon Wigglesworth?"

Gareth turned around, furious at the interruption, and because the buffoon knew his mother. "Yes, but that doesn't matter to you?"

"I'm best mates with your Uncle Brian!" Sid gave a big smile with his pearly yellows.

Gareth screamed a war cry and threw himself at Sid, punching and kicking with all of his worthless skinny might. History of Art may teach you one thing (what, exactly, is anybody's guess), but it certainly isn't fighting.

Sid looked confused. "What's he doing?" he asked of anyone who might answer. Watching a nine stone nerd laying into Sid with the effect of an annoying stray fly whilst screaming and crying simultaneously was a sight that no one wanted to witness but had to watch. Finally, after some moments, the young Wigglesworth wore himself out before running out of the Job Centre. He stopped outside the doors to take a brief puff from his inhaler.

"Next!" shouted the desk jockey, unfazed.

"Tillsley, Sid Till—"

"I know who you are, Mr. Tillsley," said the young attractive woman.

"Only good things, I hope," flirted Sid, misreading the situation.

She ignored his comment. "Room Twenty. You know the one."

"Thank you, young lovely."

* * * *

Sid knocked on the door of room twenty.

"Come in."

Behind the desk sat a beaming Wally Harwood.

"How do, Wally?"

"How do, Sid? Good to see you again. Sit yourself down, lad."

Sid wasn't often referred to as "lad," but he had a lot of respect for Wally. He didn't agree with some of his views, but he was a good man at heart because he found Sid tax-free jobs.

"What you been up to then?"

"No proper work, like. Done the odd-job here and there, bit of courier work and that sort of thing. Was hoping that you could sort me out like, Wally." Sid asked hopefully.

"To be honest, I am in no position to offer you any work at the moment. I have been getting a lot of attention from the powers above. As I'm retiring next month they're doing their best to get rid of me and me hard-earned pension. The bastards! They've wasted all their fookin' money on them fookin' immigrants, then they take it out on the hard working folk like you and me. Taxing us up the arse so we can pay for Jonny Foreigner to go on bloody holidays and buy them bloody cars to go out and find jobs…" he tailed off in a racist slur.

Sid gave him a pat on the arm. "No worries, Wally. You've been bloody good to me over the years. I'm sure I can find some work somewhere else. There's always work for a big fella around these parts. Summat will turn up for us in one of the pubs."

Wally smiled. "You're right, Sid. Made a fair few quid meself from them hams of yours." Wally threw a couple of mock friendly jabs at Sid. The smile faded. "I'll still keep you informed of any jobs that I hear of. I like to look after me lads. Not many old-school like yourself anymore. Smithson is being overrun with every fooking race under the sun: blacks, Hispanics, Chinese…"

"What, not ol' Winston?" asked a surprised Sid. "He's been here man and boy! Top fella is Winston, lovely family too. You don't mean him, do ya?"

Wally dismissed the comment as if Sid were mad. "Don't be stupid, Sid. Winston's old-school like yourself. He don't bleedin' count. He's one of us!"

"What about Rodriguez? He's been here thirty year!"

Again, Wally acted surprised, "No! He's a bloody living legend that man. Finest bullfighter in all of Cuba he was, until he retired here."

"Surely you don't mean Lau. Best fookin' food in the Northeast."

Wally was starting to get annoyed. "Of course bloody not! He don't count. Lau's been a good friend to one and all. Does all that Jap-slappin', too, don't he?"

"Aye, reet handy little bastard. Me and him have been in a few scrapes together. His hands move as fast as lightning, like." Sid tried to do a karate chop and knocked Wally's mug of tea over the floor. Wally shook his head. He was used to it. "Sorry, mon. Anyway, who do you mean?"

"Sorry?" asked a lost Wally.

"Well, you said that all them foreigners have moved in to the Smithson Estate. I can't think of anyone apart from our mates."

Wally paused and then thought hard. "Well, Sid, time you were on your way." Wally opened the door for Sid and gave him a warm handshake. "Next time you are here, though, it won't be me interviewing you, mate. You are gonna have a proper benefit officer so get your story straight. Rumour has it, there is a right ball-buster coming to the 'boro and you are her number one priority."

"Ah, fook! I'll get me story straight, Wal. Don't you worry about me." Sid stopped and turned in the doorway. "Oh yeah, do you know Sharon Wigglesworth?"

"Aye, nice looking lass. Fine set until recent years," replied the forever politically correct Wally.

"Her lad was in the queue for a job. Reet little wanker he was. Anyway I mentioned to him his Uncle Brian and he went fooking bananas, he did."

"Sid, you're a naïve young lad sometimes. Garforth was knocking her off when her old fella was away." He laughed. "Garforth has wrecked more homes than that Lawrence Llewelyn Bowen."

Sid gave him a blank look. Wally sighed.

"Garforth's an arsehole."

Sid gave a knowing nod and shut the door.

9

"Right," said the twenty-five year old, pseudo-mullet, dinner jacket with scruffy T-shirt and jeans intentionally made to look dirty, jumped-up little wanker. "Don't let anyone down this hallway. Most importantly, do not question anyone who comes from either of them staircases. Actually, do not even look at them."

"Why's that then?" asked the inquisitive Sid Tillsley as he lit up a Russian. He had obtained six hundred of the amusingly named, "Vlad the Inhalers," by helping Nickov the Russian sell a batch of ex-KGB bugging equipment. There was a definite gap in the market out there and Middlesbrough husbands and wives, suspicious of their loved ones, had snapped them up.

"Do not ask questions, either," the jumped-up little wanker added.

Sid had not experienced the new breed of trendy student types before. According to Brian there were loads of the little bastards around these days. Wasn't like the good ol' days where you knew what people were. It didn't matter if you were a Teddy Boy, a Scooter Boy, a Mod, or a Rocker, people knew what you were. These days they all looked the same. He was struggling to understand the lad because the young Geordie was trying to put on a cockney accent. Why would anyone want to change their accent to something different? Sid wondered. Well, apart from Scousers.

"Right. You can get changed in the gents' locker room. The club opens the doors at nine, and you need to get yourself here for ten-to. OK, now you can ask questions." He waited. "Well?"

"Get changed?"

The jumped-up little wanker rolled his eyes. "Into your tuxedo. You honestly didn't think that you'd be working in that, did you?" He looked Sid up and down with disgust, which greatly confused Sid.

What was wrong with his brand new Tarantula Bitter T-shirt? He had won it for drinking a whole crate in an evening, and he looked the business. "This is what I always wear, like," said Sid.

"Yes, I can imagine that it is. Listen, you are a last-minute replacement, and you were employed because you are meant to be fairly handy." He talked down to the man who was twice his age. "Tonight, you are getting paid extremely good money for an extremely easy job. I suggest you do as you are told and you may make a few extra quid in the near future, OK?" He didn't wait for Sid's answer. "Terry, the doorman, who works this patch, is off for a few weeks with a punctured lung. He didn't do his job properly and he asked too many questions. I suggest that you do your job properly."

"Not a problem, lad."

"His tux is in the gents' locker room. Terry was in better shape than you, so do your best to fit into it."

"When do I get me money?"

"You get your money after you have performed a decent job," said the jumped-up little wanker.

"Fookin' hell, mon. I've been doing this job since you were sucking on your mummy's tats. You run along and don't you worry yourself. I can do this job standing on me 'ead."

The jumped-up little wanker stood speechless. He was the "Assistant Bar Manager" and was not used to abuse from fat, drunken scum from Middlesbrough. Then the jumped-up little wanker remembered that he was a professional and regained his composure.

"You can run along now, lad." Sid lit up his seventieth Russian of the day.

"You…you can't smoke here!" The Assistant Bar Manager's composure was blown out of the window.

Sid was getting tired. "And why the fook not?"

"Listen here." The jumped-up little wanker started to go red. "This isn't some dirty little pub in smogland *'boro*," he sneered. "This is a high-class superclub and punters expect you to be polite, and to do your job professionally. They do not expect some dirty, great, fat oaf, puffing away like a fucking chimney."

"You're still upset 'cos I mentioned your mother's tats, ain't ya, lad? Ne'er you mind. Run along and don't you worry about Sid."

"Right! That is—"

Sid's fist absorbed the rest of the young man's sentence.

"Jumped-up little wanker." Sid shook his head and threw the unconscious lad over his shoulder. He needed to dump the little bastard where he wouldn't be seen until morning. Sid looked around.

"Where the fook am I?"

He was in Rapunzel's night-club in Newcastle, doing the type of work that suited him down to the ground; a bit of security work, out of the public eye, and out of the way of the benefit-bastards. It was one night of work, cash in hand. Perfect. One of the lads down the Miner's who often did a bit of door work put him on to it. And here he was, Saturday night trying to dump an unconscious body. It wasn't the first time, and it was unlikely to be the last.

He mentally retraced his steps: through the entrance, through a long corridor, cloakrooms, pay booths. No good as there would be people around. Through to the massive circular main room, through the corridor to the main pissers, and then through…

"Fook it."

It had been a trek and he wasn't going back. He looked around. There were two staircases: one that went up and one that went down. He took the staircase that went down in order to conserve energy. There was a door, but no handle.

"Shit the bed!" He looked back. There were at least ten steps. "Fook!" He forgot that he would have to climb back up. Eventually, he made it to the top, working up a hell of a sweat in the process. He looked up the other flight of steps. "Fook that."

Sid ambled down the corridor until he saw another door labelled Ale Cellar.

"Aha!"

Voices could be heard from further ahead so he ambled quicker and made it to the ale cellar avoiding any detection. He was ninja…sweaty ninja. Steep stairs descended into darkness and he made his way down carefully, ignoring the jumped-up little wanker's head which banged heavily off every stair.

"Perfect." There was many a good hiding place to stash the little arsehole.

Something caught Sid's eye: four crates of Tarantula Bitter, Hartlepool's finest. He grinned. This could be the finest stitch-up ever! If he did this properly, he could get the jumped-up little wanker sacked for stealing, and also have a tipple himself.

"Sid Tillsley, you could have been in the A-team." But then something else caught Sid's eye. Next to the bitter sat four crates of Smirnoff Ice. This was a conundrum and a half. This jumped-up little wanker would almost definitely be a Smirnoff Ice drinker. A student type would never drink proper ale, never. Should Sid complete the perfect plan and actually drink the ladies' favourite? Yes. Yes he would. He would sacrifice one of the finest brews of the North to drink the ladies' beverage. Sid unceremoniously dumped the jumped-up little wanker like a sack of spuds and set to work on his flawless plan.

* * * *

Forty-five minutes had passed and Sid Tillsley was violently sick.

"Blaaaaaaaaaahhhhhhhhhhh…mmmm, lemony." He was still standing, but only just.

The perfect plan was almost complete. Twenty-eight bottles of Smirnoff ice in forty-five minutes had to be a world record, but he had heavily underestimated the beverage designed for the feminine drinker. All he had to do was go and get into his tuxedo, stand in the hallway and the plan was complete. The alcohol would hinder him, he thought, but surely a lady-drink couldn't possibly thwart his master scheme, and the jumped-up little wanker wouldn't wake up until at least mid-morning.

"Actually–*hic*!–better make sure. Always better to be safe than–*hic!*–something."

Sid lined up his big right foot, and connected with a devastating toe-punt to the groin.

"Thatsh better."

He surveyed the mess he had made, and "mess" was an understatement. He picked up the jumped-up little wanker and laid him carefully in the sticky, multicoloured pool of sick. Voila. This really was an amazingly innovative plan.

He made for the stairs but although *he* wanted to go, his legs had other ideas and he hit the ground hard. The perfect plan was now in jeopardy, but with the will of a prize fighter, Sid got to his feet. It was a staggering eight count and the fight should have been stopped. However, the big man didn't quit easily, especially as he hadn't picked up his wages yet. He managed to get to the top of the stairs and stumbled along the corridor towards the changing rooms. Fortunately, most of the bar staff had arrived and the doormen weren't on duty yet so there weren't many people going to-and-fro. Sid was going to need a lot more luck in order to get away with this little scheme. He was in a hell of a state and one of his eyes wasn't working any more.

Meandering through the club, he bounced from wall to wall, knocking everything over that wasn't nailed down. He made it to the changing rooms and fell through the door.

"Fook!" That fall hurt. His hands didn't make it out in time to break his descent and his chin hit the floor, but luckily his belly cushioned most of the fall and he rolled back and forth comically.

"Fook!" said Sid again, getting back to his feet and commenting on the general state of affairs. There were lockers along the left and clothes-hangers along the right of the small, but smart, changing room. Three or four tuxedos hung neatly for his perusal.

Sudden panic rose with a feeling of impending doom somewhere deep in his intestines.

"Oh, God!" He set out with pure desperation for the toilets. The acidity of the lemons in the vodka had caused a lot of movement in his lower bowel and bad things were travelling south, fast. He ran as best he could, clenching his buttocks with vice-like intensity, a practised skill. The toilet was near, but so was an anal explosion that would be seen from space.

Sid was within six feet, the toilet door was open, the lid was up and the seat was down. Thank God. He felt a rumble that was indicative of Armageddon. There was only one option left, and that was to perform a manoeuvre that only hardened drinkers could perform, and only then at times of pure peril.

If he didn't make it in time, he would end the night in the worst possible predicament. If he made it in time, there would be a plumber in the worst possible predicament. If he got half way, there would be a team of cleaners in the worst possible predicament. No matter what, someone was going to have a really shit time. When he was within five feet he leapt. Sid had never made the manoeuvre from more than four feet before and this was going to be close.

"FFFFFFFFOOOOOOOOOOOOKKKKKKK!"

KAAAAABBBBBBOOOOOMMMMM!!!!

He made it. He God damn made it.

The simultaneous act of undoing your belt, pulling your pants and trousers down, turning around in mid air, landing on a toilet seat, shutting the door, and then defecating at a near-fatal rate was not the work of a man…it was the work of a god. It was a technique that could only be done justice by being viewed in slow motion with a *Matrix*-esque rotating camera.

Sid's almost nuclear-like excretion had instant sobering effects, which he was not thankful for when he realised that there was no toilet paper. When he was certain that he had not lost part of his intestines in the explosion, he shuffled to the other cubicle with hope in his heart.

"Fook!"

This was going from bad to worse. Hannibal's plans never involved the infamous "cardboard-bit-from-the-toilet-roll-wipe." Sid reached for the Card of Pain. The acidity of the lemons had done him a wrong'n. The toilet roll broke in half when he reached up inside the dispenser. It was the kind that had plastic on each end so it could slot into the dispenser.

"Fook!"

A thought crossed Sid's inebriated brain. Can you wipe your anus with plastic?

"FFFFFFOOOOOOOOOOKKKKKKK!"

No, you can't.

After a few minutes, when the pain and most of the bleeding had subsided, the wounded soldier took off his pants and used it to wipe his behind, slowly, with a grimace. It wasn't the first time that this unfortunately expensive technique had been performed on a Saturday night, and it wouldn't be the last. He strategically placed the pants behind the toilet and limped into the changing rooms. At least it had sobered him up a bit.

He checked the four tuxedos to find the biggest size.

"All these bouncers are fooking midgets!" he exclaimed as he couldn't find a size forty-six inch waist. He squeezed into the thirty-eight inch waist trousers that were available and had to wear them low so he could do them up. It left ten inches of trouser leg that needed turning up and three inches of bum crack showed itself proudly to the world. He put on the shirt, but left it unbuttoned because it was impossible to do up. The jacket was skin-tight.

Doing up the bow tie up proved beyond him and he made a complete mess of it.

Sid checked himself out in the mirror. "Lookin' good!" he said with a devilish grin. With only a few mild staggers he left the changing rooms and headed for his post. Some miscalculated corners later, he made it. Mission accomplished with only a relatively minor mishap along the way. He had had worse in his time.

It was nine o'clock and the club was now officially open although it only tended to get busy after about ten thirty. Some top DJs from the north of England were playing so it was going to be a busy night.

Rapunzel's was a high-class nightclub. There was hardly any trouble and the doormen had very strict guidelines as to who was let in. Drugs were a problem, but a blind eye was turned unless dealing was noted. None of this would affect Sid. All he had to do was stop anyone from the nightclub passing by him. Everyone who came the other way could do what they wanted. It was that simple.

A doorman approached Sid. He was short for a bouncer, well under six-foot, but he was as wide as he was tall. His head was shaven and he had a heavily scarred face. To anyone apart from Sid, who didn't care about such things, he would look menacing. "Hey, you seen Miguel?"

"Miguel?" said Sid with the same facial expression he pulled when he tasted something horrible. "What kind of a name is that?"

The bouncer ignored his comments. "The assistant bar manager. He showed you around. Have you seen him?"

"N-no, no." stuttered Sid. He was not a good liar unless he was confronted with the benefit office, their representatives, or the police. He was even worse after a few ales and worse still after twenty-eight bottles of Smirnoff Ice.

"Have you been drinking?" The doorman moved closer and reeled back quickly as if punched in the face. "Your breath stinks! You're a disgrace!"

Sid couldn't afford to lose this job, especially after all that had befallen in the last half hour. He staggered back accidentally, but regained himself with dignity. "How dare you? How dare you accuse me of drinking?"

The bouncer gave a look of disgust. "You'd be sacked if it wasn't club opening time. Aren't you Sid Tillsley?"

"Why?" Sid never liked to admit who he was, especially when out of his hometown of the 'boro.

"Thought so." The bouncer shook his head. "Word is that you are the best fighter in the town, if not the whole of the Northeast. The doormen round there are always telling stories about you. You're just a drunk though, aren't ya?"

Sid considered it. Hardest man in 'boro? He had never thought about it before. He couldn't give a crap about all that "who's the hardest" bollocks. If he had trouble then he dealt with it.

Hang on…he called him a drunk! How dare he? But when Sid recalled the last hour, his throbbing anus came to mind. "Well, I can't say that I don't enjoy a drink now and then," he admitted.

The doorman shook his head once more. "If you see Miguel, tell him I'm looking for him."

"No problems, boss." Sid gave a salute. As long as he was paid he couldn't care less what anyone thought of him. He'd already knocked someone out tonight and he didn't want to add another to the list.

* * * *

Sid was bored senseless. With every second he was sobering up and starting to feel hung over. The music of the club pounded through his skull incessantly. How could these lads and lasses listen to this garbage? And why so loud? He had not seen anyone for half an hour. A few clubbers partied down the far end of the corridor, but his orders were simply to stop people going any further so he ignored them.

Four hours to go, and no-one had discovered Miguel yet. What a stupid name. No self-respecting Geordie parent would ever name their bairn, Miguel. He must have changed his name, the jumped-up little wanker.

Click! The door at the bottom of the stairs opened. A man in a long coat wearing a wide-brimmed hat walked up the stairs. He didn't look up or acknowledge Sid but walked down the corridor, head bowed, into the club. Sid made a mental note. *Right. That fella is allowed to go anywhere so best remember him.*

Party-goers ebbed their way down the corridor as the night progressed, just to cool off or chat. It was quarter past eleven and still no one had tried to get past him. Sid's alcohol levels had metabolised enough so that now he was merely "merry." He had developed a serious headache and was in a bad mood because of it.

He spotted the guy with the wide-brimmed hat walking down the corridor with a young lady wearing practically nothing. "Ah fook! What do I do now?"

As the man approached, Sid moved into the middle of the corridor, and looked and felt awkward. "Erm, sorry, mate, I was told to let you through because you came through that door," he nodded to the basement, "but, I canna let the lass through unless I get the go-ahead from one of me bosses, like."

Sid couldn't see the man's face as he had the brim of the hat pulled low, but the voice spoke quietly in an accent that Sid didn't recognise.

"I am friends with the owner and I assure you that any guest of mine is allowed past this point. Be co-operative, and you will be rewarded at the end of the night."

Sid didn't see the guy move, but a twenty-pound note had appeared in the top pocket of his tight tuxedo.

"Go right on in, sir." Sid bowed as the couple passed, and he watched them go up the stairs. His professionalism wavered when he ducked down so he could see up the girl's skirt. No knickers! That was the best twenty quid Sid Tillsley had ever earned. He went back to guarding the corridor with a renewed sense of vigour and tried to put on a doorman's face by looking miserable.

A group of girls walked up to Sid after seeing the encounter with the couple. All three were about twenty years old and all three wore very little. Sid got excited both emotionally and a little bit physically. After all, chicks love bouncers.

"Good evening, ladies. What can I do for three beautiful vixens?"

"What's up them stairs?" asked a brunette with a lovely set of tats.

Sid talked to the lovely set of tats. "It is the room for VIPs, my young lovely."

"VIP lounge is other side of club, mate," replied a blonde with even greater tats than the brunette.

Sid bent forward to get an even better look. He wasn't very subtle because he was still a bit drunk and also high off his twenty-quid windfall. The breasts were also acting as a fantastic painkiller for his quickly receding headache. "This is for the real VIPs, darling, proper important people. That is why I am guarding the door." He gave a winning smile...to the blonde's breasts.

"Who's in there, like?"

Sid turned around to face another blonde who unfortunately didn't have very good tats at all. He ignored her.

"Can we go in there then, mister?" asked the Best Tats.

"Well, that depends?" said Sid, abusing his power.

"On what?" asked the Second-Best Tats.

"On what you ladies can do for me. I could murder a whisky."

"Fook off!" said Crap Tats. "They're about three quid a shot in 'ere. How about you let us in there, and I'll suck ya off?"

Fooking Hell! This was the best night of work ever. Sid Tillsley was about to get some action on top of the twenty quid he earned earlier.

"That method of payment will be quite acceptable, young lovely. Will any of your friends be joining you in your adventure?"

"Will we fook. Hurry up, Cheryl, so we can go get ourselves some footballers."

"Where are we going then?" Cheryl asked, one of Newcastle's finest.

"Ah, fook...yeah...err..." Sid paused. Where to go? The downstairs basement had no handle, and there were people upstairs. He had been sick all over the ale cellar. Fook! There was nowhere else to go. He was now torn. Did he walk away, take the twenty quid, take the ladies' offer and call it a day? Alternatively, did he work for the next couple of hours and pick up the eighty-five quid promised to him?

A question for the ages: was a blow job worth eighty-five notes?

"I'm sorry, love, but I canna leave me post."

It was like winning the lottery and losing the ticket.

Cheryl gave the big man a filthy look. "Fooking 'ell, how many offers do you get from a lass like me? You must be queer or summat? Come on, girls."

The girls departed. Sid put his head in his hands. That was the closest he had come to some action for two years, but then eighty-five quid was a lot of money. He could subscribe to *Razzle* for fifteen years with that sort of wedge. Sid made peace with his decision.

Midnight came. The jumped-up little wanker had said that someone would bring him a cup of tea at half eleven. Sid now had a hangover mouth and was desperate for a slash. He hadn't been to the toilet since the incident earlier (he winced at the thought, both with his face and with his behind), and twenty-eight Smirnoff Ices is a lot of liquid for one human to consume. It would be pretty impressive for a camel to drink twenty-eight Smirnoff Ices.

Another half an hour passed and the club was at full capacity. So was Sid and he was now dying for the toilet. Moving around awkwardly, he tried to numb the pressure build-up that was threatening his waterworks. His irritation was showing in his job.

"What's down the corridor, mate?"

"Fook off."

Clubbers had meandered their way as far as the ale cellar, which meant he couldn't go down there for a piss. The only option was to try upstairs. If there were people in there, they'd surely understand. Jesus, he only wanted a piss. Gingerly climbing the stairs, he found the door slightly ajar. He knocked. Nothing. He knocked a bit louder, still no response. Sid's nether regions screamed for relief so he opened the door and walked in.

The room was beautifully decorated, but not as beautiful as the drinks cabinet. Whisky! You always feel thirsty after a few whiskies, he reasoned, so maybe if he had a few whiskies it would dehydrate him a tiny bit. Then, he could have a few more whiskies before he would need a piss again. Yeah, that made sense. It made absolutely perfect bloody sense.

Sid went for the whisky and picked up the first bottle that he reached. The bottle was very old and the label had mostly perished. He uncorked the top and took a sniff.

"Fookin' Hell, that smells grand." He poured himself an extra large glass.

Sid took a large mouthful of the golden liquid. "That is without a doubt the finest thing that has ever touched me lips." For the first time in his thirty-two year drinking career, Sid Tillsley savoured every single last drop and didn't neck a millilitre. This was not the whisky that MacTavish the Glaswegian made from WD40, de-icer and orange squash. This was Heaven on Earth. "No wonder Scotsmen are drunks," said the drunk.

Sid Tillsley, whisky connoisseur, picked another bottle. He examined the bottle, uncorked it, sniffed it, and drunk a lot of it. He nearly savoured every drop. This particular brand he savoured slightly less than the one before.

"One more and I'll find a pisser. Just one more…" Three triple whiskies later and Sid Tillsley was in danger.

"Right! Time for a toilet." Attempting to make for a door on the opposite side of the room, Sid only succeeded in falling through a coffee table. "Fook!" Too much noise. Must be like ninja. Taking another step, the ninja fell through a plant next to the broken coffee table.

Sid weighed up his options: a) go forward, find a lavatory and leave no trace, or; b) piss in the plant pot and drink some more whisky.

Plan B was the easiest option at this point in time.

* * * *

It had been a bad night for Jacques Jereaux. He hated England almost as much as he hated humans. Therefore, being in the same building as a thousand English humans was the worst combination possible. All this way to meet up with the Lamian Consilium, who was third on his list of hates. At least he was meeting Richmond. Not a soul in the world could dislike Richmond, a vampire of the old code. Unfortunately, Richmond had not arrived yet. He always slept more than usual for an immortal. In these summer months, too long was spent in hiding and extra sleep was not an option.

Jereaux had arrived an hour ago and decided to pleasure himself on a young girl. Human females were at least good for something apart from feeding. He had found himself a particularly pretty specimen and bought her back to the safe house. Richmond had a number of spare rooms allocated for this very carnal purpose. The fat oaf on the door had tried to stop him, but was bribed with a small amount of money. Humans have no honour. Not that Richmond would mind him bringing this girl back.

Unfortunately, she decided to run off when the going was getting too rough for her. Stupid bitch, what did she expect? Did she think that someone like him would be bothered about pleasuring her? He would have ripped her head off if he were outside his guest's house. He had run after the girl to calm her down and ply her with some drink. The fat imbecile of a doorman had his head buried in his hands as they went past. As for the girl, she was bought easily. A bottle of champagne had convinced her that everything was fine. She would pay the price later.

Jereaux took in the sights and sounds. He was surrounded by a thousand humans playing their music at a level that would damage their delicate ears, drinking ethanol and taking narcotics until they were ill, fighting, or fucking. It made him sick that he had to eat them, but they did taste exquisite. He made his way back to the safe house, pushing aside partygoers as he went. The idiot had left his post.

"Useless bastard." He pushed open the door and in front of him was the overweight oaf, inebriated to near-unconsciousness, sat in the shards of a sixteenth century table whilst urinating in a plant pot.

Richmond entered from another door into the lounge. He had been resting in his quarters and was awoken by the commotion.

"What is going on down here!" A rather awkward silence followed.

Sid sat, cock in hand, coffee table shards sticking in his arse. "Thankss God you ladshh came in time!" he slurred.

The hostility in the air was thicker than that of the average war.

"Who are you?" asked Richmond through gritted teeth.

If Sid were wearing a cap, he would have taken it to hand. "Sshir, I am bouncing the corridor downshtairs, shir! I…errr, heard a commotion up here and investigated. I think there has been a shtruggle or summat?" Sid indicated the mess around him with a sweep of the hand.

"Why is your penis in your hand?" Richmond's anger was diluted only slightly with the mystery of the situation.

It would take a very intelligent man to think of a good explanation as to why he had his cock out. *Think fast, Sid.* "There…was…a fire! Yes, a fire. I put it out, be…because it was a fire."

Jereaux had heard enough. "Richmond, would you give me the honour of disposing of this scum?"

Sid slowly tried to get to his feet, fell back to the ground a couple of times, but a sterling third effort succeeded. "Gentlemen, gentlemen, there is no need. I have averted the danger. I ssshall continue to perform my duty downstairs. Good night."

With that he bowed and continued to bow until he fell into an unconscious heap on the floor.

* * * *

The ten seconds after you wake, after the night before, half way between the land of sleep and the dawn of the new day you experience a life which has no memory of the past and no thought for the future. That place is utter peace—until a hangover kicks in.

Sid Tillsley had just come out of that state of "peace." Flashbacks attacked. Twenty-eight bottles of Smirnoff Ice and a bottle of malt whisky attacked. Sid was sick over the side of the bed, but it was no bed. It was a cold hard surface and it wouldn't be doing his piles any good. He opened his eyes expecting to see the streets of Middlesbrough, but no. He saw a tin roof. Where was he?

He sat up (not an actual sit-up, but he rolled around a bit and ended up in a sitting position). Five men stood around him in a large warehouse full of computer equipment. He recognised a couple of them: that big Jamaican who had seemed a little peeved at him drinking his whisky, and the angry bloke who had also seemed peeved at the whisky drinking. He didn't recognise the other three. They were big lads, well-dressed and not looking too happy.

"Now then, lads," said Sid clutching his head, "about the whisky, I only had one to sort out me cold." He sniffed for effect. "Look, I'll get you another one. Not a problem."

"Whisky should be the last of your worries," spoke one of the three that Sid didn't recognise.

"Well, that is very kind of you, sir. Thank you for letting bygones be bygones. Now there is the small matter of me getting paid for my evening's work."

"You should be more worried about your own life," threatened the lad who had caught him with his cock out.

Sid considered this. "Well, I guess I do eat too many saturated fats."

"Look at yourself, human; pathetic, too stupid to know your fate. We are going to rip you to shreds. We will keep you alive as long as possible, and make you suffer until the very last."

Sid was rather confused with the whole affair. How could one of them be worried about his health, and the other want to kill him?

"Your ass is mine!" said one of the big lads.

Sid's *Pink Alert* activated in milliseconds and he was on his feet and ready to go.

"Keep away from me, you dirty bastard! I won't be having any of it! It will be a cold day in hell before your kind gets Sid Tillsley!"

"So you know of our kind, human?" asked Richmond.

Sid turned to face him. "Yes I bloody do. I've seen your kind, before, bloody everywhere, these days. Every five seconds on bleedin' telly. On them bleedin' planes with them moustaches!"

The vampires looked at each other confused.

"And in them toilets down the park. Them toilets are for pissin'! Not for you lot!"

"You have no idea, do you?" mocked one of them he hadn't recognised. "Your uneducated little mind cannot comprehend what we are. It is best that we put you out of your short-lived misery. We are the vampire." And with that he launched himself at Sid with cat-like agility.

Sid had seen cat-like agility before and not just in cats. He had fought a few of them poncy, martial arts fannies before, spinning around in pyjamas screaming things in foreign. Bloody idiots.

All the cat-like agility was wasted. The vampire had attempted a double-back-shadowless-spinning-axe-kick, whilst Sid Tillsley had attempted—and succeeded with—a big right hand. The vampire crumbled into dust making Sid cough and splutter.

"What the fook?" The remaining vampires were as shocked as Sid. "I knew you lot weren't made of the same thing that we are! Come on then, ya bastards!"

The fight was over in seconds. Jereaux and two of the vampires attacked Sid simultaneously. Sid went for the biggest one, as the others in a group normally backed off when the big lad went down. He caught Jereaux with a straight right, turning him into dust. The other two jumped back but Sid caught one on the way, which meant he had one attacker left to deal with—the vampire made the mistake of pausing, Sid's right didn't, and the hapless vampire joined his mates as dust.

Sid paused for breath, hands on knees. Pointing at Richmond, who had watched the fight in disbelief he wheezed, "You son…will get yours…as soon as I get…my breath back… otherwise, fook off!"

For the first time in six hundred years, Richmond ran.

10

Richmond paced anxiously. He had been pacing constantly since what happened, had happened. In all his centuries, he had never addressed the Lamian Consilium. They had never requested anything from him and he had never had reason to seek their help. However, this was different. How could a human do what that fat man had done? Was he even human?

"Richmond? Would you join the Consilium, please?" A young male vampire formally called him to the meeting. He didn't recognise the young and serious vampire, no doubt already trying to network himself up the ranks. Surely, he had better things to do with his youth than get involved with this political back-stabbing bullshit.

Richmond followed the vampire into the room. Archaic torches lit every corner of the vast chamber, and gothic architecture caught the eye. Hundreds of gargoyles stared down at the centre of the room in grotesque poses. Fifty vampires sat in a circle of ornately carved throne-like chairs. Grouped together opposite the entrance of the hall sat the founders of the Consilium.

Michael Vitrago sat amongst them. He appeared younger than the other elders, some of whom appeared like human gentlemen in their early sixties or seventies. One looked like a frail old man, silvered hair and bowed in his seat. Augustus and Lucia were present. They, along with Michael, were the only members of the joint vampire/human Coalition that sat on this group.

"So, we have come no closer to establishing what is feeding incessantly in the Northeast?" asked one of the elders. He was a small, wiry vampire, still tall by human standards, but dwarfed by the younger generations.

"No," answered Lucia. "Franco Stoloni is tracking through the moors as we speak. He has recruited a few lamia, good trackers, to the investigation. However, they have come up with nothing."

"Surely the humans have put their own people on it? Have the Hominum Order come up with anything?" asked a muscular, and strikingly handsome vampire. She was not beautiful but her strong features drew your attention.

"The same as us, it seems," said Lucia. "Caroline heads the Hominum Order, and she would share any information that the humans had acquired. It appears that whatever is making a mess of the human population of Middlesbrough is as silent a killer as our best assassins. It is hard to believe, considering the mess that it makes of its food. The brutality is impressive…even for one of us." The comment brought heated discussion throughout the group.

"Richmond, it has been a long time." The other vampires stopped talking amongst themselves as soon as Michael spoke. All eyes turned to Richmond who was waiting outside the circle.

"Yes, Michael, it has. I never thought that we would meet under this roof."

Michael gave a rare laugh. "True, I agree. But, Richmond, I believe that you have something to tell us. Something urgent?"

"Yes, my friends, I have. This is my first time in front of you all and it will hopefully be my last. The news I bring is, indeed, urgent." He gathered his thoughts before continuing. "Vampire hunters have been a joke to us for centuries, shadows of their forefathers…until now. This morning I witnessed something infinitely more powerful. I watched a man—a human—kill four vampires in thirty seconds with nothing more than his hands."

The revelation brought forth a tirade of questions from the congregation:

"Are you sure that he just used his hands?"

"How do you know they are dead?"

"Were they really vampires he killed?"

"Brothers and sisters, be silent!" Richmond insisted. "I will pretend that you are slightly disturbed by the news that I have just given you. That is why I take no offence from your insulting questions." He looked at them pointedly. He really had no patience for this but the situation was critical. "When he connected with his fist, it was if he decapitated them, or sunlight took them."

Michael sat with his head propped up by his massive hands. "What do you think this means, Richmond?"

Richmond shook his head slowly.

"What was he like?" asked another member of the council. "What could possibly take one of us?"

Richmond recounted the tale of Sid's unsuccessful night as a bouncer. He included every detail down to his urination into one of his orchids. "He was in a bad state due to a serious hangover, and, physically, he was in terrible condition. I could practically taste the cholesterol in his veins from the other side of the room. However, when he moved, he was like one of us, and the power…you could sense the power explode from inside him. It was almost supernatural. He killed Jacques Jereaux."

A gasp went up from several of the congregation at the news of Jereaux's death. He was an extremely powerful vampire. Richmond listed the rest. "Stefan Kahn, Winston Montero and Terence O'Hara. Not easy pickings at all."

A female elder stood. "Could the humans have a new weapon? Have they found something new?"

"Possibly, Maria, but why would they give this weapon to a wreck of a human like that?" said a blonde male, shorter than average, yet incredibly good-looking. "There is something else out there causing severe problems, for both races. We need to get to the bottom of that, first."

"I agree," said another elder of the Lamian Consilium. "Whatever is killing humans in the Northeast is more dangerous than a man that can kill vampires. If he goes to the press then no one will believe him. However, if the news of horrific killings gets to the police and then the press, I do not want to think of the consequences."

"Richmond, what do you know about the man himself?" asked another council member.

"He was hired for one evening's work. We were down a man due to Gunnar injuring one of my door staff. He was hired on a whim, the same way I hire all of my one-off staff. I asked a few questions and found out a considerable amount. His name is Sid Tillsley. He's in his forties and has a hard-man reputation in a run-down local estate in Middlesbrough. He smokes and drinks heavily, and practically lives his life in a pub. He was very adamant about getting his money paid, cash in hand. We told all the staff that Tillsley got drunk so we sent him on his way with a few quid in his pocket."

"How could this man perform these deeds?" asked Maria. "He sounds like he struggles to take care of himself, and that time will solve this problem in due course."

"Perhaps, the Firmamentum is upon us?" The speaker was the oldest member of the assembly and his eyes had lost part of their characteristic agelessness. "This hasn't happened for two millennia. That was the last time a human killed a lamia in hand-to-hand combat."

"The Firmamentum?" said Michael surprised. "That cannot be, Pontius. The feedings in the Northeast cannot be attuned to that. It would be impossible to hide."

Pontius considered this carefully. "I am often mocked when I speak of the old days. Our so-called scientists describe the Firmamentum as 'a spike in genetic evolution,' but I see it as a reminder of what it is to be a true lamia."

The vampires, spare a few, sat captivated. It was rare to hear Pontius address the group. He normally sat back and listened to the proceedings of the modern generation.

"The Firmamemtum is a phenomenon to celebrate. We should celebrate it in battle and in blood. Where we rid ourselves of mankind's petty bureaucracy and rely on our feral instincts and our lust for violence. The Firmamentum has always brought unity in the vampire race. We cannot hide away like scared vermin when the monster is set free!"

"What monster? What's the Firmamentum?"

Pontius closed his eyes and shook his head. "We have fallen so far." He looked the young vampire who had interrupted him up and down. "The Firmamentum is when the most powerful, blood-thirsty vampire is born onto the world. Every two thousand years, this magnificent vampire—this beast—

strides across the land, decimating everything in its path. However, where there is yin, there is yang, and where there is dark, there is light. There is always a balance and the Firmamentum is no different. There is always a reply: a human born with awesome power far greater than our own, the Bellator. This human is as fair and beautiful as the beast is brutal and vile—and the two are always born simultaneously. The Firmamentum is the time when the beast and the Bellator are alive."

Pontius spat on the floor, disgusted that a human could possess such gifts. "We have grown weak over the last two millennia. We need a Firmamentum to show us what it is to be a vampire. A real lamia. This modern day *arrangement* we have made with the humans will shatter as soon as the animal reveals itself. Politics do not control the mind of a beast whose instincts are as terrible as they are deadly. How will petty words control an animal that doesn't kill to feed but kills because it loves to?

"Peace?" mocked Pontius. "If the Firmamentum is here, is there a chance of it? Yes, only one. The human answer—the Bellator. However, kill the Bellator..." Pontius cast a sly glance around the assembly. "And the beast is free to bring sanity back to the world, and end the ridiculous charade of the Coalition!"

"Enough!" Michael banged his fist on the table in an unusual sign of emotion. "Things have changed, Pontius, possibly beyond the limit of your council. We cannot live like we did in the old age. Such talk is madness."

Most vampires cowered in Michael's presence, but Pontius was not affected. He chuckled to himself, amused at the rise he got out of his fellow elder. "Sparle was born from two vampires of Russian descent. They were a hardy couple that migrated to Italy out of interest in the Empire. The two vampires were nothing special. She was plain to look at and not a powerful being, yet her thirst for killing bordered on the abnormal. The male didn't share his partner's lust for killing, but did thrive on torture, whether it was human, vampire, or animal. He was a natural sadist, and the only thing that he ever loved was his wife, although it was probably her lust for murder that he loved." Once more Pontius chuckled, but this time at the sadism and torture he described, a love he shared.

"Sparle's mother died during childbirth. This was taken as a sign of the start of the Firmamentum since it is not uncommon for the male vampire to die during conception. His father, as you would imagine, didn't take too kindly to this, and tortured the baby from birth. When it was two years old, the child killed its father with its own hands. Five years later, our good friend, Ricard, was the next lamia to come into contact with the child. It had killed everything within fifty miles of the house where it was raised. By eight years old, it was six foot tall and hulking with muscle. Sparle possessed no conscience and the only thing he inherited was his mother's desire for murder and his father's lust for sadism.

"How Ricard survived, he—as usual—kept secret, but I believe it shows how dangerous the old bastard is." Pontius scowled. His contempt for the scholar was quite apparent. "He spent fifteen years with Sparle, a name which he gave him. He tried to teach Sparle how to live and hunt humanely. He watched him grow to an immense size and he knew what he was. The Firmamentum has existed since vampires and man have walked the earth, but that stupid bastard thought he could change nature's monster.

"Nevertheless, if anyone could have done it then, although it pains me to say it, Ricard would have been the one." Pontius' contempt for the scholar was quite apparent.

"Sparle, at the age of twenty-three, grew tired of the old man, and how the old man escaped death is another mystery of the age. The monster wandered for two years and killed all in its path. Lamia, animal, human, he would drink the blood of anything. It was after attacking a Roman garrison that Sparle's future was decided. He attacked the camp of fifty soldiers and killed all except one scout who managed to escape and take word to his commanding officers. With the exception of Ricard, he was the first man or beast to escape Sparle's murderous intent.

"Armies were sent against him and he relished the battle, bathing in their blood. He knew not that he was different and only cared for violence and murder. Meanwhile, in Rome, a gladiator dominated the games. The vampire had to erase his existence from history once the Agreement was established. Remo Elscachius, the Bellator, was a human who was beautiful to gaze upon. He, too, was motherless from the moment of birth and signified the fulfilment of prophesy. His body was sculpted out of rock and his eyes carried the same luminescence as his beastly counterpart. I watched him kill a vampire, with speed, grace, and nobility in the Coliseum. It was he who the Emperor sent to fight the monster and it was the most incredible battle I have ever witnessed." Pontius' voice quickened with every mention of bloodshed.

"With two swords Elscachius danced around Sparle and cut him over and over again. The earth was soaked with blood and Sparle screamed in pain and delight at the challenge he had found. Sparle was cut hundreds of times, and his body struggled to heal the wounds that had been inflicted. Then he landed a blow on Elscachius, a backhand that sent the man fifty feet in the air. The human landed hard and did not move from what looked like a fatal strike. Sparle was no tactical fighter, and he ran over to feast on his newest victim. As he knelt to feed, Elscachius stuck two daggers through his eyes, deep into his brain. It enabled him to withdraw the weapons and decapitate Sparle, ending his magnificent life."

"Remo Elscachius, the Bellator. What happened to his line?" asked Richmond.

Pontius laughed. "Oh, for the vanity of humans. He sired many bastards from the hundreds of whores he cavorted with. His bloodline was diluted and died out centuries ago. He became a hunter until his life was ended by the son of a vampire whom he had defeated in the Coliseum...Isn't that right, Michael?"

Michael sneered at Pontius. "As well you know, Pontius, as well you know. I witnessed my father's death at the hands of a human. I hunted him down and obtained the revenge that I saw fit."

"How did you...?" asked Augustus.

"That is of no concern to any, except Remo Elscachius and me. He was different to others in his line, and he and Sparle didn't belong on this Earth. The Firmamentum can damage the very structure of our civilisation. As for its reoccurrence and for all of Pontius' stories, it is absurd. If one of Sparle's power walked the earth, then we would know within hours of him coming to age. I do not think that a human like Remo Elscachius will be born again. From what Richmond has just told us, the man, Sid Tillsley, does not even appear to be in shape!"

Richmond nodded. "Yes, you're right, but he moved like one of us. He was no normal human, I promise you."

"It must be investigated," said Augustus. "An anomaly of any kind requires our full attention. I would be astonished, as I think most members of the council would be, if he turned out to be the Bellator."

Michael nodded. "I do not believe he is the Bellator. Nor do I believe the bloodshed in the Northeast can be attributed to an animal like Sparle. The Firmamentum is not here. If it was, the vampire race would be on the brink of extinction. The Firmamemtum is not something to celebrate. It never was. The Agreement is in place for our survival. If it falls, we fall. The Firmamentum would be the end of us all." He looked pointedly at Pontius before continuing. "I'll contact Franco Stoloni who is investigating the massacres in the Northeast. He will not struggle tracking this human down. I suggest that we do not kill him immediately. We need to find out exactly what he is and how he performed such feats. Comments?"

"Are you suggesting we capture him?" asked another elder.

Michael nodded. "I think we would be foolish if we didn't. But first, we should track him to determine his movements. We need to ascertain if there is anything more sinister behind his actions."

A murmur of agreement went up around the hall.

"Should the Hominum Order be informed of these matters?" asked Augustus.

"Of course they should," answered Michael. "We work in harmony with our sister council for the benefit of both species." His true feelings, he kept hidden. The humans would know within the day of all that has befallen.

"We will reconvene in a week," he said and then he left the room.

11

"So there I was in middle of this room, and the undead were upon me!" Sid lit up an Embassy Number One. He was in the Miner's, propped up by the bar. The cigarette had been donated to Sid by one of the lads and it was his first legal cigarette for nigh on ten years. It was eight o'clock on the Sunday night. Brain Garforth (reinstated drinker of the Miner's Arms—Kev could never turn down a dollar), Kevin Ackroyd, Arthur Peasley, Peter Rathbone, and the lads surrounded Sid, listening to his tale of courage and drunken haymakers.

"I'd had a few ales like, as you do when you're working the door."

Peter Rathbone interrupted. "Not me, Sid. I never use these after a drink," he looked at his fists as if they were going to go off. "When I studied Tiger Claw and Husky Kung Fu under Master Thomas, I learnt how to kill. The slight mistiming of my chi energy can kill a man dead, if that's not what I'm trying to do in the first place."

Every eyeball rose to the roof simultaneously. Every pub has a certain character that is full of shit and always trying to outdo everyone else's story. Peter Rathbone was that character. Every story that has ever been told, Peter Rathbone had one better. If someone pulled a set of twins, he pulled triplets, or possibly Siamese twins. If someone holed an eagle, he holed an albatross, etc., etc., and on it went until closing time—or until he was knocked out.

Brian Garforth didn't suffer fools lightly and had listened to the ranting of Peter too many times. "Shut up, Rathbone. Let the man tell the story. No one wants to hear your bullshit"

"How dare you? You are lucky that I was taught restraint during my teachings in China."

"Everyone knows that your 'training' consisted of Billy, the chef at Ming's Kitchen giving you a kicking for nipping his bird's arse last New Years'. Now shut the fook up and let Sid tell his story."

Peter went bright red with anger and embarrassment, but kept quiet nonetheless. After the laughter subsided Sid continued.

"As I was saying, I was in the middle of the room, and the undead were upon me!"

"Where were you, man?" asked the handsome face of Arthur Peasley.

"It was in some warehouse. I didn't really know where the hell I was. I just woke up 'cos some bastard had thrown water over me."

"How did you get there?" asked Brian.

"That's the thing, mate, I ain't really sure. I was at the club, and then I went for a slash 'cos I'd had a few too many. I must have slipped and banged me 'ead like?" Sid was genuinely puzzled by it all. Booze is wonderful at taking the memories away.

All heads nodded simultaneously and gave that "aaaaarr" sound that people make when the penny drops. All the guys knew Sid, and knew that he often passed out through alcohol abuse (and once from eating crisps, but that was for a bet, which he won).

"Any road, I'm in this warehouse thing, like, and there're five of these big bastards surrounding me." Sid described it like an everyday occurrence. "I knew it was gonna be trouble, mind."

"When studying karate, my Daddy could cope with four men simultaneously!" exclaimed Arthur. "Maybe not towards the end, with all the extra weight and all. I followed in my Daddy's footsteps, and I could never take more than three good men, even with my best stuff used on 'em. Sid, you fought the undead. I'm surprised you're here to tell the tale, baby."

The group nodded agreement.

"It were close, like. Especially with them being the undead and all that."

"Sid?" asked Kevin. "How do you know they were the undead?"

Sid lit up another free Embassy. "At first I thought they were *them lot*, which was their first mistake. They had big pointy teeth, like that fooker I knocked out when I was trying that doggin' lark out."

The group nodded again. It was now common knowledge that Sid was experimenting.

"Any road, one of 'em said summat like: 'we're fooking vampires,' or summat along them lines. I like to keep an open mind on things, you know?"

"That include gays, Sid?" volunteered Peter Rathbone, the greasy little bastard.

A horrible silence followed…and kept following.

The big man's face indicated that thoughts were racing (well, gently traversing) from one side of his massive, yet limited, brain to the other. The thoughts slowed, got a little side-tracked and were forgotten about. All part of Sid's anti-gay defence system.

"Anyway, lads," his mind finally back on track, "I am out of pocket until benefit day. My beer and tab supplies have dried up so I bid you good day." He headed for the door.

"One more beer on the house," said Kevin. Sid turned on a sixpence and returned to the arena. One of the lads passed him a free Woodbine.

"So, where was I? Oh yeah, the undead. Yeah, they were really pale and had them teeth thingies." He gestured with a sneer and a hand gesture that looked like he was pulling mustachios. "And when I hit 'em, they exploded into dust." There was a murmur around the group as none of them had experienced the undead before.

"So you reckon they were vampires, Sid?" asked Kevin.

"Well I'm not sure really, but that's what one of 'em said. I don't know much about 'em really."

Everyone looked at Brian.

"Don't you uneducated fookers know anything?" Brian let out a huge sigh. He was fed up with teaching these idiots everything. "Vampires live off blood and need to drink it otherwise they die. They can be killed by sunlight, a stake through the heart, crosses or garlic. They have been known to be extremely good at counting." Brian naturally assumed all vampires have the book smarts of Count Von Count.

"Clever bastards." offered Kev.

Brian looked at Sid. "I don't know how you managed to kill them, mate." And there wasn't much that Brian didn't know.

Sid ran through the situation in his head. "I canna remember it that well. I had the mother of all hangovers and me hangover dump had kicked in. Half me thoughts were of not being sick and shitting meself at the same time, cos that can kill ya!"

The group nodded in agreement. Drinking was a dangerous game.

"Anyway, they swore at me a bit. I think they were a bit pissed off 'cos I drunk all their whisky, and I pissed in their flowers."

The group could understand the vampire's point, and Sid sensed their feelings.

"Which I was genuinely sorry for!" Sid shrugged his big shoulders and gave a puppy-dog look. "I remember saying: 'I'm sorry, lads. I had a few too many last night. I'll get you a bottle of whisky from Aldi, and we can call it quits?' After all, I still hadn't been paid for me night's work. Then they started using profanities and calling me names. They really were quite rude."

The group shared looks of disgust. The youth of today were bad enough, but for the undead to show this sort of behaviour was quite unacceptable.

"After a few minutes of them talking silly buggers, one of 'em jumped at me and I caught him with a sweet right."

They all winced as one because they had all seen the "sweet" right before. The only thing that it had in common with "sweet" was that both were bad for your teeth.

"He turned to dust in mid-air. A few others tried it on, and they got a bit of the same. The big black pansy just bolted. After I got me breath back, I left the warehouse. Turned out I was in fooking Scunthorpe! Glad I pissed on their plants." Sid was offered another free cigarette, which he willingly accepted.

"What are you going to do then?" asked Kev.

"What do you mean?" said Sid, placing his empty glass on the bar.

"Last one. I mean it," Kevin gave Sid a stern look. "It isn't everyday that someone is attacked by the undead. Are you going to sell your story? I reckon there's a bob or two to be made."

Sid had not thought of this. A quick bob or two sounded good, but would it infringe on his benefit claims?

"Don't know, like. If I make a few quid off a story, what will happen with the benefit office? I can't afford to lose me allowance. Me 'eart canna take to work and I got to think of the future."

"You have got to think of your fellow man!"

The group turned as one. Reece Chambers had entered the pub.

"You can put an end to this war that has raged for centuries."

"Who are you, man?" asked Arthur, assuming a defensive karate stance.

"My name is Reece Chambers. I am a vampire hunter. For twenty years, I have hunted the very thing that hunts us. I have travelled from country to country, from town to town looking for hellspawn. I have put an end to many of their wretched lives and thus ended thousands of wanton murders. The undead you speak of, they have slaughtered children. When you hear on the news of women raped and killed, of children abducted and abused…it is the vampire who are responsible. Murderers, butchers, animals!" Reece ended his passionate unrehearsed speech.

"Not that twat, again," said Brian rolling his eyes. Emotions were wasted in the Miner's Arms. "Didn't you dump him in that skip, Sid?"

"Aye, but that was then, and this is now," Sid said, letting bygones be bygones. "I think it's time that we listened to what the lad has to say." Sid took a seat at the bar. "After he buys me a couple of beers."

Reece nodded to Kevin, who dutifully pulled a pint of Bolton Bitter, and took a seat next to Sid. "You fought and killed vampires. It may sound stupid, far-fetched bullshit, but, the fact of the matter is, vampires are real." He waited for the gasps, but there was nothing (except the sound of Tarrant on in the background), and the lads turned away to watch the telly. They only wanted to hear stories about Sid hitting people.

Reece watched in amazement as the lads walked off. "There are two thousand of these creatures in the UK, alone. They populate the entire world!" This did bring shock to the group. Jonny Foreigner had them too!

Arthur broke the silence, "It's true, fellas. My Mom told me that my Daddy took down one of these sons of bitches, down in Memphis once. He used his karate on him." Arthur demonstrated with a flurry of karate punches.

Reece shook his head.

"So," said Peter, "these vampires…are they actually baddies, then?" Reece didn't answer in a second, so Peter continued. "I saw that Dracula film thing, and he was a baddy in that. Bit weird when that wolf shagged that lass, but you did see her tits, like? Then there was that vampire film with that short arse from *Top Gun*. His mate from that fighting film was alright in that. I liked him."

Reece looked the horrible, greasy excuse for a man up and down. "What are you talking about?"

Peter considered his sentence. "I can get you them films on VHS for a fiver."

Reece restrained his temper. He remembered his sore head after the night in the skip. Still, there was only so much he could take.

"I can get you *Lethal Weapon 2* and *3*, *Die Hard*, *The Last Action Hero*, *A Clockwork Orange Penis*, *The Load in My Ring* and—"

Reece couldn't take anymore. "I think it is time you—"

"*Load in My Ring*? The missus wants to see that." Kevin Ackroyd could now see a way of getting back into his wife's good books after the incident a few nights previous. "She read the books and everything. Loves it she does. Thrives on it."

The pub went silent. Even Tarrant shut up.

"*Load in My Ring*…is, err, Mrs. Ackroyd into that sort of thing, like?" Peter asked carefully.

"Aye. I saw an advert for it. It's got that fella with the big white beard interfering with them little dwarfs?"

"Yeah, that's the one," confirmed Peter.

"And that short fella thinks he can destroy that little dwarf's ring. He gives it everything he's got with one of the biggest weapons I've ever seen and it doesn't even split the bastard."

"Yeah, that's the one."

"Then they go down that dirty mineshaft."

"Yeah, that's the one."

"And they have to pull out cos it gets real messy."

"Yeah, that's the one."

"And they go and see that slutty blonde piece in the forest whose got a lovely ring already, but the little fella offers her his and she ain't having any of it, like."

"Yeah, that's the one."

"At the end that fella goes a bit funny, and ends up with more pricks in him than that dartboard." He nodded at the Miner's dilapidated board. The pub turned to the dartboard, shuddered as one, and then turned to look at Kevin Ackroyd. "Aye, the missus told me all about it. I'll give you a fiver for it, Peter."

Peter took a copy out of his coat pocket and handed it over to a beaming Kevin. "If this gets me back in with the missus, then I may even get some afterwards!" And with that he made his way upstairs.

One of the lads ran outside to be sick.

Reece tried to gather his thoughts. He was not used to this sort of environment. He lived a solitary life, always on the run. He had dealt with people before, but these weren't normal people. Sid Tillsley was something different. Was he what the prophecies spoke of?

"Sid…Sid?"

Sid jumped up startled. "Eh, what?" He had become bemused by the *Load in My Ring* controversy.

"The vampires, Sid, remember the vampires? We have a duty to protect mankind."

"Well, in all fairness, Rich, them there vampires haven't actually done anything wrong to me, have they? They had a go at me while I was out doggin', but it's not like I was being an upstanding citizen. The second time they had a go, I had drunk their whisky and pissed in their stuff. I ain't got no beef with them."

Reece felt the sinking feeling, the one where you can hear the blood rushing from your head and you feel faint and sick.

"You've got 'no beef' with them?" asked Reece, distraught.

"Aye."

"These murderers…you have 'no beef' with them?"

"Aye…" he said it a bit slower as the lad seemed a bit on the dense side.

"Tens of thousands of us…*us*…were taken in this country, last year!"

"Bloody hell!" offered Kev. "Who do we know who's gone missing?"

Sid scratched his head. "Jim Heathers?"

"In prison," replied Brian.

"Ricky Morgan?"

"He went to Thailand to find a bride."

"Jimmy Parsley?"

Brian paused. He knew everything and everyone. "I haven't seen that lad for bloody ages. Last time I saw him he had just grown himself a moustache like that fella out of Magnum."

Reece breathed a sigh of relief. He was finally getting through to these idiots.

"You see, gentlemen, they are among us. They are taking the lives of your friends."

Again he was cut off by Brian Garforth. "He ain't my friend, like. He thinks he looks like fooking Magnum, does he shite. Fooking loved Magnum, me."

Reece rolled his eyes. He walked in front of Sid so that the big man could have no distractions. "Sid, listen to me please!" Sid's eyes left the television and centred on Reece. "You have managed to kill vampires with your bare hands. You don't seem to realise what this means. Vampires are immortal."

"I thought they could get killed by sunlight?" asked Brian, which obliterated Reece's train of thought and sent Sid back to watching the telly. Tarrant had finished and there was a documentary on about parrots. Sid liked parrots.

"What? Oh yes, they can."

"Not immortal then, are they?" stated the smartest man on the Smithson Estate.

"What?"

"If they can die, then they ain't immortal. It's kind of like, the very opposite of what they actually are. It's like me calling you a cock, when actually you're a cu—"

"My Daddy said that they are allergic to garlic," interrupted Arthur with impeccable timing.

Reece was now in a staring contest with Brian Garforth. "That's a myth," said Reece. "They need blood to live. The plasma in blood regenerates their bodies. They can go without it for a couple of months, after which, they wither and eventually die of starvation. They do not need to kill to live. They do not even need human blood. The only reason that they kill us is because they choose to. They say that they cannot satisfy their bloodlust if they do not take human-life. The needless suffering could end tomorrow if they had any sort of willpower."

Brian gave the vampire hunter a sceptical look prompting the man to continue.

"If the vampire feeds then they will age at an astoundingly slow rate. A vampire has never died of old age, or illness. The legends and myths that talk of silver, garlic and crucifixes are merely old wives' tales that have mutated from fact along the course of history. Vampires, I can assure you, can be killed. I know because I have killed many of them myself. They can be killed by sunlight, and it remains our greatest ally. They can be killed by decapitation, but the blow would need to be severely powerful to cut through the spinal column, the fatal step." He turned his back on Brian and focused again on the big man.

"Sid, the point is they can't even kill each other with a punch and they are incredibly strong. You have done something that hasn't been done before. With you on my side, we could end the bloodshed and live in peace."

"Do them there vampires live in London?"

"Hundreds!" exclaimed Reece.

"Well, I can't hold beef with anything keeping down the cockney population now, can I?" said Sid matter-of-factly.

Brian Garforth backed his friend. "You're right there, Sid." Brian hated cockneys more than syphilis, but not as much as cockneys with syphilis.

"Sid, you could save mankind from the vampire."

Sid grimaced. "I canna be seen working, Rich, as I claim job-seeker allowance. I cannot send that money down the shitter. I got to think of me future, like."

"I will pay you five times what you earn on the dole." Reece argued.

"But for how long? I have worked hard to maintain that money. I put a little bit aside for a rainy day. I do little odd jobs, here and there, to wet me whistle."

Reece looked on in despair. Desperate times called for desperate measures. "What would happen, Sid, if you were to lose your job seekers allowance?"

Sid's beady eyes managed to narrow a little further. "What are you saying, like?"

Reece leaned against the bar. "Well, say for instance, that the benefit office were to get wind of you working? Say they caught you on the job?"

Sid started to get the gist of what Reece was saying. "They haven't so far. Why would they now?"

"Yeah, everyone in the whole bleedin' town knows Sid will do an odd-job for the right price. Including kicking seven bells of shit out of some blackmailing scumbag!" said Brian.

The tension in the pub sky-rocketed. Arthur took an offensive karate stance. Reece held up his hands.

"Gentlemen, I am not looking for trouble. You have stumbled on to a world which could devour everyone single one of you in a heartbeat. I must see that humanity is protected from the vile abominations that share our Earth. Sid, I need you to come out with me for one night, just one night. I will pay you five hundred pounds for eight hour's work."

"How do I know you ain't from benefit office?"

"Sid, if you don't come with me I'll set you up for benefit fraud. It will be easy. How do you think you got the job working that nightclub?"

"You bast—"

Reece interrupted more abuse from Brian Garforth. He looked Sid directly in the eyes and held his gaze. "However, you come out with me for one night, and I solemnly swear that I will never contact the benefit fraud investigators, or try to set you up. On my honour, I swear it."

"Can you give me five minutes for me to discuss this with my colleagues?" asked Sid formally. Reece nodded and left the pub.

Sid waited for him to walk out and close the door. "Five-hundred notes, fooking hell I'm a millionaire! Stupid bastard, I would have gone out for two hundred Benson and Hedges. Kevin, a pint of your finest ale for every man in this fine establishment! And one for yourself, mon!"

"You could be on to a goldmine here, mate," said Brian.

"Aye, you're right. Someone get the stupid bastard back in here. He's got a round to pay for."

One of the lads knocked on the pub window and motioned Reece back in.

"Five hundred notes, one night, no killing, and you get these beers in." Sid offered out his massive hand.

Reece smiled and shook the right hand of Sid Tillsley.

* * * *

As soon as Caroline heard about the death of the four vampires at the hands of an unarmed human, she called the emergency meeting at the desolate cottage in the Buckinghamshire countryside. The Hominum Order were scattered across the country, and this was the most central location that enabled this ad hoc meeting to be called in the promptest fashion. Everyone was here except for Ben Edric. His fate was known to the Order, but no one enquired how it had happened. No one wanted to know.

Caroline's spies within the Lamian Consilium were always trustworthy and accurate down to the last detail. Humans had never had the luxury of a vampire spy before, and Caroline was the first leader of the Order to obtain one. She knew it was not her negotiating skills that built the bridge. Every passing year meant huge technological advancement in surveillance. It would be possible one day to track every vampire across the world, if the need ever arose. Already, vampires with a more colourful appetite were monitored closely.

A vampire with an incessant passion for murder had approached her, promising that she would leak any important information provided a blind eye was turned to her unsanctioned kills. It was for the greater good of the human race. Caroline tried not to think of the thousands of children murdered for the greater good. They were still at war and war was not glamorous.

"Thank you for turning up promptly, with so little notice." Caroline said to the assembled council. "I can assure you that it was for no light matter that I called you here."

This put a stop to the puzzled murmuring. There were twenty people in the small, wood-beamed cottage, including all the human representatives from the Coalition.

"I called you to this remote cottage with news that could change the world." She looked at a young gentleman in a designer suit and glasses who peered into a laptop. "Ruskins?"

"There isn't a bug within 2.3 miles, ma'am," he said with certainty.

"Very good." She gave a smile that vanished in an instant. "Two nights ago, a human killed four vampires. A week before that, this same human killed Gabriel." She paused to let the enormity of it all sink in. "He killed them all with his bare hands."

"Gabriel? He…killed Gabriel?" questioned Charles. Everyone knew of the murders Gabriel had committed. He would slay humans or vampires without a care.

"Yes. With a single blow. Gunnar Ivansey witnessed all of it and fled the scene."

"Gabriel and Ivansey, together? You'd need a fleet of tanks to bring them down, and that's if you were lucky," said Sanderson. "This is a time to fucking celebrate! A fuck-you from the thousands that he's killed over the years!" He looked around the room to see if anyone shared his joy. He was greeted with shocked, pale faces.

The excited serviceman continued unabashed. "Ivansey fleeing the scene! What I would give to witness that? Who's the hero who took that fucker down?"

"Who were the other four?" asked Charles.

"The other vampires killed were Jacques Jereaux, Stefan Kahn, Winston Montero, and Terence O'Hara."

This excited Sanderson further. "All well known bastards. I will not mourn the loss of Jereaux, the son of a bitch. The amount of his handy-work that I've cleared up." He spat. "How did it all happen, Caroline?"

"I was only informed this morning. The Lamian Consilium was informed yesterday and they have sent a team out to investigate this phenomenon, as will we. I am awaiting the official contact from them, which should follow shortly. We both know that there are leaks that go both ways. That is the reason why we will send word to the Consilium about Gabriel's death, something they are not aware of."

"Why—" started Sanderson.

"We work together," said Caroline, cutting him off. "If we don't share information then we build distrust—more so. They have their spies, we have ours. There is no point playing games." Apart from Caroline, no other member of the Order knew who Caroline's vampire contact was. If Caroline died, then the vampire would simply contact the new leader in due course.

"Richmond witnessed the death of the four. The human, Sid Tillsley, forty-six, born and currently living on the Smithson Estate, a poverty-stricken council estate in Middlesbrough He has fraudulently claimed job-seekers allowance since he left school. The Benefit Fraud Squad has never been able to pin him down with anything."

"Is that all we have?" asked Charles.

"At the moment, yes. We need to find out what Tillsley's secret is. His résumé does not make him sound like the type who would scientifically discover a weapon. His name does not link any family members to any vampire activity. So, at present, we have no motives for him to become a hunter. The team we send will discover more over the following week."

"Count me in, ma'am!" yelled Sanderson.

Charles snorted, "I don't think so, old boy. I think your temper could get the better of you. You've been under immense pressure, of late."

Sanderson's eyes narrowed. "With all respect, sir, I believe I am owed this."

Caroline cut him off. "There is no *owed*, Sanderson. You, like every person in this room, are a soldier and are fully expendable. The job will go to the most suitable members of the team."

Sanderson gritted his teeth, but held it together. After his last display, it was best to play it cool this time.

"Rickson," called Charles.

"Yes, sir?" answered a man that could have been anywhere from late twenties to his early forties. Brown hair and brown eyes with an average height and build, he was difficult to describe, which was why he was in the team. He was recruited from MI6 for the sole reason of tracking and spying on humans. He was a hardened serviceman.

"You know what to do, Rickson," said Charles.

"Yes, sir."

"Jeremy, I think it would be a good idea for you to accompany Rickson on this field mission," said Caroline.

Jeremy Pervis looked on smugly.

Rickson looked taken aback. "Forgive me, ma'am, but I work best alone."

"I don't care, Rickson."

"Do you still want me to track whatever is causing the chaos in the Northeast, Caroline?" asked Pervis.

"Yes, but we will send more help. There are difficult times ahead of us. We must remain vigilant, and the Agreement must be upheld." Caroline stood to adjourn and gave the group a curt nod. "Good day to you all."

12

It was a warm and balmy Friday night. Two nights had passed since Sid made the deal with Reece and he was under strict instructions not to drink anything at all. Right about now Sid could murder a pint or fifteen, so he took his mind off drinking by smoking a few more tabs than normal. He was on his hundred and seventh Alaskan of the day: "Eskimo's Friends." He had helped some bloke down the docks deliver three hundred-weight of salmon in the back of his Montego Estate and was rewarded with two-hundred Alaskans, three bottles of Alaskan gin and then an extra fifty quid once Sid realised that the smell of old fish would be lingering in his car for the next few weeks.

Sid had to meet Reece outside the local corner shop. Apart from the beer rule, he had been told to wrap up warm. This particular rule, Sid ignored. Men from the Northeast were bought up the hard way and they didn't need to wear coats on a night out. He still wore his leather jacket though, but that was because it made him look cool.

"You turned up?"

The voice made Sid jump. "Shit the bed!" He grabbed his heart. "Where did you come from, for fook's sake? You know I've got me 'eart."

Reece smiled. He was dressed in black and his grey hair was tied back underneath a hood. "You have to move silently in this world. You have to blend in with your surroundings or you will be dead in an instant…if you are lucky."

Sid belched loudly. "Don't you worry, I can be as silent as a mouse, me."

Reece ignored the windy Northerner. "Anyway, I thought it was your bad back that you had problems with?"

"It's me back as well, aye. I'm not a well man. Benefit's only thing that keeps me going through the long gruelling week."

Reece held his tongue as this was going to be a long night. "Walk with me, Sid."

"You never said anything about walkin', like!" This was going to be the hardest five hundred quid that Sid had ever earned.

"Sid, tonight I am going to show you how rife the world is with vampire activity. I am going to show you the ferocity that they kill with, and their merciless disregard for human life. Tonight, I am going to open your eyes."

"Is it gonna take long? I'm gagging for a dump."

Reece sighed. "Sid, I have killed thirty-eight vampires in my twenty years of hunting. Thirty-eight. That's impressive, even by my ancestors' standards.

You have killed five in a fortnight. I spent months and months planning each move. You killed one with a single punch."

"Aye, I've always had a good punch on me. I would have got into boxing, but getting hit in the head can slow your brain down." The big man was full of surprises. His head was probably the least important part of him.

"I can, to some degree, understand your reluctance to join in the battle against these monsters. You live every day in—" Reece stopped talking because his partner had stopped to take a seat on a bench.

"Give me a sec, lad," Sid wheezed. He looked up at the smog. It was a beautiful evening. He hadn't seen a completely sober night for many a year and he was getting a bit of exercise. It was all lovely stuff apart from the exercise and the lack of beer. "Sorry, Rich, what were you saying?"

"It's Reece," he corrected. "I was saying, Sid, that in my business you live every day in fear."

Sid lit up an Alaskan. He could have sworn that they smelled slightly fishy, but a tab is a tab. "Why do it then? Why hunt 'em?"

"Do you fear anything, Sid?"

"Oh aye, mon. Always got an eye out in case the benefit people are trying to catch me doing an odd job here and there. That and...*them lot*."

"Homosexuals?" asked Reece, not entirely surprised.

The orange streetlights silhouetted terrace roofs and chimneys, every one outlining a Sky dish paid for by the council, whist the smog danced magically in the moonlight. Maybe it was the beauty of his surroundings that made Sid comfortable enough to discuss the matter with Reece. He really felt he could get things off his chest. Sid spat out a massive, black, Alaskan-induced spit ball and now that was off his chest, he could chat.

"Aye, I don't get 'em. They're men...and they like the company of other men...in a family sense." He took a deep draw of the only fag that he was ever going to go near. "I just don't get 'em, like. Them and Eskimos. Eskimos live in a house of ice, which is warm. Bastards." He could get into this philosophy shit.

"Anyway," he finally continued. "How come you got into this vampire-hunting business? Why are you going round causing them trouble? Hating them for killing us and then doing the same back is a bit hyposhitical, don't you think?" Sid was high off the philosophy chat and decided to throw the biggest word he knew into the fray.

Reece wasn't expecting this. Apparently Sid Tillsley was full of surprises. "I was twenty-three years old, having finished my masters in criminology at Oxford, when a letter arrived through my door asking me if I wanted to know the truth about my past. You see, I was an orphan and never knew my real parents. I was bought up in a terrible orphanage, in Sheffield. I was beaten, abused and humiliated until I was eleven when I murdered the 'carers' who harmed me." He paused. He had never told anyone this story before. If he was to convince Sid to fight for the cause, he would have to be completely honest.

He was finding it surprisingly easy to talk to this big oaf when he was without alcohol and the call of his drinking buddies.

"I went through child counselling for my trauma, but I wasn't sick or disturbed. The people who mistreated me deserved to die. Then I was put in a foster home. A loving caring family took me in, but because of my past I could never get close to them. Nevertheless, they supported me through school, college, and then university. Then the letter came."

Sid sat smoking and listening. He was a good listener, as it didn't involve any work. "Who was it from?"

"My father. Turns out I wasn't an orphan, after all. My father was a vampire hunter. They took my mother just after my birth. My father put me in an orphanage to protect me from them. He said that he couldn't risk contact in case they found out I was his son. He would never have made contact with me, at all, if I had not made it by myself. I absolutely hated him for leaving me, but they put him in that situation. They took my mother, making me go through years of hell. That is why I hate vampires. And here we are now, Mr. Tillsley, at the place it all began for me. Tonight, this is where it all begins for you."

Sid took another drag of his cancerous cigarette. "Now then, mon, it may end here tonight as well. One night, we agreed." He waggled a sausage-like finger at Reece, which said, "No silly buggers, like."

"I am a man of my word. You will get your five hundred pounds at the end of the evening. As agreed, there will be no killing…at least not by us."

Reece pulled out a key ring from his pocket, pressed it and walked over to a black car parked adjacent to the pavement. It was black, but Sid couldn't decide what it was. It certainly wasn't a Montego Estate.

"What kind of car is this, then?"

Reece smiled as he opened the door and got in. Sid followed suit and sat in the passenger seat of the four-door hatchback. Reece started the engine and the car was as close to silent as a car could be. The big-man gave an impressed whistle.

"Made it, well modified it, myself," Reece said. "It took me an age, but it was worth the effort. If you were to identify this car to the police, how would you describe it?"

"I didn't see anything, officer," Sid stated his monotone generic answer.

Reece laughed, although Sid was not joking. "OK, pretend that you were describing it to your mates, what kind of car is it?"

"Well, you made it, like. I couldn't really say it was anything."

"Exactly," said Reece with a touch of smugness.

"But, then again," added Sid "it is the only car like it, and that makes it pretty recognisable now."

Reece sulked. Leave it to this moron to find a logical flaw in his plan. He hadn't shown off his car to anyone before and had hoped for a more impressed response. He floored the accelerator and raced away.

Sid could sense the air of tension. He was sensing many different things without alcohol in his blood-stream. "Can I put radio on?"

"There is no radio."

"My Montego Estate has a radio." One-nil to Sid. He couldn't resist. He didn't have many opportunities to win boasting contests when it came to cars.

"This is not the kind of car that you go cruising in, you know?" Reece had obviously never seen a Montego Estate. "It is a weapon in its own right," he added coolly, trying to let the sulk go.

"Class. Has it got missiles and ejector seats and shit like that?" asked Sid, a big fan of James Bond, but not Sean Connery. Sid was a Roger Moore man, just like all real men were.

Reece didn't respond.

"What about a machine gun out of the exhaust?"

Reece was not happy.

"Can it leak oil out of the back to make enemies skid?"

No answer.

"My Montego Estate can. The amount of pile-ups that bastard has caused!" He chuckled to himself.

"Look, just fuck off! Fuck off!"

Sid scratched his head. He was worried about losing the five hundred quid. "Erm…the dashboard is pretty snazzy, isn't it? I'd love to have a dashboard like this in me Montego." He gave an impressed whistle between his teeth.

Reece continued sulking for a few more miles. Sid had no idea where they were. They were in the countryside, possibly ten or fifteen miles from Middlesbrough town centre. They turned off the main country road into a bumpy dirt track, lined with large evergreens, which carried on twisting and turning for about half a mile.

Reece put his dummy back in. "The first night I saw you, you were seeking sexual gratification in the car-park of Teesside Memorial Park."

"How dare you!"

"Shut up, Sid. We are near Sunderland. This is a new spot for doggers." He talked louder as Sid tried to protest at the outrage of being called a dogger. "It may get hit fairly soon. They never attack anywhere where there are too many people. New dogging sites are perfect."

Reece drove further along the track until it opened out to a large car park, surrounded by woodland. He drove up and parked away from the other cars; a couple of them were already rocking.

"You're just a pervert, you!" said Sid, unsuccessfully trying to hide his arousal. He couldn't keep his eyes off the rocking cars in front of him.

Reece shook his head at him. "This place could get hit at any minute. Keep an eye out for anything untoward."

Sid screamed.

The Great Right Hope

He screamed like he had never screamed before. It was a high-pitched yelp that would shatter crystal and Reece's eardrums. Only utter and desperate fear could cause a grown man to make such a noise. He was staring out the side window, straight into the eye of an erect penis that was being waggled at him by a middle-aged man in a Macintosh.

Sid covered his eyes and put his head in his lap.

Reece tried to calm down the big man. "Relax, if I don't turn my light on, he'll go away. This must be a gay site."

Sid passed out.

"Sid?" He gave the man a shake. "Sid!" Reece laughed out loud. This man could kill vampires with a swipe of his hand, but being in the presence of active homosexuals was enough to make him collapse in terror. This was definitely worth the five hundred pounds alone, and he could probably blackmail him over it. Work with him, or risk the lads down the local pub knowing he was at a gay-dogging site. Possible though that was, it was probably not a safe thing to do.

"Come on, Sidney, it is time you came back to the land of the living." He opened the glove box and took out a bottle of water. He opened the top to pour a little over Sid's large and uncharacteristically pale head. Suddenly, he stopped.

The car. Did it just move? A repugnant smell filled the small vehicle. Reece sighed in disgust. "Dirty bastard."

He went to pour the water, but again, his hand was stayed. There was a definite vibration in the car, and one not caused by Sid Tillsley's anus. He looked around the car-park. A couple of cars were still rocking with men stood outside watching, which was nothing untoward considering the circumstances.

There it was again, but more intense, like a distant underground explosion. He could see nothing past the light thrown from the parked cars, and the moonlight offered only shadows.

Was that movement? This could be what he brought Sid to see. He poured some water over Sid, but the big man didn't stir. He needed him to see this, to see the horror. A worrying thought crossed Reece's mind. What if Sid approved of the vampires attacking gay-dogging sites?

A Volkswagen flew across the car park, airborne for fifty feet. It crashed into another car in an explosion of twisted wreckage. One of the spectators was flung backwards from the blast, whilst the other man was crushed by the soaring vehicle. A moment later, a tree followed, landing on the fallen victim, caving in his chest cavity, blood momentarily fountaining from the catastrophic injury. The active doggers stopped in the other moving car, whilst the remaining men ran back to their vehicles, fleeing for their lives.

"This isn't…right?" Reece was transfixed. Vampire attacks didn't happen like this. Vampire attacks were cool and calculating. They were not noticed until it was too late and there was no chance of escape. Then the bastards had their fun.

A car's wheels screeched. A large saloon car parked on the edge of the wood was wheel-spinning, the driver desperate for it to achieve traction.

"Idiot!" Reece cursed. If the man's car was trapped in mud then he was only making matters worse. The reason for the wheel spinning became apparent when the vehicle began to lift off the ground. There must be at least three or four of them! It would have taken a great number to throw that other car so far.

Shadows obscured the tormentors, but Reece remained calm as they wouldn't be able to break into his secured car, which was bullet, fire, and explosion proof. No matter what the vampires did, they wouldn't break in for hours and daylight would be here by then. He switched on the headlights and that's when fear took him.

For what seemed a lifetime he stared into the eyes of the Devil himself, straight into the eyes of Death and into the world beyond. It took all of his will to start the car and slam his foot on the accelerator, performing a sharp U-turn that threw up a trail of dust. He tried to force the image he had just seen out of his head and concentrate on the road ahead, his only chance of survival. A deafening roar erupted from behind Reece's speeding car. Blood exploded across his windshield along with a body hitting the bonnet. The body rolled off, but Reece had still noticed the extent of the mutilation.

The car automatically started the windscreen wipers after it sensed, what it thought, was rain. Reece, although temporarily blind, didn't move his foot from the floor. The vehicle began to shudder. It was following! They should be safe if he could make it to the main road, but how fast could this thing run? Surely it couldn't beat him on tarmac, could it?

"Where the fook am I?" Sid awoke with a start. He looked over at Reece. "You're as white as a sheet, mon! And fooking hell, slow down! What's a matter wit' ya?" He sniffed the air. "You haven't shit the car, have ya, ya dirty bastard?" Sid was back and his highly tuned, gay defence system had shut down his last few conscious moments. The viewing of the erect penis never happened.

Reece didn't answer. He could hear the thing getting closer. It was actually catching up, and he was travelling at sixty, on a winding road.

"What the fook was that?" asked a startled Sid. Trees crashed everywhere around them, accompanied by the rhythmic beat of giant strides.

Through immense fear, Reece understood that Sid had to see what chased them. Through gritted teeth he managed, "Look at what hunts us."

Sid turned round in his seat, struggling to get his belly into position. "All I can see is dust, mon. Hang on. I just saw a few trees fall down. Fook me!" A tree flew over the car, missing it by a matter of feet. "That could be dangerous, that!"

It was running at sixty miles an hour whilst smashing trees down and throwing them like javelins. Vampires were not capable of that, not even Michael Vitrago.

"I think I can see summat, like." Sid squinted. "Aye, some big bastard is running after us. He's fookin' quick, like. You must have really pissed him off. Did ya cut him up or summat?"

Fear subsided and astonishment filled the void. "It's running at sixty miles an hour, Sid!"

"Aye, he's pretty quick, like, but I reckon Brian could take him over thirty yards. Brian's quicker than you think."

The beast let out another deafening roar but the sound of falling trees, and more importantly, the sound of its booming strides, ended.

Reece didn't relax his speed until he was far away from the park. Eventually he slowed the car down, breathing more than just a sigh of relief. Turning to Sid he said, with exasperation. "You know what? You really are a fucking twat!"

13

Sid mopped his mighty brow. It had been a hard morning's work helping Jock the Turk make Donner Kebabs in preparation for the Middlesbrough/Newcastle friendly that was kicking off later in the week. There was always demand when the fat Geordies travelled south. He had earned thirty notes and two hundred "El Shish" cigarettes from Turkey.

"See you later, Jock. I hope you don't have too much trouble from them Geordie bastards!" called Sid from the door of the butchery. He lit up his first Turk, but not his first cigarette, of the day.

Jock waved back and let out a blood-curdling battle cry. "Ayayayayayayaya! Don't you worry about me, Mr. Sid. You watch out for them benefit bastards, too, my friend. Here, take this!" Jock threw the big man a full carrier bag, which he caught with a squelch. "Miscellaneous meat! Enjoy, my friend!"

Sid left the butchery. He had often been given miscellaneous meats from Jock the Turk, and he had never once opened the bag. Some things weren't worth it.

Sid walked from the back of the butchers to the main street. It was a warm, beautiful summer's morning, and the pubs were open. He threw his leather jacket over his shoulder and strutted along, very casually, very Arthur Fonzarelli. It was a good day and he was proper flush. Five hundred notes last night, thirty quid this morning, and tabs for the next few days. He lit up a second Turk. "Not bad, not bad at all."

The sun shone that little bit more and he started to warble, "Zip-A-Dee-Doo Dah!"

"Oi! Madonna!" screamed a Middlesbrough maiden at her young child from across the street. "Get your fookin' arse in this house reet now you horrible little bastard!"

Maybe this was not the place for bluebirds, but hey, Sid Tillsley was still a happy man.

It was a funny evening, last night. That thing, whatever it was, was damn strong. Sid doubted whether Daly Thompson could throw trees that far. It was as quick as Brian over thirty yards, too, and anything with Daly Thompson's power and Brian Garforth's thirty-yard dash was going to be a handful in a brawl.

That Rich fella had acted a bit weird. The guy was normally a gobshite, an absolute gobshite. However, after they legged it from the big bastard, he hardly said a word.

When they had pulled up to the Miner's Arms, it was too late, even for a lock-in sent from heaven.

Reece was as white as a sheet. "I don't know what that was, but it had to be a vampire. It just had to be. It was enormous. It had bitten a man's head clean off and held his body in one hand. It was more animal than humanoid. It was all muscle and teeth. First you, now this. It can't be what I think it's…" He had shaken his head and then said, "I'll be in touch."

And that was that. Five hundred quid and no chance of being caught by the benefit office. Sid was nearly at the Miner's now, and that first pint of Bolton was going to go down a treat. That welcoming smell of cigarettes, alcohol, and the undertone of vomit, greeted him when he opened the door.

The lads were all watching a repeat of Tarrant on the old set. Business as usual. Kevin Ackroyd tended the bar, engaging, the one and only, Arthur Peasley in conversation.

"Gentlemen, what can I get you to drink?"

Kevin looked at Arthur, who returned the same look. It was a look that a man would give if he witnessed a pig flying or a fifth wedding anniversary in Middlesbrough. Was this their Sid or some generous Northern imposter?

"I take it you went out with that weird vampire-fella last night, then?" enquired Kevin.

"Five hundred quid says I did!"

Kevin waited to see the colour of Sid's money before pouring out three pints of Bolton. He handed the two beers to his patrons and then took a sip of the beer bought for him, another rarity.

"Good health," toasted Sid. They all took a long enjoyable draught of the fine beer. A short silence followed as the three connoisseurs savoured the goodness of ale.

Arthur was the first to come out of his ale-induced trance. "What did you get up to last night? We were all surprised that you weren't in here, to tell you the truth."

"Well, it happened to be the easiest five hundred quid I've ever earned. We went out looking for some more vampires, but ended up going to some park and I fell asleep." He was not technically lying; part of his gay defence system involved his brain re-writing past encounters. Sid, even under regressive hypnotherapy, would never remember looking eye-to-eye with the dogger's body part. "Next thing you know, we are speeding and this 'thing' is chasing us."

He took a large swig of ale and pointed to his glass. Kevin obliged.

"You mean one of them vampires?" asked Kevin sliding over Sid's second pint.

"Well, I didn't actually see it. By the time I'd come to me senses we were getting the fook out of Dodge." He lit up another Turk and, amazingly, offered them round. The two gents turned down the cigarettes that contained thirteen per cent powdered cancer. "That Rich fella proper shat himself, like. He said the thing was proper massive, and had bitten the head off one of them dirty bastards who goes into them woods for a shaggin'."

"That's pretty scary, like," said Kevin. "Them other vampires sounded like nasty buggers, but at least they were normal size."

Arthur Peasley nodded in agreement, "You're right, I'm gonna increase my karate training." He threw a few devastating punches in mid-air. The air felt pain.

* * * *

Sheila Fishman shuffled the papers in front of her. It had been a long day, so far, and it was only eleven a.m. She loved and loathed her job with equal passion. She loved the feeling of taking the illegally acquired money from lying, lazy, worthless scum, but she loathed the times she had to speak politely to the losers who contribute nothing to the world and were parasites in the lower bowel of society. She wished the non-working class were castrated so they couldn't produce any more hellspawn, which they did at an alarming rate.

The job was everything to Sheila, but her beloved cats came a close second. She loved her cats and they loved her, but this was not the time to be thinking about her cats. This was work time, and she was wasting taxpayer's money by thinking non-work thoughts.

Back to business: Sid Tillsley.

She had ringed the date in her calendar a month ago, after being assigned the lowest of all the lowlifes in this disease-ridden, pox of a town.

"Sid Tillsley."

She had seen him in here before when he was interviewed by that cretin, Wally Harwood. She hated Harwood. She knew he was a crook, but she couldn't prove it. If she could, she would have him sacked in a heartbeat.

That would really be something, to take a cheating man down at sixty-four, just before he claimed his retirement money. Too many people were paid too much money for doing a bad job. There were no decent people left in the world. Sid Tillsley, the fat, smelly excuse for a man was now in her hands, and by God he was going to pay. He would be forced to get a job and he was going to pay back every penny that he had taken from the government illegally.

* * * *

It was one-thirty. Sid had enjoyed about six pints of Bolton Bitter with his friend Arthur Peasley. Debates were volleyed back and forth, and it had been an enjoyable time for Sid who had completely forgotten about his forthcoming benefit interview.

"Well, Sid, I thank you for the drinks that you have bought me on this fine day, but I have some jobs to attend to so I best be on my way, baby."

"See ya, mate."

Arthur gave Sid a friendly pat on the back, which the big fella couldn't even think of taking the wrong way, and Arthur Peasley left the building. Kevin joined Sid after he had finished cleaning some glasses.

"So what you got planned for the rest of the day?" asked the landlord, hoping that Sid was going to continue spending the five hundred pounds that was calling Kevin from the back pocket of Sid's ultra-tight jeans.

Sid scratched his head. "Don't know, but I swear I've got to do something this afternoon, and I think it's something which isn't enjoyable, either."

"What about washing? I doubt you enjoy that, and you reek, mon. What have ya been doing this morning, like?" asked the nasally assaulted barman.

"Been graftin,' mate. I was helping Jock the Turk make kebabs, like."

Kevin sneered up his nose. "That's a nasty, nasty job, mon. Them donners are horrible things. Big, dirty, elephant legs, and I'm sure that Jock's are far worse than your everyday kebab. He's a reet dirty bastard, he is."

"He's a good lad," defended Sid, who liked anyone who paid him well. "His donner kebabs are just a little more continental than most. 'Extravagant animals' is what he calls them."

"Extravagant? What? Bloody German shepherds?" joked Kevin.

"Nah, mon, but I didn't know you could get a whole hedgehog in a mincer."

Kevin laughed. "I didn't think you'd be in to that sort of thing.'

"What do you mean?"

"…Errr…ale on the house?" backtracked Kev.

"Well that sounds—shit the bed!"

"Ah man, not again! Get in that bathroom and sort yourself out, ya dirty bastard! It ain't bloody right for a man of your age to have so many bloody accidents!"

"What?" asked Sid confused. "Oh no, not that, well…I don't think I have, like. I've just remembered, I've got another fooking benefit meeting and it ain't with Wally Harwood!"

Kevin rushed the big man into action. "Hurry up, mon. You need a change of clothing at the very least. You stink!"

Sid scrambled out of the door at a slightly quicker pace than normal.

* * * *

Sheila looked at her watch. It was two o'clock and it was time. She had the office arranged in the most intimidating fashion. Grey walls were scientifically proven to be the most depressing colour that could be applied.

The Great Right Hope

There was nothing on the walls, to make it look like an interrogation room, the exception being a mirror which was there so that the scumbags might think it was a two-way mirror, like in the movies. Her desk was massively oversized, as was her executive chair. The interviewee's chair was a tiny stool, designed to make the suspect as uncomfortable as possible.

It was two o'clock, and he was late. She wouldn't show leniency. She wouldn't show mercy. Sid Tillsley was about to meet his maker.

"Mr. Sid Tillsley?...Mr. Sid Tillsley!"

* * * *

Sid ambled up to the front entrance of the job centre. He had managed to change into another pair of jeans, a *Police Academy 4: Citizens on Patrol* T-shirt and his killer-look leather jacket. A whole can of deodorant from Wilkos had done a poor job of hiding the smell of rotten hedgehog meat, but this was probably because Sid had bought hairspray in his mad rush. His substantial level of armpit hair wouldn't be moving for the next two months.

He burst through the front door. The quick amble had built up a lot of sweat, which was competing with the smell of hedgehog.

"MR. SID TILLSLEY!"

The roar ripping through the building caused children to cry into their mother's laps. Sid had not received this kind of reception before. He followed the voice until he found the door of Sheila Fishman. A second bellow of "TILLSLEY!" informed him that he had found the right room. Sid stubbed out a Turk, and put it in his pocket for later consumption. Regaining his composure, he knocked and entered.

His ample frame perched comically on the stool, as he weighed up his adversary. She wasn't bad looking. A bit rough around the face and the lenses of her glasses made her eyes appear to be the size of swan's eggs but, nevertheless, if she did a sexy strip like a secretary...yeah! The wrinkles didn't matter, and at least she nearly had a full head of hair. She wore very frumpy clothes, but that didn't hide the considerable pair of tats hiding under the stripy jumper.

"I am Sheila Fishman, Mr. Tillsley. I am your new case worker."

"Call me Sid," he said coolly.

"Down to business, Mr. Tillsley. I believe that you are well aware of the drill by now. You have been through it more times than anyone else in the UK. However, Mr. Tillsley, you have not gone through this drill with me," she said threateningly.

"I'm looking forward to it already, Sheila." This was going to be the best interview ever. Sid was not very good at reading people's tones at the best of times, and he was even worse when a sexy lady was involved.

"That's Miss Fishman to you, Mr. Tillsley. Do not use my first name."

Sid's eyes twinkled. "So there's no Mr. Fishman, I presume?"

"Presume nothing. That is of no importance to you. I remind you to keep your simple mind on the business at hand. Previous work experience, Mr. Tillsley?"

"Now, Sheila…"

"Miss Fishman," corrected Miss Fishman.

"Sheila, we have these interviews regular, like. I think you'll find all the details in me file, pet."

Sheila's complete disdain for Sid was turning rapidly into hatred. *Pet!* Not only was he a lying, cheating, thieving benefit fraudster, he was also a sexist pig. "How many jobs have you had in the past five years?"

Sid scratched his chins. "Well, first there was…"

Sheila's eyes opened wide for a moment. Was he really going to slip and confess to having worked?

"Me angina. Played up for the first couple of years, pet."

Sheila tried not to look crestfallen.

"It has been a proper hard five years, like. Me back has given me a world of pain over the last three, that's for sure. I think that there was a brief spell where I…hang on. You said five years, didn't ya? Reet, I have actively been seeking employment for the past five years," he said officially.

She knew he hadn't worked, but it still made her feel sick hearing the words come out of his despicable mouth. "How many interviews have you had in the last five years, Mr. Tillsley?"

He paused as he recollected the past five years. It was all a drunken blur if truth be told, but one hell of a drunken blur! He chuckled to himself. "Well, there's been a few interviews, like."

Sheila shuffled through Sid's rather extensive file. "Let's see, shall we? You had an interview for a position for 'Meet and Greet' at Asda. Apparently, your previous employment officer thought you would be suitable for the job because of your familiarity with the local neighbourhood. You were not offered the job. Can you tell me what happened at the interview?"

"Oh, aye, I remember that." He gave a nervous laugh. "I didn't quite get to the interview on that one."

"Really?" said Sheila with a hint of excitement. Was this a chink in his armour? If he was in a fit state of health and failed to attend an interview then he might be liable for paying some of the money back. "So, you didn't attend?"

"I did attend, like. I was walking to the manager's office at the back of the store when fate played a cruel trick on young Sid Tillsley. Some inconsiderate beast had set up a tasting stand for that new white and brown creamy-booze-shite that had hit the shops. You know, the one with the fancy bottle?"

"What has that got to do with anything?" asked Sheila impatiently.

"Well, I tried a few, like. The lady on the counter said that it was the most sick that she had ever seen come out of one person," said Sid, not being able to hide the pride he connected with the event.

"OK, OK, OK!" Sheila put her head in her hands. "Let's just ignore the past five years. Let's pretend that you want to find a job." Sid attempted to interrupt. "No, Mr. Tillsley, please. Let's just pretend that you want a job. What skills or characteristics do you possess that could help you to find a job, any job?"

Sid took a deep breath. "Well, I'm quite good at darts I suppose."

Sheila gave him a blank look. "I am sorry, I think I misheard you. Did you say darts?"

"Aye, pet. Had two 137 finishes, last year."

Sheila let the "pet" go because this was another chance for her to get the scumbag. If he had won money playing in darts tournaments then he may have earned enough so that he was claiming benefit illegally. "Are you a successful darts player?"

"Aye, pet."

Yes! Sheila thought and picked up a biro and prepared to take notes. "How well have you done in the last year, Mr. Tillsley?"

"Been me best year. Came fifth in the Miner's Open," he said proudly.

"How much did you win in this tournament?"

Sid gave a triumphant smile. "Quite a prize actually, Sheila. Twenty-four beef burgers, two pounds of pork sausages, and mince—both beef and turkey." He gave her a knowing nod.

"And that's…it?" she asked, all hope vanishing.

He looked around to make sure no one was listening. "No, there was also a big bit of frying steak in there." He gave her a wink, leant back, and rubbed his belly.

"Take a five-minute break, Mr. Tillsley. I need to speak to my superiors."

As soon as he was out of earshot, Sheila took a stress-ball from her desk and squeezed it, desperately trying to relieve some of the tension of being in a room with twenty-stone of scum. The stress-ball didn't work so she went up a level by taking out a cuddly teddy bear from the bottom drawer of her desk and violently stabbing it with her biro until there was nothing left but stuffing. She felt better.

Sheila picked up the telephone and asked reception to let the oaf back in. Sid returned after he had finished a couple of Turks.

"Mr Tillsley, you are forcing me to be frank. We believe that you are claiming benefit, whilst working." She gave him the most serious of looks, one normally reserved for convicted murderers or dog-owners.

"How dare you, Miss Fishman?" Sid gave his most hurt and sorrowful look. "I am an upstanding member of the fair town of Middlesbrough."

Sheila Fishman was having none of it. "Everybody in this town knows you, Tillsley. Everyone knows that you can be found wasting tax payers' money in that hole, the Miner's Arms. Everybody knows that you will do odd jobs, door work, anything for money, cigarettes or any of the other disgusting habits you have picked up in the last forty-six years of your worthless life!" She had moved round from behind her desk and was almost shouting at the end of the sentence. All professionalism was thrown out of the window.

"The problem is that no one will bear witness to your lying, cheating ways. None of your fellow scumbags will say a word against you."

Sid attempted to speak but the tirade of pent up abuse continued over him.

"You're all in it together, aren't you? You, that pretty boy Peasley, Rathbone, and that Brian Garforth. I hate Garforth. Everyone knows how he skives maintenance payments for all the little bastards that he has released into that overcrowded cesspool!"

Sheila Fishman was only inches from Sid's ear when she finally realised that her temper had run away from her. She was bright pink and sweat poured down her face. A silence filled the office. It was a big silence, not a long silence. It was a big silence because the silence filled the entire floor of the job centre. The entire building had heard Sheila's rant. She smoothed down her skirts and sat down.

"I apologise," she said calmly. "I should not let my temper get the better of me. It was unprofessional and rude. Please accept my sincere apologies. If you wish to make a complaint, I can give you the address of our complaints department." She offered a microsecond smile before awaiting his response.

"Ah pet, guess the 'boro are playing at home, like?" He gave a wink.

"I'm sorry, I do not follow?"

"'Boro at home lass. Painters are in. Women's curse…You're dropping clots, reet?"

Sheila threw the first thing that came into her hand, the name plate on her desk, with such velocity that it smashed through the glass of her office door. Sid dodged it with his characteristic fighting speed.

"Shit the bed, pet! Calm yourself down! Don't let the hormones beat ya!" encouraged Middlesbrough's finest woman's rights activist. He dodged a flying stapler, but Mr. Croaker didn't.

No one wants to be struck by a flying stapler. However, if you had the choice of someone throwing a knife or a stapler at you, and your life depended on it, you'd pick the stapler every time. A knife is a fifty-fifty, blade or handle. Surely, a stapler would only inflict a nasty bruise. But what are the odds of the stapler actually hitting you in a stapling area? And what are the chances of the stapler ejecting a staple through your scrotum and on to your inside thigh? Pretty low, but it's a funny old world.

The Great Right Hope

Mr Croaker, who had come to see what the shouting was about, went down like a lead balloon. He passed out immediately. A big silence filled the Job Centre again.

"Did that hit him in…?" Sid winced.

"Yes."

"Is his leg stuck to his…?"

"Yes."

"What are the odds of that?"

Big silence.

A pretty, young blonde put her head around the door. "Mr. Croaker?" When she realised that nothing else was going to be thrown, she edged herself through slowly. "Sheila, what did you do?"

Sheila Fishman took her eyes away from Mr. Croaker's private region to look at her work colleague. "I…I…"

"She went fooking mental and stapled that lad's knackersack!" said Sid, never afraid to get to the point.

"I think you better leave, Mr. Tillsley. We will contact you later if an inquiry is necessary." The lady ushered Sid out. He stepped over Mr. Croaker, shaking his head. That was no way for a man to go down. Sid hoped the man didn't have the ambition to have children.

It was definitely time for him to have a few beers. It wasn't his biggest disaster in a benefit meeting, but it was up there. No one had received a stapled knackersack before, that was certain.

Sid looked back. Mr. Croaker was still unconscious and the pretty assistant had attempted to unzip him to check for blood loss. She was now retching into the paper bin.

The poor man had suffered one of the worst office supplies injuries in the history of local government bureaucracy. At least it would take the heat off Sid for a while.

He ambled off to the Miner's Arms off for a pint.

14

It had finally arrived: Ladies' Night. This was not the regular fortnightly ladies' evening where ladies got twenty pence off a pint of Bolton Bitter, oh no. This particular event was so special that Sid was banned from using the ladies as "a shit-stop." That was how prestigious this night of glamour, beauty, and sex appeal was.

Kevin Ackroyd was a very excited man. There were not many opportunities to see many different women. He saw Mrs. Ackroyd a great deal, and that was not a gift from God. She wasn't speaking to him after the controversial "Load in My Ring" viewing. The only other women he saw were Garforth's slags and he couldn't bear to look at them in that sort of way because he could imagine Garforth's filthy hands, and worse, all over them.

Arthur Peasley. Now there was a man who always had a proper stunner on the go, but he hardly ever brought them in here, unfortunately. It would have been great for business if he did. Yep, slags and the missus were the only women in Kevin Ackroyd's life…oh, and the mother-in-law.

However, tonight was a night when ladies, far and wide, came to one place, and that one place was his place. And in typical Northeast tradition, they would turn up wearing, at most, nothing. These red-hot firecrackers were horned up at the best of times, and tonight, when they saw what Kevin had lined up for them…they were going to explode in a sexual frenzy!

Because tonight, and at the expense of thirty-eight quid, "Obi-Dong-Kenobi and his Pink Lightsabre" was going to get the ladies wetter than your average Bank Holiday Monday. It was the first male stripper to ever appear on the Smithson Estate. Kevin had always considered himself a bit of a trailblazer; he was the first landlord to put a condom machine in the bogs. There still hadn't been any sold, but it was trailblazing, nonetheless.

Through all the excitement, he was still slightly apprehensive at the prospect of a male stripper. He had done his market research and the results were quite satisfactory (Sid said he wouldn't knock him out). Ladies' Night was to begin at seven, Obi-Dong would do his ten-minute act at about half ten, and Kev had a few surprises lined up for later in the evening. It was going to be a rip-roarer!

Arthur Peasley and Peter Rathbone entered the pub. Peasley was dressed all in white, his thick black hair styled to perfection. He looked a million dollars. Rathbone looked the same as ever, a greasy, little, horrible bastard.

"Gentlemen!" greeted Kevin Ackroyd. "I hope you are excited about this evening's entertainment? How may I serve you on this fine afternoon?"

"You're unusually perky today. You're normally a miserable bastard." Peter Rathbone took away Kev's happy face—he was good at that. Kev pulled two pints of Bolton. "Four pounds."

"Fook me," said Peter, not expecting the price hike. "That's the second time that you put bloody ale up!"

"That ain't on, man!" backed up Arthur.

Kev's smile returned. His two favourite past-times: annoying people and making money. "Relax, gentleman. It is only for tonight, and we have an official late license. An extra two measly pence on a pint of ale doesn't really come close to the price of pulling a beautiful lady, does it? Believe me. Tickets have sold like hot cakes for the stripper."

"How many then?" enquired Peter.

Kev gave a nod and a wink. "Let's just say about fifteen."

"Fook me! That will be a record won't it? Fifteen lasses in the Miner's!" Peter rubbed his greasy hands together.

"Aye, it won't disappoint, lads," assured the pimp-daddy.

"KEVIN! SOMEONE'S ON THE PHONE!" The yell filled the bar and carried out onto the street. Poor Kevin Ackroyd. Everyone could understand why he was a bitter little man.

"Coming dear!" he tried to yell sweetly. "You two bastards better not touch anything when I'm gone," he growled before running up the stairs to grab the telephone.

"Miner's Arms?" he answered.

"Ackroyd. It's Terry Fenton 'ere," replied a gruff Northeast accent.

"Who?"

"Terry Fenton. You know, Obi-Dong Kenobi."

Recognition dawned on Kevin. "How are ya, big fella? You got that thing of yours ready to get the ladies gagging for more ale?" The barman let out an excited chuckle.

"Sorry, boss, hate to do this to ya, like, but I gotta cancel. The Pink Lightsabre will be out of action for a while."

"What do you mean?" A cold sweat washed over a panicked Kevin Ackroyd.

"How do I put it?…I've got nob-rot," replied the unsubtle, wounded Jedi.

"But…but…you can still perform, can't ya? You must be able to perform?" asked a desperate party-organiser.

"I'm pissing puss, mon! I can hardly swing it around now, can I? If I drop it in a lasses' sherry, it's gonna look like she's drinking Baileys by time I pull it out!"

Kevin was, well and truly, up shit creek. There was going to be at least fifteen of Middlesbrough's muckiest slags all baying for cock, and his cock-for-hire was banged up with the clap.

"HOPE IT FALLS OFF, YA BASTARD!" yelled Kev before slamming the telephone down. This was trouble, he had just six hours until Ladies' Night and the entertainment had gone down the shitter (or rather down the clap-clinic). Fifteen birds at three quid a pop meant that there was no way he was going to offer a refund, and they were all expecting a donkey-dick at ten thirty. Alternative entertainment was the only choice.

Six hours…

* * * *

Sheila Fishman fed Alfred his fresh tuna steak from the local fishmonger. She had cut the skin off because Alfred preferred his tuna steaks without the skin. She had prepared the other nine cats' meals just as meticulously. It took her an hour to prepare their evening dinner and it had to be served just the way they liked it.

Sheila Fishman lived in a two-bedroom terrace on the outskirts of the Smithson Estate, alone, with her ten male cats: Alfred, Bartholomew, Edward, Graham, Marcus, Perseus, Quentin, Reginald, Ulysses, and Wilson. The house was extraordinarily clean considering it housed ten animals, although Sheila Fishman would castrate any man who dared call them "animals." To Sheila, they were little furry people.

The cats' food was served on the dinner table, which Sheila headed. When the cats had finished eating, they left the table accordingly, but Sheila didn't care about their lack of table manners. Her darlings could do anything they wanted, bless them. She finished her dinner and gathered the plates, taking them into the kitchen for washing up. It was like any other day except this day was ruined by Sid Tillsley.

Sid Tillsley was everything that a cat was not. Sid Tillsley was the reason that she might lose her job at the benefit agency. Sid Tillsley was the reason that Mr. Croaker had his scrotum stapled to his leg and was awaiting surgery in hospital. Sid Tillsley was the reason that Alfred may soon be eating tinned tuna instead of tuna steaks. Sid Tillsley was a sexist, arrogant pig of a man. Sheila would never have a boyfriend because of men like Sid Tillsley.

Tonight, at the Miner's Arms, she would have her revenge. Tonight she would find out where Tillsley was working.

* * * *

He circled the fat oaf. How a human could let itself fall into that condition still amazed him. Gabriel leapt and he disintegrated into ash through the fat man's fist. The pain struck as his brother was taken from him. He felt like he could vomit. Gabriel killed by a human. He ran. The moon never changed…how he hated it.

Gunnar awoke. He knew he was dreaming. That night went through his thoughts every moment of every day, whether asleep or awake. It was about three o'clock in the afternoon, six hours until nightfall. Tillsley was revealed to him at last. At least the Lamian Consilium had given him something of use in the last millennium—a name. He hadn't given a human a name for centuries, not since the last tragedy.

Tonight, Tillsley would begin his slow journey into the afterlife.

* * * *

Sid Tillsley looked in the mirror and liked what he saw. He was looking good, extremely good, in fact. The leather jacket shone in the neon lit toilet of the Miner's Arms. His Esso Tiger Token T-shirt gleamed. He had even managed to get the curry stain out. Even his jeans didn't smell! Ladies' Night was going to get much more than it was bargaining for.

* * * *

Brian Garforth looked in the mirror and liked what he saw. He was looking good, extremely good, in fact. His red tailored suit contained more Rohypnol than the female population of Middlesbrough Polytechnic. He never needed it, but better to be safe than sorry. Hands checked for the little blue pills, too, hidden carefully like a concealed pistol. Brian Garforth was ready for war.

* * * *

Arthur Peasley looked in the mirror and liked what he saw. He was looking good, extremely good, in fact. He was indeed a beautiful, beautiful man. Sideburns cultivated to perfection, black thick hair swept back with lazy grace. He had been blessed with his Daddy's good looks. Arthur was dressed to impress. A white suit, tight in all the right areas, gave an insight into his religion and his lady killing abilities. He was gargantuan. At least fifteen chicks were out there tonight. If he didn't leave with at least three of them, it would be a disappointment. He threw a few karate punches to warm up, checked out perfection one last time, and Arthur Peasley left the building.

* * * *

Peter Rathbone looked in the mirror and liked what he saw. He was looking like a greasy, horrible, little bastard, like an extremely greasy, horrible, little bastard, in fact. His disgustingly thin hair fell limply over his pitted oily skin. His poorly-fitting clothes were stained, ripped and stinking. He hated everyone and everyone hated him. He had no chance of pulling a woman or making any new friends. Should be a good night.

* * * *

Franco Stolini had been given what would normally have been the mundane task of tracking a human. It would have been his worst job for years if it wasn't for the exceptional circumstances. A man that could kill vampires was unheard of. He hadn't heard the story of Sparle and Remo Elscachius before. That was kept quiet outside the Lamian Consilium for reasons he didn't know. Ironically, for a spy, he hated secrets.

Out of all the vampires walking the earth, he looked more like a human than any other. Short and of slight frame for a vampire, but still large for a man. He was not as fair as his brethren, but he would still be considered a model by human standards. His eyes, for some reason, lacked luminescence, which was the most startling feature of an immortal. If war broke out between the races, then Franco Stoloni would be a deadly weapon.

He was given very strict orders from Michael, whom he had never seen so agitated. Although he hated to admit it, he was terrified of Michael Vitrago, whose impossibly large hands had mercilessly killed thousands upon thousands. A cold shiver ran up his spine as he considered the consequences of failing the mission. Blending in wouldn't help him if Michael wanted him dead.

"Follow him closely for one night and do not arouse suspicion," Michael had instructed. "We have reason to believe that Reece Chambers has contacted him. Chambers is pathetic, a shadow of his ancestors, but he can get to us through this man. Find out his character, his motives, and his weaknesses. There will be great reward for this, Franco. Failing is something that you should not consider…"

Franco shuddered. Failing. He knew what would happen if he did. Michael had never threatened him like that before. Tillsley must have him spooked. Tonight he would make contact with the target. Franco had watched the man over the last couple of days and was seriously wondering if he justified Michael's cause for concern. The human had spent most of his time inebriated in the Miner's Arms, and on two occasions he had messed himself. Nevertheless, orders were orders and tonight he would discover Sid Tillsley's true character.

* * * *

The Great Right Hope

Kevin Ackroyd was in desperate trouble. Desperate, desperate trouble. He was without a stripper. In any normal pub, in any normal town, this wouldn't be a problem. However, this was Middlesbrough, and this was the Miner's. You didn't find your average lady in the Miner's. When they wanted cock on show, by God they wanted cock on show. He had two hours to find a guy brave enough to flop it about on stage in front of some of the roughest tarts in the Northeast. It was going to be difficult...especially because he didn't want to spend a lot of money.

15

It was seven o'clock. It was Ladies' Night. Kevin Ackroyd polished the last of the champagne flutes. Every lady would get a complimentary glass of the finest Yorkshire champagne at the complimentary price of ninety-nine pence. Though there were only fifteen ladies in guaranteed attendance, he had polished thirty. He had found a replacement for Obi-Dong Kenobi and he was feeling lucky.

The ladies' toilet was fully functional and Kevin had invested in some potpourri, which he placed seductively in an ashtray on top of the khazi. He himself was in his finest of fineries: brown corduroys, ironed and clean, and a paisley silk shirt which billowed with each of his sexy flourishes. His remaining hair was slicked back into a Willy Thorne-esque shine. He poured himself a fine ale and enjoyed every mouthful. The door opened and his heart fluttered. What beauty could this be?

"Maggie! What a fantastic surprise," wooed the barman.

"Fook off, Ackroyd. I'm only here to see how big that stripper is and whether he's worth a shag or not. Pint of Bolton." The Middlesbrough beauty took a seat by the bar, and what a beauty she was. Twenty-eight stone of sophisticated lady-love fell out of the tiniest of outfits. "And giv' us a pack of pork scratchings, and a Mars bar, and a Baileys, and a Twix."

"Coming up, li'l lady. Someone's flush this month?"

She let out a loud guttural belch that Kevin could smell from four yards away. "Spat out another couple of sprogs, last week, so I'm raking it in this month." She lit up a cigarette.

"Who's the lucky father?" asked Kevin, bringing her the chocolate, scratchings, and the drinks.

"It's either Reg—that lad with the Nova SR—or it might be John—the lad with the fake arm. Thinking about it, it could even be Jimmy who was put in nick for kicking that Kosovan to death. Or possibly Denzel from round block."

Kevin nodded until it occurred to him. "Denzel's black! Surely you'd know if it's his?"

"Well, the sprogs are pretty dark, but that could be dirt. Get us a half pint of Tia Maria."

The door opened and in walked Arthur Peasley, possibly the sexiest man in the world. Maggie wolf whistled and exposed a little more of her colossal thighs, which was quite an achievement considering she was wearing a mini skirt for a size twelve.

"If it isn't Arthur Peasley, himself! Fook me, I'm slipping off me chair here I'm so fucking w—"

Arthur didn't look at her. He raised a finger and cut her off, such was his effect with women, and thankfully, she kept quiet. "A pint of ale, man."

Kevin looked on impressed. Arthur Peasley was the finest ladies' man without the use of Rohypnol in all of Teesside. "There you go, pal," said the landlord. "I must say you are looking a million dollars, this evening."

Arthur gave a wry grin. "Hey man, it's what I do best. If this is the standard of lady that we are getting tonight..." He shot Maggie a glance. "Then Arthur Peasley is not gonna be a happy man. You understand me, baby?"

Kevin did. He was well aware of the deadly karate skills that Arthur Peasley had learned from his daddy. Nevertheless, he was not a worried man because of the classy women he knew were attending. He was hopeful that the bastard Garforth was going to bring some beauties from the local hospital as well. If the substitute stripper could fire up the women, then the regulars would be happy. "Don't you worry. This place is gonna be heaving with fanny by the end of the night."

Maggie gave a dirty laugh. "Me fanny is heaving already, lads."

* * * *

It was half eight, a few hours before the stripper excited the crowd. Kevin looked around. Most of the patrons that had bought tickets were here, soaking up the atmosphere. The complimentary champagne had been a huge success with seven glasses already sold. Kevin smiled. This was turning into a right little earner. He surveyed the crowd. Maggie was near paralytic already. She would only be able to handle another eight to ten pints at best. Her skirt had rolled up into a belt and her monstrous gut hung over it giving the impression that she was half-naked. How could a girl so fat have tits so small? Kevin wondered. A dilemma for the ages. Even so, the lads were all around her trying their luck for a quick jump in the gents—Tarrant had been turned off for the evening and they had to occupy themselves another way.

Three ladies surrounded Arthur Peasley and they were all tasty. Actually they were really tasty and couldn't possibly be locals. Garforth was in as well, sleazy little bastard. He had a gaggle from the local hospital with him. All were married, but he had probably done the lot of them before, the absolute bounder. Kev had seen him with his hand on a few buttocks. He was not a hundred per cent sure, but he thought he had seen him come back from the ladies with one of his harem. She had bought a pack of extra strong mints afterwards.

There were a few unexpected guests in the crowd. In particular an extra group of girls he hadn't expected, all top-notch lasses, but they had a raging poof with them. Kevin himself was not homophobic in Smithson Estate terms.

He may punch one to the ground, but he wouldn't set fire to it afterwards. What he was concerned about was the imminent arrival of a certain Mr. Sid Tillsley.

There were also a few extra people from the local area, which was nice to see. He felt good about bringing the community together like this. There were a few strangers in the crowd. There was an old battleaxe that, at every opportunity, gave the men in the room evils. She had only bought one small sherry since entering the pub. There was another stranger in the Miner's. He was a tall fella Kev had never seen before. He was a good-looking lad who was probably out for a jump.

Kevin was a happy landlord indeed. He pulled himself another pint of fine ale, took a deep draught, and smiled.

* * * *

Sid Tillsley could hear the buoyant crowd from the bottom of the road. He was going to let his hair down tonight. Who knew? Maybe he'd get lucky with a lass? He opened the door and walked into the Miner's Arms.

* * * *

It was now nine-thirty and the Miner's Arms was completely packed as even more locals had joined the fray. There were about twenty-five women in there now. All of the newly-arrived ladies were friends of Maggie, and unfortunately for the boys, they were of similar ilk. Maggie was hammered. Her top was now permanently around her belly, revealing breasts that pointed straight to Hell. She had propositioned every man in the pub, and amazingly, not every man in the pub had turned her down. Her mates were not as drunk as she was, but they were equally as colossal and equally as negotiable into lovemaking. Three had already been outside with various gentlemen from the establishment.

The alley behind the Miner's often witnessed the beautiful creation of life; adding a few more quid to these beauties' pockets was just a by-product of the mutual thirty seconds of shared love.

Arthur Peasley was impressing, just like his Daddy used to. He hadn't ventured outside with any ladies yet, but he currently had three stunners on the go. Tonight he was going for the ménage à quatre, a mighty feat he had only pulled off twice in the past. If there was one man who could obtain a hat trick of lady-foursomes then Arthur Peasley was that man.

Brian Garforth was not sure what he fancied next. He had already serviced all the ladies from the hospital on previous encounters, and he could fall back on one of them if need be. Maggie's mates were not his style at all. Seventeen-year olds with two stone for every year of life and mothers of five didn't float his boat, unless he was desperate and Arthur had already picked up the only three beauties in the pub.

Both Brian and Arthur were fine swordsmen, but they were very different beasts. A sniper was the best way to describe Brian Garforth. He had his target, and only needed one chance. Bam! He got the job done and only one round was required.

Peasley was more like Rambo. He would take down six or seven women without pausing for breath, spraying bullets with no remorse. The one similarity between the two was that they were both absolute bounders. Peasley had these lasses booked. Arthur and Brian didn't step on each other's toes. That was the rule.

Sid was already on the road to ruination. As normal, he had sank a considerable amount of ale in a considerably short amount of time whilst smoking an incredible amount of tabs. He was smoking a Bangladeshi "Ring of Fire." He had earned two hundred smokes and forty quid for helping Dilshan, the owner of Smithson's local curry-house, put a competitor out of business. The mission had been simple. Dilshan had cooked him up an extremely potent Sprout Phaal. Sid had to eat it and then use the competitor's facilities. The plan worked perfectly although the first couple of sorties were unsuccessful as the "dirty bomb" was dropped too early.

"How do, Brian?" asked the big fella. "You got your eyes on 'owt special?"

Brian shook his head. "Nah, mon. There's a lot more lasses than I thought they'd be, but there's n'owt new worth doing. Probably stick to one of the hospital Doris's. I haven't done the one with the glass eye in a while. How about you then? You seen owt special?"

Sid smiled. "In fact, I have, mate."

Brian was happily shocked until he thought it through. "You ain't gonna do one of Maggie's lot, are ya?" He shook his head at Sid. "Mon, you'll get nob-rot and a bairn for your troubles. It ain't worth—"

Sid cut him off. "Nah, mon, don't be silly. I've got standards you know."

Brian remembered Sid's ex-prison guard and shuddered. "Aye, sure you have. Sorry I doubted ya."

"There's a reet ol' crowd in here tonight ain't there, Brian? Quite a few people I ain't seen before, like."

Brian surveyed the crowd. "Aye, you're reet, Sid. I haven't seen this many in here for donkey's years." He eyed the group with the young gay guy. They were getting a little bit too close for comfort. He really didn't want a "Sid incident" tonight. Dumping another body in a skip was not desirable.

"Look at that fella over there, Brian," Sid nodded over to the camp young man, frolicking around. "He's dressed very flamboyantly, don't you think?"

Brian winced. Flamboyant wasn't the word for skin tight white trousers and a tight shirt with a bright flowery pattern. He was impeccably dressed, but *them lot* always were.

"He's doing reet for himself. Look, he's got three birds on the go!"

Brian thought it wise not to explain to Sid why he was in company with the fairer sex, or the reason why he was extravagantly dressed.

"He's got a funny walk, too, hasn't he? He really uses his hips to strut his stuff. Guess that tells the lady where the power comes from." Sid demonstrated some lewd thrusting movements. "He's got very dark eyes as well. I bet the ladies go for that sort of thing, Brian, the mystery man!"

Mascara thought Brian. It was only a matter of time before all Hell broke loose.

"And who is this big brute of a man, then?" asked a scandalously feminine voice. It was not camp. It was far too gay for camp.

Brian's worse fears were realised. It could only be seconds before this poor defenceless lad was thrown through the Miner's Arms' window onto the hard street outside. He beckoned over Kevin Ackroyd and said, "You may want to get an ambulance on standby."

Kevin looked puzzled until he realised what Brian was talking about. In fact, the whole pub had stopped talking and they all watched the opposite ends of the spectrum: yin and yang, chalk and cheese, arse and twat, confront each other.

No one dared intervene. Everyone knew it would make no difference if they did. Everyone looked. There was nothing that anyone could do now.

"I must say that is an adorable tee-shirt you are wearing, my big friend." He rubbed Sid's belly where the Tiger stared out at the world, demanding blood and for the wearer to buy more four-star.

Sid laughed and looked at Brian. "He's even got a funny voice, Brian." Brian remained silent. "I got this from Esso for collecting them Tiger Tokens. Probably before you were born, little fella. Your shirt is pretty flowery. Is that what the hip kids are wearing these days, like?"

"Well, some people are quite stiff and don't like the shirts I wear." The lad picked up his Bacardi Breezer and took a long provocative swig from the bottle. A big gasp went up from the Miners' Arms regulars. "How about you, mister? How...stiff...are you?"

A few of the knowing locals entered the foetal position.

"Me, I think I'm pretty hip with the kids, like. I may get myself one. Reckon it'll suit me?" asked Sid hopefully.

The lad grabbed Sid's lapels. "I think anything would suit you, you big hunk o' love!" The lad winked before turning to dance with his girlfriends.

For a second, Sid said nothing, he just sat there looking confused…and then he laughed heartily. Every local in the pub breathed again. Brian took a big gulp of his Bolton Bitter.

"What a nice young fellow, Brian. The modern generation could learn a lot from a good straight lad like that."

"Yeah…sure, Sid. Kevin, two more pints of Bolton, over here."

Kevin poured three pints and downed one in a single draught before giving the patrons their refreshments. "On the house," he said before walking over to serve Maggie another half of Tia Maria.

"You remember me telling you about that lass from Benefit Office?" asked Sid.

Brian winced at the thought. Even though that Croaker had been from the benefit office, every man had felt sorrow for the poor disabled bastard. "Aye, mon."

"She's here, like, and she's all dolled up and everything. I haven't dared say anything to her, yet. I'm just getting some Dutch courage down me first," he said, draining his twelfth pint of Dutch courage.

"Easy, big man! You don't want to drink too much in case things get a little, shall we say, intimate." He gave Sid a wink.

Sid stared at Brian blankly for a minute. Had something been said untoward? Was Brian propositioning him? Hang on, no, he was talking about Sheila. A smile slowly cracked Sid's face and he gave Brian a slap on the back, which took the wind out of the much smaller man's sails.

Gathering his breath back, Brian asked. "So, which little lovely is it?"

"Her," said Sid, pointing in the direction of Sheila Fishman.

Brian spat his beer out. She was hideous! She was even worse than the nipple-cigarette-extinguishing monstrosity from two years ago.

She stood next to the jukebox by herself, scowling at anyone who ventured near, scowling if anyone even looked at her. Her small sherry was untouched. She looked about fifty, but was probably younger and had just aged badly. She wore big frumpy clothes and a short, balding-lesbian haircut. She looked as miserable as she was hideous. Nevertheless, Sid liked her and he needed a jump more than any man on the Smithson Estate, or maybe the whole of the Northeast.

"She seems…nice, Sid. Why don't you go and talk to her?"

"I'm too shy, mon."

"Don't be silly, Sidney. Buy a sherry and take it over to her. Ask her if she is enjoying the evening or something like that. What harm can it possibly do?" Brian was torn. He wanted to see his best friend do well, but not with that thing.

Sid nodded. "You're reet, mon. You're absolutely reet. Kevin, a pint of Bolton and a glass of your smallest sherry."

Kevin nodded, he knew what Sid meant. He obliged the gentleman and gladly took his money.

Sid Tillsley was on the prowl.

* * * *

This was surely Purgatory. Franco Stoloni had been here for an hour now, and for an hour he had desired to rip out every throat in the room. He didn't fit in with this crowd at all. They were all hideous except for a man with immaculate hair who reminded him of someone, and the three attractive women that were desperate for his loins. So far, he had been groped dozens of times by a disgusting group of teenage girls. They all stank of sweat, semen, alcohol, and baby faeces. Three drinks had been spilt on him and he had passively inhaled about a thousand cigarettes. He did appreciate the ale, and this beer was very good.

He had watched Tillsley drink himself into an inebriated state. The man was a machine and must have been on his seventeenth pint. First impressions were that he was an overweight, drunken idiot. After being in his company for an hour he had come to the conclusion that he *was* an overweight, drunken idiot.

Franco could smell the cholesterol in Tillsley's blood. However, his heart pumped slow, strong and steady like a bull elephant's. He was extremely overweight, but muscle bulged underneath the fat, hairy flesh. He was certainly a handful for a human, but to a vampire?

From overhearing conversations between patrons, he had discovered that Sid Tillsley claimed jobseekers and disabled benefit because of various fabricated ailments. Franco could sense nothing wrong with Tillsley's heart, whatsoever. The man was an obvious liar, and a lazy liar at that. This was the weirdest assignment that he had ever been given, but Michael Vitrago was involved so he would report his findings, to the letter.

The oaf got up, looking very nervous for once. He was talking to the weasley man in the disgusting suit and the greasy beard that reeked of sex. Both of them kept looking over at one of the most disgusting-looking creatures Franco had seen in four hundred years.

This was a repugnant town at the best of times, and for someone to stand out in this way was impressive. The reason for Tillsley's nervousness became apparent when he attempted to make conversation with the woman. He was nervous because he was attracted to the woman, genuinely attracted! Four hundred years and humans could still shock you. Another weak link that the human possessed. This was all too easy.

* * * *

Sid snubbed out a Bangladeshi, picked up the small sherry in his massive hand, and walked over to try his luck with Sheila Fishman. She saw him coming over and scowled.

"I knew you'd be here, Tillsley. I knew this was your kind of disgusting entertainment." She spat each word with pure hatred. She was here to gain his confidence, but she couldn't hold back the rage inside.

It was not the best of starts for Sid. It appeared that he was on the ropes from the first round.

"Howay, flower, I've bought you a drink. I'm here to make amends for what happened the other day at the office. How is the poor fella and his sack?"

Sheila knocked back the sherry from her own glass and then snatched the sherry from Sid. She was not a drinker, but these were unusual and distressing circumstances.

"He'll be fine, as if you care. I could lose my job because of you. I love that job." She drank half the sherry. "You make me sick!"

Sid rubbed the rolls on the back of his head, awkwardly. He had just taken a standing eight count. "Come on, love, it wasna me who stapled his knackers to his leg. I don't know why you hate me so much. I'll get you another sherry, pet."

She drank the other half of the small sherry at the mention of stapled knackers. Before she could tell him where to stick his sherry, he had ambled off to the bar.

He returned seconds later and gave her the sherry. "Look, if you get to know me I ain't so bad. None of us are, really."

At the most inopportune moment, Maggie asked the bar who wanted to see her "nought."

"Well, most of us are decent folk, like," he smiled, trying to cover up the situation.

"Burdens on s-s-society, all of you!" Sheila finished the sherry, and it was going straight to her head. In fine Northern tradition, Sid saw his chance. He disappeared, and in a second, reappeared like ninja…with large sherry!

"Have another sherry, love," said the Casanova. "When I saw you in that office the other day, it put a smile on my face. I said to meself, 'Sid, there's a lass who takes pride in her job.' I tell a lie. I actually said, 'Sid, there's a beautiful lass who takes pride in her job,'" he beamed at her.

"R…really?" she said, letting a small amount of rage drift peacefully from her coal black heart.

"Oh, aye. I really admire you, Miss Fishman. I'd love to do a job like yours, it's just that…I canna. I'm not the smartest of men. I ain't the brightest penny in the pile, not by a long way. All I can use, Miss Fishman, is me hands…and when you're crippled with a back like mine, then, Miss Fishman, the world is not your oyster." Sid let his heart out to the benefit investigation officer.

"I…didn't realise that you fffelt like that, Mishter Tillsley," she slurred, "I didn't realise at all. I thought…I thought you were scamming the government out of thousands." The corner of her heavily wrinkled mouth turned almost to a—was it a smile?

Mission accomplished. Brian Garforth wasn't the only silver-tongued fox in Middlesbrough. Sid smiled back at Sheila and casually reached down to tweak her breast. "Howay the lads, mon!"

The glass in Sheila Fishman's hand shattered. The colour drained from her face and ever so slightly, she began to shake.

"You alright, pet?" asked her concerned lover.

The rate and the magnitude of the shaking increased. Her lips peeled back to reveal gritted yellow teeth. Her veins visibly pumped blood up her neck and colour returned to her face. Her eyes bulged with the increased pressure, and her face reddened to the same hue as Sid's. Things were not going as planned for Sid. Maybe he had been a little forward?

Her teeth started chattering as her shaking body accelerated to an unnatural frequency. "T...T...T..." she stuttered with each breath.

"I better be going, petal." Sid made a quick beeline for the gents.

"T...T...TILLSLEY!...YYYYOOOOOUUUUU CCCCCUUUUUN...!"

"LADIES AND GENTLEMAN, IT IS TIME!" Kevin Ackroyd roared the announcement from behind the bar to rapturous applause and shouts from the women (and one man). Groans came from all the men who were not big into musical theatre. There was a general migration of the men towards the bar and they stood with their backs to the stage, which consisted of a cleared space near the broken jukebox, whilst the women fought to get to the very front.

"Tonight, we have a replacement for the advertised Obi-Dong-Kenobi…" He was interrupted with jeers and boos from the incensed women. He held up his hands. "Don't fear, ladies, we have a replacement and he is—MR. NEWCASTLE!"

Screams erupted from twenty-five women and one flowery shirt-wearing gentleman.

"Two Tribes" by Frankie Goes to Hollywood blared out at full volume from a ghetto blaster that Kev had borrowed from a mate. A lad of about twenty-five years jumped out from behind the bar dressed as a fireman. The women went wild. He jigged his way to the makeshift stage, whilst being groped and probed as he passed. To the music, he took off his hat to reveal an extremely good-looking young man. Kevin Ackroyd beamed with pride as the ladies from the Smithson Estate roared in appreciation. Maggie threw her knickers and Mr. Newcastle skilfully dodged to one side.

The knickers stuck to the wall behind him with a stomach-churning squelch.

Off came his overalls to leave a pair of tight white trousers, rippling abs and a beautifully sculpted torso. The baying women loved it. He danced around and the ladies pawed him in a way which was tantamount to rape. After a few minutes of prancing around, he ripped off his trousers in a magnificent finale. All that remained was an impressively filled thong above well-muscled legs. The women went wild. They cheered, they roared, and they screamed obscenities against nature itself. The atmosphere was absolutely terrifying and the men rubbed their hands in glee. These ladies were going to be red-hot, after this.

The music ended in perfect time with his routine. Mr. Newcastle took a bow and started to pick up his equipment.

"Oi, ya fooking bastard!" yelled a drunken harpy. "Where the fook do ya think ya fooking going?" Her face was red with rage, or possibly a hot flush.

"You fooking arsehole! Get that fooking thong off now! We paid good fooking benefit money to see cock!" screamed one of Maggie's drunken gaggle of girls.

Poor Mr. Newcastle.

"Sorry, I only strip down to the pants, like."

This incensed the women further. Obviously, Mr. Newcastle had never worked a venue like the Miner's before.

"Kev!" called the stripper, "Kev, you knew the deal!"

Kevin Ackroyd looked on. He had sold his soul to the Devil that night. He knew the score, all right. He knew what he had thrown the poor lad into and he was willing to face judgement for it before going to Hell. Kevin slowly put out his hand in a fist. He didn't look sad and he didn't look sorrowful, for he had made peace with his own demons. Looking Mr. Newcastle straight in the eye like a Roman Emperor, he turned his thumb down.

"COME 'ERE, YA BASTARD!" One of Maggie's clan reached out and grabbed at Mr. Newcastle's thong. He recoiled too late and as his pants were pulled away, a pair of socks fell out and rolled across the floor before coming to rest at Maggie's feet.

Silence fell upon the pub.

The gents who had their backs turned for the past five minutes had regained interest after hearing the fracas caused by the angry women. They knew what was coming.

Some say that the anticipation of pain is worse than pain itself. It isn't. Four cock-crusaders attacked Mr. Newcastle. All grabbed for the G-string. The silence was broken by blood-curdling screams of rage by the women and screams of fear from Mr. Newcastle. There was an almighty *twang!* as the G-string snapped under the ferocious tug of the 'boro ladies. Karma had come to Kevin Ackroyd, and it had come with vengeance.

"THAT'S A FOOKIN' MAGGOT!"

"THAT'S A BABY-COCK, YOU BASTARD!"

"THREE QUID TO SEE THAT WORM!"

Mr. Newcastle stood frozen. Perhaps it was smaller than average, but the fear that consumed him had shrunk it, considerably. It was practically an "inny." He stood transfixed by his attackers until the barstool hit him between the eyes.

The men roared with laughter and the women roared with sexually frustrated anger. Chairs now filled the air. Many were aimed at Ackroyd, many were aimed at the laughing men, and many were just thrown randomly in rage. Kevin pulled down the shutter of the bar. He knew when the ship was going to sink and that time had come. All he could do now was watch the mob destroy his beloved pub. This would require rubber bullets, tear gas, and half of Middlesbrough's finest to calm it down.

Obi-Dong-Kenobi had a lot to answer for.

Glass started to shatter through the shutters and Kev left for higher ground, hoping that this time they wouldn't set the place on fire.

* * * *

Gunnar Ivansey approached the Miner's Arms. He doubted whether this night would quell his sadness, but it didn't matter. As long as Tillsley was killed by his hand, he would have revenge. Fifty yards from the Miner's, a figure approached from the opposite direction. The scent. He recognised it and it caused him to laugh. He had heard about this human and his line many times before and had had the pleasure of meeting him once.

The human and the vampire arrived at the pub at the same time.

"Hello, Reece."

Hearing his name startled Reece. He, like Gunnar, was deep in thought about Sid Tillsley.

"Who's that?" He looked closer and answered his own question. "Ivansey!"

Gunnar smiled, "Yes, the very same. Have you missed me?"

Reece didn't respond to the vampire's taunt.

"Tell me, Reece, how many have you killed since I let you live on that beautiful night?"

"Sixteen bastards I have sent back to Hell," he spat at the vampire.

Gunnar laughed mockingly. "Sixteen! Fifteen years and you have managed to kill sixteen of my brothers and sisters. Reece, you amaze me. How someone can disgrace an already pitiful line is beyond me. You are better than your father, though, if that is any consolation?"

Reece's blood boiled. Fifteen years previous, he and his father had killed two vampires in a single night. They were young, and had the habit of preying on young walkers around the Yorkshire Moors. His father tracked them down to an abandoned mine where they hid from the daylight. He remembered the satisfaction of severing the sick animals' heads.

Their surveillance, however, was not perfect, and they didn't realise that these two adolescents had a father figure whose great wing they sheltered under: Ivansey.

Reece snarled, "What are you doing here?"

"The complete opposite of you, I should imagine. I am here to kill Sid Tillsley in a slower and more excruciating way than I killed your father. Would you like to watch this time, as well?"

Reece fought desperately to hold back tears of frustration. He longed to kill Ivansey, but he had to keep his head as the powerful vampire could kill him in an instant, or even worse, a lifetime. "What makes you think that you can manage the job? Gabriel died with a single punch."

Before Reece could blink, Gunnar's right hand had lifted him a foot off the ground, and his fangs had descended to their full length. His voice was as a guttural growl, which penetrated into Reece's heart, saturating him with fear.

"You are not worthy enough to mention his name. How that thing came to kill him, I do not know. How or why, I do not care. I will avenge my brother, tonight!"

He threw Reece against the wall, which took all the wind out of him and he was left a wheezing wreck on the ground. As Gunnar turned towards the Miner's, a window exploded out into the street. A barstool followed shortly after and struck him hard in the windpipe, crushing it. He fell to the ground. It would take a couple of minutes for him to regenerate to full strength.

"FUCKING SMALL-COCKED BASTARDS!"

Another stool smashed through the window of a car parked behind Ivansey's prone body. About fifteen to twenty men herded out of the door and watched the carnage from the relative safety of the street. Through the crowd, Gunnar could see overweight, drunken, tattoo-covered, jewellery laden, behemoth-women rampaging uncontrollably.

He surveyed the group of men that had gathered outside, recognising Franco Stoloni. The Coalition were already on to Tillsley. Another two didn't seem to be locals and were most certainly agents from the Hominum Order.

Tillsley! Gunnar's figure of hate stood in front of him with a pint of ale in each hand. He was obviously drunk, but it didn't matter, he would feel pain no matter how much alcohol he consumed. His throat was beginning to heal.

Chambers.

Reece had managed to get to his feet, although he still found it difficult to breathe. "Sid…S-Sid!" He struggled between coughing and wheezing.

"Eh!" Sid turned round. "Ah fook me, mon! Canna you leave me alone for one good piss-up? It's just started to get going in there, and I'm definitely on for a jump, like."

"There's…there's a vampire here to kill you!" he spurted out in a single breath.

Many heads turned round at once. Local hero, Brian Garforth, picked a bottle up from the ground, whilst local hero, Arthur Peasley, adopted a defensive, yet deadly, karate stance. Both took up their position behind Sid.

Franco Stoloni tried to mingle into the crowd, as did the two agents from the Hominum Order. They didn't do a very good job as they were the only three people not completely hammered and near unconsciousness.

Gunnar rose to his feet. His throat had completely regenerated.

"Sid Tillsley!" he shouted in a booming tone. Everyone in the street turned round, whilst the women inside the pub continued to rampage. "Do you know what I am?"

"A tosser!" shouted a few drunks at the back of the group.

Sid scratched his head, and then his bum crack. "No idea, mon. Actually, don't you play darts for the Tap and Spile?"

"He's a vampire, Sid," said Reece.

"Really? All them years and I never knew. To be honest, I should have realised. He's a pale fella and I only ever see him at night, and he's good at counting too." He gave Brian a nod. Sid Tillsley did learn some things.

"My name is Gunnar Ivansey."

"I thought it was Stan."

"...I am here to kill you."

"I've been calling you Stan all these years. It's embarrassing when that happens."

"You killed my brother, Gabriel. I am here to repay the debt...and to add to it!"

Sid looked at Brian. "I thought Stan's brother was killed by that horny bull, in Stockton-on-Tees?" Whilst Sid's head was turned, Gunnar charged and fired four inconceivably powerful punches into Sid's face.

Gasps filled the air. Sid had taken a step back!

The crowd looked on in excited apprehension, whilst chaos still reigned inside the pub. Maggie was sitting on the unconscious face of Mr. Newcastle and a paramedic was a necessity.

Gunnar stepped back. He had unleashed all he had, and the man had only stepped backwards. The crowd were impressed though. This vampire fella must be pretty handy if he can move Sid with a punch.

Sid gave his chin a wiggle.

"Now then, lad, I nearly spilled me beer there." Sid held on to his tankards of ale. The ground was dry. Sid did a mighty biceps curl and downed his right pint, then repeated on the left side, like all good athletes.

Ale was down, now it was fighting time. The spectators surrounded the group as if it was a school fight. Gunnar held up a guard. He was shaken that Sid was still standing.

Sid fired off a left jab and Gunnar's nose broke. His knees buckled, but he managed to keep his feet. In his heart, fear began to overtake hatred because his nose hadn't started to re-heal immediately. It must be badly broken.

Gunnar threw a couple of quick punches but Sid dodged both with expert timing.

"Now I'm gonna go easy on you, lad, 'cos you're upset about your brother and all. I'll wait 'til you get ye senses back and we can call this a day."

The Middlesbrough Marauder fired off another jab, which caused Gunnar to lose the use of his right eye. He was so fast there was nothing that Gunnar could do. He spat the blood out that had gone up his nose and down the back of his throat. "If I can't kill you now, then I'll kill all the people you care for, you bastard!" Gunnar screamed the words in desperation.

"Reet, no more silly buggers." Sid put his left foot forward to step into the finisher, the coup de grace, the Big Right. However, as he threw the cruise missile, his left foot came down and slipped on a pair of knickers that had been left outside after a loving encounter. The punch was thrown and there was no calling it back. The cruise missile missed its target and landed square on the jaw of the spectator, Franco Stoloni, who instantly exploded into a cloud of dust.

Gunnar stared into the space where Franco Stoloni had once stood. He had suffered the same fate as Gabriel. It was no fluke of nature that he had died. Gunnar looked at Sid, who stood scratching his head, slightly embarrassed about killing someone. Gunnar had hit him with four punches that would have felled an oak and he only stepped backwards. His left jabs were more powerful than the impact of a car. There was no other choice. Gunnar fled.

Sid looked around at the group of spectators. He knew everyone apart from a couple of young lads. "I didn't mean to kill him, like." He rubbed the back of neck awkwardly. "I tried to give that other wanker a proper smack, 'cos he deserved it."

Brian squatted over the remains of Franco Stoloni. He picked up a bit of Franco and rubbed it between his thumb and forefinger. "Is this what happened after you hit them other vampires, Sid?"

Sid nodded. "Aye, mon, but them bastards deserved it. This poor fella was only down here for a few jars at Ladies' Night. He didna deserve this!"

"Casualties of war, man," commiserated Arthur Peasley. "The undead want to start throwing their fists around then someone's gonna get their ass kicked. He was one of them, man."

"Aye." Peter sighed. "I kicked fook out of three of the bastards, earlier in the gents. Caught 'em looking at me tackle."

"Shut up, Rathbone!" said numerous voices in the group.

Reece stepped forward. "Sid, he was not here for Ladies' Night. He was here for you, and he was either here as an assassin, or here to spy on you. Just like those two agents, there." He turned to look at Rickson and Jeremy Pervis.

Rickson stood stony-faced, whereas Pervis looked as if he was about to burst into tears.

"Tell the gentlemen where you come from," commanded Reece.

Pervis wilted immediately. "We are from the—"

"Shut up!" Rickson shouted at the young statistician. He pointed at Sid. "It doesn't matter who we are. What is important is *what you are.*"

He was interrupted mid-flow by the sounds of police sirens. The riot inside the pub was escalating and Mr. Newcastle was in serious need of medical treatment and, unknown to him, a STD test. As in every corner of Middlesbrough when sirens are heard, everyone legged it.

16

Gunnar awoke from his troubled sleep and winced. His broken nose still hadn't healed. The human's power was immense. He was stronger than anyone Gunnar had ever battled with. Stoloni—the poor bastard. It was not a great loss to the vampire world. The wretch was born more like a human, but to die by accident…worse luck couldn't happen to an immortal. A month ago, Gunnar would have scorned any vampire killed by a human, but now things were different.

He left his crypt and followed the stairs up to the grand hallway. It was one 'o clock in the morning, which meant he had slept hours more than normal and his body was struggling to heal the wound to his nose. He walked up the curving staircase and into his massive shower room, turned the power to full and the heat to high, and allowed the water to massage his body vigorously.

There was only one thing that mattered in the world now, and that was to destroy Sid Tillsley. He wouldn't rest until he had ruined the man completely. He needed to move fast as the oaf could die, any day, from ill health. The dilemma was: how to ruin the man?

He couldn't beat him in unarmed combat. The man was drunk and still could take blows that would knock out a bull elephant. Gunnar would be damned if he would take a weapon to the man; his honour held him firm to that. His honour was the only thing that outweighed his want for revenge. But how could he hurt him? How could he hurt him so badly that he yearned for death? Gunnar recalled the fight. Reece Chambers witnessed the ordeal, but he would prove tricky to find. He had eluded better trackers than Chambers for over a decade now. There were many people present who were obviously local and there were definitely two from the Hominum Order.

They thought they had blended in so perfectly, but Gunnar could have told who they were with his eyes closed. The bespectacled ugly agent, the stench of fear, revealed that he knew what was happening before the confrontation had begun. The coward gave away his counterpart. The coward would scream everything that Gunnar needed to. However, the fun that he could have with his cool accomplice would be exquisite. He would soon lose that hard exterior.

Gunnar cut his shower short. There was work to be done. He dried off quickly and got dressed. He needed the names of the humans and he knew exactly the vampire who would give him the answers he sought.

* * * *

Gunnar sped along to Rickson Flatley's residence, the human who he desperately needed to…interview. He hadn't enjoyed what he had just done, not in the slightest. The name he wanted came from Augustus, member of the Human-Vampire Coalition. They were once good friends, and if Sid Tillsley didn't walk on this earth then they still would be. Augustus would live, but Gunnar didn't enjoy the actions he took acquiring the information.

Rickson Flatley. Torturing him would make up for the treatment that he had just inflicted on his former ally. It was lucky that he lived locally because the sun was soon to rise.

He was sure that Flatley would offer him his hospitality. There was no wife or kids to deal with, but there was the possibility of a gay lover. Gunnar didn't care what mess, or what clues he left for Sanderson and his team. This was more important than his life was worth. Honouring the great existence of Gabriel was all that mattered now.

He feared no other vampire and only Michael could defeat him in combat. Would Michael remind the world of what he was capable? It would be a difficult situation for the former-tyrant. Gunnar was almost there and his questions would be answered. His impatience led him to drive faster into the suburbs of London.

* * * *

Rickson awoke with a start. Had he just heard something? Probably not, he was suspicious at the best of times and was the first to admit that it bordered on paranoia. Nevertheless, that was why he was in the job he was in. He glanced over at the bedside clock: three thirty in the morning. It was exactly five hours until he met the Hominum Order and briefed them on all that had befallen in the past week.

What a week. It felt like the seven days would never end. It was a living nightmare being in the company of Pervis, the most pitiful man he had ever met. Not only that, he was away from his beloved for a week. At least he would be reunited with Lee, tomorrow night.

Tracking the movements of that overweight scumbag had been painful, but it finished with the most amazing sight he had ever seen: the slaying of a vampire. Was this a chance to wipe the bastards from the face of the planet?

He jumped out of bed. That was definitely a noise! He reached into his bedside cabinet and pulled out his berretta handgun. One good thing about working for the Order was that he could put a magazine through the bastard and have it all taken care of.

As he walked through the house, he held the gun with both hands in his line of sight. He thought the noise had come from below him, in the lounge, so he crept down the stairs without making a sound, years of military training working perfectly. It could only be a burglar. Lee was the only other one with a key, and he was out of the country until tomorrow.

He peered slowly around the doorway of the lounge. *There you are, motherfucker.* How did this burglar bypass the security? No matter. Rickson fired a double tap into the burglar's central line. The burglar fell backwards and spun, with the impact, to face Rickson. One more double tap left the burglar lifeless, slumped in Rickson's armchair.

"Boooyaahh!" Rickson blew the smoke from his pistol and turned on the light.

"Aren't you meant to shout a warning first?" asked Gunnar.

Rickson stepped back startled. A vampire! That thought had never entered his mind. "I-I am with the Hominium Order. You cannot touch me!"

Gunnar rose from the armchair and walked casually over to Rickson Flatley. He slowly lifted his finger up until it was pointing at Rickson's forehead, and gently tapped him twice. "Guess what? I just did."

"Get the fuck out of my house!" Rickson regained his confidence and Gunnar could smell that it was not a front.

"You remember me, don't you, Rickson? You remember me from last night, outside the pub in Middlesbrough?" asked Gunnar calmly.

Rickson smirked. "I know who you are, Ivansey. More importantly, I know exactly *what* you are."

Gunnar smiled. It was extremely rare for a human who knew of him to show so much courage. Maybe he would finish him quickly, after all. "Pray tell, what exactly am I? What tales have you been told to scare you when the lights go out?"

"You are evil, Ivansey, evil…" spat Rickson.

Gunnar waved his hand dismissively, as if he had had just been given a compliment.

"You are worse than a murderer, worse than a rapist, worse than a fucking paedophile."

"Enough of this flattery." Gunnar got up from the bloodstained chair. He was a fast healer, even for a vampire, and the gunshot wounds had gone. "Now, young Rickson, please take a seat whilst I ask you a couple of simple questions, and then I'll be on my way." He walked over to the window and looked at the sky. "That is, unless the day comes and I have to stay the night. How would you explain that to your boyfriend?"

Rickson's face contorted into rage. "You leave him out of this you fuc—" his words curtailed into an agonising scream and he collapsed in a heap on the chair behind him.

"There's a good chap," comforted Gunnar, who had leapt across the room and stamped through Rickson's knee, snapping his leg to an impossible angle and ripping every ligament in his kneecap, ensuring a life of disability.

To Rickson Flatley, the few seconds he was conscious before he passed out seemed to last a lifetime. Mercy was not a word in the vocabulary of Gunnar Ivansey. He massaged part of Rickson's neck, influencing the blood-flow back to his brain and the agent was thrown back into consciousness and agonising pain.

"I believe I have your full attention," laughed Gunnar. "Now, that can be the only injury I inflict on you. You can walk away—well, limp—a relatively unscathed man. Let's be honest, Rickson. If you know of me, and I mean you *really* know of me, you'll know that your wound is equivalent to a paper cut."

Rickson did know. This thing's hatred for humans was well documented throughout history. If this animal wanted to know something then it would find out. The torture was just for his sick amusement. "What do you want to know?" he finally conceded.

Genuine shock appeared on Gunnar's face. "I thought you had more courage than that? Oh, well. That human that I fought, what do you know of him?"

"His name is Sid Tillsley and he is forty-six years old. Jeremy Pervis and I were assigned to follow him and gather information on his activities." He struggled to talk through the pain.

"So, you monkeys know of his ability to kill vampires? You know that he killed Gabriel?" It was the first time since Gunnar's meeting with Ricard that he had spoken to another soul about Gabriel's demise. His shame for his friend's death had passed since his confrontation with Tillsley. He knew what power the man possessed, and the death of Franco Stoloni had proven that it was no fluke.

For a second Rickson forgot about the pain. The death of Gabriel was the greatest news he had heard in years and he couldn't hold back a smile. He instantly regretted it as Gunnar drove his foot through his other leg, snapping it like a twig. This time he had aimed his blow at the middle of the shin. The bones ripped through the flesh, causing a catastrophic injury to his leg. Rickson screamed with all the pain and anguish in the world. He screamed for the pain, and he screamed because he knew the best situation that could come from this was that he would be crippled for life.

"If you smile again at the death of one of the greatest vampires ever to walk this earth, then I promise you that your arms will share the fate of your legs."

"We knew of the death of Gabriel." He quickly tried to give what information he had to Gunnar. It was difficult with the agony he suffered. "We know that he has also killed four other vampires. The Lamian Consilium sent us the report filed by Richmond…"

"Four more?" Gunnar interrupted him, unaware of the death of the four at the hands, or rather the right hand, of Sid Tillsley. "Tell me all you know of the report."

Once Rickson had finished telling the vampire of Richmond's report, Gunnar took a moment to think of all that had befallen. Tillsley was extraordinary. Had there been people like him before? Gunnar's history on his own kind was poor and he would have to consult Ricard once more. Nevertheless, one thing was certain, Sid Tillsley couldn't be beaten in unarmed combat.

"Tell me all that you know of Tillsley."

"He is nothing more than a drunken bum. He spends all of his time in a small, run-down pub, which was demolished in the riot that ensued during your…encounter."

"I bet you loved watching last night, didn't you?"

Rickson tried to keep his face blank as he knew the consequences if he lied and said no, or if he told the truth and said that it was the greatest sight that he had ever seen. Gunnar smiled. It was the one response that kept Rickson Flatley from losing his arms.

"Please, continue," said the amused vampire.

"We never managed to track him to his home. He was extremely elusive once he left the pub. We…" He winced, the pain in his legs was almost impossible to bear. "…We found out that he has been claiming job seeker's benefit for thirty-two years. He has also claimed numerous fraudulent sickness benefits revolving around his heart and bad back. We were going to consult the Job Centre tomorrow to find out more information. He would have run up a considerable sum in illegally claimed benefit monies."

Was this Gunnar's way to destroy the man? He couldn't beat him in unarmed combat, and he had accepted it, although it cut him deep. No vampire would ever take a weapon to a human in a one-on-one confrontation because the shame would be impossible to bear. These monkeys would shoot one another in the back, but vampires were a noble race. Nevertheless, destroying the man's wellbeing could hurt him in a way more than death could.

"What else do you know about his benefit fraud?"

"When you fought Tillsley, did you see the woman who was outside? She was the only woman outside of the pub, hideously ugly?"

"All of you monkeys are hideous to me," said Gunnar as he spat into Rickson's face. "But yes, I do remember one female more grotesque than the rest, why?"

"Her name is Sheila Fishman and she works at the benefit office. She is a man-hater and she hates Sid Tillsley more than any other. She has declared it her life's work to bring him to justice."

This could be Gunnar's best chance. He would have to contact Sheila Fishman and find out everything he needed to know to put Tillsley behind bars. It would be worth it, even if he had to work with a monkey. "Is there anything else that you can tell me?"

"No. I was going back to Middlesbrough after I had reported everything to the Order." Rickson couldn't hide the anxiety in his face. He had given all he had, and knew that this animal had no use for him now. He was not looking forward to the rest of his life.

"Now, Rickson Flatley, are you telling me everything that you know?" Gunnar knelt down in front of him and reached out slowly towards his right eye. The crippled human tried to pull his head back but Gunnar grabbed his eyelid between his thumb and forefinger. "Are you really telling me everything?" He pulled gently to let Rickson know what was going to happen next.

"Yes! Yes, I swear to you! I fucking swear it!" he screamed. Pure desperation and panic filled him, but it didn't stop the sadist. Blood poured into Rickson's right eye, half blinding him. He grabbed at his eye and wept. The pain was nothing compared to what he could feel in his legs, but all he could find in his heart was utter despair.

Gunnar grabbed the left eyelid. "Are you sure?"

This time Rickson didn't even answer. He knew what was going to happen, and he was right. The other eyelid tore off and he was now totally blinded by the blood filling his eyes. He yearned for death.

Gunnar laughed to himself. He had forgotten that he had said to himself earlier that he would make the death quick. No death was quick if he had the opportunity to play. Sanderson's team would know who had done this, but Gunnar didn't care. All that was important was that he took Sid Tillsley's livelihood away. He would claim benefit no more!

There was a click at the front door as a key turned in the latch. A male voice called through the house. "I'm back early, babe."

Gunnar put his hand over Rickson's mouth before he could yell to his boyfriend to run. Gunnar leaned down and whispered gently into Rickson's ear, "I have just thought of a way for you can survive this night."

17

It was about half past eleven on the Saturday night and Sheila Fishman was still hungover. It was the first time she had been hungover and it was the reason that she was in a terrifyingly bad mood. Normally, she would just be in an extremely bad mood, but the demon drink had taken its toll. She should be fast asleep, but she couldn't find the land of dreams after what happened the previous night. She would never forget the horror for as long as she lived.

Tillsley.

The name made her feel sick to the stomach. It went past the sherry sickness to her very life essence. Tillsley had claimed benefit for decades, illegally. Tillsley had spent it all on cigarettes and alcohol and worse. She only wanted to speak to him for information that would bring the bastard to justice. Everything after that was blurry…except the grab. To think, she had accepted drinks off the man, drinks bought with illegally acquired money! Her own hypocrisy burned her like a hot iron.

"Tillsley. Tillsley was the reason!" she yelled at the top of her voice with fists raised to the heavens. She had let her guard down. Up until he arrived, she only had a single sherry, and that was to fit in with the scum. She would have had a glass of mineral water, or something else equally respectable, but every other woman in the place was drunk and out of control. She recognised ninety per cent of them from the office. They seemed to have a child every nine months and then they sponged more money. Her rage was getting sidetracked. Tillsley had caused all of this.

She remembered the pain of smiling sweetly at his hideous face and the pain of listening to his horrible language. But, as she found herself at the bottom of her third glass of sherry, she found the worst moment of all. That moment would haunt her dreams for the rest of her natural life, and it would probably follow her all the way to Hell. For a second, just a second, she had thought that maybe, just maybe, he wasn't so bad…

Sheila spat on the floor. A large, oyster-sized piece of saliva landed on her impeccably clean floor with an almighty squelch. Feeling anything but utter disdain for the man filled her with a shame so great, that nothing could cleanse her soul. She gave the spit-ball on the floor a bigger and slimier twin-brother.

The grab.

She had washed her right breast thirty-six times that morning. She didn't know it was going to happen. The pervert! It was tantamount to rape! Sid Tillsley epitomised hate for Sheila Fishman and she would get her revenge.

Alfred the cat walked up to her feet and purred because he wanted feeding…again.

"Fucking cat!" she let lose a toe-punt that sent Alfred fleeing for one of his nine lives.

"Fucking Tillsley!" It was the third time she had sworn in twenty-three years and it was all because of Sid Tillsley. He had more to answer for than any other man did, including Hitler.

She was off to visit poor Mr. Croaker, tomorrow. He was recovering in Middlesbrough Hospital. She hadn't seen him since the stapler incident.

"Tillsley," she growled through gritted teeth.

If it wasn't for him, Mr. Croaker would still have the ability to achieve an erection. The word erection made her shudder. Croaker was a worm of a man, and was not the supervisor that the benefit office needed. The benefit office needed an iron fist to crush all that do not contribute to this great country. She had to visit him in order to keep this job, and she had to hope that he wouldn't launch an official complaint.

She walked into the kitchen to finish a cup of tea and, in a reflexive move, unleashed a mighty toe-punt into the groin of the man that suddenly appeared before her. She felt the stern leather of her pointed shoes puncture both testicles with a satisfactory pop.

Gunnar Ivansey dropped like a sack of concrete. Vampires healed to blows almost instantly, but two split gonads were complicated pieces of machinery and the pain was immense. He took the foetal position and hoped things would go back to normal, as soon as possible. Boiling water poured into his eyes.

"Have that, you bastard!" Sheila Fishman poured a kettle's worth of boiling water into his face. "Try and burgle a defenceless lady? You're gonna pay, you horrible little bastard! I'm going to get the blowtorch and stick it up your arse…just like I did to your accomplice, last week!" She ran out of the kitchen to get the tool of unthinkable torture. After the last burglary attempt, Sheila kept the torch handy.

Gunnar raised a hand. "Stop! I'm not a burglar!" He needed to get to his feet. Vampire or not, he didn't need to feel what a blowtorch in the rectum felt like. His testicles were healing fast, but it would be a minute before he could see. He rose to his knees as he heard the strike of a match. "I want to get even with Tillsley!" he yelled.

"Why didn't you say so?"

Sheila Fishman blew out the faeces-stained blowtorch.

* * * *

Gunnar sipped his tea from a bone china mug. Cats purred around him and rubbed themselves against his leg. He hated cats. The past five minutes had been some of the strangest of his life, and things were not getting any less surreal. Sipping tea with a human who had just put him to his knees. It was the second time in a weekend that a human had him at their mercy. Tillsley was not a normal human, but this hideous woman was nothing out of the ordinary, except for her revoltingness.

There was nothing he could have done after the attack. Her kick to the groin would have been fatal to a human. It was as if her shoes were designed to puncture a man's genitals. And once he had lost his sight, then he was very vulnerable indeed. A blowtorch in the anus? This woman shared his sadistic streak. Maybe working with her might not be as bad as he had imagined.

"I want to ruin Tillsley's life. I have heard that you have the same goal," Gunnar said.

Sheila put down her cup of tea. "I hate that man more than anything. I hate him more than disease, more than cancer, more than starvation, more than war. I'd go through anything to bring that bastard down."

Gunnar smiled at her aggression and hatred. "Then I guess we are not as different as I once thought. I want to bring this man to his knees, but physically I was not able to out-power him."

"You want me to run him over in my car?"

"No. If I cannot beat him in unarmed combat then the route of violence I will not take. I thought of killing his loved ones, but it appears that he has no one except the people he drinks with, and drinkers never have proper friends. I have researched his life and it seems the best way to get to this man is to take away his livelihood. Sheila, this is why I have contacted you. I understand that you are trying to take away his illegally acquired income?"

Sheila nodded with vigour. "I am gonna catch him and bring him to justice…but…" There was the possibility that all of this might be taken from her. If Mr. Croaker decided to launch a complaint then things would become very tricky indeed.

"But what? Name the problem and it will be dealt with."

"What can you do?"

He laughed. "I am sorry, my dear, for I have not introduced myself fully. I am Gunnar Ivansey, and I was born centuries ago in the forests of Germany. I am not a human…I am a vampire."

"Well, you still went down with a kick to the stones, didn't you? Look, I don't care if you are a vampire or a dark-billed platypus. If you help me get even with that bastard, Tillsley, then you're alright by me."

Gunnar smiled. She didn't believe him. It mattered not. She would believe soon enough. "Tell me your problem."

"Very well, but if you don't sort it out then you're on your own."

Sheila told Gunnar about Mr. Croaker, and of how he had lost the use of his genitalia in one of the nastiest desktop stapler accidents ever seen by the A&E team at Middlesbrough General Hospital. She told him that if she lost her job, she wouldn't have the powers to bring Tillsley to justice, and the only chance of her losing her job was if Croaker complained.

"Where exactly is he staying?"

"C-Wing, Ward Four."

"I will be back once the problem is sorted," and with that, he left the room.

"When you coming back?" called Sheila. She walked into the hall for a response, but Gunnar Ivansey was nowhere to be seen.

Sheila put the kettle on.

* * * *

It was one o'clock in the morning and Sheila couldn't sleep. She was excited about having her first ever partner. No one at the benefit office shared her passion for the job. They were only there for the money.

"Bastards."

She couldn't stop swearing, but she didn't care as it enhanced her rage and focused her on the battle ahead.

She now had an ally in her fight against benefit fraud and against the bastard, Sid Tillsley. It didn't matter that Gunnar was a complete and utter loon, thinking he was a vampire! What mattered was that she had someone who was willing to fight by her side, for nothing else than sweet revenge.

There was no way that she was going to sleep tonight. She was far too excited. Maybe a warm cup of cocoa would settle her. She kicked back the covers and Ulysses the cat flew across the room and hit the wall before scurrying for cover. She swung out her legs and landed with both feet on Alfred, who screeched before fleeing to join his friend in hiding.

Sheila didn't notice any of this and she put her large, repugnant feet into her shoes, the nearest footwear to the bed. Her cats used to be one of the most important things in her life, but now she would skin every one of them alive to bring that bastard to justice. She walked through to the kitchen to put the kettle on and swung a lightning toe-punt into the groin of the man standing in front of her.

Gunnar Ivansey hit the floor like a sack of concrete, again. Both gonads destroyed for the second time in the evening.

"I'm sorry!" she yelled before he had reached the floor. "You shouldn't sneak in like that! I thought you were a burglar!"

Gunnar didn't respond. He breathed deeply to allow the healing to take place.

"You alright? Do you want a cup of tea?"

Gunnar got to his feet slowly and took a seat at the breakfast table. "Yes, please…Where do you get those shoes of yours?" he asked through gritted teeth.

The Great Right Hope

She looked down. "I made them myself. I call them my 'nutcrackers'. A lady cannot be too careful in this day and age."

He rubbed his swollen scrotum. "Your problem is now sorted. Croaker will not launch a complaint and you are likely to gain a raise for all your hard work over the last few months."

She nodded. "Good, we can press on then."

"There is one problem with our mission. Daylight will kill me. If we are to go out together in the day, then I must be enclosed by complete darkness. I have a van with a light proof compartment in the back. It is a surveillance vehicle and I can work the equipment whilst you drive.

Sheila smiled. Video surveillance! If he had a surveillance vehicle, she couldn't care less about his strange nuances. "When do we start?"

"Tomorrow."

18

Caroline was enjoying a long, hot bath in her extensive flat in Kensington. This was her time. This was when she let all the troubles in the world and all the blood on her hands wash away. This was when she forgot about the hundreds and hundreds of children who were dead because of the decisions she made.

Johann Sebastian Bach played softly in the background and candles burned fragrances from around the world. She was finding it harder than usual to forget the troubles of the week, but then the weeks were becoming more taxing. Could the Firmamentum be here? She hoped not. Were the murders in the Northeast caused by a vampire born stronger, faster and more vicious than the most powerful vampires of the old age, something even more terrifying than Michael? Could this Sid Tillsley be the answer? Tomorrow Rickson Flatley and Jeremy Pervis would hopefully provide the answers that she was looking for.

"Sweetness?" called Caroline's husband through the closed door. He knew she didn't like being disturbed during this personal time.

"Please, Jeffrey, give me an hour," she called back with a touch of annoyance.

"It's the office. They say it's very important. I told them that you'd phone them back, but they are adamant to talk to you?"

The office knew that Caroline needed this time. It must be urgent indeed.

"Bring me the phone."

Her husband opened the door and handed her the cordless telephone. He promptly left, not wanting to hear the conversation. Two minutes later, she was out of the bath and rushing clothes on in order to get to the local hospital.

Caroline arrived to find the Order waiting outside Rickson Flatley's hospital room. The mood outside was extremely grave.

"How is he?" she asked as she approached the group.

Charles shook his head. "He'll survive, but I don't think he'll want to."

"What do you mean? What do we know?"

Charles got to the point, as Caroline didn't like to mince words. He looked around to check that no one was near. "We don't know for certain, but it looks like a vampire has tortured him and his now-deceased boyfriend."

Caroline raised an eyebrow. "How do you know it was a vampire?"

"His wounds are unbelievably severe. Only a vampire could commit such atrocities and not kill. He—" Charles swallowed to fortify himself. "He has had his eyes and his genitals removed. His body has been horrifically carved up, and all of his limbs and ribs are broken. The boyfriend had similar injuries except some of his veins were opened. The doctor said that the veins that were opened would have contained the least pressure. It would have taken him a long time to die."

Jeremy Pervis ran over to a paper bin and emptied his stomach. Tears streamed down his face that were not caused by the sickness. Caroline looked on, her face still stone, but inside her mind raced. A vampire wouldn't attack a member of the Order. It was part of the Agreement, and there would be Hell to pay for whoever was responsible.

"When can we speak to him?"

"The doctor said he would be awake in about an hour," replied Charles.

"OK, Pervis, we need a full report."

With a few words to one of the nursing staff, a meeting room was set up. Members of the Order carried the sort of papers that meant things were done for them, instantly. It gave them authority over police, paramedics and the fire service. They were extremely powerful, yet unknown, politicians. Once the room had been scanned for bugs, the impromptu meeting began. Jeremy Pervis gave an accurate account of all that had happened at Ladies' Night at the Miner's Arms. He told the group of the riot that had ensued, about the emergence of Reece Chambers and about the amazing fight that had occurred between Sid Tillsley and Gunnar Ivansey. When he had finished the group sat quiet.

Sanderson was the first to break the silence. "This is fantastic news. We have a real vampire hunter. A real warrior that can kill these fucks!"

"We know your views, Sanderson, and they are not the views that the Order holds. We do not want a war," Charles said sternly.

"War? I see war every day! When you say war, what you mean is that some of them fucks may take some casualties," he said aggressively.

"If Franco Stoloni is dead, then the vampires will not know any of this. We must inform them," said Charles.

Sanderson almost choked. "Are you fucking crazy? We have a weapon that they do not know about. Why should we just give him to them?"

"Charles is right," said Caroline. Her calmness contrasted Sanderson's manner. "They will find out eventually. Both sides have their spies and there is no point in holding back information. Both sides will need this man if he is the answer to the vampire Firmamentum. It seems like too much of a coincidence that this man is discovered, just as the abominations in the Northeast come to light."

"If it is the Firmamentum that has happened in the Northeast, then it is not the only beast on the loose," said Jeremy Pervis. "Gunnar Ivansey is the most likely culprit for Rickson's torture. He has thrown off the shackles that have restricted his kind. If he will do this to a member of the Order, what else will he do?"

"This is one of the reasons that the Lamian Consilium must be told," responded Caroline. "I can promise you that Michael Vitrago will come down on Ivansey like a tonne of bricks. He will not have the Agreement broken, not by anyone."

"Can we be so sure?" asked Sanderson. "Everyone knows what those fucking animals did together."

"Absolutely. The Agreement is the only thing that Michael cares for. Trust me, he will…" She stopped speaking immediately as there was a knock at the door. "Come in."

A nurse popped her head round the door. "The doctor says that you can see him now. He is conscious, although it is a miracle that he is alive."

"Thank you," said Caroline, before following the nurse with the other councillors.

Rickson Flatley was a mishmash of bandages. Only his jaw-line was left unscathed.

"Rickson?" asked Caroline gently.

"What's left of him," replied the wounded operative.

"What happened?"

"Ivansey left me alive…so I could tell you what he did…and why he did it." Rickson managed to talk between wheezed breaths. He was barely audible because of his broken ribs. "He tortured me for hours. He made me carve…he made me kill Lee. If I didn't do it…he said that he would leave him alive…in a worse state than me. I…I had to…He did this to show that he would…do anything to get to Tillsley. He said he… would avenge Gabriel's death at any price. The only reason he didn't kill me…was so I could tell you this."

"What else did he do, Rickson?" asked Charles.

Rickson ignored the question. "If there is any decency in you, Caroline…I will be dead by the end of the night."

"You have my word," she replied. As ever, she was stone.

"Thank-you."

"Goodbye, Rickson." She left the room and was followed by the rest of the group. There was much to be discussed.

* * * *

"Hello, Ricard."

"Michael! What an unexpected visit." Ricard's look of total surprise passed in the blink of an eye. "Please, do come in."

It was midnight at Ricard's dwelling in the North York Moors. He never had visitors here, especially not visitors like Michael Vitrago. Ricard walked through to the sitting room of the seventeenth century cottage, ornately decorated with trinkets of the past few centuries. A fire raged in the hearth of the small, yet cosy dwelling.

Michael took off his long black coat and threw it over the chair. He wore it to disguise his immense size rather than to stay warm. Underneath the coat, he wore a well-tailored black suit. "How long has it been, Ricard?"

"Fifty-seven years, two months, and a day if my memory serves me well."

Michael offered a brief smirk. "I'm sure that it does."

He took a seat in one of the large armchairs surrounding the fire. Ricard poured two large single malt whiskies from the drinks cabinet. "Is it business, or pleasure, that brings you to my humble dwellings?"

"I think you know," said Michael.

"I'd be lying if I said that I couldn't remember the last time we met on a social occasion, but it has been a great number of decades, hasn't it?"

The huge vampire nodded his head slowly. "Happier, greater days, which I miss dearly."

Ricard smiled. "I'm sure that's not your official line on the matter though?"

His question was greeted with a mirthless laugh. "Very true." Michael looked long into his glass. "Nevertheless, if anyone had to change with the times, it was I. I am not ready to leave this world yet, although sometimes I wish I were. Until that day comes, I will do what is best for the unity of the world."

"Of course, Michael. So, what brings you here?"

"Two things. The first: Gunnar. I must take him," he said plainly.

"The death of Gabriel was more destructive to his vulnerable psyche than I imagined. What has he done?"

"He has broken the Agreement and tortured a human agent. He was very thorough in his work, although I have seen him do things a hundred times worse. He let him live so that he could tell us that he no longer holds any oaths."

Ricard nodded. It was never a question whether Gunnar would go off the rails; it was always a question of when. "Why do you seek my council?"

"When did you last see him?"

"The last time that I saw Gunnar Ivansey was thirteen nights ago, the night after Gabriel died. He didn't come for advice, he never did. He needed to pour his heart out."

There was a brief silence. "You never told the Lamian Consilium about Gabriel's death. Why?"

"Gunnar needed time and was not ready to face an interrogation. I gave him the chance to seek his revenge. If someone else had intervened, I wouldn't like to have stood in their shoes." Ricard answered the questions calmly and carefully. He knew this was an interrogation, and he knew that Michael would kill him in a second if he jeopardised the Agreement in the slightest.

"Gabriel." Michael paused after the mention of the name and stared into his, now empty, glass of scotch. "His blood line has ended now, and I do not see another lamia ever matching his feats. I miss him dearly. How could he fall to the empty hand of a human?"

Ricard paused before answering. "That was one of the reasons that I didn't immediately tell the Lamian Consilium. I wanted to investigate the matter further because I wanted to know how a lamia could be killed by a man…"

"Which brings me on to my second reason for being here," interrupted Michael.

"The Firmamentum," said Ricard softly. "I know that is the reason you are here, old friend. I know that you wanted to tell me about Gunnar too. I appreciate that, and I thank you. I shall mourn his loss deeply…"

"As will I," said Michael.

"When Gabriel died, I thought it was a freak accident. The Firmamentum didn't cross my mind as there was no balance. The human is called because of the lamia, it has always been so. A vampire of such might couldn't be hidden in this modern world. You saw Sparle, Michael. How could you stop the world knowing? How could you stop the war that would be certain to follow? It was for this reason that I didn't suspect Tillsley of being the Bellator."

Ricard pointed to Michael's glass and got a nod in return. Ricard went to the drinks cabinet, returned with a decanter of whisky and filled both glasses.

"But, it seems that the increase in humans killed has not been a coincidence at all," said Ricard. "It seems that there is something out there with an appetite for killing that is larger than ours, or should I say yours? Nevertheless, the Firmamentum. You saw Sparle. You saw the answer that mankind produced. From all the reports that have been filtered through to me, Tillsley is a drunken bum. The human bloodshed has not been that great and how many would Sparle have killed by now? Tillsley is forty-six!

"My council is this: the Firmamentum may be here, but if it is, then it is a very weak strain. You are not going to have to kill the man that you did two thousand years ago."

Michael considered Ricard's council as he sipped his whisky. "Why are you living back here?"

"I have been here a while. I travel from house to house, and at the moment this is where I hang my hat," he said, undeterred by the accusing line of questioning. "I cannot deny that I am interested in what has happened here over the last few months."

"And what have you discovered?"

"I have discovered very little, if all truth be told. I have found no vampire answer to Sid Tillsley, even though the brutal killings have been plentiful."

Michael stared deep into the eyes of the scholar. It was a look that went deep into the soul and would scare any living creature on the Earth, but not Ricard. Ricard was one of the oldest of his line, and though he had never possessed physical power, his mental prowess was second to none. He looked straight back at Michael with equal intensity.

It was Michael who broke the deadlock. "It surprises me that you have not uncovered any clues. It also surprises me that the vampires that I assigned to watch the area have found nothing. My respect for you is unquestionable, but I know your power does not lie in your fangs. If there was something to be found in these parts, then no matter what it was, you would have found it. I assigned good lamia to the area, quite capable of tracking whatever is causing the unrest, unless there was someone better to hide it."

Ricard laughed. "If it wasn't you I was talking to, I would assume that you were joking, but everyone knows that no mirth lies in your heart. This puts you in a difficult situation, Michael, a very difficult situation, indeed."

"That it does, old friend."

"Taking my life wouldn't be difficult as ties mean nothing to you. However, these accusations I can guarantee are yours and yours alone. I know the Lamian Consilium wouldn't believe any of this nonsense and believe me, it is nonsense. I have nothing to do with the blood that has been spilt across these lands."

"I hope so, Ricard. It may surprise you, but it would pain me to take your life. It would pain me, not for the loss of our greatest source of knowledge, but it would pain me to take someone of whom I am fond. It galled you that you couldn't change Sparle. Up until that point, you had never failed at anything, and it must have hurt inside not being able to tame him. If the opportunity arose again, I do not think that you could turn down the chance to right the wrongs of the past, and to succeed where before you failed."

A stern look came over Ricard's face. "You offend me by assuming that my pride is greater than my intelligence. I saw what Sparle did. I witnessed it first hand and it petrified me. If the beast was reborn, then I wouldn't let it loose on the world for a minute longer than necessary. It does not belong on this Earth. Nothing that desires murder as he did deserves life."

"I hope you speak the truth." The huge vampire stood up and placed his glass on the side of the table. "I bid you farewell."

* * * *

Michael arrived back in London well before daylight. He threw open the grand double oak doors of the vampire meeting hall and was greeted by a wall of noise. Conversation was ripe and it wasn't until Michael had taken his seat that the group settled. They had waited for hours, wanting to hear about his meeting with Ricard and to discuss what should be done with Sid Tillsley.

Michael began. "I have met with Ricard. I questioned his involvement with the Northeast. He said he has no clue as to what has caused the bloodshed over the last few months."

"Is he telling the truth?" asked an elder.

Michael cupped his chin in his hands. He had pondered over the very question since he left the old lamia in his cottage. "I don't know. He is too old and wise to give anything away. Whether I believe him or not comes down to my gut feeling. I think that Sid Tillsley will have the answers. The disturbances in the Northeast looks like the destruction Sparle caused two-thousand years ago. But Tillsley, by all accounts, does not match Remo Elscachius, the Bellator."

An elder female vampire with white streaking her red hair addressed the floor. "We need to meet with him. Then we can decide on what he is and whether we can dispose of him or not. We may need him."

Michael nodded, as did most of the Consilium. "You are right. Reece Chambers has latched on to him, but reports shared between us and the Hominum Order says that Tillsley is not a man of action. He does not pose a direct threat to us. We will send a greeting party. There is no rush to apprehend him. It is the blood flowing in the Northeast that ails me."

19

Sid Tillsley had a wicked hangover. He hadn't been able to drink in the Miner's, the night before, due to its temporary destruction. This meant he had to drink in town and the unusual beer had done him a wrong'n. The hangover was worsened by the guilt that he was suffering. He still felt bad about killing the vampire fella as it really was an accident, the poor bugger. The other gobby lad was different, a right arsehole. Sid hadn't a thing against these vampires, but if they were going to start acting like that on a regular occasion then a few slaps would need to be handed out.

It was nine o'clock in the morning and he was on his way to do a bit of construction work for Pervez, Middlesbrough's only Asian docker. He would get a fair few quid for the day's work and hopefully a few ciggies as well. Sid was a bit of a dab hand at the old construction lark and a bit of an artiste, even if he did say so himself. Bit of hard graft today should set him up with beer tokens for the next week. At least the Miner's would be back open tomorrow.

Sid lit up another "Chickboyo" Thai cigarette. He had come into two hundred for helping some Welsh-Thai prostitute get rid of a couple of unwanted gentlemen trying to seek her attention. She had offered Sid a freebie, and she was red hot, too, but Sid had this job to get to and he was a professional. He may go back later to see if the offer still stands…though she did have a very deep voice for a lass.

He finally arrived at Pervez's. It had been a tough walk and it was going to be a tough few hour's work, but it was money in the bank and tabs in the lungs.

* * * *

Sheila Fishman sat in the drivers' seat of Gunnar Ivansey's transit van. The unlikely couple had trailed Sid to the entrance of Pervez's docks. Gunnar was setting up the surveillance equipment in the light-proof rear of the van, whilst Sheila Fishman sat in the driver's seat with a pair of binoculars.

"I can see the bastard," growled Sheila. Swearing was now a regular part of her vocabulary and she swore like a trooper, every blasphemy fuelling her hatred further.

"I've nearly got it set up to record." Gunnar said. The van had cameras looking from all angles. The lenses were camouflaged by writing on the side of the van: Morgan O'Connor, Building Contractors.

"Hurry up, I can see him bloody working! I can see him bloody working!" she yelled excitedly. "The bastard just picked up three sacks of concrete! Three sacks of concrete and he reckons he's got a bad back! He's claimed thousands on his fucking bad back!"

"Calm down, otherwise you'll give the game away," Gunnar barked through the intercom.

Sheila suppressed her excitement with difficulty. "I'm sorry, but we have never got this close before."

Gunnar continued tweaking the surveillance equipment. "OK, we are ready. Film is rolling."

* * * *

Arthur Peasley hummed a very tuneful tune as he strolled along. He occasionally broke into a few words of song, much to the delight of the passersby. Ladies' Night had been a good night for Arthur. He had booked the forthcoming weekend to settle some unfinished business with some of the lovelier ladies of Middlesbrough. The ménage à quatre hadn't come off, as everyone legged it when the police turned up.

"Hey, little lady!" Arthur stopped off to speak to a beautiful young brunette who was passing his way. Arthur was not looking particularly dapper at the moment because he was dressed in his plumbing overalls and it had a few of the nastier stains on them. However, whilst not looking particularly dapper compared to his normal sleek appearance, he still looked a million dollars compared to most film stars.

The girl stopped to talk to the beautiful man, but found herself tongue-tied, intimidated by his lady-killing looks. Arthur was used to this and, as usual, he took care of business.

"How about a drink sometime?" he asked. The question was rhetorical, of course. "Well, here's my card. Just drop me a phone call one evening when you're lonesome that night." He offered her a wink over his shades, and went on his way.

It had been the third card he had dropped off to beautiful women, that day. Certainly a good day for the ladies, but then he was on the posher side of town. He would have three messages on his answer phone when he got back home. At this rate, he would start to get booked up for next week too. It was a hard life, the life of a swordsman.

Arthur was on the posher side of town because a top-notch hotel had problems with one of the toilets and he had been called in to take care of business. He reached his destination: The Royal York. It was a lovely hotel and very stylish. He had never done a plumbing job anywhere this swanky, but he had performed a few jobs on some rich wives and widowers in places similar.

He walked through the marble foyer to the impressive reception where three attractive girls were taking telephone calls and dealing with guests. Arthur walked over to the only free (and most attractive) of the receptionists who was busy looking through the current guest list.

"Miss, I'm here to do the plumbing job," he said professionally.

"You are meant to come in the tradesmen's entran…" She trailed off when she looked into the eyes of the beautiful man.

Arthur gave a cheeky wink. "Hey baby, I don't mind coming in your tradesman's entrance."

Most men would have been slapped, but the receptionist giggled like a schoolgirl with a crush. "I'll get the porter for you, Mr…?"

"Call me Arthur, baby," He gave her one of his infamous calling cards and she rushed off to get the porter.

* * * *

"Where's he gone? Where's he gone?" screamed Sheila. Sid had wandered out of sight of the van. "This is what he does every time we have ever tried to get him. He gets away!"

"Calm down," Gunnar said impatiently, "You didn't have me with you last time."

"I'm sorry, I'm sorry," she said excitedly. "It's just that the prospect of putting him behind bars is the only thing that holds my rage at bay. If we can get some shots of him holding that concrete then we can put an end to Sid Tillsley!"

"Why are you so driven to put these people behind bars and take away their money?"

"It's my job and it's in the rules. Breaking the rules is against the rules," she replied logically.

Gunnar didn't question her any further. What a horrible existence these humans had, working their fingers to the bone performing the most menial of tasks. Then, after working over half their lives, they retire. He had concluded that retirement meant 'waiting to die.' They may live longer now, but their existence was as pointless as it was a millennium ago.

"I can see him over by the forklift truck! Have you got him?" she screamed.

"I won't if you keep jumping around, calm down." Gunnar took control of the appropriate camera. "Yes, I have him clearly." He zoomed in on the fat oaf who, unsurprisingly, was taking a break. He was smoking his life away and occasionally lifting a buttock to pollute the atmosphere. Bestowing this gift on this man made the situation all the more frustrating.

"The bastard!" sneered Sheila through gritted teeth. "Not only is he getting paid benefit money by us, he is also getting paid to do a manual labour job. The ultimate insult is that he is not even working. The lazy bastard is taking a break!"

The vampire ignored her. He watched Sid finish his cigarette and then instantly light another, and then another...and then another. He surely couldn't see many more years if he carried on the way he was.

Sid got up from his seat on the front of the forklift truck and walked behind some crates. He was still visible to the camera.

"This is it!" said an excited Sheila, through the intercom.

"I have him on the video."

Sid bent down, out of view.

"He's picking something up. This is it!"

* * * *

"There you are, my good fellow. This is the bathroom that has been quite ghastly of late. Apparently, the flushing mechanism won't flush." The porter was an extremely well spoken, middle-aged gentleman. His rotund torso strained against his immaculately turned out uniform. "Is there anything else that you require?"

"I'll sort it, baby." Arthur gave the porter a respectful nod and went about work in his professional manner. The porter smiled and left the hotel room. The room was strange to say the least, but not in its layout as it was a very well equipped five star hotel room. The peculiar thing was that the room was underground and he had no idea how far. They had walked down a staircase in the foyer to a separate lift and travelled down for what seemed a considerable length of time.

The lift only had one other stop, this long corridor, which offered a number of different rooms. Why they were underground, Arthur had no idea. He concluded that it must be in case of a war or something. Oh well...to work. You saw some strange sites as a plumber and Arthur had seen much stranger than this.

Arthur was a good plumber and this was going to be a simple job. All he needed to do was replace the siphon diaphragm and he would be on his way. Well, if it was in a residential area he would be, he was a good man. This hotel had money coming out of its ears and the rich assholes could afford to pay a few extra quid.

Arthur took the cistern to pieces and laid everything neatly on the floor. He then went into the main bedroom to watch a bit of telly. Making himself comfortable on the bed, trying not to get some of the nastier stains from his overalls on the clean sheets, he flicked through the satellite channels and was disappointed by the lack of porn.

"Man, I may as well get back to work." He got off the bed and headed back to the bathroom but, through no fault of his own, he walked past the mini-bar. Arthur stopped dead, not being able to walk past the call of the miniature bottles of whisky, rum, and brandy. He opened the door to see what magic waited inside.

* * * *

"We're gonna get him picking something up! We're gonna get him!"

Sid was indeed bending to pick something up, and he emerged clutching a rolled up magazine in his hand.

"Lazy bastard!" Sheila shouted.

The bookworm sauntered back towards the forklift and took a leisurely seat on the side of the vehicle. He opened the magazine and began to read, or rather, he began to look.

"Dirty bastard!" she screamed.

Gunnar shook his head. So far, all that they had was video footage proving that Sid was an avid reader of *Tits*.

"I hate him, Gunnar, I bloody hate him! Wasting the government's money on that...on that—filth!"

Through the intercom, Gunnar heard her spit on the floor of his van.

* * * *

Arthur was not drunk. He was definitely *in drink*. By Middlesbrough standards he was still alright to drive. He was definitely too drunk to replace the siphon diaphragm though, and he had managed to snap the toilet seat with his mighty karate-grip.

"Ah, man!" There wasn't any more booze in the mini-bar for drowning his sorrows at the unjust misfortune.

The beautiful plumber was, however, a clever man. He was not as clever as the cleverest man on the Smithson Estate, Brian Garforth, but he could certainly think on his feet. He decided that the best course of action was to go into one of the other rooms and change the toilet seats over. If they ever noticed, he would have already been paid and he would have got some free booze out of it as well.

Arthur sneaked out of the front door using his karate training. He looked both ways for the porter before darting across the corridor without making a sound. The door on the opposite side of the corridor was locked. "Damn." It was one of the card-activated doors, which meant that Arthur couldn't pick the lock.

A little light bulb lit above the great one's head. He took one of his remaining calling cards from his inside pocket and placed it into the cardkey slot on the door handle. The light went green and the door unlocked. Arthur smiled. Apparently no slot could say no to the most beautiful man in Middlesbrough.

Still not making a sound, Arthur edged around the door. He didn't know if there would be anyone in there, but was certain he could sweet talk his way out of any situation.

At first, the room appeared to be identical to the one where Arthur was fixing the toilet, but there were more doors coming off the main chamber, and behind one, Arthur could hear a voice. He was a very confident man, and after a fair amount of alcohol, he was a tremendously confident man.

If he had heard a man's voice then he would have simply turned around and tried the next room. However, the voice was female, and it was extremely sexy. He could only hear one voice, so she must be talking on the telephone.

Arthur sneaked up to the door. His plan was to assess the situation and make sure that only the fairer sex resided behind the door. Then, when he was fifty per cent certain that it was a lady, he would make his move.

He put his ear to the door.

"I agree, but Sid Tillsley is the key!"

* * * *

Sheila continued her torrent of abuse and Gunnar turned off the intercom. It didn't make much difference as the reverberations of her language still managed to get through the soundproof wall. He continued to watch Tillsley pour over the naked girls in a lewd study of the female form. Patience was the key to this. Tillsley would have to do some work, eventually.

He turned the intercom back on to tell Sheila to calm down for the umpteenth time.

"—unting motherfu—"

Gunnar turned it back off and continued to watch the object of his hatred. The man's face had reddened considerably. It was now heart-attack purple. He was either dying or was getting himself into a state that would turn Sheila homicidal.

Gunnar watched Sid look around quickly and hide the magazine behind his back. Gunnar turned up the outside microphone and turned the intercom back on so he could speak to Sheila Fishman.

"What's going on?"

"Keep quiet or we will never find out," he warned. He was thankful that she heeded his advice.

Gunnar watched as Sid's employer stormed up to him. The small Asian man with a moustache was pointing his finger aggressively at Sid.

"Mr. Sid! Why are you sitting around?"

The van started bumping up and down due to Sheila's excitement. "We will get him if he mentions payment for service..."

"You are a lazy, lazy man, Mr. Sid!" he lectured in a Bangladeshi accent. "What have you been doing, all morning?"

"I-I…" stuttered Sid.

"What are you hiding behind your back, Mr. Sid?" he asked after seeing Sid struggle to hide his magazine.

"N'owt, mon!"

"What are you hiding? Tell me, or this will all end now! Show me, Mr. Sid!"

"I got n'owt!" His attempt to hide the magazine failed miserably as it fell onto the ground between the guilty Sid Tillsley and the accusing Pervez.

Gunnar panned the camera down. The magazine had fallen open on a page with a revealing picture of a middle-aged Asian lady with enormous breasts. He panned back to the face of the Asian man who was shaking with anger.

"It says that she's from 'boro. You know her, like?" asked Sid.

"Mr. Sid, that is my wife!"

* * * *

Arthur listened intently to the sexy voice. His mind had raced since he heard the mention of Sid's name. He wasn't sure what the conversation was about, but he was concerned that the woman was a benefit agent. More importantly, he wanted to find out if she was as pretty as her voice was sexy.

"Vladimir and Sven are making contact tonight at the Miner's Arms."

There was silence as the person on the other end responded.

"Six at the moment, but I am going to help this evening. Hopefully we can get three more vampires to join the hunt."

Arthur gasped, she was a vampire! The female voice stopped. Had he been rumbled?

The door flew open, and Lucia charged out with her fangs fully drawn.

* * * *

"Get out, Mr. Sid! Get off my property!"

"But—"

"Get out!"

Tillsley ambled away from the seething dock owner who charged back from where he came from, screaming obscenities in his native tongue.

"Where's he going!" yelled Sheila.

"He's been sent away, Sheila. The man's wife was in the magazine."

"Fucking hell!" Sheila whined. "That was our chance!"

Gunnar put his head in his hands and turned off the intercom for some peace and quiet. He felt the anger through the truck's vibrations as Sheila punched and kicked at the van, screaming for all she was worth. He felt the door of the van open and then slam shut. He looked through his camera system to watch Sheila storm round the site kicking and punching the crates that were stored there.

"The fat cun—"

He turned off the intercom, deciding to wait until her rant waned enough for him to get a word in edgeways, and watched her disappear around the crates where Sid had first picked up his magazine. When she reappeared it was with a gigantic nail gun that she could barely lift.

Gunnar shook his head. She was certainly the most psychologically demented human he had met. He watched as she uncontrollably fired nails at everything in sight. There were nails sticking out of every crate in the dock, and the forklift truck now sported two flat tyres and ruined paintwork. The only thing that stopped the tirade of nails was her strength. She dropped the gun down and panted heavily.

The amazed vampire deduced that this would be a good time to calm her down, but before he had reached the intercom she had gained her second wind. She lifted the gun and began her assault on the world once more. She turned the gun on the van and unleashed a couple of missiles.

"You stupid, stupid woman!" yelled Gunnar, not unlike the great René Artois.

Her rage was finally halted by Gunnar Ivansey's scream. She dropped the gun, finally coming to her senses, and hurried back to the van and buzzed through the intercom.

"Are you alright, Gunnar?"

After a brief silence he muttered. "Just drive back to base."

"But Tills—"

"Fuck Tillsley!" he yelled. "Drive back to base!"

She complied with the ferocity of his voice.

Gunnar felt the car start back for home and the vibrations of the van caused him extreme pain. If he had been hit with the nail then it would have taken a few minutes to heal. However, he had been hit with the worst thing that a vampire could face: sunlight. The nail had ripped through the van and caused a beam of sunlight to strike Gunnar, like a laser, in the groin. The agony was immense, but Tillsley's pain would be worse.

And so would Sheila fucking Fishman's!

20

It was the night of the grand re-opening of the Miner's Arms. It wasn't particularly grand, but it was the re-opening and some things were different. Different furniture now decorated the pub, although the new furniture appeared to be older and tattier than the previous. There were also a record number of people barred from the pub, as well. All those involved in the riot that were not in the custody of Her Majesty's finest were not allowed to set foot in the Miner's. Kevin, being the money-grabbing bastard that he was, would let them all back in come the next Ladies' Night.

It was Monday and the bar had been open for two hours. Tarrant was not on television because the television had been smashed in the riot. The lads sat around in silence supping their pints, bored out of their minds with nothing to say to one another. Still, it was better than being at home getting nagged by the missus, or sitting alone wondering where everything went wrong. At least they were in company where things were just as bad for everyone else.

Celebrating the reopening of the establishment were none other than Sid Tillsley, Brian Garforth, and Peter Rathbone. They were all propped up the bar, chatting about the usual: Brian's sexual conquests and Sid's lack of.

"Haven't you been knocking off that bird from that deaf charity shop on Mondays, Brian?" asked Sid.

"Aye, but tonight is a special occasion, like. The Miner's refurbishment doesn't happen too often now, does it?" replied the swordsman.

"True, mate, true. Ain't that bird deaf, as well?" asked Sid as he lit up a Japanese cigarette, a "Smokyo." He had obtained four-hundred for helping the Japanese restaurateur Onicchewa Hagasaki move a dead porpoise from Seal Sands to his Japanese restaurant in Hartlepool.

"Sid!" said Brian, offended. "They prefer to be called 'audio-impaired,' and yes she is."

"How does that work?" asked Rathbone.

"Well, it has its ups and downs. I have had to learn a bit of sign language, like." The impressed looks he got encouraged him to demonstrate.

"This..." He mimicked drinking tea with his little pinkie up. "...means: make us a cup of tea, pet."

"And doing this..." mimicking pulling a chain before putting both hands on his head in dismay, "...means: your shitter's blocked!"

"And this one you can guess at!" He mimicked something obscene, which was acknowledged with knowing nods from his audience. Sign Language!

Brian Garforth was indeed the most educated man on the Smithson Estate. If he wasn't such a swordsman then he'd be known as "the Professor."

Peter Rathbone was not a man who liked to be outdone, especially after a few pints. "I once did a lass with no senses at all."

It took a few seconds for Sid and Brian to work this over in their heads.

"Was she dead?" asked Brian.

"Course not, dickhead," retorted the idiotic Rathbone after he realised that he was in trouble this time.

"Coma?" asked Brian.

"Nooo," shooed away Peter. "She was…sort of like…a cabbage… but a cabbage with great tits."

They went back to ignoring him. Kevin bought over three pints, which Brian paid for. "You get any repercussions for killing that vampire fella, Sid?" asked Brian.

Sid shook his head mournfully. "Nah, not as if he left any evidence like. I have been feeling pretty bad about that 'cos it was a proper accident. That other twat deserved a smack, tho.'"

"Yeah, he was an arse that one, but you shouldna feel bad about the other fella, Sid. If what that Rich says is true, then they ain't a good bunch of lads, are they? All that drinking blood stuff…it's a bit weird if you ask me."

"Aye, you're reet, mon," he lit another Japanese.

Reece Chambers entered the pub.

"Aww, bollocks," said Brian. "Not that twat again! Do you want me to give him a smack, Sid?"

"Nah, mon. He may know something about that lad I killed," said Sid the Humanitarian.

Brian unclenched his fist and took the keys out of his hand. Kevin Ackroyd breathed a sigh of relief. At least his pub wouldn't be smashed up on its opening night.

"Sid, I am glad I have found you. I have much to tell," said Reece.

"I'm pretty busy at the moment, you know?" Sid looked at his glass that had magically emptied.

"Very well. Take a seat over there." All three of the group went and sat on the new furniture. "I want to speak to you alone, Sid."

Sid gave him a grave look. "I am sorry, Rich, but that cannot be. These fine gentlemen are my entourage, my advisors, and my friends. They look out for my best interests, and they are drinking with me on this evening and are all very thirsty."

Two empty glasses appeared.

Reece rolled his eyes. "OK, three pints and a mineral water over here please, Kevin…and one for yourself," he added as he saw Kevin's face at the mention of bringing the pints over. The Miner's didn't offer a waiter service, but anything was available at the right price.

"I have researched everything that might explain the mysteries of the past few weeks: the increase in killings, the death of vampires by a human hand, the monster that we saw in the woods…I believe I have the answer to it all."

Kevin brought the beers over and took a seat to listen to Reece Chambers' news.

"This is not the first time that these events have occurred. Over two millennia ago, this very same thing happened. A monster was born. A vampire so powerful, that nothing could withstand its murderous intent. It killed armies of humans and vampires, alike. Everything fell before it, and it drank blood for nothing but the pleasure of it. In nature, everything has its balance. There was an answer to this beast: a man born with the power to kill a vampire in battle.

"Two thousand years later and history has repeated itself. There is a monster out there committing hideous atrocities except this time he has help…he has a master. That is the only explanation for why it didn't catch us the other night."

"Aye," said Sid. "You should have seen it, lads. I reckon it was as quick as Brian over thirty yards."

The statement got an impressed whistle from the audience. Reece had forgotten that he was dealing with idiots.

"Sid, you are the answer to the monster. You must face it and you must kill it, or I do not know what will happen. Thousands may die."

"Aw, mon, I've just sat down!"

Reece put his head in his hands. "Do you not understand what you are? Do you not understand the reason you are here? You are the chosen one!"

"But me back, mon! Brian, tell him about me back."

"He's got a bad back." Brian confirmed.

"You must come with me and fulfil your destiny. You have to fight for mankind and I will pay you anything!"

"Bollocks to it, mon. I've got a sneaky suspicion that you took me to where *them lot* go…"

"London?" interrupted Rathbone.

"I don't know, but I ain't getting involved with any of that funny business."

"OK. Kevin another round of beers, please," Reece decided to regroup.

"Certainly," called back the barman. He saw a big wad coming his way and had no problems with the new waiter service. Kevin saw it as being very continental and realised that, once again, he was trailblazing.

"Sid, do you have any idea of how different you are to normal people?" Reece said. "You have a gift, a gift that has not been seen for over two millennia."

"Don't be daft, mon!"

"Sid, you are going to be a wanted man. Both races have seen what you can do. The men who were present at your battle with Gunnar—"

It was time for Brian Garforth to get involved. "'Battle?' What do you mean, a fooking battle? It was no better than a pub car-park brawl, ya posh twat."

Reece shook his head. "Gunnar Ivansey is a gifted predator. That day will go down in the secret history of this country for as long as records are kept, that, I can assure you."

A nervous look crossed Sid's face. "Hang on, mon, what do you mean by 'records?' I canna be seen fighting outside pubs with me back the way it is. It may put me benefit money in jeopardy and I've got to look after me future, like."

"For God's sake, there are more important fucking matters than your benefit money. The world will not care whether you are claiming benefit if you are fighting vampires with your bare hands, and winning!"

"You listen to me, mon, there are people out there who would love to catch me working, or to find me doing something that would compromise my disability benefit. I don't give a fook about a punch up I had on a Friday night outside me local pub. In fact, I'm a little bit embarrassed about hitting that other fella."

"You weren't fighting a normal human being. You were fighting a super strong, super fast, immortal fucking vampire!" Reece was practically foaming at the mouth with excitement. "Everyone who is involved in the real world, and I mean the *real world*, where murder takes place every hour, will want a piece of you now. And it has nothing to do with your bad back!"

Brian Garforth rolled up his sleeves. "I think it's time for you to leave, or I'm gonna kick seven bells of shit out of ya, ya posh Southern bastard!"

"Shut up, little man. This is beyond you."

Brian rose from his chair, but was halted by Kevin Ackroyd.

"If one of you even raises a fist, they are barred for life, I promise that. I ain't having this place smashed up twice in a week. Now, sit down!"

Both men sat. Reece regained his composure, but Brian seethed in his seat.

"Sid," continued Reece, "there are going to be humans and vampires coming at you, all with different motives. Some humans will want you to help them, just like me, but some will put a knife in your back and you won't know until it is too late. You are in grave danger, do you understand?"

At that moment, in walked Arthur Peasley, survivor of a vampire encounter. "Hey fellas, you are never gonna guess what happened to me!"

He didn't wait for the response as everyone knew it would have something to do with shagging. "This morning, I ended up nailing one of those vampire chicks whilst doing a plumbing job at the Royal York. She was the most beautiful woman that I have ever slept with."

This did surprise the Middlesbrough locals. The standard of Arthur's conquests was a thing of legend. For him to say that a lady was his finest would be like Da Vinci picking out his finest painting, or Beethoven choosing his greatest symphony, or Meat Loaf having his biggest dump.

Brian Garforth was not a man who went for beautiful women, although did get the odd stunner now and then. "Was she was better looking than that lass who used to do the football pools?"

His question was answered with a smiling nod. Brian could only be impressed.

"You...had *sex* with a vampire?" asked Reece incredulously.

Arthur gave him a double finger point and a wink of his beautiful eye. "Ah, man, sex is such a dirty word for something so beautiful, baby!"

"You can't have had sex with a vampire! Not without being killed afterwards. It's unheard of! How do you even know she was a vampire?"

"I overheard her talking to someone about Sid, and when I tried to get closer to hear what she was saying, she rumbled me. She charged out of the door catching me by surprise. She was unbelievably quick. If it was a fella, then it would have been different as my karate speed would have taken care of business. She was so beautiful though. For a millisecond, I was stunned and she had knocked me off my feet and pinned me to a table." He changed the subject and looked at Reece. "Hey man, all this talking is thirsty work."

Reece shook his head and sighed. "Kevin! Another round of drinks please?"

"Coming right up, Mr. Chambers!" acknowledged the friendly barman.

"OK," started Arthur once he had taken a large refreshing mouthful of beer. "So there I am, and this red hot lady is on top of me with my arms pinned to the table and she has these teeth," he points to his canines, "and they ain't like a normal chick's teeth. They're long and pointy and that's when I say to myself, 'Arthur Peasley, this little lady is a vampire and it is your duty to make love to her.' So I gave her my look."

"Your look?" asked Reece.

The beautiful man gave Reece another knowing nod.

"Man, the look that no lady can resist. Anyway, she looks into my eyes and the lady knows that I ain't no normal man. She pauses before going for, what I assumed was, a bite...so I give her the look and I know I've got her.

"'Hey, pretty lady,' I said. 'Who are you?' she asked. She was a little breathless because I had given her a look which would rate about 8 out of 10 on my Irresistibleness-O-Meter. So I say, 'I'm a peacemaker, baby. I'm the man who gives love to every single lady out there whether she is a human, or a vampire.' That's when I knew I had her. She didn't expect a plumber to know about vampires. That's when I went in for the kiss. Then it went on from there. Man, it went on and on from there! Rock-a-hula, baby!"

"Who was she?" asked Reece. "How did you escape? What did she say about Sid? Who was she talking to?"

A man to sleep with a vampire and not become an active part of the food chain would have been the most amazing event that had occurred in Reece's lifetime if he hadn't met Sid Tillsley. How? Why? There were so many questions!

"Did you do her in the ar—"

"Why didn't she kill you?" Reece interrupted Sid with a more relevant question.

"Kill me? Why would she want to do that? She said in four-hundred years she had never been pleasured that way before. I even took her number."

Now that really surprised the congregation.

"But…but you have never taken a birds' number…ever," said Brian.

"I know, man, I know. It's the first time that I haven't given out a calling card and it's gonna be the first time that I ever phone a chick."

"For the love of God, you idiots!" screamed Reece. "The fact that he has hasn't handed his number out is insignificant compared to a female vampire having sexual intercourse with a human and not killing them! Arthur, did she tell you her name?"

"Yeah, man, but I kinda forgot it?"

"Oh for fucksake!" yelled Reece.

All eyes (except the lads who wanted to be watching Tarrant) turned to the door because two strangers had walked in. It was still dusk so they had to be human. Silence filled the pub. The tension in the air was incredible. The two young men stopped and stared at the group that they had captivated. They walked to the bar, not expecting the hostile reception.

Kevin stared at the one who looked like he was going to speak first. "What do you want?" he said gruffly.

"Can I have two bottles of Smirnoff Ice, please?"

Brian Garforth crossed the room and landed an ungainly, but accurate, haymaker on the man's jaw. The impact put the man straight on to his arse.

"I fooking knew it!" he yelled wrathfully. "Get the fook out, before I really start losing my fooking temper!" He kicked the man's behind as both turned and fled.

The punching maestro sauntered back to the table. Reece Chambers couldn't hide his astonishment. "How did you know that they are involved in the world of the vampire?"

Brian gave him a funny look. "Eh? Oh nah, mon, they looked like students."

* * * *

The night went on and by ten-thirty the group, with the exception of Reece, were completely wasted. Many different people had entered the boozer, but all were locals enjoying the Miner's renovation. Reece had used this time to really understand the group's mentality and he had realised that his first diagnosis was completely and utterly accurate.

They were a bunch of twats.

He surveyed the group.

The Weasel, Brian Garforth, was a horrible little man. He had regaled stories of his past that had made Reece feel sick. He had had sexual relationships with hundreds and hundreds of women, and whoever said that Northern Man lacked diversity should meet this fellow. He had put his genitals in, on, and at, dwarfs, midgets, amputees, the deaf, the dumb, the blind, the terminally ill, giants, lesbians, and every creed and every colour. He seemed to possess no morals whatsoever. Sid described him as "cock on legs." The scariest thing of all was that the others in the group really respected his opinion. He was treated as a scholar in this uneducated group.

There was Peter Rathbone, who was basically a piece of shit. He lived to outdo everyone else, yet lacked the skills, and the physical or emotional presence, to outdo an amoeba. The others didn't even talk to him. He was just sort of there like a limpet sticking on to the group, yet the others didn't seem to mind him tagging along.

Arthur Peasley, now he was an interesting character. Not the smartest of men, but he wasn't a complete idiot. He was an incredibly handsome man and there was something so familiar about him, yet Reece couldn't quite put his finger on it. He was a karate master and his libido matched the weasel, yet Peasley's taste seemed to be reserved for the beautiful women. Between the two, they had probably slept with every woman in Middlesbrough.

And last, but not least, there was Sid Tillsley. The most powerful human to walk the Earth with the answer to the vampire question stored in his right hand. He was what stopped man being the prey. He could be the ultimate hunter. Yet he was stuck in his ways more than anyone Reece had ever met before, unwilling to take his rightful role as a hunter and live his life as a king, because he didn't want to jeopardise the pitiful money that he claimed illegally. Nevertheless, Reece was still confident that he could recruit Sid to his cause. Soon the Coalition, the Lamian Consilium and the Hominum Order would be coming down on Sid, and his life would change in a way that he couldn't possibly imagine.

The door of the pub opened. A tall figure ducked to get through the door, and was followed by a man equally as tall, but far broader.

Reece had been waiting for this. Night was here, and so was the vampire. He knew there would be contact, tonight. He was armed to the teeth under his black trench coat: grenades, pistol, and a sub-machine gun. He wouldn't be able to kill them unless he managed to get a grenade in one of the bastard's mouths. Nevertheless, he still had the firepower to make them think about their actions. What he didn't know was what their intentions would be. To kill? To befriend? He was about to find out.

"Sid…Sid…"

"…And that's why you should never sit sideways on a bog…Eh? What is it, mon?" He was extremely drunk.

The vampires approached the group. They stood side by side, both standing six foot six. The table was arranged so that Reece faced them and the door, Sid had his back to the two, and the others sat round the sides of the small bar table.

"Sid Tillsley," said the vampire with hair slicked back over his head. They both wore contemporary clothes that fit in with the local style of dress. Not that it was worth it—they stood out a mile. It wasn't just because of their height; it was because of the beautiful features of their faces. Only Arthur Peasley could compete, but then he also stood out a mile in Middlesbrough.

Sid turned around carefully in his chair because he didn't want to fall off. "Yesh, gents."

"I am Vladimir," said the vampire with the slicked back hair, "and this is Sven." His companion had long flowing blonde hair that fell gracefully over his face. Both vampires had the most brilliant blue eyes. "I take it that you know who we are?"

Sid squinted, it had been a hard nights drinking. "Brian?" he ventured. "Is that you?"

"You twat, Tillsley, I'm 'ere ya…ya—fook it!" It had been a hard night of drinking for Brian Garforth too.

"May we join you, Mr. Tillsley?" asked Vladimir.

Sid sobered up (not that much) at the mention of "Mr. Tillsley." He was only called "Mr. Tillsley" by one group of people.

The Benefit Office!

"You…may. But, first I must first try and get to the gents." Sid made an awkward attempt at getting to his feet. "Me back! Me back! Why has God cursed me so?" He limped dramatically towards the toilets, stopping every now and then to clutch at the thing that deprived him from his dream of becoming a working man.

"Gentlemen," started Reece, addressing the group around the table. "These two characters are not what they seem."

"What? They're not bummers?" said a drunken Brian Garforth. He wouldn't have dared make the comment if the big man was still in the room.

"Be careful, maggot," hissed Sven. "We are not here to fight with Tillsley, but we will not hesitate in showing you your beating heart."

"And I won't hesitate in putting the nut on you either, you lanky twat!" Brian Garforth had fought people taller than him all of his life, and he'd put the nut on lads taller than these.

"Baby, he's got back-up like you wouldn't believe." Arthur jumped up from his seat, which was an impressive feat after twelve pints of Bolton Bitter, and fired off a rapid succession of demonstration karate punches.

"You'd be making a mistake to mess with the friends of Sid Tillsley, vampires," said Reece. Realisation dawned on Brian and Arthur, but this didn't quench their spirits in the slightest.

"Chambers! I thought you might have crawled from under your stone to come and see this man," said Vladimir. "I look forward to taking your life after this meeting."

Reece smiled. "I wouldn't be so sure. I have developed quite a relationship with Sid Tillsley. I know his power and I have witnessed it firsthand. Do not cross me."

"He thinks you're a prick!" said Brian, destroying the front that Reece had tried to build. Both vampires laughed. Brian joined in. He would gladly put the nut on either two of the undead that now sat next to him, but he preferred them to Reece by a country mile.

"Listen, if you wanna impress the boy in there," he pointed over to the toilet where the occasional groan could be heard. Sid's acting was over and he was completing the coup de grace on another, soon to be retired, piece of Royal Dalton. "Then you wanna get the beers in for the lads. That's the only reason that he talked to that tosspot in the first place." He nodded scornfully at Reece. Brian Garforth was a fickle man.

Vladimir smiled. "Very well. Barkeep!"

"Who are you calling fookin—" Kevin Ackroyd halted mid sentence. Could it be? Could the legends be true? Every eye in the pub was fixed on what Vladimir held in his hand, raised high for all to see.

A fifty-pound note.

A fifty-pound note was a legend that had been told on the Smithson Estate for years, but one had never been spotted.

"A drink for every man in the pub, and keep them coming." The fifty pound note turned into four fifty pound notes that resulted in a massive gasp from the patrons.

Sid returned, limping, from the gents. This time he didn't need to put a limp on because his excretion had done him a wrong'n. He looked at where the group was sitting. There was beer, there was whisky, and there was brandy. Had he died and gone to heaven?

"Sid! Sid! They ain't benefit bastards! They're vampires—and they got the beers in!" said an excited Brian Garforth.

"Howay the lads!" shouted a miraculously-cured Sid Tillsley.

A few drinks later the entire pub was in a dangerously drunk state. Kevin Ackroyd was having the time of his life. These were record takings for a Monday night. The problem would be at last orders when he had to throw the lads out. He couldn't risk a lock-in as the coppers would have an eye on the place.

"Tell you what, lads…you're alreet. I mean…you're alreet." Sid was the most sober man out of the group with exception to Reece, but even though he was close-to-dead drunk, he could still just make conversation.

Arthur Peasley had passed out with his head laid on his forearm. His karate skills were unlikely to be called upon if the need arose. Peter Rathbone had thrown up in the toilets and made his way home. Chances were high that he would fall asleep in a hedge along the way. Brian Garforth was still awake although he had lost the powers of relevant speech. He just took turns staring at the vampires, and then Reece. He was trying to work out whose side he was on. There was still a desire to put the nut on the lanky twat, but then again, he did buy him free drinks. That fella, Rich, was a complete wanker but felt that he should be on his side because he was a human, and he had bought him a few drinks before. He concluded that whoever went down first would get the boot and he couldn't be fairer than that.

"Thank you, Sid," said Sven. "That is very kind of you to say so. Sid, would you be interested in earning a substantial amount of money?"

Sid took a while to work out what "substantial" meant, but then moved on when confusion set in. "I canna deny that I like to earn the odd pound, here and there. What do you…*hic!*…want me to do?"

"All you have to do is to come with Vladimir and me. We'll put you up in a five-star hotel and tomorrow evening you will meet some of the senior members of our group. They'll ask you a few questions and then you will be free to go…with a thousand pounds in your hand, cash."

Reece had remained quiet for a long period of time because he was nervous about his position. These two would love to take his life and Sid was his only protection. If he left now, then one would stay and the other would kill him. If Tillsley passed out, then it would be the end.

"They'll kill you, Sid," Reece warned. "They'll kill you as soon as you walk outside of the pub. Trust me. I've seen what they can do. They know that you killed one of them on Friday. They want revenge. A life for a life."

Sid still regretted accidentally killing Franco Stoloni. "Lads, I really am sorry about that. It was an accident, like, and I was aiming at some other twat who really deserved a good hiding. I slipped and caught that other fella and…and I'd thrown a good'n." He drained the last of his beer and put it down with noticeable force.

"Barkeep!" called Vladimir. Once the beer was brought over, Vladimir continued. "I can promise you, Sid, we understand that the death of Franco was a complete mistake. You are pardoned by the vampire factions. We just want to find out how you managed to do it. We just want to chat to you about your past, and whether you have had any contact with us before. The benefit office will not find out. I promise you that nothing will come of this, other than a thousand pounds."

"Ladsh, you canna say fairer than that." Sid was in a vulnerable place: drunk and open to suggestions.

"Sid," said Reece, "They will kill you if you go. You will not survive the night."

Sven interrupted sternly. "Reece Chambers, what can you possibly give this man? You skulk around in the bushes with the worms and the dog shit, in hope of bringing us down. You are pathetic. You are holding this man back. Sid Tillsley is heading for greatness. The vampires revere him, and we will learn a lot from his methods of combat."

Sid smiled. "Ladsh, please give me five minutes to relieve meself, and then I will accompany you to the hotel." Sid got up slowly, and with considerable difficulty, before heading for the gents, once more.

Reece had to move fast. If Sid left with the vampires then it would be the end of both of them. Reece tried to keep the vampires talking. "I am surprised that a great species would have to lie to a drunk. Is this a sign of your power waning?"

Sven laughed. "You have nothing to worry about anymore as you will not see the day. Fear not, it will be quick as there isn't time to give you the death you deserve."

Fear contorted Reece's insides, though he tried not to show it. "So what do you intend to do with Sid? You will not find him easy prey, even though you are employing a knife in the dark technique."

"Tillsley will not be murdered, as you suspect," said Vladimir. "We need to discover his secret. We need to know where this power comes from."

"He is the answer to the Firmamentum. He is the answer to what resides in the woods of the North Yorkshire Moors," said Reece.

Vladimir and Sven glanced quickly at each other surprised at Reece Chambers' acquired knowledge. "Speak of what you know."

"I have seen what resides in the forests. I have seen the monster, and believe me the word 'monster' is an understatement."

Vladimir and Sven were two of the trackers sent by Michael to uncover the mysteries in the Northeast. So far, they had found absolutely nothing, except human remains.

"Perhaps, Chambers, you, too, will survive the night. You will come with us to meet the elders," said Sven.

Sid came back from the toilets, staggering from left to right in a drunken stupor. Brian Garforth had joined Arthur Peasley, asleep on the table. Sid's back-up was out of action.

"Reet, gentlemen, I am ready to join this meeting of yours. Would you mind if I had a little something for the road? A little livener against the cold night ahead?" asked Sid. It would have been against his nature if he didn't try to milk the vampires for all that he could. He propped himself up against the bar.

Sven rolled his eyes. "Barkeep!"

Reece contemplated the dangerous situation. He needed to get Sid and himself out of it as soon as possible. Sven and Vladimir joined Sid at the bar, one either side of him. Vladimir kept his eye firmly on Reece who had to think on his feet.

Reece walked slowly over to the group at the bar. His mind raced as he tried to decipher a plan that would enable him to live another day. As he approached behind Sid, he bent down to tie his shoe-lace. An idea came to him. It was a gamble but he had no other choice.

Vampires are quick, but Reece didn't have far to go, and once he had reached his target, no speed could save them from their fate. As he began to tie his shoe lace, Reece rolled forward, commando-style. Half way through the roll he reached back and reached for the buttock of Sid Tillsley...and gave it a delicate pinch.

Even though almost lethal levels of alcohol controlled Sid's body, he felt the pinch, and *Pink Alert* fired him up to maximum homophobocity. He turned to the direction of the pinch, but Reece had rolled to his opposite side. It could only be Sven.

"You fooking vampires are *them lot*, ain't ya, ya bastards?" roared Sid.

"What?" Sven began. "What are you talking abo—" Before the sentence had finished he exploded into a pile of dust. The punch, as always, was perfection, but the balance was not. Sid drunkenly fell through the table where Arthur Peasley and Brian Garforth sat, waking them from the land of the drunk.

Vladimir stared at the floating dust of his associate and friend. He had heard the reports, but to witness it with his own eyes...If Gabriel could fall to this man, what could he do?

Sid Tillsley regained his feet and rolled his sleeves up. Beside him stood Brian Garforth, two broken bottles in his hands and a small quantity of sick tricking down his chin. To the other side stood Arthur Peasley who had adopted an aggressive karate stance and was firing punches at a less than blistering pace.

"Right yous!" shouted Sid. "I ain't having it anymore. I ain't having you dirty bastards getting into my personal space and trying your... *things*...with me. Have you fooking got it?"

Vladimir was confused because he hadn't seen the pinch that Reece Chambers had performed on the homophobe's rear. Reece positioned himself behind the three friends, smiling at what had befallen.

"I-I don't understand what you mean."

"Yes you fooking do, Tarquin. You're fooking acquaintance thought that he could try and get me drunk and then get involved with me, and it ain't fooking reet!" shouted Sid, angry, upset and violated.

"But, a minute ago, you were happy to come with us!" pleaded Vladimir.

"That's before you started with ya wandering hands!" He turned to his allies in battle. "Are you gonna settle this, or shall I?"

"What's he done, man?" asked Arthur.

"He…" Sid struggled to mention the most heinous of crimes. "…grabbed me, like."

"I didn't grab anything!" shouted back Vladimir defiantly.

Arthur, Brian, and Reece all struggled to hold back the laughter. Sid's *Pink Alert* was always a matter for careful amusement.

"I think this one's yours, mate," said Brian.

And with that, the shortest pursuit in history took place. Sid ambled after the vampire who immediately turned and fled the wrath that confronted him. Before Sid reached the space that Vladimir had occupied, the vampire was out of the door and fifty yards down the road. Sid got to the door in a sweat, but the vampire was nowhere to be seen.

"Bastards!" Sid went back inside for last orders.

21

Brian Garforth sat in the passenger seat of his Ford Capri 2.8i. It was a beautiful, jet-black motor vehicle without a scratch on it. It was half-eleven at night and he had just experienced one of the worst days of his life. The hangover was a killer, and he had slummed it on the sofa all day, missing yet another day of work.

He was feeling better now and he was ready to go somewhere different. It was Tuesday night and he hadn't got his leg over all week. Perhaps he was losing his sex drive? He had needed the help of the little blue pill a few times now, but the lasses of late were red hot and he needed the edge. One of the lasses was a bouncer in town, and she had to take the weekend off sick after he had finished with her, and it wasn't because he had give her a bad dose of the clap, either. Nah, he'd never lose it!

Brian had about four lasses on the go at the moment, but none were too exciting and he wanted a change. He remembered back to a night with Sid, when he had suggested that he try his hand at dogging. He wanted to see his good chum get some action, but he was curious himself and it had been bugging him ever since.

Tonight he had decided to give it a go. After all, what did he have to lose? The answer: his reputation. Yes, he did have something to lose. He was very proud of his reputation. It was a reputation that was known, not only on the Smithson Estate, but over half of Teesside. He loved being known as a lady-killer, loved it that men outside his immediate group of friends would put their arms around their loved ones when he walked by. Everyone knew a lass that the great Brian Garforth had nailed. It was a good thing that his best friend was the one and only Sid Tillsley. Otherwise, he'd have the shit kicked out of him on a weekly basis.

Yes, his reputation did matter to him and going to car-parks for sex with strangers was not the kind of thing that Brian Garforth needed to do. It was a little too seedy for him and he preferred the title of "cad," or "bounder," not "pervert." Therefore, he needed to err on the side of stealth so that no-one would know where he was going. Nevertheless, he was still going to try it out as he had been fired up ever since he got his ten o'clock hard-on, and there had been no lasses to satisfy his needs. The answer was dogging.

He started the Capri that roared into life on the first go. All attempts of stealth were blown out of the water as the Capri's engine roared with sexual energy.

"Easy, baby, easy," soothed Brian, stroking the dashboard seductively. He touched the accelerator gently, but the natural growl of the man's-man's car caused several residents to investigate the noise.

"Garforth, you wanker!" was yelled from several windows simultaneously. Everyone knew the roar of the Capri.

Brian Garforth, being the opinionated fellow that he was, couldn't let this sort of thing lie. He rolled down the window and yelled back, "Go fook yourselves, ya bastards!" He accompanied his point of view with a one finger salute.

"It's gone half-eleven, Garforth," shouted a naked man leaning out of the window of one of the terraced houses. "Where you bleedin' going at this time at night? Doggin'?"

Brian stalled the car.

"He bloody is! The pervert's going doggin'!" yelled the naked man.

Brian slumped into the comfortable seat of the 2.8i Capri. A few more windows opened and more lights came on, further down the street.

"EVERYONE! GARFORTH, THE LITTLE PERVERT, IS GOIN' DOGGIN!" The naked man was in his element. He had Brian Garforth on the ropes and about bloody time. He had no proof that Garforth had been near his missus, but he had a hunch when he was working off-shore.

Brian tried to start the Capri. It didn't start until the fifth attempt. Only when all the lights in the street were on did he manage to get the car going. He raced down the street away from the jeering voices of the wronged husbands of Teesside Terrace.

"Bastards!" spat Brian Garforth as he drove through the town centre. He knew something like that would happen. The Capri was a beautiful car, perhaps the most beautiful of all cars, but it was not a quiet car. It was a car that screamed: "Dogger."

He tore down the country roads as he headed to Middlesbrough's Memorial Park. Not even the jeers of the street could suppress his ten o'clock, or seven-pint hard-on (whichever came first). A curse he had been afflicted with since the age of twelve. Was Brian Garforth addicted to sex? Absolutely. How could anyone not be? The Capri made a few untoward noises from under the bonnet.

"Come on baby, hold together!"

It was not a one-way ticket because he needed to get back. If the local bill caught him up there, they would have a bloody field day. The clanking sounds stopped and Brian breathed a sigh of relief. It was not far now.

The Capri pulled into Middlesbrough's Memorial Park. This was the place that Sid had his first encounter with the undead. Brian was hoping there wouldn't be any here tonight, but not because he was frightened. Brian Garforth wasn't afraid of anything except sexually transmitted diseases, and he had built up a natural immunity to eighty-seven per cent of those. No, he didn't want to get into a scrap as that was the only thing that would quell his ten o'clock affliction. He was here now, so he might as well do some shaggin'.

He did a three-sixty in the car-park to check out what other cars were there. One bleeding car: a silver Mercedes. He was hoping to have the pick of a few birds, at least. Ah well, he thought, might as well make it clear what my intentions are. He flashed his headlights, the local sign for: "I am a red-blooded heterosexual male who is interested in full-on-fun that goes no further than meat-and-potatoes in nature."

The silver Mercedes flashed three times saying: "I am a female interested in having full-on-fun with you."

"Reet!" Brian rubbed his hands. "Howay the lads." He got out of the car and headed towards the Mercedes, which turned its full beams on to take a look at the catch it was about to make. It caught the catch giving itself a quick rub on the sly, trying to gain an extra inch. The full beams went down.

"Shit," said the guilty party.

Brian walked around towards the driver's side, but he couldn't see anything because of the blacked out Mercedes windows.

"In for a penny…" He opened the door and immediately wished he hadn't.

"Oh, God, no…"

* * * *

Sid was working the door of the Claggy Mat. He had worked this particular venue in Yarm, North Yorkshire a few times. He didn't work the door in Middlesbrough as it was too risky. If he worked the door anywhere, it was a suitably rubbish shithole where cash in hand was always offered and no operational CCTV cameras were present.

It was quarter to midnight and it was a relatively quiet night. There had only been a few punch-ups, so far. Just kids throwing their weight around after a few too many shandies. He'd get fifty quid for tonight's work, plus petrol money and two-hundred decent cigarettes. The shift had started at eleven and he still felt a little hung-over. Like Brian, Sid hadn't managed a day's work, but that wasn't unusual for Sid.

"Sid!" shouted the manager, as he ran through the backdoor. Sid refused to work on the front door of clubs, and normally sat out the back and someone would give him a shout if his services were required. "It's all about to kick off."

"Aye, mon, I'll come and sort it out." He followed Gary the manager through the door of the Claggy Mat and into the heart of the small, cramped dance floor. There were two groups of five lads causing the commotion. All had fuzzy moustaches that would have blown away if the wind got up. Their furry lips looked pathetic, but the lads were too proud to shave off their first piece of facial hair.

The dance floor parted to allow the big man to walk through, and it was only the arguing kids that didn't notice. They began to push each other a little more aggressively whilst shouting various threats that they had picked up from their favourite gangster films. Neither group wanted to throw the first punch, or to back down because there were girls watching.

Sid didn't say anything. He just picked up the first two lads he came to, one from each of the boisterous groups of teenagers. The lads were held at arms' length by the scruff of their necks, hanging limp like submissive kittens, staring fearfully at the scariest bouncer they had ever seen, and by far the scariest bouncer that they had ever heard of.

"Right, lads," said Sid loudly. "If I hear of any more funny business between you lot again, there's gonna be trouble. I don't give a fook who started it, or what's it about, or any bullshit, like. You lot…," he indicated one group of teenagers with his head, "…go play over there, and you lot…," to the other group, "…go play over there. Now then, is there going to be any more trouble?"

All ten teenagers shook their heads as if their lives depended on it.

"Lovely stuff," said Sid, dropping the lads and returning to his post. He remembered what he was like when he was a lad and gave a chuckle. He didn't like it if he had to get heavy with a young'n. He only did if they pulled a blade on him; then they needed to learn. Sid lit up a Tibetan "El Monko." He had obtained four-hundred after helping Dave the Buddhist hand out some rough Karma to some Jehovah's Witnesses who had been messing with his turf.

"Not long to go," he said, watching the clock.

* * * *

Sheila Fishman and Gunnar Ivansey sat together in his white Ford Transit. They had followed Tillsley all the way to the Claggy Mat and needed to get some footage of him doing something physical in order to prove that he was capable of work.

The vampire sat behind the wheel, staring intensely at the door of the club. Living for hundreds of years gave the gift of patience, the like of which a human couldn't comprehend. "We need him to throw someone out of the club. That should be sufficient in showing that he is work-capable."

"You're right," agreed Sheila. "But we haven't seen the fat bastard since he went in there." She tapped her fingers on the dashboard, impatiently.

"Patience," said Gunnar calmly. "It is still only early. Most trouble starts towards the end of the night."

* * * *

Brian Garforth stared into the eyes of the thing he didn't want to face, the only thing that could take away his ten o'clock hard-on. Confronted with the animal that had ruined thousands before and would no-doubt take thousands more. He stared into the eyes of the Devil…and the Devil stared back.

A fat lass.

He was hoping for a stunner, not this. Brian "Any Port in a Storm" Garforth decided to make the best of it.

"Alright then, lass, best we get this over with as I haven't got all night, like." He dropped his red woollen trousers and then ripped down his pants to reveal the marriage-wrecker.

"Come on then, pet. You canna be shy if you're up here in the first place, like." He pointed to the bonnet where he wished to perform the act of lovemaking.

The girl got out of the brand new Mercedes. "Hi, I'm Sadie."

Brian gave a shrug of his shoulders and shuffled around to the front of the car, "Howay lass."

"What's your name?" she asked.

Brian sighed and shook his head. "Listen, pet, this lark ain't about all that talking bollocks. If I wanted to talk then I'd phone a porn line. This lark is about ruttin', n'owt else, so if you hurry up we can get on with it." He pointed at the bonnet.

Sadie looked down at the ground. "I was hoping that I'd meet some new people. I thought this was more than sex."

"Well ya thought wrong, didn't ya? Now to business, or do you want me to get in me motor and fook off?"

"No! No…OK, I'll…I'll do it," she said sadly and walked around to where Brian was already doing something obscene.

"Now, pet, if you could grab on to the badge of ya nice motor, then we can begi—" Brian was silenced by an almighty crash that occurred in the woods. "What was that?"

Sadie looked scared. "I…I don't know."

A blood-curdling scream filled the air and both Brian and Sadie grabbed their ears to protect them from the din.

* * * *

Sheila and Gunnar had watched the club for over two hours. It was one o'clock in the morning and Sheila was verging closer and closer to death as she was annoying the hell out of Gunnar. Patience was something that Gunnar learnt during the weeks he was trapped in the Canadian avalanche. However, even the threat of death couldn't compare to the annoyance he was suffering in the cramped transit van.

He snarled at her through gritted teeth. "If you don't calm down, Sheila, you are going to blow our cover."

"He hasn't shown up for hours! He's probably on to us. One of us needs to get in there and see what he's up to!"

"Very well!" he snapped back. His patience had reached breaking point. "I've had enough of you going on. I have a camcorder in the back of the van. You can go in and try to catch him working, if you want to."

"Me!" she exclaimed. "Me in there? With them horrible little bastards. I am a lady and wouldn't dream of entering such a place."

He had expected as much. "You were in the Miner's Arms, were you not? This is a much classier establishment than that."

Her eyes glazed over as she looked into a distant place. "After the Miner's I-I cannot bring myself to…I cannot, Gunnar. I will do anything to bring that bastard down, but please, do this for me," she begged.

Gunnar was in no mood for games. "Very well. Be ready to start the engine."

* * * *

A tree crashed into the clearing, and into it walked something from a nightmare. Brian and Sadie both froze at the sight of it. It walked slowly towards them and the ground shook with each footstep. It stood twelve foot high, its shoulders as wide as a man was tall. Heaving muscle occupied every square inch of its frame. Not a hair was visible on its entire body, but veins bulged across every muscle, tendon and bone. Tattered clothes covered its bronzed skin.

The face of the monster contorted as it unleashed another deafening scream. Its massive shoulders heaved with each breath and sweat evaporated from its hulking body. Saliva and spittle flew from its mouth and dripped down teeth the size and shape of a shark's. Its eyes were blood red and the pupils as black as coal. It looked humanoid but it certainly wasn't human.

It crossed the clearing until it reached the two doggers. It bent down until its face was a foot away from Brian Garforth's. Sadie was the first one to regain her senses and she turned and fled, running mindlessly away from the beast. The beast bared back its lips to fully reveal its immense teeth and Brian's life flashed before his eyes…

* * * *

Gunnar walked into the club, glad to be away from the hideous woman that was plaguing his days. His moment of relief was tainted by the stench of human sweat. He passed the sorry excuse for doormen and grudgingly paid the entrance fee. It amazed him that humans paid to get into this place. It was decorated in a heinous fashion. Fluorescent lime green and pink walls were adjourned with modern so-called "art." The ceiling was probably white, originally, but now it was sickly-yellow through the years of smokers cramped into one place.

The clientele suited the club perfectly, a mixture of humans that hadn't yet come of age, and humans who were well past their prime. They danced and cavorted with each other under the influence of alcohol and narcotics. There was an aggressive atmosphere on the small dance floor as groups of adolescent boys tried to impress the scantily clad, intoxicated females. The bar was relatively empty compared to the rest of the club. It appeared that the penniless clubbers had drunk themselves stupid before coming in search of a fight or a fuck. There was no sign of Tillsley, but there were many nooks and crannies where the fat oaf could be hiding.

"Oi, mate! Take a picture of these!"

Gunnar turned around to see a disgusting woman in her forties, colossal in size and covered in the most vulgar tattoos that the vampire had ever seen. Her greasy hair hung down lankly over an amazing quantity of cheap jewellery. She had pulled her top down her to reveal two heavily tattooed breasts.

Gunnar winced. It appeared that she had suckled a herd of elephants. He looked away and went about his business.

"Oi! I said take a picture of these, ya bastard!" The horror stormed after Gunnar and grabbed his arm with a vice like grip.

"I suggest that you let go of me, woman."

"Hey girls, this fella taking pics for the website is fit as fook!" she yelled at her drunken posse.

"Fooking 'ell, Dot, he's fooking gorge!" shouted a lady of similar ilk. "Hey, mate, we're on a hen night from Doncaster. Get a pic for the website."

Ten hammered ladies from Doncaster ran over, and as one, displayed their mighty mammary glands. Gunnar reluctantly picked up the camcorder and filmed the horrific display. He didn't need to arouse suspicion, and these women would certainly kick up a fuss if he didn't yield to their will.

The hen displayed far more than her breasts to the camera. Gunnar was amazed that he felt sorry for a human who was going to marry the harpy. At the sound of a commotion, he looked up.

"Where the fook are they? Where the fook are they?" Sid Tillsley bounded through the club knocking clubber after clubber out of his way. Gunnar could sense his heart pumping at a dangerous rate and hid his face behind the camera as Sid approached. This could be just what he needed.

*　*　*　*

The repugnant breath of the monster washed over Brian's face, causing him to regain his senses. He put the nut on it, turned and tried to leg it. The monster roared with anger and held its arms aloft as Brian waddled away like a penguin, still with his kecks around his ankles. He reached down and pulled them up with speed and agility, a move perfected from years of jumping out of ladies' bedroom windows and sliding down drainpipes when husbands came home.

The monster smashed its giant fists into the ground before charging at its first ever attacker. It was unbelievably powerful, but Brian Garforth was indeed spectacularly quick over thirty yards. Brian pumped his arms and legs as hard as he could as he ran for the safety of his Capri 2.8i. The beast charged and Brian didn't look back as he could tell how far the monster was behind him from its footsteps. Over the first ten yards of pursuit, Brian put more distance between them. Over the next ten yards the distance between them increased further, but Brian knew he was at least fifty yards from the Capri and he only had ten yards of explosive power left.

Brian hit what is known by marathon runners as, "the wall." The only difference was that marathon runners hit the wall after twenty miles, whilst Brian hit the wall after twenty-seven and a half yards. He managed two and a half more yards before he began to slow and he could sense the monster gaining ground.

* * * *

"Howay the lads, mon!" yelled Sid as he caught sight of the exposed breasts and the other, more intimate, areas of the Doncaster beauties. "Which of you red-hot lovelies wants to meet the boun—"

Suddenly, Sid bent over double and clutched his back. He had seen the camera and the situation he thought was too good to be true, was indeed too good to be true. He limped away from the Doncaster hen night.

Gunnar stormed out of the Claggy Mat and into the van. As soon as the door shut, Sheila floored the accelerator.

"Have you got it? Have you got the bastard?" she asked excitedly.

"No. He ran through unexpectedly and as soon as he saw the camcorder he feigned back injury. There is no way of getting him tonight."

Sheila hit the brakes hard and they ground to a halt. "What did you get, then?" she asked. She snatched the camcorder out of his hands so she could see what footage he had captured in the nightclub.

"You fucking pervert!"

"What?"

"You fucking pervert! You were in there perving at those rotten slags! You weren't trying to catch Tillsley at all!" She got out of the car and started walking home, even though it was several miles away.

Gunnar flipped a coin. Heads: he would get out of the van and talk her back round. Tails: he would run her over.

Heads.

He tossed again; still heads. He reluctantly got out of the van.

"Sheila, wait!" he called. "I was hiding behind the camera and as soon as those women saw it, they started revealing themselves. They thought that I worked for the nightclub and was taking footage for the website. That's when Tillsley bounded over to have a look. He saw the camera and grabbed his back."

Sheila continued her journey home. She was angry with Gunnar and she was angry at the slags spending their benefit income in that sordid nightclub. More than anything, she was angry with Tillsley for perving on them like a lecherous beast. She was angry that they had spent the entire night trying to catch him working and had come up with nothing. She was angry that he had grabbed her breast.

She stomped over a bridge that ran over a canal, only intending to stop stomping as soon as her wrath had subsided to tolerant levels. A hand landed on her shoulder, which reminded her of the hand that had grabbed at her breast.

"Get your fucking hands off me, you rapist!" she yelled. She spun around and threw her hands up to relieve her shoulder of its unwanted attention. For once, the vampire was not nimble enough to avert the attack, and he fell over the side of the bridge.

He tumbled over the railings and fell face-first onto a barge moored below. Sheila looked over the bridge and her rage was replaced with worry. She hadn't meant to push him over the edge. He was her only ally in the fight against the tyranny of the non-working class and she didn't want to see him dead. He lay motionless, his coat raised up like a tent.

"Oh no!"

He had landed genital-first on the chimney of the barge. Her misfortune in inflicting crippling injuries to male genitalia was amazing.

"I've killed him!"

* * * *

Brian ran through the pain barrier. Luckily for him, his Olympian start and Sadie's lack of athletic prowess meant he had caught up to her, thirty-four yards from where he had started running. Brian Garforth was not a gentleman, and in all fairness to the man, he never pretended to be, but Brian Garforth was not a coward either, even though his next action would appear cowardly to an outsider. He saw it as an act of self-preservation, and for the greater good of woman-kind.

As Brian drew level with the fleeing Sadie he gently, but effectively, tapped the back of her left heel, which in turn, kicked the back of her right heel. Her legs tangled beneath her and thus began the long and slow process of falling. Although Sadie was not running quickly, she was travelling with a lot of forward momentum and it took a while before she eventually hit the deck, face first.

The monster was intent on ripping Brian to pieces and didn't notice the prone body of Sadie until it tripped over her, and suddenly it too was heading for a nasty landing.

Brian jumped into the hot seat of his 2.8i Capri and hoped to God it would start. Against all karma and everything in the world that was decent and holy, it did start first time. With a mighty flooring of the accelerator, Brian Garforth roared out of Middlesbrough Memorial Park with no chance of being caught. He was in the fastest and the most beautiful thing ever to come out of the nineteen-seventies.

Brian raced for home. This must have been what that Chambers wanker was talking about. Brian put the radio on and cruised along to the enchanting tunes of Toto. His conscience was clean. Brian Garforth was a cunt of immeasurable proportions.

* * * *

"Nnnnngghhh…" Gunnar moaned and stirred. Excruciating pain ran through his lower regions. He dared not think what damage had been afflicted, or the length of time that it would take to recover from it. That woman. He couldn't wait for this whole section of his life to end so he could torture her for weeks and weeks. His genitals had only just recovered from their last injury.

The door of the barge opened and an elderly gentleman carrying a torch and a frying pan looked gingerly over the top of his boat. He was wearing stripy pyjamas and slippers, certainly not equipped to deal with the situation that presented itself. Seeing Gunnar prone, he climbed onto the roof and sleepily made his way over to investigate.

"Are you alright, young man?" he asked, not noticing that the chimney had impaled the vampire.

Gunnar grabbed the old man's leg and threw it as hard as he could. The old man fell hard to the floor with the audible breaking of bones. Gunnar pulled him over by his hair and desperately bit into the man's neck. He needed blood for the strength to push himself off the chimney. He needed it so that he could start regenerating.

The old man was dead within seconds. He wouldn't have felt anything as he was unconscious from his fall. When Gunnar's thirst was satisfied, he pushed himself up hard from the roof of the barge and escaped his captor with an agonising scream.

"Edward!" yelled the concerned voice of the new widow from inside the barge. Gunnar leapt from the roof to the deck and rushed inside to drink more blood, vital to his recovery.

Sheila looked on and her jaw dropped. She could neither shout, scream, nor even move after witnessing the horror on the barge below. After a few minutes, smoke began to appear from inside the cabin. Gunnar walked casually outside and up across the roof. His jump on to the bridge was superhuman. He faced Sheila.

"If I were you, I would forget all that you have witnessed." Then he leaned close enough for Sheila to smell his blood-soaked breath. "And I suggest that you do not put me into that situation again."

"I thought you were mad…" she managed.

"It matters not. The hunt for Tillsley is the most important thing. Come. We must leave before the authorities arrive."

The two left for the van as the fire took the barge. The remains of the elderly couple would be cremated along with all evidence of the vampire's involvement, and the truth behind their tragic end.

22

Sid, Brian and Arthur all entered the Miner's Arms within five minutes of each other. All three had stories to tell, and all three had copious amounts of ale to drink. Peter Rathbone sat drinking at the bar, waiting to hear the stories so he could better them. Reece was waiting at the bar, away from Rathbone, drinking mineral water. All three of the heroes groaned when they caught sight of Reece. The only reason that they hadn't given him another pasting was because he got the beers in.

Kevin Ackroyd was enjoying the increase in business. There were loads of people flashing their cash at the moment, and the best thing of all was that he had kept it hidden from the missus. He pulled a pint of Bolton when he saw Sid, the last of the three to enter the pub.

Reece joined the group only after Sid had arrived. "Good evening, gentlemen," he said warmly.

"When are you going to fook off?" said Brian coldly.

"Once all the problems in the Northeast are solved, and once Sid takes his rightful role as vampire hunter."

Sid raised his eyes. "The more beers you buy, the more I get tempted, Rich."

"It's Reece," he said fleetingly. "Kev, can we have a round over here, please?"

The four lads smiled. Everyone had a price and these lads were cheaper than most.

"I have discovered some shocking facts about the thing that lives in the woods," he said grandly.

"Oh, aye. I had a scrap with that fella, last night," said Brian.

"You had a fight with it?" Reece smirked. "I thought it was that Rathbone fellow who told lies?"

Brian gave Reece a stern look. "A, Peter Rathbone doesn't lie, he tries to better other people's stories, which results in lies, and B, are you calling me a fooking liar?"

"How can you have survived? It is not just a vampire, it is an abnormally powerful, bloodthirsty animal?"

"Well, it weren't really a proper scrap. I stuck the nut on it and legged it, like."

"Stuck your nut on it…and legged it?" Reece was unconvinced. "Where did this battle take place, exactly?"

"Ah!" exclaimed Brian. He realised that he would need to divulge more information. "Well, I was kinda up near Memorial park, last night."

"You out dogging?" asked Sid.

"Err..."

"I didn't realise you were into that sort of stuff, man?" asked Arthur with a little bit of disappointment in his voice.

"I'm not, I'm not," retracted Brian. "Rich is right. I didna fight the monster thingy. I just thought I'd make it up, you know, for a joke." He gave out an unconvincing fake laugh.

"Brian, I have been your friend for a long time and I know that you are not a man to lie," said Sid.

"Ah fook," said Brian. "Alreet, I was out looking for a bit of action in the car-park," admitted the dogger.

Reece looked startled. "So you did fight the beast?"

"Aye."

"Did you get any action?" asked Sid.

"It was a bit disappointing, actually, mate. There was only one car there."

He was interrupted mid sentence by Reece. "He has just been in a fight with the monster that is plaguing your local area, and you are more worried about whether he got any 'action?'"

Sid scratched his head. "Aye, guess I am, aren't you?"

Every time Reece thought that Sid Tillsley couldn't surprise him any further, he surprised him further.

Brian continued with news of the female dogger. "There was only one lass and it was a fat lass."

Arthur Peasley winced and recoiled from the table as if struck, whilst Sid had the opposite reaction.

"Well?" said Sid rubbing his hands together. "Did you do the deed, you mucky git?"

"I was going to," he said, ignoring the groans from Arthur Peasley. "Had me kecks round me ankles and everything. Then that thingy turned up, kicking off."

"So you didn't get any action?" asked Sid with a hint of desperation in his voice. He often tried to live his sex life through the loins of Brian Garforth, vicariously of course, not in any other way.

Reece looked to the heavens for help, exasperated. As he did so, two strangers entered the Miner's and everyone in the pub turned to see who was entering their turf. Reece spoke under a hushed breath. "I want no one to speak of what Brian has just told the group. Those men work for the Human Council that deals with vampire activity. Say nothing!"

The two gentlemen walked to the bar and ordered a couple of pints of ale. Both were dressed in a smart casual manner meaning they immediately stood out.

"Who are they?" asked Brian.

"They, gentlemen, were sent here to make contact with Sid. They are taking a different tact to the vampires and appear to be trying to find information, inconspicuously."

"That's shit, mon! Them vampire fellas bought loads of ales. We're gonna get n'owt with these tight-wad bastards!" exclaimed Sid.

"Keep quiet, gentlemen, and let them come to us."

Sid decided to completely ignore the advice. "Oi! Ya tight bastards!"

The two men at the bar didn't even try to pretend to ignore Sid's cries. Instead, they walked up to the group and sat down to face the object of theirs, and every member of the different faction's, interest.

"Good evening, gentlemen," said the older of the two operatives. His smart, casual look was obtained from the most expensive cut of clothing. He was a good-looking man in his late forties and grey hadn't yet touched his thick black hair. "I take it you know why we are here?"

Reece took the mantle as he knew the four men with him were only interested in drinking as much free ale as was humanly possible. "We know why you are here, but we do not know who you are, or what your intentions are."

"My name is Grant Adams," said the older well-spoken gentlemen. "My partner here is Timothy Orton." Orton was in his late twenties, and as well dressed as his older counterpart. His head was shaven as he wanted a harder image than the soft features of his face gave him. Orton nodded to the group as he was introduced.

"What are the intentions for your visit?" asked Reece.

"Aye, ya bastards. When are ya getting the beers in?" asked Sid, getting the important question in.

Timothy Orton smiled at Sid. "That is not the reason why we are here, Mr. Tillsley. There are more important things to discuss than the arrival of your next beer."

This comment was greeted with dismay from the Smithson Estate locals. The vampires always put their hands in their pockets; even Reece did, and he was an annoying bastard. They all looked to Reece for alcoholic support.

"Why are you here, then?" he asked.

The 'boro lads groaned.

"We are here to hold discussions with Mr. Tillsley here. We want to know what he will do if it comes to the crunch, and war between humans and vampires breaks out."

"You're getting fook all unless you get the beers in!" said Brian Garforth.

Timothy Orton sighed and, to the delight of the Miner's Arms locals, rose to his feet and alighted to the bar.

"That's better, like," said a satisfied Brian Garforth. He had become very used to free beer coming his way. If these bastards weren't going to get him drunk then he was going to make sure that Sid knew exactly what he thought of the situation.

Grant Adams carried on the proceedings. "Mr. Tillsley, you are the object of many people's attention, both human and non-human. We understand that the vampires have contacted you recently about your remarkable execution of several of their brethren. We understand that you sent them away with another execution, to hand. Firstly, we thank you for ridding the world of some of the most dangerous predators in existence." Grant could tell that he had lost Sid's attention.

The lads were all staring at Timothy Orton, who was bringing back four thirst-quenching pints of Bolton Bitter.

"There you go, gentlemen, please enjoy your—"

He was cut off by four empty pint glasses being slammed on the table. Timothy Orton turned on his heel and returned to the bar. He didn't join the service to keep drunks in alcohol.

Grant Adams continued where he left off. "So, Sid, what will you do with your newly found power?"

"Well, to be honest with ya, pal, pretty much n'owt. As long as they don't start playing silly buggers and they leave Sid alone, that is."

"They will not leave you alone because they cannot afford to. If it turns out that the Firmamentum is upon us, then none of us can afford to let you go. We will need you to fight for the benefit of the world. Do you understand what I am saying, Sid?"

"Aye, ya bastards are gonna keep bothering me like that bastard over there!" He pointed to Reece, who nonchalantly waved back.

Adams turned to Reece, someone whom he had heard many stories about. He had only seen a picture of him as a young man, but he was easily recognisable. "Good evening, Mr. Chambers. How long have you been involved with our good friend here?"

Reece didn't respond to the agent. Kevin Ackroyd approached the group with a round of whiskies.

"Howay the lads!" exclaimed Sid. Timothy Orton had grown tired of fetching drinks for these men who clearly had a severe drinking addiction, and instead left a fair chunk of money behind the bar thus prompting, for only the second time in Miner's Arms history, a waiter service.

"You are not prepared to fight the vampire, Mr. Tillsley?" Timothy said. "You are not prepared to help rid the world of sick, violent, depraved individuals? You are not prepared to put an end to paedophilic rapists that walk your very streets?"

Sid thought about it for a minute and realised that it could be a trap. "Aye, I would love to gentlemen, but me back, me back wouldna won't allow me to take up such strenuous exercise. I could do meself serious damage, like."

"We will pay you, Mr. Tillsley," said Adams. "We can also arrange it so that you are never investigated by the benefit office ever again."

"Shit the bed!"

Kevin Ackroyd made another trip to the table where all of his dreams were coming true. This time he was carrying a tray full of very dusty blue and red bottles. He plonked them down on the table with a giant smile.

"What are they, Kev?" asked Brian.

"I have a treat for you lads. Dooley's Toffee Cream Liqueur!"

"What the fuck is Dooley's, man?" asked Arthur.

"Glad you asked, my friend, glad you asked. Dooley's is the drink that Baileys could have been if the paddies had the gumption and the sheer brilliance to fuse Baileys with a Werther's Original."

"Hang about, mon!" interrupted Sid. "That Werther's fella from the telly is dodgy as fook! Always had that bairn on his knee an' offering him candy. Fooker wants locking up he does. He must be one of them fellas that you lads were going on about. You know, them diddling bastards!"

Brian Garforth rose to his feet and rolled up his sleeves. His friend couldn't dish out justice with these potential benefit-investigating bastards at the table and it was time to take matters into his own hands. He walked over and punched the paedophile at the bar that had recently walked in for a beverage, in the side of the head.

"Garforth! What the hell are you doing?" screamed Kevin as the elderly gentleman hit the ground, unconscious.

"He's one of them diddlers, Kev. Them lads over there were telling us about him, dirty bastard!" He landed a big toe punt into the prone body of the war veteran.

Grant Adams shouted at the O.A.P. basher, "Stop that, you idiot! He isn't a vampire, he's an old man! It's broad daylight outside!"

Brian's face dropped. He hadn't hit a pensioner in months. It was really bad for his Karma.

"Ah shit, at least he's still breathing. I assumed he was one of them Werther's diddlers! None of you saw anything!" he said, pointing at every man in the room. He didn't need the threatening point, but all nodded anyway, even the two agents.

The O.A.P. beater took the pensioner by the legs and dragged him outside. "I'll stick him in the skip, Kev."

The barman nodded. "Aye, make sure no one sees ya, like."

"Don't worry, mon." A light came on in the quick thinking head of Brian Garforth. "I'll nick his wallet and then ring the coppers and tell 'em I saw some kids beating the ol' bastard. Should get meself a reward! See you lads in a bit."

"Clever bastard," said Sid, Arthur, Kev, the Lads and Peter simultaneously. The two non-Middlesbrough residents shook their heads in complete disgust.

"Anyway, lads, as I was saying, Dooley's is the nectar of the gods. Actually it's a bit of a poo…" Kevin Ackroyd very nearly said "poof's drink". If he had, he would have lost the sale of his untouched stock of Dooley's, and also the use of his jaw. He had bought a crate a few Christmas's ago and he had hoped to shift it on Ladies' Nights, but the 'boro beauties just weren't interested.

"Poo…?" enquired Sid.

"Nah, I meant to say 'winner'."

"Ah well, in for a penny…" The big man unscrewed a bottle and took a massive gulp of the sickly spirit.

"We are not paying for those as well!" said Timothy Orton, pointing at the nine remaining unopened bottles (Peter and Arthur had followed suit and were drinking their Toffee-tastic treat straight from the bottle).

Sid wiped away his Dooley's moustache. "If negotiations are to continue, you fooking are," he threatened. Grant Adams put his hand up to Orton, to calm the younger recruit down. All the lads took another mighty gulp.

Negotiations did not really progress much over the hour-long Dooley's marathon. Brian Garforth had returned with fifty pounds in his hands. He had put the blame on two lads that looked like wrong'ns. They were quite near the vicinity and the old man couldn't remember anything so it was an open and shut case. He celebrated with a bottle of Dooley's, much to the annoyance of Timothy Orton.

Nine empty bottles now stood in front of the heavy drinkers of the Miner's Arms. The four pals were not in good health and it had been a difficult hour for the agents. Early on, they thought that they had fulfilled their mission of bringing Sid in for questioning. They had offered Sid the destruction of all the files held by the benefit fraud agency for the last twenty years. All he had to do in return was to go with them to their office in Newcastle. Unknown to him, he would then be tested extensively by the agencies' scientists for any abnormalities.

However, as the Dooley's had poured, or rather oozed its way out of the bottle, negotiations had fell by the wayside. Reece Chambers had looked on in silence, occasionally laughing at the human agent's predicament. He had been in the same situation many times.

Each of the Dooley's drinkers had been sick several times over the course of the evening. The only reason that they had managed to get drunk was because they were drinking malt whisky chasers with their bottles of toffee cream. Even the Jolly Green Giant wouldn't be legally allowed to drive if he consumed the level of alcohol that these individuals had.

The subject of conversation had been as diverse as it was pointless. They had discussed one-on-one combat using any weapon that could be found in a garden shed. They had gone over a huge range of adversaries including a flock of penguins, a rabies-enhanced badger set, Shadow from *Gladiators*—and Jesus—if he took steroids. They had then spoke at length on what was the worst thing that you could lick.

The conversation that worried the agents of the Hominum Order the most was: How much Dooley's does a man need to drink before he goes blind?

The last question was the only one that was going to be answered. Arthur grabbed at his stomach in a concerned manner. "Hey, man, I think this Dooley's is taking away my sex-pack." He pulled up his immaculately pressed, white, sequinned shirt to reveal rippling abs of steel. "Hell, I think I've put on an ounce of fat drinking this funky shit."

Sid pulled up his Esso Tiger T-shirt to reveal the hairiest, roundest belly in all of Middlesbrough. A sweater could have been knitted from the fluff in his cavernous belly button. "Aye, you know I think I have put a few pounds on, meself," he said gripping massive handfuls of flab.

"Ooh! Hang on, bit more cream to get rid of. Excuse me, lads." Sid struggled off in the direction of the toilets.

"You're wasting your time, you know?" said Reece to the agents. "He won't come with you. I've tried numerous times and the vampires have tried too. He wants to live his life here and be the king of his own tiny kingdom. For him, it has enough mystery, enough money, and enough romance. Everything he needs is right here on this small estate."

Brian laughed into his creamy bottle. "Enough romance? He hasn't been laid in the last two fooking years!"

Reece ignored Brian's comment. "You might as well go back and tell the rest of the Order, your righteous Order, who watch every day as their own people are murdered, raped and savaged."

"Spare us, Chambers," said Timothy Orton disgustedly. "Your idealistic bullshit can only be believed by the truly delusional. Think what it would be like if it wasn't for us. Think about the carnage that would reach the streets if vampires were discovered by the public."

"At least the truth would be known. We wouldn't live the lie that we have lived over the last few centuries," said Reece.

Sid returned back from the toilets and settled down to another bottle of Dooley's and an extra large malt whisky chaser. He caught the back end of the conversation and waved a big hand at the agents and Reece. "For fook's sake, will ya stop being boring bastards and enjoy a drink and have a fooking laugh?"

"So, Sid, will you come back with us tonight? We will pay you substantially for the night's work. We will put you up in a hotel, all expenses paid, and then wipe all benefit records for the last twenty years," said Adams.

"Can we have a few more here, like?" he asked hopefully.

"Yes," sighed Grant Adams and he nodded over to Kevin Ackroyd who watched the group with eagle eyes, loving every minute. He was getting rid of loads of unwanted stock and also the expensive booze that none of the locals could afford.

More alcohol passed the lips of the locals at inflated prices. They had all built up a tolerance to the cream and the vomiting had subsided allowing more time for the whisky, beer, Dooley's, and now Warninks, to enter the blood stream. They had reached a level of alcohol abuse that opened up a lottery in potential violence, and if women entered the establishment, guaranteed debauchery.

"Shall we alight, Mr. Tillsley?" asked Grant Adams.

Sid looked into the bottom of the last bottle of Dooley's and saw double. "Yessh, yessh I think that it is time for me to alight." He attempted to rise and hit the ground hard. The two agents helped the big man to his feet. "I'm alreet, lads. It was just a little slip, thatssh all."

His three friends were in no state to stop Sid taking the trip with the human agents. They all sat with their head on their forearms in a comatose state. The mother of all hangovers awaited them the next day. Again.

"Gentlemen, we cannot say goodbye without one last drink for the road," said Reece Chambers, uncharacteristically.

"We must be on our way," insisted Timothy Orton, struggling under Sid's weight.

"I canna say no to one last drink, ladsh," said Sid, miraculously regaining his balance. Reece smiled and went to see the grinning Kevin Ackroyd.

"We must be leaving after this last drink. It's getting late," said Orton, fearful of the vampire.

Sid waved his big paw for not the first time in the evening. "Shurrup, mon, it's just a little drink. I said that I'd come with ya, didn't I?"

Reece returned with a drink for the big drunken fella, a big, flowery, grandiose drink.

"What the fook is that?" questioned Sid, in an ungrateful and unimpressed way.

Reece smiled again. "Well, Sid, after seeing you enjoy some exotic drinks, I thought I'd get you something a little special. This drink is well revered by all ladies' men across the South American continent and the Mediterranean. This, my good friend, is a Mojito."

A Mojito is a cocktail comprising of mint leaves, white rum, sugar and limejuice. The Miner's Arms didn't stock any of the above, except for an abundance of fake Bacardi. But, at the flash of a twenty-pound note, Kevin Ackroyd ventured into the lion's den of Mrs. Ackroyd's kitchen to find the required resources for the cocktail. He returned with icing sugar, a jar of mint sauce, and the active ingredient for Reece's master plan: lemon juice. Four Jif lemons to be precise.

Reece's plan required a change to the composition of the beverage. In the pint glass was a whole jar of Colman's finest mint sauce, eight teaspoons of icing sugar, a third of a pint of rum, and to finish, it was filled to the brim with Jif lemons. As long as Sid could smell alcohol, he would drink what was put in front of him. If he drunk the lemon juice then Reece's plan would come into fruition.

"A Mahhh…a Mahee…fook it, it's booze. Howay the lads!"

Down the drink went in a trademark Sid Tillsley mighty draught.

"Have a good night, Sid."

"Cheerss, Rich."

The two agents accompanied the drunk out of the pub. Timothy Orton gave Reece a very smug look as he took Sid from under his nose. Reece took a seat with Sid's unconscious friends, and banged on the table hard. The vibrations ran through the heads of Arthur, Brian, and Peter, bringing them back to the blurry world of reality.

"What the fook?" said Brian looking around quickly. "Where's Sid gone, like?"

"Sid left with the human agents, a second ago."

Arthur threw him an aggressive, but drunken, stare. "What the Hell are you thinking of, man?"

Reece got up. "Come and have look." The three men struggled to get up with the alcohol weighing down their struggling bodies, but they all heroically made it to the street outside. They all watched forlornly as the black Mercedes pulled away with their good friend inside, travelling to meet his destiny.

"You see," lectured Reece, "even though you have each vomited a significant amount of cream, you are all currently in the process of digesting pints of the stuff. Whilst you were asleep, I gave Sid half a pint of lemon juice. Have you seen what happens when cream and acid mix?" He didn't wait for the various answers that he would undoubtedly receive. "It curdles. At this very moment in time there are about five pints of cream curdling with half a pint of acid in the stomach, intestines and bowels of Sid Tillsley."

"Oh my God!" said Brian Garforth.

The Mercedes skidded, and slid across the street before a parked car brought it to a metal-rendering stop. Timothy Orton and Grant Adams collapsed out of the doors of the luxury car, projectile vomiting astronomical distances. Their clothing and their features were indistinguishable. Each man was covered top to toe in thick brown faeces.

"AAAAAAARRRRRRRRGGGHHHHH!" the men screamed in unison as they clutched at their eyes and gagged. They continued to retch long after they had emptied their stomachs. The back door opened and out fell Sid Tillsley. He was not completely untouched, but was in a much better state than the agents. He had felt the warning and got his head down and his arse up, just in time.

His pants and jeans had been ripped asunder, and Timothy Orton had been hit hard in the back of the head. Grant Adams would have been safe if the agents didn't have the air-conditioning on. Faeces were distributed around the car in an unrelenting fashion. Shit everywhere.

Sid got up and headed towards his friends who held their noses when he got within fifty feet.

"Get away! Get yourself home, ya dirty bastard!" screamed Brian as he ran in the opposite direction of the smelly culprit. The other lads, including Reece, followed suit. The agents now lay unconscious on the road. Sid had successfully alienated the humans and the vampires, and there was no chance he was going to be served last orders in the state he was in.

"Shit the bed...," he moaned, before heading for home.

23

It was midnight. The telephone rang twice and Michael answered it. He was in his office in London, a massive room deep beneath the grounds of his manor. It was beautifully decorated in oak. Many manuscripts and tapestries hung on the walls. One wall was completely dedicated to weapons from the ages, from basic flint hunting knives to beautifully polished samurai swords. Every kind of weapon adorned the wall, except firearms.

"Yes?"

He was greeted by sobbing. "I am sorry, Michael. I couldn't help it. I had to try."

"Ricard, what have you done?"

"I-I thought I could handle him. I thought that after my experience with Sparle that I could—I thought—I am sorry, Michael."

"Where is he?" said Michael, all his fears realised.

"We lost him in the North Yorkshire Moors. He was doing so well, Michael, but we just couldn't tame him."

"You will be dealt with accordingly along with your accomplices. Nevertheless, the important thing is to end this abomination now. We will be with you in two hours. You will help us end what you have started, Ricard." He slammed down the phone and initiated the mission he had already prepared for.

* * * *

His team was ready within the hour. When rumours of the Firmamentum had first arisen he had assembled the vampires. It could have been the finest group to grace the earth in living memory. However, with the death of Gabriel, and the exile of Gunnar, the effectiveness of the squad had diminished. All twenty would be nothing compared to the might of Gabriel and Gunnar combined.

Two hundred and eighty-four years ago, Michael made the Agreement. Actually, it was Ricard, and others, who dealt with the logistics, but if he hadn't agreed, it would have all been in vain. Back then, it was he that was the superpower.

Michael was the same vampire that he was all those years ago, and he still lusted for power more than anything. Back then, he had foreseen the end of the vampire domination. Humans had fought back for the first time since they had swung down from the trees. With the technological advancements they were making, they would soon have the upper hand. The loss of a few key figures in the vampire world had convinced him it was time to lie low, no matter how much it pained him. The establishment of the Coalition and the Hominum Order ensured that he would still hold his seat of power, even if kings and queens no longer bowed before him. Everything moves in cycles. Soon, he would rule as a God once more.

He snapped back to the present. Once tonight was over, he could think of the future.

Briefing the team would only take minutes. They knew what they would be up against. Most of them were old enough to remember Sparle and the destruction he caused. All they needed briefing on was the place he was last seen. The team of twenty were equipped with full Kevlar body armour, sub-machine guns and grenade launchers. It would be a different story this time. With this technology and raw power, the monster would have no chance.

The prophecy predicted that the Bellator was the only one who could end the Firmamentum, and the Bellator had to be Sid Tillsley. Michael Vitrago hated the prophecy and would be damned if he would rely on it. A lamia needing a human…the thought made him sick. The last human born from the prophecy killed his father, and it had haunted him for two thousand years. Michael had ended the original Bellator, but it was the beast that he longed to face.

 Tonight it ends, and then it was time to think of bringing about a new beginning.

* * * *

Two gunships flew, with all haste, to Ricard's home. Michael Vitrago briefed the troops in the air via intercom.

"We meet with Ricard in forty-five minutes. We have trained for this moment. Death will come swiftly to the beast. When it is spotted, press your homing device and then all other troops will rendezvous, immediately. Once we have convened, we will open fire with everything we have. Beheading the thing is the only thing that will stop it. I will perform this personally…no matter what the circumstances."

"Five minutes to landing, sir," buzzed the pilot.

Michael surveyed his chosen team and it made him realise how the times had changed. For centuries, the fashions had changed, but the weapons remained similar. Over the last two hundred years, however, things had evolved at a frightening rate. Humans certainly had a knack for developing weapons that destroyed one another.

They touched down and the troops made their way out of the back of the helicopter. They were not finely ordered like a regiment because they were not trained for discipline—they didn't need to be.

Their task, in principle, was a simple one: search and destroy at any cost. Their natural killing instinct was their greatest ally. How easily could the beast be taken down, though? Would their killing instinct and their cutting edge weaponry be enough? Many lives would end tonight, but this was of no consequence to Michael.

Ricard was waiting for the group. He ushered Michael and the more senior members of the team inside. The small house could barely contain the massive lamia and their equipment, but once they were all in the house, Ricard disclosed all that he had held secret for so long.

"I am sorry, Michael. I am sorry for what I have done." He had managed to regain control of his emotions.

"That is of no issue now. You will be punished in good time. For now, all that is important is that we find and destroy it."

A flicker of pain crossed Ricard's face and was gone in an instant, but Michael picked up on it. "I will end your life without trial if you do not give me all the information that I require. I will not hesitate to feed your corpse to that beast before ending its miserable life."

"I do not doubt it for a second. Remember though, I didn't have to contact you. I contacted you because I couldn't keep Sparle under control…"

"Sparle? How sentimental of you to name him after your pet from two-thousand years ago." Michael shook his head in disgust. "Did you, for a second, think you could tame it? Was I right? Would your ego not allow you to let go of past failures?"

"My ego? No, I couldn't condemn an innocent being to death before it was given a chance."

"Your missionary voyage was doomed from the start. Why did you call me? What has happened?" said Michael impatiently.

"There were five of us to begin with, but I am the only one left alive. All of us helped to keep Sparle at bay. We placed electrodes under his skin when he was an infant. If he became too boisterous, we would electrocute him until we could bind him and take him back home. He needed to run free. It would have been cruel to deprive him of what he was put on the earth to do.

"Everything was fine. All his kills were sanctioned for the others and me. However, as he grew, so did his bloodlust, not to mention his incredible strength and speed. On more than one occasion he evaded us. That is the reason that some of the clean-ups, performed by Sanderson and his team, have been considerably messy.

"We always managed to recapture him for he would spend a great deal of time feeding and playing with his prey. Sadism is in his genes. He has had no external influence of violence. We stopped taking him out into the open, but the effect was degenerative. I should have ended his life, but I couldn't. My weakness, as you well know, is my compassion." Ricard's voice faltered once more as his feelings got the better of him.

"What happened?" pressed Michael.

"This evening, the electricity that we passed through his body didn't affect him at all. It didn't even slow his pace. He killed the others and I knew he was past my control."

"I take it there is a tracking device?" asked Michael.

"Of course."

Michael pointed to the door and the troops immediately began to fall out. "We must find him before he reaches any populations. If he does, we will have no chance upholding the Agreement."

* * * *

The helicopters passed low over the hills of North Yorkshire. Ricard's tracking device showed that Sparle was travelling at a rapid pace across the moors. "We are lucky that he has gone west," said Michael. "It would have been catastrophic if he had turned east and hit Middlesbrough. Why has he not stopped to feed?"

Ricard stared at the laptop screen in front of him. "He has been held captive all his life. He is running free. I am the beast, Michael. I am the beast for imprisoning him."

Michael ignored Ricard. The sentimental old fool was starting to annoy him. He would kill him if there were no use for him. He could become a useful distraction if he has built up any sort of relationship with the animal.

Michael reached for the intercom. "ETA, pilot?"

"Five minutes, sir."

"Troops!" called Michael through the intercom that connected both gunships. "As you know, we can pinpoint his location to three hundred meters. He will not be hard to find. Let's end this quickly."

Five minutes later, the gunships set down twenty feet from the moorland heather and the two squads of vampires dropped down to the ground. To them, it was like jumping down from a doorstep, and they hit the ground running. The two squads spread out and covered the ground at pace, as the gunships wheeled overhead surveying the land with infrared heat detectors.

Their surroundings were far more tranquil than the business they attended. The warm balmy night was pleasant, and the gentle breeze blew the sweet smelling heather across the moonlit hills. The gunships would have impeccable vision as there was not a cloud in the sky. If this thing was anything like the original Sparle, there would be no chase as it would be yearning for a fight.

The vampires all kept pace behind Michael as he ran through the night. He was the only one that didn't carry a firearm. He detested them, though equally respected them. They were the only things that would give humans an edge if there was full-blown war. Instead he carried two butterfly swords, although in his massive hands they were more like daggers. He would need these deadly weapons against Sparle. He accepted it, no matter how much it hurt his ego.

In the distance, he could see a large farmhouse and the lights were on. He took the radio from his jacket. "Make a perimeter two hundred metres away from the centre. Remain invisible." As soon as he had barked his order, the vampires began to make their formation. He changed the frequency of the radio to that of the gunship.

"Pilot?"

"Sir."

"Contact the Coalition and have Sanderson's team follow Sparle's path from Ricard's to our present co-ordinates. Also, block all telephone lines and mobiles."

"Yes, sir."

"What heat images are you getting from the farmhouse?"

"From this height, sir, it is difficult to be accurate. There seems to be several people in the house and heat is radiating from all. Whether they are alive or not, I cannot tell. There is movement though."

"We'll investigate and kill all inside. Inform Sanderson he is going to have a busy evening. Over and out."

Michael stared at the farmhouse and his instincts told him that Sparle was feeding. It would have heard its pursuers from a mile away. Trying to satisfy its unquenchable thirst would be the only reason it hadn't attacked them.

A few outhouses occupied adjacent sites, but these didn't concern Michael. If they contained animals then Sparle would have massacred them first, as the smell of their flesh would have been stronger than the human's.

The lights were on in the farmhouse. It was late and unlikely that the whole family would be up. The lights were on because the inhabitants were not alive to turn them off.

In the blink of an eye, one of the windows turned blood red. He was here.

"Troops, it is in the farmhouse. Hold the perimeter. Move in to one hundred metres."

He could see the shadows move closer in unison. He hadn't expected to be this fortunate, expecting the beast to find them before they found it. Catching it feeding and completely unaware of them was a bonus.

"Shall we move in, sir?"

"No, Viralli. We will force it out and then hit it with all that we have. We do not know where it will appear from so all blindsided soldiers will have to move with haste. I'll call in a strike." He changed the radio frequency. "Gunship Echo, one missile. Centre of the building."

"Aye, sir."

As the farmhouse exploded, Michael drew his swords. The blaze lit the night sky, and debris showered the waiting vampires. Sparle's roar of agony could be heard clearly over the fire that consumed the farm. He leapt from the centre of the inferno and ran at astounding speed away from the burning building. The tattered clothes that he wore had burned away, as had most of his skin. He ran, whilst leaving a trail of smoke.

"Open fire!" yelled Michael.

Twenty machine guns burst into action, but didn't slow the monster. The two gunships followed Sparle with their mini-guns blazing, but he easily dodged the slow-manoeuvring weapons. With every step, his skin healed, the pain lessened and his rage increased. Without warning, he turned and faced his merciless attackers.

The sight was terrifying. He was larger than the last rendition of the animal, quicker and stronger. Nature had seen fit to bring forth a life form that could cope with the technology of the modern world.

The gigantic vampire ran straight for his nearest attacker, faster than a cheetah in full flight. The redness of his skin could be seen by the moonlight, stretched across heaving muscles that ached for vengeance.

His first victim was Otto Klaisman. He had walked the earth for fifteen hundred years and once ruled the Bavarian lands, butchering thousands. After running through a wave of bullets, Sparle ripped his throat out in a second. He tore his head clean off with a second swipe of his hand, before lifting the body to shield him from the bullets that constantly bombarded him.

The gunships were not agile enough to get close to the super-fast monster and seeds of doubt started to enter the minds of the hunters. They watched Sparle charge into Julius Alberto. For two thousand years, he was a power to behold and in an instant, Sparle ripped him in half. The beast screamed with delight as the blood of his victim soaked him from head to toe. He drank from the carcass as he hid behind Otto Klaisman's dismembered corpse.

"Rally to me!" ordered Michael. Fear didn't touch his heart, it never had and it never would. Only fifteen of the twenty lamia managed to reach him before setting lines of covering fire. Sparle, strengthened by the blood of his victims, screamed a roaring challenge before charging at the fifteen machine guns.

He reached the firing squad without losing any momentum. Carlos El Rivia, the youngest vampire of the squad, turned and ran in fear. He lost his head to Michael's flashing blade.

"Hold your ground or die!" he roared. Cowardice couldn't be forgiven, even by death.

Sparle bowled into the firing squad, sending several flying back with his momentous power. Those who didn't lose their feet tried to fire at him, but it was all in vain. Many lost their lives until only nine of the squad remained.

The sound of metal scraping on metal filled the air and the firing stopped. All turned to look at Michael, and even Sparle stopped in his tracks. Michael stood holding his swords at his side. He had stripped to the waist and cut himself deeply from the top of his chest to the bottom of his stomach. The others watched as the cut visibly healed. His powers of regeneration were staggering.

Sparle knew that this was a duel challenge. His head was a mess of rage and murder, but the lust for fighting was strongest. Even his simple mind could tell that this was a challenge, and a worthy one.

"No matter what the situation, no-one will interfere," Michael said calmly. He charged at Sparle with all his might, butterfly swords gleaming. A second later, Sparle replied and was up to full speed in a heartbeat. The clash would have been fatal to all but the two vampires that battled under the moonlight.

Michael plunged one of his swords deep into Sparle's chest but the sword was not long enough to reach the heart that lay deep within his massive torso. Sparle caught Michael's other hand that held a sword millimetres from his eye. With his free hand, he gripped Michael Vitrago's throat and squeezed hard. Blood oozed from his fingertips, causing Sparle to grin in delight. The sword wedged into his chest didn't seem to affect him, nor did Michael seem concerned about his crushed windpipe. The two stood in stalemate. Neither Michael nor Sparle were willing to relinquish their hold and neither was able to finish their opponent.

"Sir, shall we shoot it!" shouted Viralli.

Michael could say nothing due to his crushed larynx, but he didn't need to. The look that he gave Viralli told the loyal vampire all he needed to know.

Sparle sunk his long fingernails into Michael's wrist in an attempt to remove the threat of momentary blindness. The pain didn't faze Michael in the slightest, but if his tendons were ripped apart then he would lose a weapon. Michael's ego was not big enough to believe that he could defeat Sparle without weaponry. He relinquished the sword in Sparle's chest and pulled it out with a spray of blood. Twisting the sword meant Sparle's concentration was directed to his own pain, which gave Michael the opportunity to slip the vicelike grip that held his throat.

As Michael retreated, he slashed at the hand that had held his throat, severing it between the middle and index finger to the outside of the wrist. Sparle screamed with rage as the vampires yelled victoriously. Michael licked the blood off the blade, taunting the beast. The animal's scream of rage turned into insane laughter as it looked upon its enemy. It had finally found a worthy foe and it relished in its own pain and blood. Sparle charged once more.

Michael flourished his swords and Sparle's blood flicked from the blades. The weapons shone in the moonlight, which was mirrored by the gleam of the monster's giant fangs. Sparle leapt with the intention of crushing Michael into the ground. Michael swiftly dodged to one side and cut powerfully downwards into Sparle's descent.

Sparle roared with pain and frustration as he collapsed into the moorland heather. Michael had cut deep into the giant's hamstrings, disabling him from his constant attack. He didn't allow Sparle to rest and he turned back and attacked with renewed vigour, seeing his opponent weakened. Michael cut deep into Sparle's right arm, which he held up to protect vital areas from the razor edge of the butterfly swords. Even under such vicious assault, Sparle still lusted for blood and lashed out at Michael, ripping open his cheek and destroying his left eye.

Michael fell back. He would have been dead if Sparle could have moved fast enough, but his hamstring was still regenerating from the deep wound that had been afflicted.

"Sir!" shouted Viralli, "Are you OK? Shall we—"

"I will rip your head off with my bare hands if you think of interfering!" he shouted in between spitting out copious amounts of blood. The complex eye would take a long time to heal, even for him.

Both parties stared at one another. Michael assessed Sparle's injuries against his own and decided not to attack. Sparle crawled towards Michael, uncaring for his own physical state. All he desired was blood and violence. His hamstring had almost healed, the strength returned and he powered into another ground-shaking charge.

This time, Michael was not able to dodge as effectively because of his afflicted depth perception. Sparle was upon him before he was able to bring his swords down into the beast's flesh. They bowled over until Sparle came to rest on top of Michael. Michael was deft enough to hold his swords out so that the monster's entire weight fell onto the upturned blades.

Sparle screamed as the swords plunged deep into his internal organs. Nevertheless, even this wouldn't distract him from his goal. With Michael's hands trapped in the sword hilts, he couldn't defend himself from the onslaught that beseeched him.

"Open fire!" screamed Viralli, disobeying a direct order. The remaining vampires unloaded entire magazines into Sparle, but it was too late. He was away before they could save their leader. The troops ran to Michael Vitrago's desecrated body.

Constance Smythers called desperately through her radio. "Gunships! Get us out of—" she was cut off as a giant fist ripped into her spinal column.

* * * *

The Hall of the Lamian Consilium was full to the rafters. All the chairs were pushed to one side and for the first time since its formation there were humans within its great walls. The emergency meeting had been called by the elders after hearing of Michael Vitrago's demise. The Firmamentum was here, and Sid Tillsley was the only answer.

Only three of the twenty strong team survived Sparle's onslaught. They had made it to the gunships, which then held position in an attempt to hold the beast from travelling any further west. The survivors had briefed the elders by radio and the area was sealed off to the best of their limited capabilities. To keep this a secret would require a miracle.

The humans were called as soon as the elders knew the truth. Before Sparle's emergence, both sides had contacted Tillsley to see what they could gain. Now it was obvious, they must work together to put an end to this.

"This is the first time that humans have entered this chamber," spoke an elder, Nawa Bwogi, an ancient and fair vampire. He was a wise being that accepted Michael's rule as he saw it, the best thing for the species. With the death of Michael, the hierarchy of the Lamian Consilium would be in a state of unrest for many years. He had ruled a non-official dictatorship, but to his credit, the former warlord had upheld the Agreement. That was, until the Firmamentum caused personal vendettas to overshadow sanity.

"Michael Vitrago has been killed in combat by the beast spawned from the Firmamentum."

Bwogi waited for the gasps and outbursts from the humans to die down. The news was an immense shock to all.

"We have the beast in the North Yorkshire Moors and are pinning it down with helicopter gunships. We are trying to stop it reaching any populations, but we do not have much time. Only a beast born from the prophecy could bring down Vitrago. The stories of his battle prowess were not exaggerated. We have no alternative but to find Tillsley, and force him to fight."

"What happens if Tillsley won't fight? What happens if he is killed?" asked Caroline.

Another elder answered the question. "If Tillsley does not fight, then Tillsley will be killed. If Tillsley dies, then we will have to attack the beast with heavy missiles."

"But…" began Caroline until she was pre-empted by Bwogi.

"What other option do we have? The cover-up operation will be more difficult than anything that has been required since Lockerbie. We have no alternative. If Sparle is not bought down then he will reach a major population density and the cover-up will be impossible."

Caroline nodded in agreement. Their hopes relied in the right hand of Sid Tillsley.

24

Ricard sat in the helicopter with the few squad members who had survived the ordeal. A variety of emotions raced through his head: relief that Sparle had survived, hope that he would somehow escape, guilt at the death of Michael and the squad, disgust at himself for not being able to help Sparle.

The remaining members of the squad stared at Ricard. Each had lost friends. Each had sustained horrific injuries because of the idiocy of the ancient vampire. The reinforcements had arrived and they were leaving this catastrophic mess.

Ricard looked up at the team. "I am sorry for what I have put you through. I am sorry for the death of your comrades."

None of them dignified him with a response.

He put his head in his hands. Never had he felt such guilt, but it was not for the death of Michael. It was for turning Sparle into the Consilium.

Sorry, Sparle.

Did he have an option? No, once Sparle had escaped there was only one course of action. He did, however, have one more choice to make, and it was a decision that was possibly the most important one of his entire life.

* * * *

Over the last few weeks, Sid had made a few quid doing odd jobs here and there. Most of the beers had been bought for him as well, and he had stacked up a fair bit of dollar. It was time to treat himself to a good, old-fashioned, all-dayer in the Miner's.

He strolled down the road with a skip in his step and a gleam in his eye. That was until the riot van pulled up in front of him and mounted the curb. Six big policemen, dressed in full riot gear, jumped out and approached him, whilst keeping their distance.

"Sid Tillsley. You are under arrest for benefit fraud," stated the nearest riot policeman. "You have the right to remain silent, but any—"

"I'm not Sid Tillsley," said Sid Tillsley in his rehearsed voice.

"Like fuck you ain't! Now get in the fucking van!" shouted the copper. His aggressive nature was due to his nerves. He would have heard about the great right hand of the heavy-drinking hero.

"I ain't taking that from you, young'n!" said the man who deplored rudeness.

Sid suddenly winced, then grabbed at his buttock and pulled out a dart. "What the fook?" Two more darts replaced the one he had removed and the effects began to take their toll. Sid spun round to look at his attacker, a police marksman in the passenger side of an unmarked car. "You…you…"

The tranquillisers began to kick in as they were forced round the big man's narrow arteries. He staggered towards the car in what would have been a vain attempt to stick the gun up the copper's arse.

Sid only made it half way before he fell. Sleep took him before he reached the ground.

* * * *

Sid awoke with a start. He was pretty sure that he was in a cell. He sat up slowly and was surprised that he was not drowsy after the tranquillisers. Cowardly bastards, hitting him in the arse with darts. He had been arrested a few times before and had always come quietly, so he must be in deep shit this time. If his benefit fraud was at the end of its long and financially lucrative road, then the next few years were going to be a struggle that he could do without.

He settled back down on the bed. This was not the type of cell that he was accustomed to. The bed was extremely comfortable, and most prison cells didn't have a bottle of water and sandwiches waiting by the bedside. Something was going on here.

In an immediate answer to his question, the door to the cell opened. Light streamed in to reveal a room that couldn't come close to being called a cell, not by the most lavish of standards. An amazingly attractive woman was silhouetted in the doorframe. The tranquillisers hadn't affected the blood flow to Sid's loins, apparently.

"Good afternoon, Sid. I am Lucia. Please follow me as there are many of us who wish to speak to you."

"Aye, pet, I'll follow you anywhere," he said lecherously. No lass at the benefit office looked like that. She was red-hot. Sid began to feel a bit suspicious of the situation, but following that magnificent behind made all the suspicious thoughts drift away.

"I suppose you are wondering why you are here?" asked Lucia over her shoulder, spilling her immaculate hair across her back as she turned.

"Eh? Err…wassat?" managed Sid, dragging his eyes away from the tight trousers of the beautiful vampire.

"I said, Mr Tillsley, I should imagine that the question: 'Why am I here?' is going through your head, right now?"

"If I'm honest, pet, that weren't on me mind at all," said the crooner.

Lucia smiled, although it took all her willpower. "All your answers are waiting through these doors, Mr. Tillsley," she said as she threw open the doors of the silent Lamian Consilium.

Sid wasn't the brightest penny in the pile, but he was clever enough to realise that this wasn't just about benefit fraud. He surveyed the crowd and realised that some of these "suits" weren't all human. In fact, he recognised that most of the people here were them vampire fellas. If any of the dirty buggers made a play for him then he didn't care how many of them there were, the first one would end up with a black eye.

Vampires were quite distinguishable to Sid now. Some of the angrier looking ones had those pointy teeth going on. All of them were big lads though, with big, bright, sparkly eyes. He hadn't seen the lasses before. If they had sent the lasses to see him in the first place then things would have been different. They all had great norks. Not a poor pair of tats in sight.

"Sid Tillsley?"

Sid looked at the vampire addressing him. He hadn't seen him before. Big, black, African fella by the looks of things. It was best that he was polite, just in case he was in shit and needed to sweet talk his way out of something.

"Yes, sir, I am Sidney Tillsley."

"Do you know why you are here?" asked the African.

Sid had a few ideas and all of them ended up with him in a world of shit. He thought it best to plead ignorance, as usual. "No, sir."

"Sidney, the reason that you are here is that we urgently require your help," the speaker was a short, black, English woman. She reminded him of a female version of Trevor McDonald. "We need your help to save humanity, and to prevent the world from descending into civil war."

"Can ya get someone else to do it? Me back. Me back is in terrible shape and I canna work, ya see?" He grabbed at his back, as if to emphasise.

The congregation gave him looks of disgust and several unpleasant comments were uttered. Sid made a note of a couple of the more offensive comments. He would be meeting the culprits in the car park after this little meeting was over.

"Do you know what your purpose in life is, Sid?" the question came from a young vampire with a ponytail. He was a good-looking lad who must have got his fair share of action.

"Young'n," he said to the six hundred old immortal, "why are you asking me a question like that? I need at least six or seven pints to start talking shite like that. Has this place got a bar?"

Everyone ignored him except for an old looking fella who was sitting next to the African. "Sid, have you ever wondered why you are able to kill a vampire with a single punch?"

The big man looked down at his right fist. "Not really, mon. I've always had a pretty good punch on me, like."

The old timer continued. "No, Sid, the way that you kill our kind is not possible through strength alone. When you first showed yourself to us, by slaying Gabriel, we were amazed. You killed one of the greatest warriors in living memory and our gut instinct was one of fear. We thought that you had a secret weapon that threatened our existence. After the death of four vampires with your bare hands, we knew something was afoot. We knew that you were here for a reason. Do you know what that reason is?"

Sid opened his mouth to answer but was cut off as the elder realised that Sid would just say something stupid.

"There is a prophecy, well it was once a prophecy, that is now a way of life. The original prophecy predicted that…Sid!"

"Eh, what? Sorry, mon"

The elder's voice removed Sid's attention from Lucia's cleavage. "I'll continue, shall I?"

"Aye, sorry, mon."

The elder continued, but not before taking a sneaky look at Lucia's breasts himself. "The original prophecy predicted that there would be a vampire born, unlike any other. It would be tremendously powerful and have a bloodlust unlike anything seen before. However, there would be an answer. The answer would be a human with the strength and the will to defeat it, and thus bring harmony to the balance. Do you know why you are here, Sidney?"

Sid didn't have a clue what the old twat was on about, and he didn't give a shit, either. What he did know was that none of them had mentioned benefit fraud, and that the black-haired piece had the most wonderful pair of tatties that he had seen in forty-six years, man and boy. Best to act ignorant…and it wouldn't be difficult.

"No, sir," he said politely.

"Sidney, *you* are the human! You are the man who will save the world. You are the man who must kill the beast that is ravaging through your homelands. You are the only one who can stop it murdering hundreds and thousands of innocent people."

The penny dropped at last. Sid realised that this was what that twat, Reece, was going on about.

"Oh aye, oh aye. Look lads, lasses," he nodded at Lucia's cleavage a little bit more than was comfortable, even for an immortal. "I don't want to get involved in these shenanigans. I am a simple man, a simple man with simple needs…"

"If you don't," said the female Trevor McDonald, "then we will imprison you for benefit fraud. When you are finally released, we will make you pay back all the money you have taken, by working legitimately. We will kill all your friends and burn down your local pub. And then, when you think that things cannot get any worse, we will torture you until you die."

"Fooking 'ell, lass! Bet you haven't had a good shaggin' in a while, miserable bitch!"

Sid's comments drew gasps from the other humans, but it didn't deter the female Trevor McDonald.

"However, if you help us, all your previously obtained benefit money will be forgotten about and you will be paid a million pounds for your one night's work."

Sid considered it. It sounded like a trap to him and he wouldn't put it past them benefit bastards to set something up like this. He scratched his head in thought. Most likely, he didn't have a choice, but Sid was a man who didn't like being pushed and Sid Tillsley would rather go down with his head held high.

Bwogi sensed that it would take more than bribery to win the moron to fight for their cause. He needed something, anything, to clench the deal.

"If you help us, Sid," said the African vampire, and all eyes turned towards the elder. "Lucia will show you her breasts."

* * * *

Sid sat in the most comfortable armchair that he had ever sat in. He was enjoying a glass of two hundred year old brandy and a Cuban cigar that was absolutely wonderful. The vampire lads were against him having a couple of brandies, but he always had a couple of drinks before a big fight and he had managed to convince them to give him a little shot of "confidence."

A large cloud of sweet smelling smoke rose steadily to the high ceilings. It was a magnificent room, grandiose and gaudy. If he were to become a millionaire, he would have to get used to it. He was ninety per cent certain that it was a trap, but the chance of seeing them heavenly tats after the punch-up, was a chance that couldn't be given up, no matter what the consequences.

The lass was not too pleased about it, and he thought that she was going to rip that African fella's nuts off. Thinking about it, none of the others looked particularly amused either. If he hadn't have shouted out that they had a deal, it would have probably kicked off!

It was eight thirty in the evening. They were going to be flying out in helicopters in an hour. Because of them vampire fellas not liking the sunlight, this lad that he had to put the nut on wouldn't be out until about ten thirty. Then it was a case of giving him a hiding and earning a cool million before going on to see seeing something very special indeed.

There was knock at the door.

* * * *

Ricard knocked on Sid Tillsley's door. He hadn't yet been tried for his crimes against the Agreement, but what of his crimes against the being he swore to protect? He had been ordered to advise this man, Sid Tillsley, on the best way to defeat Sparle, and to detail his strengths and his weaknesses. Sparle he would further betray, but his crime against the balance he would begin to pay back.

"Aye?" said a deep Northeast accent. Ricard was familiar with the accent after spending the past twenty years amongst the likeable folk.

He opened the door and walked in to see the overweight figure of Sid Tillsley, killing himself on a giant cigar. The man lounged in the huge armchair and appeared to be in his element, not perturbed by the horrors that he was about to face. This was the man who had killed Gabriel with a single punch. He was the man who had defeated four vampires whilst hungover. Was it possible that he could defeat the raw power and aggression of Sparle? Ricard very much doubted it.

"Good evening, Sidney. I am Ricard," he said, offering his hand.

It was shaken vigorously. "Please to meet you, Rick. Call me Sid. I understand that you are here to tell me about the fella I'm gonna be doing a few rounds with later?"

The human threw a few shadow punches, as if he was in for a light sparring contest. It was obvious that this man had no idea what he was up against. His pulse was not racing, although through the cholesterol, it was definitely struggling. He was not dressed for combat. He should be wearing full Kevlar battle armour and be equipped with copious blades and firearms. Instead, he wore jeans that were three sizes too small for him. A fading tiger stared back at Ricard with the words "The Collection" written underneath.

"The first thing that I am going to suggest is that you change your attire. You will need all the protection you can get."

"Nah, mon, this is what I always scrap in. I'll be reet."

"Sid, this isn't a normal vampire you are going to be fighting. You do understand that, don't you?" Ricard realised that he was not dealing with one of the smartest members of human society.

Sid nodded. "Aye, mon. Me mate, Brian, had a tussle with him up in Memorial Park a few nights ago. Big ol' bastard apparently, good chin. Brian said he got all his balls into a head butt and it didn't even shake the bugger. Brian did a runner and the thing was nearly as quick as him over thirty yards! Fast hard fooker, by all accounts."

Ricard looked into the eyes of Sid Tillsley and saw no fear. "Sid, how old are you?"

"Forty-six, Rick."

Ricard had never been called Rick before. He quite liked it. "When did you realise that you had the gift of battle Sid?"

"Eh?" asked Sid, screwing his face up.

Ricard dumbed down the question. "When did you first realise that you could fight?"

"Oh, reet. Let me think…"

Ricard watched Sid scratch his head like a great bald gorilla. Maybe he was the Missing Link.

"I was always big as a kid, like. I was always a lot bigger than the other lads at school. When I started school, some of the older lads tried to bully us 'cos I stood out, like."

"Really? What did they to do to you?"

"Well, n'owt. You see, that's when I first realised that I could fight. One of the older kids came up with a group of his mates, showing off, like. He tried playing silly buggers, so I give him a right hook and none of the others wanted any after that."

"How old was the boy you hit?"

"He was about fifteen, but he had a shit jaw."

"How old were you?"

"Five."

Ricard blinked. Sid really was not like other humans, but Sparle would tear him to shreds in seconds. He didn't deserve that, not under the circumstances. He was not Remo of two thousand years ago. Ricard knew that he should never have allowed the situation to reach this point. He had no idea how similar this Sparle would be to the one born two thousand years ago. They were born with identical personalities, although the modern rendition was undoubtedly stronger. Now he was to send this human against him…this human with a "gift."

"Sid, I don't think that you can beat Sparle. I don't think your right hand will work." His comment was not taken seriously.

"Don't be wet, lad. This right hand has never failed to knock out a client. It's just you buggers react a bit differently, which is unfortunate for yous, like. He'll go down the same way as the rest of yas. Don't you worry."

Ricard realised that he wouldn't be able to convince Sid of anything else but a round one victory. It was futile to tell him Sparle's weaknesses. Weaknesses! Only his intelligence held him back from being a perfect killing machine, and that wouldn't help Sid, as it was likely that Sparle had the higher IQ. The only thing Ricard could do was to tell him of his strengths. At least then he'd know what it was that would kill him.

"Sid, Sparle has no weaknesses, but let me tell you his strengths."

"Aye, you should know your opponent before going into a fight. Clever thinking that, Rick," commended Middlesbrough's answer to Sun Tzu.

At least he isn't that stupid thought Ricard. "You already know about his speed, and you already know about his ability to regenerate?"

"Eh? Regen…regenter…Eh?"

Ricard smiled. "He heals very quickly, almost instantly in fact. The blow that your friend landed on him would have felt like a fly landing on his face. He could be hit by a car and heal within a minute."

"Shit the bed, mon!"

Ricard hoped that he was finally getting the point across.

"Poor bastard! Means he has no hope of getting anything on the sick from benefit office."

Ricard hadn't expected that, but he was quickly learning to expect the unexpected from Sid Tillsley. "That's not the only thing, Sid, his power is immense."

He was cut off by Sid's recollection. "Oh aye, I saw the bastard lobbing trees like darts, very impressive, like. Thing is, darts ain't a power game, Rick. Darts is about accuracy and nerve. Got two 137 getouts, last year, ya know?"

"The only other things are his teeth and nails," continued Ricard, unfazed. "His teeth are the size of your little finger, and his nails are like a tiger's claw. If they catch you, you will die."

Sid didn't look impressed by this latest revelation. "Scratching and biting! Is he a fooking girl, or summat? I don't like that, Rick, I don't like that at all. But, if it's fighting dirty, then Sid Tillsley is willing to go there. I don't like it, but I ain't having some fairy trying to pull me hair." He noted that Ricard looked at his shiny bald head. "Me chest hair…or worse. He'll regret it if he plays silly buggers."

Ricard looked at the benefit cheat, the obese, drunk and disorderly, drain on human society. He still didn't deserve what he was about to go through.

A knock at the door preceded the beautiful Lucia entering the room.

"Mr. Tillsley, your helicopter awaits."

"Howay the lads!"

25

Sid sat in the helicopter, as excited as a schoolboy when his mum's new edition of the Littlewoods's catalogue came through the post with an extra large lingerie section inside. He had always wanted to have a go in a helicopter, especially as he had never flown because of his fear of air stewards. A helicopter was different, it was man-travel. None of them orange-hued feminine fellas putting your seat belt on and…He went into a cold sweat and grabbed the armrests of his chair.

"You OK?" The voice came through his ear-guards from the vampire opposite.

"Aye, mon," he said through his own intercom. "Never been in a chopper before, that's all," he lied about the reason for his unrest.

The vampire looked away in disgust at what he thought was Sid's fear of flying. The big-mans anxiety began to pass. *Relax, mon! Just think about the chopper, just about the chopper and not the air steward's chopper…Hang on.*

Sid was sick into a paper bag.

* * * *

Ricard paced the room where he had conversed with Sid Tillsley. Two thousand years ago, there was no way to control Sparle. The world was not as populated then and communications were painfully slow. Sparle, of that generation, could destroy a village before any warnings were sounded.

This time was different. With modern technology, metallurgy and hydraulics it was possible to contain him. Ricard had known that it would be virtually impossible to change Sparle from what he was, but he had to try. Trying was the reason that so many would die tonight, and was the reason that the Agreement might fall. Two thousand years ago the world was a different place and things could be disguised in legend, in myth, in religion. This was a different age…and Sid Tillsley was on his way.

* * * *

The helicopter soared high above London and raced towards the north of England. After a quick shot of whisky, the taste of cigar-smoke flavoured vomit had subsided and Sid really began to enjoy the ride. There were some beautiful views of the towns and cities that were lit up below. It was almost a shame that he had to give someone a pasting at the end of it. He had no choice though, and this might make him a rich man. However, if they had proof of his benefit fraud then all that money would be flushed down the shitter.

Sid tried to focus on the fight, but it was difficult with the fantastic views and the constant whirring of the helicopter blades. He didn't know where they were going to have the scrap, and apparently, they had to find the fella first. What was his name? *Spam?* He was hoping that they'd scrap in a nice barn or something. He didn't like fighting in fields as there was too much mud, which made it easy to lose the footing if the right was being thrown with a little extra venom.

That Rick did go on. He was a funny fella, but the best vampire Sid had met so far. All the rest had been nonces that were due a slap, although the African fella was a good lad; he was gagging to see that lass's jubblies. But with Rick, he got the impression that he didn't want the fight to kick off, for some reason or other. It didn't matter now. He had no choice but to get on with the job.

"Eh' up, fella, when we getting in?"

The pilot spoke through the intercom. "Half an hour. We have helicopters scanning in the area. It won't be long. Prepare yourself."

* * * *

Ricard walked briskly though the corridors of the Lamian Consilium. He was about to stand trial for his crimes against the Agreement. He would be tried by the elders, and then he would be sentenced immediately. This would be the first trial without Michael being present since the setting of the Agreement and he was curious to see how the elders would function without the Bloodlord. Who would replace the irreplaceable? Would they rule as a council rather than a dictatorship now there was no obvious figure of power?

Ricard reached the doors of the courtroom, grand double doors similar to that of the Great Hall. He pushed them open into a room surprisingly larger. Several pillars were required to hold up the ceiling, high above the stone floor of the gigantic oval hall. At the far end, were twelve identical ornate chairs set in a semi-circle surrounding a dais where the accused would be interrogated.

Eleven seats were occupied with eleven vampires dressed in blood red robes. There was no way the Consilium, or the elders, could possibly foresee Michael Vitrago's death, but Ricard did. Michael held the Agreement above everything, except his own ego. It was ironic that Michael had accused Ricard of the same mistake. There was no way that he could resist the chance of fighting the most dangerous creature ever born. He would have broken the world to face Sparle in battle. It haunted him that a human, who killed his father, defeated the last beast in battle.

Ricard stood on the dais. He was older and wiser than every elder present. He knew it and they knew it, but it would do him no favours in this trial. Ricard cast his gaze over the elders. There was a mix of friends and enemies in this group, but all would judge him fairly. It wouldn't be difficult. Bwogi sat in the centre of the elders, but Ricard doubted he was striving for leadership. He was a good vampire with a righteous heart. Ricard didn't like putting him through this nightmarish situation.

To his left was Helga Khan, a Bavarian he had known for fifteen hundred years. She was not much younger than he, and was as striking as when he first met her. Grey now flecked the long dark curls that fell gracefully over her slender shoulders. Her eyes irradiated with the intensity they did all those centuries ago. They had worked together many times over the years, but their mutual fondness for one another wouldn't hold any sway this day.

These were the only elders that Ricard could call friends. Henrik Sleant sat before him. He was an animal, but not in the same sense as Michael was. He would have killed and tortured thousands of humans though his many years. Being an accomplished diplomat, in Ricard's eyes, was no excuse for being an abomination.

Who these people were was not important. He was the one standing trial.

* * * *

The helicopter's warning signals screamed at the pilot as he lost control of the vehicle. The helicopter regained stability and the reason for the loss of control became apparent. A fireball rose hundreds of feet above the moors, and the thermals had sent the chopper spiralling up into the atmosphere. "Looks like we have him," said the pilot.

"Never mind him!" shouted Sid. "Watch how you're flying this bastard. I nearly shat myself then. I canna fight with messed up kecks!"

The pilot ignored the cries from his unhygienic passenger. "This is Prophecy. We have Sid Tillsley with us. Can you update us on the ground status?"

"Glad to have you on board, Prophecy. This is Alpha Gunship. Apologies for the explosion back there. We suspected Sparle was in—" The transmission cut off abruptly.

The pilot of the Prophecy attempted to regain contact. "Come in Alpha…Come in Alpha!"

"This is Alpha. We have contact, repeat, we have contact. We will patch you the bearings."

The vampire opposite Sid lifted the visor of his helmet. "This is it human. You had better be all that you are hyped to be, because if you're not…you are a dead man." said Viralli. "I watched that thing kill twenty powerful vampires whilst taking constant machine gun fire. What can you do?"

"Death from above!" Sid loudly broke wind to the tune of "The Ride of the Valkyires."

Viralli couldn't help but be impressed.

* * * *

Bwogi began the proceedings for the trial. "Ricard, you are accused of jeopardising the Agreement. How do you plead?"

"Guilty," said Ricard in a far away voice.

Bwogi nodded. "It is understood that you have harboured 'Sparle,' as you have named him, the vampire born from the Firmamentum. You attempted to educate him to our ways and tame him, is this correct?"

"Yes."

The council members looked at each other, passing different comments with their eyes. It was Helga who spoke first. "Ricard, what did you hope to achieve by this? Did you really think you could succeed where you failed, two millennia ago?"

"I had no choice, Helga…I couldn't forsake my son."

It took a moment for the enormity of Ricard's confession to sink in.

"Sparle…is your son?" asked Rita Ilcladis, an Italian vampire. "What about the first Sparle? What other lies have you told us through the years?"

"The first Sparle was also my son. I have told two lies in my life, both to protect my blood. The first time I harboured Sparle, the death of thousands on my conscience was my punishment. This time, I realise that the consequences of my actions could change the world."

"For someone so 'wise,' surely you would have realised this when you set the beast free?" asked Miguel Samorro. He had always considered Ricard a weak entity because of his love of the human race. If it weren't for the severity of the situation then he would have enjoyed the predicament entirely.

"I have no excuses. My love for my son stayed my hand, and I am willing to accept any punishment that is deemed fit."

"It is lucky that the Bellator has been found. He is the only hope we have left," said Helga.

Ricard shook his head. "Tillsley…He is not what you think."

* * * *

The gunship Prophecy raced over the Moors with Alpha following closely behind. The monster took refuge in an abandoned mine and left to hunt as soon as the sun set. Since his initial escape, Sparle drove west, killing everything in his path. Houses were evacuated wherever possible, and excuses made to the locals. The vampires plotted his path by using herds of cattle and sheep. They placed them at strategic points for him to feed. However, all attempts to trap the creature were unsuccessful.

"Are you ready, human?" asked Viralli. "We are pushing him towards an old quarry where we will be able to hold him for a short while."

Sid threw a series of quick jabs and stretched his arms across his chest a couple of times. "Aye, mon, that should do it. I don't want to peak too soon, like."

Viralli didn't comment. What was the point? He was not someone who believed in prophecies. Sparle was real, and putting this human up against him would be like setting a child on a bear. Prophecy or not, Sid Tillsley was going to die.

* * * *

"What do you mean, Ricard?" demanded Helga.

Ricard played with his hands, anxiously. It was the first sign of nerves that he had shown since the trial began. He had betrayed Sparle once, and that is why his son endured the chase over the moors. Could he let him down utterly?

"Ricard! Explain yourself!" shouted Harold Stewart. He wasn't old enough to have seen the Firmamentum of two-thousand years ago.

This was it. This was the time where he made his decision. His son would die whether he faced the Bellator or not. Modern artillery was too powerful and had the ability to atomise his son if the need be. It would be at great risk to the Agreement, but not compared to Sparle running through the streets of Leeds. It wouldn't be right for things to come to that. If Tillsley fought Sparle he didn't know what would happen.

"I am so sorry, son."

* * * *

"We can't touch down within half a kilometre of the target," said the pilot. "Sparle bought down a helicopter that was flying low. We cannot risk losing another bird."

"Affirmative," replied Viralli. "From the drop off point, we will proceed to the quarry, on foot."

"Eh?" For the first time, Sid was shaken about the mission. "What the fook you talking about? How far is half a kilothingy, when it's at home?"

"Five hundred metres."

"Eh? Stop playing silly buggers, mon. How far is it in real distances, in yards?"

"Five-hundred and fifty."

The Great Right Hope

Sid put his head into his hands…five hundred and fifty yards! He would be absolutely spent after five hundred and fifty yards. This was going to be harder work than he bargained for.

Viralli assumed that the magnitude of the situation had finally hit home. "It will all be over, soon."

Sid looked up from his hands. "You're having a fooking laugh, ain't ya? Five hundred and fifty yards! It's gonna take me a good half an hour to make that sort of ground. No one said anything about me walking anywhere." He finished the sentence with a look that said: You come out with some smart-arsed remark you little fooker, and you ain't going to be eating solid food for a week!

"But five-hundred and—"

"You come out with some smart-arsed remark you little fooker, and you ain't going to be eating solid food for a week!" Sid turned his look into words.

The pilot announcing that they were beginning their descent breached the awkward silence. Viralli said nothing after the threat. His mission was to accompany the human to the battle, and as ever, he would follow his orders to the letter.

Viralli looked the big human up and down. Gabriel's bane. Viralli had fought beside Gabriel many times and had seen him defeat overwhelming odds on numerous occasions. Viralli would love to have a go at Sid Tillsley, this champion of humans. He was a wreck of a man, but his eyes, though small and beady, showed something else. Where the eyes of the vampires were bright, beautiful, and piercing, Tillsley's were like dark pools, which reflected no light. He was unlike anything that Viralli had seen before.

The landing was a smooth one. Viralli jumped out of the helicopter whilst Sid climbed awkwardly, but safely, out. The helicopter took to the air to avoid attack. The two began the long arduous walk to the quarry. The quarry was still active, which made it a perfect place to fire missiles as they could be made to look like an explosives accident. The gate to the quarry could be seen in the distance.

"What is your strategy of attack?"

"Eh?" said Sid, screwing his face up at the stupid question.

Viralli raised his eyes to the heavens. The man was an idiot. "What I mean is: how do you intend to fight your opponent?"

"I knew what you fooking meant, you smart-arsed bastard, but it's a stupid question, ain't it?" Sid didn't like this vampire, in fact, he had met loads of vampires now and he didn't like many of them, all *them lot*, and wankers.

Viralli didn't like humans, especially Sid Tillsley. "How is that a stupid question? You are about to fight a ferocious animal, you need to have some sort of plan!"

"Well, I don't do that running around bollocks. I'll wait until it comes to me. Then I'll fooking smack the bastard!" Sid was getting wound up. It was probably for the best as it was getting him fired up for the scrap ahead, and more importantly, it was taking his mind off the walk. They were nearly there.

"And then what?"

"What do you mean, 'then what?'" asked Sid.

"What are you going to do after you've 'smacked it?'" Viralli did the two finger dittos when he said "smacked it." It took all of Sid's willpower not to head butt the prick.

"I guess I'll leave him to you bunch of wankers. You seem keen to get your hands on the lad," said Sid through gritted teeth.

"What I mean is: what are you going to do after you've smacked it," Viralli survived the evening by refraining from the two-finger dittos, "and your blow does not even shake the creature? What are you going to do when it is ripping your head off with its bare hands?"

Sid gave his right fist a trademark kiss. "Don't you worry about Sid." Sid turned from his newly found enemy to see how far he had to walk. He was pleasantly surprised to see the gate only a hundred yards away.

A deafening roar filled the air. It echoed round the quarry walls, making the sound even more terrifying, if that was possible.

"Noisy bastard!"

"He awaits you, human." Viralli was torn between wanting an end to Sparle and wanting to see him rip this ridiculous human being to shreds.

The two approached the gate and looked into the quarry- it was a bloodbath. A large herd of cows had been left in the quarry to keep Sparle occupied whilst Sid got into position. Carcasses, ripped to pieces, were thrown the length and breadth of the vast pit. The moonlight glistened over the rocks and it would have been beautiful if it wasn't blood that was causing the effect. It was impossible that Sparle had fed on all the cattle, but he had killed all for the fun of it.

Sparle stood in the centre of the quarry. His naked body gleamed in the moonlight. In each hand, he gripped the decapitated head of a cow. He held each aloft to the moon and bathed in the glory of murder. He roared again and threw the heads of the cattle out of the quarry.

Viralli marvelled at the strength and savagery of the beast. He had seen him in combat and seen how he had destroyed Michael, even after sustaining horrific injuries. Missiles couldn't stop him- there was no way that this idiot could achieve anything.

"That bastards got no kecks on!" cried Sid. "I ain't fighting him if his tackle is flying all over the place!"

"Ssshh," hissed Viralli. Sparle looked up and saw them silhouetted against the moon. He unleashed a challenging scream and bounded towards them.

"Too late."

* * * *

"Ricard, no one has challenged the Agreement with such severity before, so do not make the situation worse for yourself. It is imperative that you tell us everything that you know, and everything that you have done," Bwogi pleaded.

Ricard's attempt at holding his emotions at bay broke down completely. "Do you think that you can do anything to me that can come close to the pain I am suffering for betraying my son?" Tears filled his eyes.

"Your crime against the lamian race and the continuation of the species is even greater, Ricard!" shouted Miguel Somarro. The comment hit home. The fact that it came from a paedophilic animal gave more weight to his words. Ricard had allowed Sparle out into the world, but Miguel Somarro had killed and sexually abused thousands of children. Yet, their deaths meant nothing compared to the war that would rage across the planet if the Agreement were endangered. Ricard had known this all along and it took the words of the lowest life-form to make him truly understand.

"Tillsley…" Ricard gathered control of his emotions. Grieving could take place another day. It was time to do his duty. "Tillsley is not the Bellator."

His revelation was like a dagger to the heart of every vampire in the room.

"When Sparle was born I knew immediately what he was. My partner died during childbirth, and the similarities to the birth and the baby were mirrored two thousand years ago. Her relatives were distraught at the loss, and the baby was their link to their loved one. It is they that helped me raise Sparle. I couldn't have done it without their help.

"As soon as Sparle was born, I knew, from personal experience, that there would be a human born to oppose him. I had to find him, but not to kill him. I knew that, one day, I might need him. More importantly, if I found him then no one else would. If the Bellator were discovered then the hunt for my son would begin.

"Finding the human was not a difficult task. History suggested that he would be born in close proximity to his vampire brother. As soon as Sparle was born, I monitored medical records for all deaths during childbirth and there were only a few cases, making my job easy.

"I abducted the child, soon after. He was overdeveloped for a human baby and by three years old, he was as strong as a human adult. He was incredibly intelligent and a beautiful, wonderful child. I raised him as my own—Jacob. Jacob was what she wanted to call the child, but when I saw what came out of her womb…I could only give him one name.

"I built a home for Jacob underground. The home, if I am honest, could only be described as a prison. He grew until he reached six foot ten and three hundred pounds of muscle. I educated him in history, the arts and the sciences. I told him that there had been a nuclear war and fallout meant we couldn't breach the surface. I grew to love him as a son, but my need to tame my biological son outweighed my love for my adopted one.

"After Sparle's escape, I couldn't let Jacob out. I couldn't bear for them to fight, but I have now accepted that they were born onto this world to confront each other. I will give you the co-ordinates to his whereabouts, but I will have to come with you. I have to talk to him. That is all you need to know, right now. Call to the gunships on the moors and cancel Tillsley's futile attempts."

Bwogi pressed a part of his chair that doubled as an intercom. "Cancel Tillsley's mission. Arrange helicopters with the utmost haste."

None objected to the decisions made by the African vampire. All looked at Ricard with utter disdain, even the members who once considered him a friend.

Bwogi shook his head sombrely. "This is a grave day, Ricard, a grave day. Your trial will continue when we return, but first Sparle must be destroyed. If Jacob cannot complete the task then I am afraid that we will have no option but to use force that will be seen across the world. This could have been averted years ago if it wasn't for your deluded sense of love."

Helga nodded agreement. "You have let your own race down and you have let humankind down. How have you fallen so far from grace? Your punishment cannot come close to the magnitude of your crime."

"Helicopters are ready, sir," announced a voice from a hidden speaker.

The vampires rose as one and headed towards the chamber doors followed by the dejected figure of Ricard.

****

"Reet!" Sid rolled up his sleeves as Sparle charged up the quarry walls. This fella was in a real rush to get a bust lip. The monster scrambled up the walls, but was unable to climb the sheer rock face. He manically scrambled up the loose rock in desperation to taste human flesh. It realised that it couldn't reach its prey that way, and bellowed in frustrated anger.

"TAKE YA TIME, YA DAFT BASTARD! I AIN'T GOING ANYWHERE!"

Sparle looked around desperately for a way to reach his future victim in the quickest time possible. Sheer walls meant that he had to go backwards to go forwards. Another cry of frustration echoed around the quarry as he sprinted to a shallower gradient.

"Twat!" yelled Sid. He had never been good at witty patter, or damaging putdowns before a big fight.

Viralli had backed off to a safe distance from the imminent battle. Once Sparle had finished with Sid, it wouldn't take it long to find him.

"Viralli. Come in," buzzed the radio.

"Viralli here."

"This is base. Tillsley is not the Bellator. Tillsley is not the Bellator. The gunships will keep him in the quarry. Retreat and you will be picked up. Your orders are: take Tillsley back to Middlesbrough, await contact with Reece Chambers. Kill both. Clear?"

"Affirmative, sir!"

Viralli sprinted back to the gate where Sid stood shouting obscenities at the monster below. "Tillsley! Tillsley!" he yelled when he was within earshot.

"Eh?" Sid turned round to see Viralli. "Get out of here, mon! I need to get ready for this bastard!"

"Change of plan, Tillsley. We do not need you anymore. We are going to hit it with heavy artillery instead. There is another coming to fight him, the real Bellator."

On cue, a missile rattled into Sparle's path, which sent him tumbling back down the quarry. He roared at the burning pain of the explosion, and at being denied his prey a second time.

"Come on, before we are hit in the crossfire."

"I ain't walking all the way back. I'd prefer to take me chance down here, like. Them lads of yours seem like pretty good shots, and if he gets away then I'll put the nut on him."

Viralli really couldn't believe that a human like Sid Tillsley existed. If he wasn't the one born to fight the vampire monster, what was he? It was best for all that he was finally taken out of the equation. "Come, Sid, orders are orders and you will be paid in full."

"That's all you had to say, mon. It's your round when we get to boozer."

The helicopter swept in low, picked up the soldier and Middlesbrough's hero and left the explosions and gunfire behind. Sid's ordeal with Sparle was over, and he could finally get back to what he was best at: drinking. He may even get last orders in.

26

Sid strolled down to the Miner's. It was a beautiful day and Sid was glad to put all of last night's events behind him. Luckily for him, he had managed to reach the Miner's whilst they were still serving. Kevin Ackroyd was having a cheeky lock-in. Lock-ins weren't the common event they once were, not since the Rozzers were called in to break up Ladies' Night.

The lock-in had been an eventful one too. Them vampire bastards had played silly buggers before Sid could get his first beer down him. Four of them had taken him back home, and, at first, they seemed a decent bunch of lads. That twat Viroply, or whatever the bastard's name was, had ordered them to give him a lift all the way back to the Miner's, but as soon as they got to the pub they started getting a bit rowdy. They all came in for beer, which Sid could understand as it had been a long night, and the beer in the Miner's was really special. Even vampires would want to kick back, now and then, with some of the finest beer ever to be served in the great town of Middlesbrough.

Some of the lads were in, Arthur and Rathbone were there, but when Rich came out of the bogs, it all kicked off. It was the roughest punch up Sid had been in for a while because the vampires were tooled up to their balls, which is out of order in a pub brawl. Truth be told, if that Rich weren't there then it could have all got a bit hairy.

"Sid!" shouted the familiar voice of Brian Garforth.

Sid turned to greet his drinking partner of many magical drunken years. "Eh' up, mate, you going for a pint?"

"Aye, mon, I am. Called in sick after hearing about what happened last night. Thought I'd get the rundown whilst enjoying an all-dayer of monumental proportions," said the supportive chum.

"Lovely stuff, mate. I'm gonna be getting meself proper pissed up tonight. I've been away from me Bolton Bitter for far too long. Yesterday, I only got to have a warm up pint and a chaser, all day, like!"

Brian shook his head. "Poor bastard. You must be gagging for an ale. I hear you had a bit of trouble last night, like. I'm sorry I weren't around."

Sid dismissed his apology with the wave of his deathdealer. "Don't be silly, Brian. Though I will tell ya, it was some nasty shit that went on, and Kev even shut up shop afterwards. Normally, he only shuts if the pub is wrecked."

"Jesus Christ, what happened?"

Sid regaled the story of Sparle; the vampire's bollocks about the million pound fight; his benefit immunity, and his escort to the Miner's.

"Anyway, the lads said that they were coming in for an ale, and more importantly that they would be buying."

Brian nodded. "They haven't been too bad actually, Sid. There was that nutter at the woods, but I guess I didn't actually know if he was gonna kick off or not, and I did stick me nut on him first, like. Them lads who we met in the Miner's weren't too bad and they put their hands in their pockets, which you canna argue with. I preferred them to that wanker, Rich."

"Aye, you're reet, Brian, but them two were playing silly buggers, if you remember? One of 'em wasn't our sort of man, was he, Brian?" Sid went as near to the subject of homosexuality as he could without blacking out. "Anyway, these four lads were alreet, but when we got to the Miner's they started playing up."

"What do you mean?" quizzed the scholar.

"Well, they went in and they asked what was the 'house speciality?' or some bollocks like that. I ordered five pints of the 'good stuff' and then Rich came out of the pissers."

Brian sighed. "Aye, he hasn't stopped hanging around here. I haven't had a pint without that twat asking where you are every five minutes. Pain in the arse that is gonna get a kicking…"

Sid interrupted him in mid rant. "Actually, mon, he proved himself to be a good lad, last night. You see, I turned to look who came out of the bogs 'cos I was gagging for a dump, and it was Rich, and the fooker was drawing a gun out of his coat jacket!"

"A gun?" asked Brian surprised. "We haven't had a gun in the Miner's for nearly three months!"

Sid nodded. "I know, mon. We were saying a little while back, how it was going soft. So I see Rich drawing his gun, which takes me by surprise, like. I knew he's always had a bit of a problem with these vampire fellas, but a gun is pretty extreme. He was quick as fook with it too. I dodged sideways with my back to the bar so I could see what both sides were doing. Out of the corner of me eye, I noticed that the vampire chap nearest to me had drawn his gun, too. I gave him a shoulder barge to put him off, and he went flying into his mate. Don't know me own strength sometimes, as ya know. Turns out all the bastards were drawing fooking pieces!

"The two I knocked over lost hold of their guns and Rich shot one of the other fellas in the head. It was a brilliant shot, Roger Moore style, in the centre of the forehead! I managed to land one on his mate, and he went into that dust stuff they go into when I connect with a good'n. I managed to land another on the one I shoulder barged and he exploded, whilst Arthur was doing his stuff on the other fella."

Brian was peeved. "Ah, I haven't seen Arthur do his stuff for ages! Has he lost any speed?"

Sid smirked. "What do you think, mon? He was lightning! You know I think all that martial arts crap is a load of bollocks, but seeing him in action…" Sid whistled. "I reckon he was quicker than his Daddy was. He worked the guy over pretty badly, but the guy had an iron jaw and he couldna put him down. Guess it was 'cos he was one of the undead or summat. Anyway, he spun him round with a big spinny kick and I caught him with a right when he was on the way. Seriously, mon, before he exploded his head was facing the wrong way!"

"That's a proper good punch up, that. I can't believe that Kev called last orders, tho'."

"He didn't. He was well fired up after seeing the scrap. He was that pumped that he called: 'Drinks on the house!' But he got real spooked 'cos the fella who got shot in the head got up."

"You're joking…" Brian was wide-eyed. "Drinks on the house?"

"I know, I know," said Sid solemnly. "Nearly the greatest day in the history of the world, but the lad getting up with a hole in his head scared the shit out of Kev. I knocked the bastard into dust, but it was too late by then."

"Well, let's try and put that behind us," said Brian cheerfully. "Because now we drink. Now we drink until we can't stand up."

Sid smiled. "All the lads are meeting us too: Arthur, Rathbone, and Rich will be there for the first round."

Brian rolled his eyes. "Not Rich. He's a proper twat."

"I know, I know. But last night if he hadn't put a bullet in that vampire, then things may have been different, and he said he's buying."

"Well if he's buying…Howay the lads!"

Sid and Brian arrived outside the locked doors of the Miner's Arms. It was two minutes to eleven and not quite the magical time. Arthur Peasley, Peter Rathbone, Reece Chambers and the lads were outside waiting, gagging for that first magnificent taste of well-kept ale.

A small cheer erupted from the group at the arrival of Brian and the triumphant Sid. Guns, although not a rare occurrence in the Miner's Arms, were an unwanted part of an evening's entertainment. None of the regulars carried such weapons and it was just non-locals who weren't man enough to fight with just a pool cue.

"Good morning!" greeted Sid who was pleased to have so many drinking buddies on the fine glorious summer's day. He took a deep breath of fresh air. "It's good to be alive, isn't it, lads?"

His question was not answered because the doors of the Miner's were unlocked and the lads crashed through. Sid passed the magical boundary and took out a large Cuban cigar, one of several he had stolen from the vampire's underground headquarters. He lit it with a gargantuan puff of smoke. "Good to be alive," he coughed.

The lads rushed to their television corner and warmed up the box. Kevin had picked one up at a bargain price at a charity shop. He had even managed to short-change the stupid bitch behind the counter. They were all disappointed that Tarrant wasn't there to entertain them, but that Judy lass on ITV had a pair of jugs that were, quite frankly, magnificent. Sid and his motley crew took seats near the gents as this was going to be a day when a lot of urination would take place. The river Tees would be running high tonight.

"Landlord, four pints of your finest ale please?" requested Reece Chambers grandly. His request was greeted with a salute from the Landlord and a cheer from the vampire fighting heroes. "And a mineral water."

"Bummer," said the fickle Garforth.

After Kev had poured all the beers, to not a millilitre over the legal requirement set by trading standards, he took them and the mineral water to the thirsty patrons. Glasses were chinked and mutual praise was shared. All four took that first draught of ale, the most satisfying feeling that a man can experience.

"To Sid Tillsley!" cried Reece, "Vampire hunter!"

In a millisecond, he was drenched in ale.

"Hang about, lad," said Sid as he wiped the beer from his chin. "We've been through this before, and I told you that I ain't getting involved in that shit. Them lads last night will be the last of it. They came at us heavy and got what they deserved. The other lot will know that if they play silly buggers then they'll get summat similar." He waved the right atom bomb.

Reece rubbed the beer out of his eyes. "OK, I won't mention it again, but you will see a repeat of last night, I can guarantee you. You will have to join me eventually to survive. From what you told me last night, you are not the prophesied one, which means that you are something different entirely. The vampires and the humans will be here for you after they kill the monster. However, you're right. Let's not talk about that now. Four more beers, lads?"

With the prospect of first class premium ale, Sid completely forgot about the disagreement. Reece made his way to the bar.

"Sid, he's fooking minted, mon! You should have a go at this vampire fighting thingy," said Brian.

"Hell yeah!" said Arthur. "I'd love to have another go at one of them son of a bitches, man. You have got to show me how to make them explode like that, Sid. You had 'em all shook up, baby!"

"I'll show ya, Arthur."

"Shut it, Rathbone."

"It ain't about the money, lads. I'm comfortable in what I do, and the odd job here and there suits me perfectly. A few quid from the government gets me through the week. If I'm honest, though, I came close to vampire hunting last night when them guns came out. Don't like that shit. Sleeping on it, it's nice having an easy life…a beer in your local, a cigarette from the corners of the globe, good friends and the love of a good woman."

"The love of a good woman?" said all three in the same surprised tone. Reece returned with the beers.

"Aye, lads. The love of a good woman." Sid smiled lovingly at the thought of her.

"Who is it then?" asked Brian hurriedly, unable to curb his curiosity.

Sid gave Brian a funny look. "Who do you think? Sheila Fishman, of course."

The three lads and Reece tried to hide their grimaces. It was similar to trying a beloved relative's cooking, and finding it disgusting.

"But, Sid," began his best friend, "I thought that you only grabbed her tit once, and she hasn't spoken to you since?"

"You are right there, Brain. I did indeed grab her titty, and beautiful it was. It was a proper romantic moment as well, I can tell ya. That was the last time that I spoke to her, but she's gagging for it, like. She's been following me about in some big transit van for the past few days."

Everyone knew what it meant, apart from Sid. These were mates, proper mates that would tell the truth no matter what. Brian, the bestest of his best friends, was the man who had to break his heart.

"Mate, sounds to me like she's trying to catch you working. There's no reason a lass like that is gonna be driving a transit van, is there? There's got to be video cameras and shite in the back. Why would she follow you around in a transit if she likes ya, mon?"

Sid considered it. "Because she's shy? Anyway, she told me that she was gonna lose her job 'cos she stapled that fella's family jewels to his leg."

"Sorry, mate, she was probably lying. She's trying to catch ya working." Brian offered a sympathetic pat on the back.

Arthur also offered a pat on the back. "Hey, man, women are always fucking with men's heads." He considered this and realised that it had never ever happened to him. "…I should imagine. Rich, get the beers in, this man needs cheering up."

Reece didn't appreciate getting ordered to buy beers, but this was not a time to upset Sid. He looked quite dejected and Reece needed to stay close to him as he was convinced that he would turn against the vampire eventually. Once you were involved in their world, you couldn't help but become exposed to the pain, misery and death that they brought. He bit his tongue and went to the bar. Hunting was turning into an expensive venture.

"Fooking 'ell, how could I be such an idiot? I canna believe that Sheila would try and get me done. We connected!"

"You grabbed her tit."

"Exactly!"

"Listen," said the smartest man on the Smithson Estate, "I've got an idea. Sid, I know how you work, mate, and you need closure on this. You need to know for certain that she is trying to get you done for benefit fraud otherwise, in your heart of hearts, you won't believe it."

Sid nodded as he finished his ale and puffed away at his Cuban cigar. Oxygen levels in the Miner's Arms were now dangerously low. "You're reet, mon."

Brian went through the plan with the lads. "Rick can drive us in his motor 'cos I've had one too many to take out the Capri, or rather…I will have done."

The designated driver returned with another round of ales. He was really beginning to grudge having to buy Peter Rathbone beer as no one else liked him. "There you go, lads. That's the last round you're getting for a while."

"That's ok," said Brian, "'cos after the next one, we've got ourselves a mission and we're gonna need that nice big black motor of yours."

"Fuck."

* * * *

Sid walked down the road trying to keep to a straight line. The "just one more round" had turned into a few rounds that had turned into a session. He was definitely on the drunker side of sober. He looked around. Nothing. There had been a lot more walking in this plan of Brian's than he had been hoping for. Still, if it proved that his lass was on the straight and narrow, and not trying to send him to prison, then it would all be worth it.

Brian hadn't disappointed with his plan. It was very simple thanks to some of the gadgets Rich had up his sleeve. When Sid suspected that Sheila was following him, he was to simply press a button on a little gizmo and they would track him down. He was then to walk down Bishop Close, the nearest cul-de-sac to the docks, and then Rich and the lads would block the road and give Sid the opportunity to confront his lass. It was a win-win situation. He either obtained closure on the relationship, or had a guaranteed jump in the back of the transit.

He had been walking a full five minutes and he reminisced over the last few days. He had hardly touched a drop and the amount of exercise performed would impress Roger Black. He could have sworn that his jeans were slightly less constrictive than they were a week ago. The next few days of solid drinking would put an end to all that.

Was that a glimmer of white?

He risked a look over his shoulder and was disappointed to see the white van of Abdul the Butcher. He was not up to all this secret agent stuff. Roger Moore was the only man who could really pull off a caper like this. Him and Boon were the only Southerners that Sid liked. If truth be told, Roger Moore was his favourite and he would have loved to emulate his hero, but knew he didn't have the chic to pull it off…not that he'd called it "chic."

Sid took another look over his shoulder with only a hint of a stagger. His heart beat quicker and his loins stirred. "Shit." It was her. It was Sheila.

He played it cool, trying to be the man he admired so much. It was only a minute's walk to Bishop's Close and he was convinced that he could make it, although he was starting to need a piss.

He pressed the gizmo.

* * * *

"The gizmo's going, Rich!" yelled Brian who had "shotgunned" the front seat. Arthur Peasley and Peter Rathbone sat cramped in the back.

Reece sighed. "I can see that, thank you, Brian. He is a minute away. As soon as he gets to the top of the road then we'll rendezvous."

"What kind of car is this, man?" asked Arthur.

"What do you think it is?" asked Reece hoping to impress the man who looked a million dollars.

"Escort?" ventured Rathbone.

Reece really didn't like Peter Rathbone, the horrible greasy little bastard. He thought about the grease that the horrible little bastard was getting on his upholstery and his hatred grew.

"I don't know what it is, man, but it sure as Hell ain't a Cadillac."

Reece smiled. "You can't recognise it because there is no other car like this in the world."

"That's bollocks," stated Rathbone. "Me brother's got one just like it."

Reece started thinking about opening a whole magazine into the fucker's heart, but luckily Brian spotted Sid heading into Bishop Close, on the gizmo.

"Let's roll," said Arthur in a way that only he could.

They rolled.

* * * *

As Sid reached the end of the cul-de-sac, he notices Sheila had taken the bait and she had parked up, unsuccessfully trying to blend in with the background. This was a great plan of Brian's and all that was needed now was—lovely stuff!—Reece blocked her in and the mission was accomplished. Sid turned on his heel and walked purposefully and confidently towards the van. Women love a man who is confident.

"Fuck! He's on to us!" yelled Sheila hysterically. The last week of surveillance work and finding out that vampires were real, had taken a toll on her already fragile nervous system. Gunnar was finding it more and more difficult not to rip her throat out, and as soon as Tillsley was behind bars...

"Relax, if you keep jumping around like that then he'll know for definite that something is up!" he snarled through the intercom.

"We're boxed in!" she screamed.

Gunnar felt his eardrum knit back together. He looked through the cameras mounted on the rear of the van to see a black car parked across the road. It used the other parked vehicles to block any chance of escape. The car was unlike any that he had ever seen before. Only Reece Chambers could be so pretentious to drive such a thing.

"Calm down," he said coolly through the intercom although he knew that his words would be in vain. "Confrontation was inevitable. Wait to see what Tillsley does."

Confrontation was not in Gunnar's plan. He was armed with many blades if it did happen, but gutting Tillsley wouldn't be a complete victory, although it would still be pleasurable. "I have a plan so, no matter what, don't panic." He was really looking forward to killing this woman.

Sid approached the van. He could see that Sheila was wearing a snazzy baggy jumper and its appeal tickled his loins. She looked gorgeous. Perhaps she had a mattress in the back of the van, anticipating the event.

He walked up to the window and gave it a seductive *rappety-tap-tap*! She ignored him—must be playing hard to get. She eventually wound the window down.

"Eh' up, pet, I see you've been following me around, like?" he said with a wry smile.

"Yes."

"Why have you been following the young Sidney Tillsley?"

"Yes."

"Eh? You're a bit pale there, love, you alreet?" he said, concerned. Sid was not just a physical being.

"Yes."

"Anyway, what you got in the back of this van?" he asked suspiciously. She wasn't acting like she was up for some action. He looked through the window at the van's interior. It looked like a normal white Ford Transit, except it had no pornography or McDonald's wrappers scattered inside it.

"Nothing."

Sid looked at the outside of the van. "Morgan o' Co…you don't work for…What's tha…?"

Sid's heart dropped like a stone. The love of his life! How could she do this to him? He could see that the O's were not stickers, and he could see they were the shiny coverings of lenses.

"Pet, I am pretty upset now and I think you should close your ears after you have answered this question. Who is in the back of the van?"

Sheila didn't answer Sid's question. She didn't even have the dignity to look him in the eye.

"Very well," he said calmly. He walked to the back of the van where the most indecent and offensive torrent of abuse was directed at whoever sat in the back. After thirty seconds, the abuse was accompanied by right and left hooks. Each punch came closer to smashing a hole through the metalwork.

"Jesus, woman!" Gunnar screamed through the intercom. "If he gets through that door, the sunlight will kill me! Distract his attention otherwise I will perish along with the chances of you catching him! You need me!"

Sheila considered it for a moment. She had grown to hate Gunnar Ivansey as much as he hated her, and the idea of him being burnt to a crisp by the sunlight appealed to her immensely. But he was right. He was a useful ally in the prosecution of Sid Tillsley.

"Sid, stop!" she yelled from the window. A second later he stopped, only because he was out of breath, not because of her plea.

"Wh-wh-who?" he managed in between breaths and pointed into the van.

She didn't reply, as she didn't know what to say or do. Gunnar would have to think of something.

"I'm gonna open them doors up, Sheila. You better tell me who's in there 'cos I'm gonna find out either way, you understand?"

Gunnar buzzed through, "I have a plan. Repeat after me."

"Sid," Sheila repeated the words that Gunnar spoke into her ear. "I can't show you who is in the back because the door is locked. There is a computer in there and it is controlled back at base. I can take you there, if you want." she said monotonously.

Under normal circumstances Sid would have ran for the hills, but he was hurting bad. He wanted to meet the man who had used this underhand tactic of using the woman he groped to put him behind bars. He walked round to the passenger side and got in the van.

"Reet, let's go meet the bastard."

Reece watched as Sid got into the van of his own accord. He decided to follow the van at a safe distance to see where she took him, and backed off to let the van out when it turned to leave the cul-de-sac.

Sheila drove past the docks into the industrial estates of Middlesbrough. Sheila had told Sid that they were based in a big underground warehouse where they launched all their surveillance work.

Sid was going to find the bloke responsible, stick the nut on him, and then go and get pissed. Sheila was not saying a word. Sid had definitely found closure on the matter. Bitch. Could he ever trust a woman again? Maybe it was worth meeting up with his ex, the prison guard. Although by all accounts she had let herself go since he had dumped her.

"This is it," she announced. It was a warehouse just like any other on the estate, except to Sid this was a place of evil. She kept the engine running and got out of the car to open the warehouse doors. It revealed a vast space that contained absolutely nothing except a ramp down to a lower level. She got back in the van, drove into the warehouse and headed for the ramp.

Sid didn't know what to say to Sheila. He wanted to ask her why she had done this to him. He just couldn't put anything into words. It was going to take at least eight more pints to get over this romantic entanglement. If she let him grope the other tit then he would have the grace to forgive her, but he was just too upset to ask.

The lower level of the warehouse was pitch black. As the van's wheels touched the tarmac of the lower level, lights came on and a heavy shutter came down, blocking the entrance. The warehouse was the same size as the one above ground and empty—completely empty.

"What the fook? I thought you said—"

"I lied," said Sheila, speaking for the first time since they had left the cul-de-sac.

"Fooking hell, woman, you really are a miserable ol' cow!"

"You bastard!" she screamed. She had kept calm on the exterior, but now the internal rage flowing inside her exploded. She threw herself at Sid in a frenzy of teeth, claws and greasy hair.

But Sid was a wily old fellow. He was quick out of the way of raging women, and quick to put the nut on raging men. He was out of the door before she could cause any damage.

"Tillsley!" boomed a voice from a speaker on the van. "It was I who turned your woman against you. It was I who tried to put you in prison for benefit fraud. It is I, Gunnar Ivansey!" Gunnar leapt out of the rear doors of the van to confront Middlesbrough's hero. Sid turned.

"Who the fook are you?"

Gunnar was caught unaware. "We had a fight. About a week ago? You killed a spectator in the crowd? No?" Gunnar realised he would have to be less cryptic. "I am a vampire trying to arrest you for benefit fraud."

"You!" Sid's face flushed with rage. "You're a vampire wanker, ain't ya? You bunch of bastards! That's it, I've had it up to here with you fookers. You are all going down, all of ya!"

"No, human. It is you who will die this evening," said Gunnar coolly and confidently. "I am not here to kill you in an honourable way. I am here to end your life." He picked a slim throwing knife from his coat and hurled it at Sid, who only just managed to get out of the way. He was really regretting those extra six pints.

"You sissy bastard…needing a blade. Fight me like a man!" challenged the old-school brawler.

Gunnar laughed. "I just want you dead, Tillsley. I toyed with ideas of a duel, and then I toyed with the idea of seeing you behind bars. Now, all I want, all I care for, is to see you dead this day."

A second knife was thrown and didn't find its intended target, but it did find Sid's left hand. He couldn't get out of the way in time and could only get his hand up. The knife skewered through the middle of his palm, spilling blood over the concrete floor.

"Bastards!" he yelled as if he had just hit his thumb with a hammer. He knew he didn't have a chance if he stayed where he was and, in an attempt at a sprint, ran for the cover of the van. A knife stuck out of his right buttock as he made it to safety. "Bastards!" he said as he pulled the weapons out of his arse.

Gunnar laughed heartily once more. He was enjoying causing Tillsley pain, and he felt alive again. "Sid, come out so I can turn you into a living pin cushion!"

"Fook off, ya twat!" came Sid's witty rejoinder.

"The prophesied one, scared of a little blade. Who would have thought it?"

"I ain't him, mon. They've found some other fella." The two circled the van at the same time. Gunnar took his time, enjoying the build up to the murder while Sid tried not to get any more knives in the arse whilst contemplating a plan. Sheila just sat in the van thinking about her cats. The whole ordeal had sent her over the edge.

"So you are not the one? So what are you, then? Shame we will never find out."

"Fook off, ya twat!"

Sid had to think of a plan and fast. He was so desperate for a piss now that it was starting to hurt, and this bloke really was a wanker.

"Think, Sid, think." he whispered to himself. "What would Roger Moore do? Dress up as a crocodile and float across the river with no one suspecting a thing. That ain't gonna work."

"I can sense the panic in you, Tillsley. Your heart gives you away!"

Sid ignored him and continued to think of a plan. *You're not Roger Moore, you are Sid Tillsley. What would I do?…Run up to him and put the nut on him.*

Sid ran round the van and charged into Gunnar Ivansey. Sid took a knife in the leg, but it didn't matter as the momentum carried him through and he got hold of the bastard. He landed three consecutive head butts on the nose of the knife-wielding vampire.

Gunnar's nose was obliterated and he only just managed to keep consciousness. Staring into the eyes of Sid Tillsley, he saw his fate coming. The right hand that had taken his brother would soon take him. He could see it drawing back slowly and he knew that his time was up.

"You are the biggest twat out of all them bastards," said Sid angrily. He had never fought anyone who threw knives before, and he didn't like it. "I have been saving up the old Tillsley Special for a while, and it looks like you're the poor sod who's earned it."

"Do your worst, human." Gunnar managed the words with difficulty as blood filled the back of his throat. "I am not afraid of death."

"No?" said Sid unconvinced. "But you may be afraid of this."

And with that he launched it—the Tillsley Special. Gunnar saw the right hand that was pulled back clench even harder so that the knuckles whitened. Then, as if in slow motion, it started its arc of destruction towards his jaw, for the deathblow.

However, something changed, and the punch altered trajectory. Sid seemed to drop in stature, as if he was falling. Had Sheila struck him on the back of the head and saved him? As Tillsley fell, Gunnar could see that Sheila was still in the van. What had happened? Why did he fall?

The answer presented itself.

Tillsley's secret weapon. Its target was not the jaw. The pain that Gunnar expected didn't come. He stumbled backwards as he was released from the Sid's mighty grasp. Tillsley stood with a hand on one knee and the right hand still clenched, shaking with tension.

"I'll give it to ya. You're the toughest man I've ever fought. I've landed that punch twice before and both times the unlucky fella ended up in a coma."

Gunnar looked confused. "What are you talking about?" The punch had been aimed at his genitals and he could have sworn he only felt initial contact. Gunnar felt for any dama—Hang on...

He grabbed desperately.

"What the fuck?"

Gunnar pulled the belt off his trousers and pulled the waistband out. A fine dust drifted up into the atmosphere.

"H...h...how?" he stuttered, before turning and running for the door at the end of the warehouse. Sid heard the door lock after the vampire wanker was through it.

Sid looked at his right. It had brought him justice once more. He walked to the transit van where Sheila Fishman sat bolt upright with her eyes wide open, unblinking. The lights were on but no one was home.

"Sheila, it's a shame that it ended like this. I hope you leave me alone from now on, pet." He was a gentleman to the last. She wouldn't bother him again and Sid hoped that her days of taking away the benefit-cheque of the unfortunate, like himself, were over.

He limped over to the ramp and found a switch to raise the shutter. When he was out of the warehouse, Reece and the lads were waiting anxiously for him.

He needed to drown his sorrows. It was only three o'clock, which meant he had the rest of the day to drink in the Miner's and hopefully get some plasters on these bloody knife wounds.

Reece and Brian rushed out of the car to help him. They weren't expecting him to be covered in blood. They had no idea that Gunnar Ivansey could be behind Sheila's evil scheme.

"What the fook happened to you, mon?" asked Brian.

"I'm reet, mon. She was working with a vampire twat. I'll tell you all about it over a beer."

"Is he still down there?" asked Reece.

"Nah, but don't worry, he won't be bothering anyone for a while. Come on, Rich, it's your round."

27

Sid looked into his sixth pint of Bolton Bitter. For the lads, the session so far had been a very forlorn affair because Sid was moping like a broken-hearted teenager. The more beer he supped the worst he got. He took out another blood stained Cuban cigar and attempted to light it, but it was too wet and Sid's mood worsened.

"So let me get this straight…it came clean off?" asked Brian incredulously.

Sid gave a depressed nod. He put down his empty glass and looked at Reece with puppy dog eyes. At least the beer was free.

"Tell me about the fight once more and I will buy you another beer," replied the out of pocket vampire-hunter.

Sid rolled his eyes as he was not enjoying the talking. "When I saw that the van was full of surveillance shite, the red mist came down, and when he jumped out of the back of van…" Sid shook his right hand, re-living the anger. The others drew back slightly just in case he re-enacted the punch and they got in the way.

"He made the mistake of throwing bleeding knives at me and that was it. He was gonna get The Special. It was weird, like. It normally feels like I've popped two balloons." All patrons in earshot winced. The "special" had been seen in the Miner's before, and three people who witnessed it had fainted.

"What did it feel like this time?" asked Reece.

"Well, it's hard to explain really. It's a bit like when I hit them in the jaw and they disappear. I know I've hit 'em, but I don't get much feedback through the ol' right. Anyway, when he pulled his kecks out to have a look, he went white as a sheet and a shitload of dust blew out. He legged it after that. I reckon summat exploded, like."

"No-one wants to lose the use of their old-fella," announced Brian, "but you shouldn't mess with a Northern-man's benefit-cheque."

"Gunnar Ivansey will be back," Reece warned. "He will not rest until you are dead. You have killed his best friend, you have taken away his honour, and now you have taken away his genitalia." The hunter smiled. "You can understand why you won't be on his Christmas card list this year."

"But he didn't send me one last year," replied Sid.

Reece decided not to make any more jokes.

"Anyway, the wanker tried to get me done for benefit fraud, and he used the woman I love to do it." He looked tragically at his empty beer glass.

Reece shook his head and went to the bar.

* * * *

Ricard stood in the elevator heading deep underground. Bwogi, Viralli, and two other warrior vampires, armed to the teeth in case the Bellator needed a calming influence, accompanied him. Ricard was dreading this moment. It would be nearly as difficult as turning his son in to Michael Vitrago. It wouldn't be an easy task telling his adopted son that he had lied to him his whole life. This was a day when all of his misdeeds were punished.

The elevator reached its destination and the large doors opened to reveal a corridor of concrete, twenty feet long. At the end of the corridor stood the double doors that were the gateway to Jacob's home; Jacob, the man who would end the battle that was raging across the North Yorkshire Moors.

"What does he say when you leave him?" asked Bwogi. "How do you account for your absence?"

"He trusts me completely. I tell him that I need my own space, and my own time to meditate. He meditates himself and understands the benefits. However, this is the longest I have ever left him. He cannot escape because the gates are secured from the outside. Nevertheless, even if he could run, he wouldn't. He trusts me absolutely and you have no idea how hard the next few moments will be."

Bwogi didn't respond. Although he would judge him to the full extent of the lamian law, Ricard was still his friend and he hated seeing his discomfort.

Ricard opened the door that would lead them to Jacob.

* * * *

"So what are you planning to do with yourself? You can't hang round here forever, can you?" asked Brian in a tone that said that Reece should "four-letter expletive" off.

Reece gave him a patronising smile and Brian Garforth's hatred for Reece was reciprocated. "Nice of you to take an interest in my affairs. I have to know when the beast has been dealt with. I have to know it is dead. I would dearly love to see the human answer to the monster, the Bellator, but there is no way that I could risk it. After that, my plans depend on the activities of our large friend over there," he pointed to Sid who was limping back from the toilets.

"You alright there, man?" asked Arthur.

"Dunno, like. I'm still bleeding a bit, even with the plasters. I'm not sure if the blood in the pan was from me leg, or if it's a new batch of piles…Just my fooking luck."

"You need to get those wounds stitched up, Sid. Do you want me to take you to the hospital, or I can perform the task myself." offered Reece.

Sid scowled and shook his head. "No way, mon. I ain't doing anything until I am completely and utterly shitfaced! Then, all I am gonna do is pass out and possibly spew me ring."

The three lads around the table raised their glasses. There weren't many things grander to drink to.

"You were saying that your plans depended on our Sid, Rich. What did you mean by that?" asked Brian in an attempt to get him into trouble with the broken-hearted Sid. The big man wasn't listening, though. He was too busy concentrating on drinking, and it was definitely starting to go to his head.

"Glad you should ask, Brian," said Reece sarcastically. "With the emergence of the Bellator, it has raised the question that was asked all them weeks ago: What is Sid?"

"I'm broken-hearted, mon!" he said and went to the bar for the comfort of every depressed man's favourite depressant—beer.

"Sid is completely unique. There is no other human or vampire in history who has had the power to recreate the effect of sunlight in a punch. The vampires will be back, the humans will be back, and I have to protect him. He will have to join me eventually. I will not let him down."

Sid arrived back with beers for all except Reece. Sid begrudged paying money for bottled water, and the fancy bastard had enough money.

"I was just saying, Sid, you are different to any other—"

He was interrupted by Sid flapping his hands and jeering.

"Not now! I've told you once, and now, I've told you twice. This is a day of mourning so just leave it out!" He downed half his pint to show he meant business. "Why do all them bastards want to pick on me? There are millions of bastards committing far worse benefit fraud. Why do they want to get me? The bastards."

"Hey, man, don't think about it," said Arthur. "Let's just have a laugh and a joke and forget about benefit investigators, vampires and women and…" He spotted two beautiful women at the bar who he hadn't yet given his seed to. "Be back in a minute." And then he went over to take care of business.

"He's right, Sid. Forget about it all and just enjoy the evening." soothed Brian. "I'll get the beers in."

Sid looked at Peter Rathbone for some words of confidence. Peter Rathbone drank his beer in silence. He didn't like this moping around for he was a man of gloating and a man who bettered the deeds of others. Miserable bastards can take a running jump as far as he was concerned, but if that Reece kept buying him ales then he was not going to complain in a hurry.

"Nice T-shirt," said Rathbone.

Sid looked down at his white tiger…it was a good T-shirt.

"There you go, mate." Brian laid down a pint of fine ale and a large glass of very cheap whisky. "Get that down ya. It'll put hairs on your chest."

"Cheers, mate, you're a diamond." The whisky was washed down with half a pint of bitter. "I can't believe that I'm a single man, again. I can't believe that she did it to me, lads. Poor old Sid, a born romantic, shot down in a moment of madness by his beloved."

Brian decided that it was time to calm him down. "Whoa, fella. You only grabbed her tit once, and she didn't want you to."

Sid dismissed it with a wave of his giant hand. "There was electricity in that titty and it screamed at me to grope it. Its mate was jealous 'cos it wanted a grabbin' too. Sheila didn't know it, but her titties did."

Arthur came back with another round of beers. "Sid, see those chicks over there?" He nodded at the two who he had chatted up.

"Aye, what about 'em? They gonna try and get me done for claiming a little bit more than I'm entitled to?" he said miserably.

"No man, don't be stupid. I've arranged us a double date for tomorrow night and you're guaranteed some action!" The beautiful man had promised it to both of the beauties tonight if one of them did the deed with his moping mate.

Sid waved his palm again. "Naaarrrggh, all bitches, mon! All prick-teasing bitches! They all hate Sid, and Sid has nothing but love to give in return!" A look of realisation came over the drunken being of love. "It was that bastard that put them thoughts in her head. It was that vampire bastard that turned my Sheila against me."

Reece saw his opportunity and took it. "It's what the vampires do, Sid. They manipulate people and will do anything to take your benefit from you."

The smartest man in Middlesbrough saw Reece's intent. "He's talking crap! Bloody 'ell, Sid, they've been trying to catch you for years! It has nothing to do with vampires. It's them benefit bastards who you should blame!"

"But Sheila only came onto the scene once you had killed one of them, Sid. They have used her against you," said Reece.

"Fooking bastards, mon! Get me another pint! Rathbone, you tight-arsed bastard, get the beers in!" He took out his last Cuban cigar which, like the last, was soaked in blood. Sheer force of will (and possibly the increased alcohol in his blood stream) had the cigar smouldering instantaneously.

"You'll forget it all in the morning. Just have a few more beers and the world will be reet again." Brian could sense the mood darkening around Sid like a storm clouding the earth beneath it. "Come on, snap out of it."

"I gave them bastards a chance, Brian. I admit, I killed a few of 'em, but they were either accidental, or they were trying to kill me, or they were trying to cop a feel. I tells ya, they've got it fooking coming to 'em. The bastards!" His face reddened in what was either anger, or a heart attack. "I am getting to the stage where I ain't gonna take anymore."

It was anger.

Peter Rathbone returned with the beers and no one thanked him. He wanted to tell everyone about the time the benefit office tried to catch him working. He wanted to tell them that they used satellite surveillance and benefit officers dressed as hookers who he had steamy encounters with, but he didn't bother. He was getting the impression that his drinking buddies didn't like him.

"What are you going to do, Sid? I haven't seen you this fired up since Michael Barrymore asked you to that pool party."

"I don't know, Arthur, but it's gonna be pretty fooking violent."

"Sid, mon," cautioned Brian. "What are you thinking? Even you can't fight all the buggers! If you go do something stupid now, then them bastards are gonna do everything they can to stop you claiming benefit. You won't be able to work again, or you won't be able to claim benefit. It will be the end of your career."

Reece struggled to contain his excitement. "Sid need not worry about finance. If he joins me then I will be able to back him financially for the rest of his life."

"Look, you!" Sid pointed threateningly at Reece although the booze had affected his depth perception, which meant he pointed past Reece to a man at the bar. The man ran out of the pub, never to return. "I've told you that I am not joining you, or any of them…*them*…I ain't into all that funny business that you get up to!" The memory of the erect penis in the car-park was still in his head somewhere, though heavily repressed.

Sid got up shakily and went to the bar to drink the lager that the scared patron left. "Sid is gonna go and sort all this out for Sid. Kev! Another round for me and me mates!" he yelled.

Kev obliged, he hadn't seen Sid this fired up since Will Young won *Pop Idle*. Sid paid and walked back to the table, spilling beer as he went.

"Cheers, man," thanked Arthur. "Maybe you should take it easy with the beers. There's an hour until closing time and you've had at least eighteen pints since we got back. I think that Kev is gonna do another stoppy-back to cheer you up."

"'Cos of her Arthur!" he slurred, "'cos of her and them bastards is why I'm drinking like this. Them vampire bastards drove me to it. They drove me to drink because they took away my girlfriend and they took away my fooking benefit! Bastards!" He downed the entire pint in a world record time for a man's nineteenth pint and then stumbled off to the toilet, swearing as he went.

"He's in a bad way," commented Arthur. "I haven't seen him this angry since he bumped into George Michael in that public toilet."

"That twat ain't helping." Brian snarled at Reece.

"You can blame me all you want, but the fact remains that he is right. Sid's life will no longer be the same as he is in their world now. I can help him, and in return, he can help us all. You've seen how they ruin lives. You've seen how they control what we do. Sid can help to regain the balance. He gives us the opportunity to fight back!"

"You mean your fight, your vendetta. I can see that you are using him for your own fooking personal war!" shouted Brian.

Sid returned from the toilets and from the state of his trousers, it was obvious that the urinal was not a target that he had successfully attacked. "What are you lot shouting about? You arguing about me?"

"Yes, Sid," said Brian, his honest and trustworthy friend through thick and thin. "This bastard is trying to get you to fight for him. He's trying to use you."

Sid stumbled into the table, picked up Brian's beer, and drained it.

"Everyone tries to use me. Sheila, my love, she used me. She tantalised me with her titty and then she used me!" He was close to tears with the memory of his one true love. He slammed the empty glass down on the table.

"No more! I am gonna do summat about it. I'm gonna tell them bastards what I really think and I am going to give them bastards a slap, as well."

"Have a drink and sleep on it. Decide tomorrow. Tomorrow's another day," said Arthur in a vain attempt to calm the big man's aggression.

"No!" he shouted and stood up in a way that suggested action was afoot. He grabbed the last remaining pint on the table to make it number twenty-one. "I'm off lads, off to avenge my honour and to avenge my benefit cheque!" He ended his mighty speech and made his way, with difficulty, to the door.

"Where are you going?" asked Brian.

"You ain't going to stop me. I'm going to the Moors. If they want Sid, they're gonna get him!" A belch of monstrous proportions ruined his movie-star line. With the lingering smell of ale and smoky bacon crisps, the bald Angel of Vengeance left in search of justice.

Peter Rathbone, Reece Chambers, Arthur Peasley and Brian Garforth rolled out of the pub to see Sid Tillsley staggering down the road.

"Where are you goin', mon?" called out Brian.

"To my wagon of justice!" he called back without slowing his mighty, staggering stride.

"Not his Montego?" said Arthur with rightful worry in his voice.

"We canna let him get behind the wheel of that death-trap! That car has caused more accidents in the 'boro than lasses missing the pill! It is not a vehicle to take charge of after twenty pints of ale!"

"Where is he parked?" asked Reece.

Brian scratched his head. "Outside his house, I guess."

"Where does he live? We can jump in my car and cut him off," suggested the fast thinking Reece Chambers.

His question was greeted with silence. The three Smithson locals looked at each other and shrugged their shoulders.

"Dunno," they said in unison.

"What the fuck do you mean, you don't know? How long have you known each other?"

"Years. But what's that got to do with 'owt?" said Brian.

"Yeah!" agreed Arthur. "We don't do afternoon tea. We meet down the boozer!"

"Fucking idiots, the lot of you! I'll go grab my car and meet you here." He looked up the road for the striding figure of Sid. He didn't find the striding figure, but the urinating figure was clear for all to see. "He won't get very far."

* * * *

Bwogi, Ricard, Jacob and the guards ascended to the surface in the elevator. The man couldn't be classed as human. He was as fair and beautiful as Sparle was terrible and vile. His beauty surpassed most vampires and his body was Herculean in stature. It was rather ironic that they suspected Tillsley of being Sparle's negative. He was dressed in a tracksuit because it was the only type of clothing that would fit him. Blonde hair trailed gracefully across his face and bright green eyes seemed to fluoresce, just like a vampire's, from his perfect face. His face wouldn't be beautiful after the battle. Bwogi wondered what strength and speed Jacob possessed. Did he have the regenerative abilities of the vampire? Would he have the killer instinct he would need to survive the night?

Ricard had visibly aged over the last few days. Bwogi hadn't enjoyed witnessing Ricard tell his adopted son about the lie he had lived for twenty years:

"Hello, son."

Bwogi was impressed with Ricard's control. The ancient had been on a roller coaster ride for the last twenty years and it was all coming to a head. "This is Bwogi, he is from the surface. I have some explaining to do."

"Hello, sir." Jacob's voice was surprisingly light and musical for such a huge man. There was not a part of him that was not fair.

"Jacob, I have not been truthful with you over the years. There was no nuclear war, there is no contamination, and the earth is untainted."

Bwogi was surprised that Jacob didn't react to the revelation. He was regimental in his manner: a natural soldier.

Ricard continued the speech that he would have had rehearsed since he made the decision to imprison the child that would grow into the man. "You were bought up as a warrior because I told you that we would have to fight for survival when we breached the surface. I am sorry to tell you, that part of the tale is true.

"You are different to other men, and you are the only man alive who has a true purpose. Your purpose is to fight, my son. You were born onto this world to fight a monster, and tonight, you fulfil your destiny. Come."

Even though Ricard had been completely truthful with Jacob, he had left out the details of his abduction as a baby from his true biological father. Bwogi was shocked at how Jacob had taken the news and the only explanation could be his devout love for his father. That must have cut Ricard all the deeper. So many questions begged for answers, yet Jacob was surprisingly quiet. His manner seemed that of an excited schoolboy. His curiosity of the outside world outweighed the tension of the imposing fight.

The helicopter was waiting outside Ricard's house. Jacob was not enthralled by the sights that surrounded him as he had seen them in books and in film. He closed his eyes and for the first time since he was a baby he breathed fresh air.

"We must go, Jacob," called Ricard. Jacob followed without hesitation.

* * * *

Reece arrived back at break-neck speed. His impressive driving skills were wasted because Sid was still dispensing his thirteenth to sixteenth pint onto the pavement. The lads got in the car.

"GET OUT OF MY DOORWAY, TILLSLEY, YOU DIRTY BASTARD!" yelled Doreen Smith as she threw a plant-pot, with deadly accuracy, onto the head of the offending gentleman. Sid staggered backwards and fell onto a parked fiesta where he unwittingly covered it in the same offensive liquid.

"GET OFF MY FIESTA, TILLSLEY, YOU DIRTY BASTARD!" yelled Edith Smithers as she threw a frying pan, with deadly accuracy, onto the head of the offending gentleman. Sid clutched at his throbbing head as nature took its course and halted the flow.

"Vampire bastards," he mumbled, channelling his rage. He headed for his Montego Estate.

The concerned friends followed slowly behind him down the narrow roads of the Smithson Estate. Cars were parked both sides of the road and it meant that Reece Chamber's black car was holding up several angry motorists. This was of no concern. The important thing was stopping Sid Tillsley's death drive. Eventually Sid stopped and marvelled at the car that would carry him towards his goal of vengeance.

"There it is!" shouted Brian.

The men jumped out of the car, much to the annoyance of the cars that waited behind them. A wave from Arthur Peasley swooned the lady drivers into a state of calmness. Brian pointing towards Sid, and then sticking his finger up scared the male drivers into an equal state of calm.

"That can't be his house, can it?" asked Peter Rathbone, who was more interested in gossip than the safety of the country.

"Shut up, Rathbone," said Arthur, but he couldn't help notice the frilly, lace net curtains in the house that was adjacent to Sid's car. "Can't be, man."

"Sid!" yelled Brian, covering the thirty yards between them in Olympic time. "For God's sake, knock this on the head 'til morning!" He jumped in front of the driver's side of the Montego to stop Sid's entrance.

Sid, however, was going for the boot, as he required fuel for his long journey. "Don't try to stop me, Brian. Love has turned my hand. I am at war!" he said dramatically as he pulled out a rubber pipe and petrol can. He looked around for the biggest car and picked out a Jaguar, a very rare beast on the Smithson Estate. He didn't feel bad stealing the Jaguar's petrol as the owner was obviously not local.

"Sid, he is right," said Reece, agreeing with Brian for once. "You cannot fight this war tonight. Tonight is a day of mourning. You can begin your quest, tomorrow!"

"No!" yelled Sid as he used a screwdriver to gain access to the petrol tank. He threaded the hose into the pipe and sucked with all his might until free fuel was his.

"Did you drink some of that, man?" asked Arthur Peasley.

"How dare you!" said an outraged Sid. His petrol-flavoured burp gave him away. Once he was satisfied that he had enough petrol for the trip ahead, he rose awkwardly and made for the Montego in order to refuel the beast. Sid noticed that his best friend had taken a position in front of the driver's door. "Please, Brian, you more than any bugger should know that I need to do this."

Brian shook his head. "You cannot drive in this state. It ain't gonna happen, mate."

"You drive pissed all the time!"

"But not thirty odd miles, and not to fight vampires! You are gonna have to trust us on this one."

"Bah!" The wily old fox dodged Brian by getting in the Montego on the passenger side and climbing across. However, his attempt to climb across the car to the driver's side was not as graceful as his masterful dodge to gain entry. The gear-stick caused all sorts of bother with his piles. He screamed out at the interference with his behind. The vampires would pay for the intrusion.

He started the Montego and a huge billow of smoke disguised his escape, which would have been seamless if he hadn't driven into three parked cars. He left a trail of wing mirrors on the road. Even the most inept of trackers could follow his escape.

Sid was away, and he would have his vengeance, although he wasn't sure how he was going to achieve it. It most likely involved finding as many of the bastards as he could and then handing out slaps until he got bored, or tired.

He put the radio on. "Wind of Change" by the Scorpions rocked the Smithson Estate.

"Howay the lads!"

* * * *

The helicopter raced over the Moors to the quarry that Sparle, for the moment, called home. It was perfect for him as there were abandoned mines littering the surrounding area and he could travel underground at pace, avoiding the helicopters. The supply of cattle that had been transported to the quarry through the day would ensure that he had no want to run…yet.

Jacob was not given a helmet. The vampires didn't want him to hear the conversation about the approaching battle. Bwogi stared at him, unable to believe that he was actually human.

"Why does he not question anything you say? How can he accept that his own father has lied to him over the years? Is he less intelligent than normal humans?"

Ricard laughed. "He has an I.Q. over two-hundred and fifty. He is beyond a genius—he is perfect. As for his manner, he was brought up in love. He is kind, fair, and gentle but he is a natural born soldier. It is as if his personality was pre-programmed for the battle with my biological son."

"How can he be ready for what he is about to face? He will be ripped apart and all of this will be in vain. We will still need to use heavy bombing," despaired Bwogi.

Ricard looked at Jacob. He still found it hard to believe how the gentle giant could turn into a killing machine. "I first built a gym for him. He was lifting human world records before he had reached puberty. My wife's brother was responsible for the evolution of many of the modern martial arts; there was nothing he could teach Jacob that he didn't already know. His body mechanics are perfect in everything that he does. He can use any weapon to its deadliest potential. As I said, it was as if it was pre-programmed, like Sparle's sadism."

"That's all well and good, but he has had no opportunity to fight. Sparle has, and he has taken every chance. That will give him the advantage."

Ricard shook his head. "Jacob has experienced combat. He has fought, and killed three vampires…another crime that I am to account for."

Bwogi looked to the heavens. "There will be much more to discuss once this night is over."

Ricard nodded. "With his bare hands he simultaneously fought Peter Stalzburg, Carlos Ganchuri and Abdul Shahn. All carried bladed weapons."

"Three old and powerful lamia. How come this was not picked up in the Coalition's reports?" quizzed the elder.

"It happened recently. When Sparle became difficult to control, I had to test Jacob. If he passed the test then I could continue taking Sparle to the surface. If he didn't, then Sparle would never see the moonlight again. I asked them to my house in friendship, and I told them of the human I had captured. I asked them if they would like to try and kill him for sport, of course they accepted. They knew that something was afoot, but their love of combat outweighed everything else. He decapitated all in seconds."

"They will be missed," said Bwogi forlornly. "Tillsley kills with a single blow, a punch that seemed to mimic the effect of sunlight or decapitation. Can Jacob do this?"

"His punch does not have the same effect as Tillsley's, but if you ever saw Michael Vitrago punch in anger then you will realise the extent of his power. Jacob's punch is twice as devastating as anything Vitrago could muster. Tillsley needs to be captured, and we need to discover the secret to his power. He is a danger to us."

"ETA: twenty minutes," buzzed the pilot.

"I have already ordered his death. A group was sent yesterday to kill him and Reece Chambers. The next time the two are together, they will be assassinated. Tillsley is too dangerous, and anomalies are best nipped in the bud along with the legends that flourish from them."

* * * *

"HIGGGGHWAY TO HELL! Sid's on a HIGGGGHWAY TO HELL!" Sid sung out loud to the rock classic by AC/DC as he powered the Montego Estate through the balmy evening. He was making good time considering he had fallen asleep four times and ended up in three hedges.

Hot on his heels were Reece Chambers and the locals of the Miner's Arms. They kept their distance and hoped to God that nothing bad happened to Sid. They had watched him crash four times, and each time, they had hoped that the Montego would give up the ghost, but there was no halting the King of Cars.

"Surely that cow he went into should have done summat to the engine?" said Brian.

"He caught it with the corner of the car. The shock wouldn't have done the engine any damage. It would be more structural than anything. That cow, on the other hand, is gonna know about it when it takes its next shit, I can assure you," contributed Peter Rathbone.

"How do you know?"

"I watched a lot of *All Creatures Great and Small*, in the nineties," he replied.

"I mean about the car?"

"I'm a qualified mechanic."

"Oh."

Things were much more exciting in the Montego. Sid was nearing his destination and it was a race against time. Could he arrive before pints seventeen to nineteen won their battle for freedom? He wanted to show these bastards that he meant business, and having a trail of piss running down his leg wouldn't help matters. Up ahead in the distance, Sid could see a roadblock. A copper had his car parked across the middle of both lanes and his lights were flashing.

"Fook!"

If Sid turned back now then he would look suspicious. If he drove up to the copper then he would be arrested for being smashed in charge of a motor vehicle.

Turning back was the best option, but Sid had a point to prove and tonight the point would be proven. Sid pushed on, singing.

"OOOOOAAAA-hic!-OOOOOOAAAAA, LIVING DAYLIGHTS!"

* * * *

The helicopter touched down and the guards jumped out to check that it was safe for the elders to leave the vehicle. At the guard's signal, they alighted along with Jacob. They were dropped at the same point that Sid had been the night previous. Ricard faced his adopted son, the man that he would send to kill his own blood.

"Jacob, tonight you will fulfil your destiny. You are to face a monster. You are to face a living vampire. He is as powerful and as fast as you, but he can regenerate. Only decapitation will kill him. You may not survive the encounter, my son." Tears welled in Ricard's eyes. "Do you wish to take a weapon?"

"Is he armed?" asked Jacob without a tremble of his voice. Fear was something he was not born with. It was something that he had only read about.

"His teeth and nails are like daggers. He will not fight with honour for he is savage and wild. You will not face a noble enemy. It is a monster whose rage is uncontrollable," advised Bwogi.

"Then I will take my mace." Jacob took off his top to reveal bulging muscles. A shoulder holster held the mace that he spoke of. It was three feet long with a narrow, rectangular, metal head on the end. It was a simple weapon, yet undeniably brutal. He removed the holster and gave it to Ricard.

Jacob looked up at the full moonlight. "Its beauty was not done justice." He spun the huge mace around his hands as if it was a baton, and stopped it dead with perfect control. Closing his eyes, he breathed in the warm evening air. "I can sense him. Father, leave us."

* * * *

There was no going back now. Sid's days of benefit fraud were over and the bastard vampires had taken it from him. They had also taken his woman and were to blame for the unconscious copper with the broken jaw five miles back. He would have to get rid of the Montego after this as well.

The Great Right Hope

Them vampire bastards were really gonna get it.

The quarry was just ahead now. He had relieved himself by the roadside and he was ready for a scrap. The lads were following behind so if things were getting a bit hairy, they could help out. He had sobered up enough to ensure he wouldn't fall asleep again and the radio was pumping. This was the night he was going to avenge his lover.

The Montego's last ride hadn't let the big man down and he reached his destination in good time, whilst in comfort. It truly was God's Car. He burst dramatically through the gates of the quarry to see the helicopters circling above. "Bastards!" he yelled seeing the vampires in the air and out of the range of his mighty fists.

* * * *

Jacob walked slowly towards the quarry, his heart beating slowly. He didn't know how, yet he knew that it beat in harmony with his opponent whom he could sense beneath him. He looked up, once again, at the moonlight. It really was far more beautiful than he had imagined. Never again would he venture underground. He had too much to see and too much to do. Whatever he was about to face wouldn't take that away from him. He wouldn't allow anything to take his future from him, not even his father.

However, his lust for the world was not as strong as his want to meet what was travelling at a remarkable pace beneath his feet in the tunnels of the quarry below. He felt his want reciprocated by what his father had called a "monster." He was connected to this animal, and he could feel the bond that joined them. The closer their proximity, the more intense was his need to face it, to fight it, and to kill it.

He reached the edge of the quarry and looked at the carnage. Animal bones, blood and gore were scattered everywhere. He could recognise bits and pieces of cattle and sheep. He could also see parts of humans scattered amongst the animals. The sight of the slaughter didn't turn his stomach; it made him keener to see what had caused such destruction.

Jacob's destiny walked slowly out of the mineshaft, and into the moonlight. It held the bloody thighbone of a cow like a club. Both stared at each other, trying to sense the strengths and weaknesses of their enemy. Both knew they were linked together. Both knew why they were here. Both were finally complete.

Sparle held the bone aloft and unleashed a blood-curdling scream.

Jacob held his mace aloft and yelled a deep, powerful bellow that matched his enemy's in magnitude. Both ceased their cries simultaneously and then continued to stare at one another, in silence. And then...

Pain, the likes of which he had never experienced, overcame Jacob like a tidal-wave.

28

The gunship transporting Viralli, Bwogi, and Ricard circled the quarry at low level.

The vampires were dismayed at the sight of the maroon Montego Estate smashing into the Bellator.

They helplessly looked on as the car carried him towards the edge of the quarry. Jacob could do nothing. His feet were trapped under the car and momentum held him fast.

"That's Tillsley!" shouted Viralli.

"Tillsley?" screamed Bwogi. "I thought he was dead? Why is he not dead? Why is he attacking Jacob?"

"He should be dead, sir." Viralli picked up his binoculars. "Oh my God, he's asleep!"

Bwogi barked orders through to the pilot. "They are heading for the edge of the quarry! We must intercept!"

"Affirmative," called the pilot as he rushed across the moors in an attempt to catch the speeding car.

* * * *

"He's fooking hit someone!" cried Brian. "Ah, fook, he'll be in trouble with the Rozzers for sure!" The car in pursuit of the drunk driver had just witnessed Sid crash mercilessly into Jacob.

Reece floored his modified vehicle. "That can only be the Bellator. Look at him! He's still moving! Only someone superhuman could survive a car hitting them at that velocity."

"Ah, shite, and Sid's ran the bastard over."

Sid woke up and stared at Jacob, the man that everyone thought was he. None of this occurred to Sid because he had just woken up after a short, but devastating, drunken nap and he still wasn't firing on all cylinders. Things gradually fell into place.

"Shit the bed!" he yelled as he realised that the man he was staring at was taking the full brunt of another Sidney Tillsley and His Magical Montego Drink-Driving Mystery Tour. He slammed on the brakes, but it caused the car to skid on the quarry gravel and he lost what little control of the vehicle he had in the first place.

* * * *

"He's going to go over the edge of the quarry!" yelled Ricard.

"Pilot, we don't have much time!" Bwogi shouted.

"There is nothing we can do. It's a three hundred foot drop the other side. Our hope is gone. We must call in the air strike," said Viralli.

Ricard looked on. "There is still hope! He is the chosen one!"

* * * *

"They're done for!" said Reece Chambers solemnly.

All four watched the car as it skidded, ever closer, to the edge of the cliff. "SSSSSSSSIIIIIIIIIIIIDDDDDD…YAAA…BASSSTTTAARRRRDDDD!" screamed Brian Garforth, in Hollywood slow-motion style.

The car slipped and slid across the gravel causing all who looked on in terrified anticipation to hold their breath. Would the car stop in time? Would the Agreement still hold? Sid managed to pull the car around so that it was sliding sideways, passenger side first, towards the edge of the deep precipice. Still, Jacob couldn't pull himself free as his leg was terribly broken and mangled beneath the wrecked undercarriage of the Montego.

Sid watched the edge. He was still drunk enough so that he could see two quarry edges growing at an alarming rate. He could see from further down the quarry that it was going to be a long drop. If he was a more agile man, he would jump to safety, but he was far too drunk and far too fat to get his gut past the steering wheel of the bumpy ride. The bloke on his dashboard didn't look very happy either. It would take a few pints to sort this little mess out, or failing that, a big right hand and a runner.

The only thing left to do was to hope; hope that the Montego Estate could muster the will to stop in time, and that the mechanically perfect brakes would muster the strength to halt the car's progress towards certain death. Hope that he could drink for just one more night and that he could give some of them vampire bastards a slap as well.

He had nearly forgotten about them.

With the might of the gods the Montego slowed. With sheer will, gritty determination and immense luck it slowed.

* * * *

"It's stopped! It's stopped!" yelled Bwogi.

Viralli pumped his fist. "Pilot, get down there. We need to get a winch on that car, ASAP!"

Ricard looked to the heavens. The gods smiled on Jacob this day.

* * * *

"YEEEHHHAAAW!" was the ecstatic cry of Arthur Peasley as they watched the car precariously balance over the precipice.

"They still may need our help. Hold on!" Reece hoped that his brakes would be a little more efficient than that of the Montego's.

The car was indeed precariously balanced. The passenger side wheels hung over the sheer drop that would lead to the death of the driver and the unsuspecting passenger. The driver's side wheels sat firmly on the quarry gravel, anchored down by the weight of the hard-drinking, dangerous-driving Sid Tillsley. Jacob was wedged between the edge of the quarry and the car. His leg was trapped so there was no way that he could possibly climb free. Sid got out of the car.

He was bursting for a piss.

"NOOOOOO!" screamed everyone in unison who looked on at the loveable but idiotic drunk.

The car rocked dangerously. Its state of balance was a matter of milligrams. Jacob couldn't call out to Sid for the entire weight of the car rocked rhythmically on his smashed leg. He couldn't call out because it caused too much pain to allow anything to leave his lungs but laborious breath.

"AAAAAAARRRRRRGGGHHHH!"

It was not a scream of anguish…but the scream of relief as Sid's last few pints went home to Mother Earth.

Reece's car stopped, and the gunship touched down in close vicinity to Sid, who was zipping himself back to full dignity. All had their eyes on the car and Jacob, who rocked from safety to death and back again. Drink is a dangerous master and a master that can control a man through all emotions. No matter how angry, horny, sad, happy; when in drink, you will always be limited to her wants and needs. Even though Sid wanted to help the man under his car, drink had forced him to use the bathroom first. Drink also made Sid stumble backwards into the car.

As the vampires and humans left their respective vehicles they all gasped as one, as the car took an even bigger bank around its fulcrum, the leg of the Bellator and the car did not fall.

In the corner of Sid's eye appeared two monstrous breasts that were paraded on the front cover of his regular literary read, *Tits*. He knew the man under the car was in danger, but *Tits* was just under three quid and there were some sluts from Billingham in it this week.

"NOOOOOO!" the onlookers screamed in unison as the loveable but idiotic drunk reached through the window to pick up his periodical from the dashboard of his drinking chariot. He emerged triumphant with the one hundred and fifteen page "Boobanza of Bazookas," clutched in his fist.

One hundred and fifteen pages of normal breasts wouldn't have held the pure presence, or spiritual weight of this mighty tome, but removing a

"Boobanza of Bazookas" was enough to topple the car over the edge of the quarry taking with it the last hope of mankind.

"Shit..."

Seconds later a huge explosion erupted as the first-ever Montego and the unique human fell to their untimely demise, crashing into the rocks, hundreds of feet below.

"You *twat*!" Brian Garforth shouted over the whirring of helicopter rotors with the most apt statement that could possibly be made, considering the circumstances.

Ricard and Bwogi both stood with their heads down and spirits broken at what they had witnessed. Arthur Peasley and Peter Rathbone both looked everywhere except at Sid and the vampires, as they were a little embarrassed about the situation. Reece and Viralli's thoughts were similar; they needed to get out of the area quickly. Their fears were confirmed as Sparle's roar filled the air.

Sparle had watched as the only being that he had felt anything for, apart from pure hatred, was taken from him. Sparle remembered the challenge that was administered to him a few nights previous. He remembered the man who had challenged him and that man had just taken away his destiny. That man would experience all of Sparle's hatred and feel all of his pain.

"We have to go!" yelled Viralli and Reece simultaneously.

"We must call in a full air-strike immediately," said Bwogi.

"Oi!" bellowed Sid. "Now I didn't come all this way for n'owt, ya bastards! I've come to tell you a thing or two, and the first thing that I'm gonna tell ya is that I ain't fooking happy."

Reece pulled at Sid's shirt. "Sid, we must leave before the beast arrives."

"No, Rich! These bastards ain't going anywhere until I have it out with 'em. I didn't waste all me petrol, knock out a copper, and knock that fella down that hill for n'owt!" He turned to the vampires who were heading towards the helicopter and the safety of the skies.

"Oi!"

The vampires couldn't hear Sid over the helicopter rotors, not they would have stopped anyway. He would be dealt with later and they needed to get off the ground. They needed to get away and have this place turned into an even bigger crater than it already was.

Two giant hands came down on the shoulders of Bwogi and Ricard.

"I said fooking '*Oi*,' ya bastards!"

The elder vampires had no choice but to listen.

"Now, I am here to tell you fookers that I have had enough with all your silly bugger games! You bastards used the woman I loved to try and get me done for fooking benefit fraud and I can tell you lot that it ain't gonna happen anymore! Sid's here to hand out a few slaps, and I might as well start with yous twos!" He let go of them, ready to hand out a jab with each fist. They were spared the brutal strikes because Viralli bundled Sid over before he could unload.

"Fooking cheap shot!" said Sid, as he struggled to get back up.

Viralli stood to face his opponent. His previous wish of facing the Middlesbrough legend had finally come true.

The rotor blades gradually began to slow as both parties turned to face their fears to see the cockpit of the helicopter was opaque with blood and gore.

Sparle walked slowly around the helicopter, chewing on the remains of the head of the helicopter pilot. His demeanour had changed. He no longer rushed for the kill. The loss of Jacob had affected him and the balance had been disturbed. This was as close as Sparle's intelligence would take him to mourning. But he would relish killing whatever had taken his desire from him.

Viralli and Bwogi backed away slowly from the beast. Ricard held his ground, waiting for his son to approach. Only he could sense the difference in his bloodline's character.

"That's the bastard! That's the one that I put the nut on!" shouted Brian. "Have him, Sid!"

"Shut up," said Ricard. He needed to calm his son, but before he could try, Sparle charged past his father and straight for Sid.

Sid saw Sparle close in at lightning speed, but he was past caring. This bastard was going to pay! He wound up the right.

Sparle launched himself, intent on tearing Sid to shreds, and straight into the right hand launched by Sid Tillsley. The unstoppable force hit the immovable object. A thunderclap that hurt the ear rumbled over the hills and valleys of the North Yorkshire Moors.

Sid shook his right hand.

"Ouch!...Bastards!"

The men from Middlesbrough drew mighty gasps.

Sid's punch hadn't worked. Sparle stood, unaffected by the biggest haymaker in all of the 'boro. He looked at the humans and the vampires surrounding him and didn't know what to kill first. He decided to kill—

Sparle blew up.

Silence spread, ever so briefly, across the quarry.

"That fella was one tough cookie, man," commented Arthur Peasley as the dust that was once Sparle fell to earth.

"Reet!" Sid chaffed his hands together. "Now all you bastards are gonna get a slap 'cos I've had enough of it! I'm giving up me career in claiming benefit and I am giving up the love of me life who yous bastards used to get me. Sid Tillsley is going into vampire hunting and you twats are the first on me list!"

Bwogi stood shell-shocked, whilst Ricard fell to the ground. He was distraught at the loss of both of his sons whilst amazed at the astonishing feat he had just witnessed. Viralli was a soldier and had trained to battle through the most diverse of circumstances. He grabbed each of the elders by their collars and unceremoniously dragged them to the helicopter.

Sid's first official vampire hunt was under way, but unfortunately his pace meant that Viralli had started the helicopter and winged his way to safety by the time Sid had made ten paces. Reece, although ecstatic that he had a new weapon in the hunt for the vampire, realised that actually catching them was going to be a real problem.

Sid shook his fist at the helicopter as it made its way across the moonlit sky before turning to his friends.

"Come on, lads, I need another beer."

29

Lucia awoke with a start. She could still sense daylight, hundreds of feet above her underground chambers. Her stomach felt terrible, as it had done for the past week. She left her bedroom and ran to the bathroom where she was violently sick.

She washed her face and looked into the mirror. She knew what was wrong with her, but she didn't know how it had come to pass. She was pregnant; impregnated by that human being…a *mortal*.

Arthur Peasley.

With the emergence of Sid Tillsley, the world had been rocked to its very core. How will it react when it finds out something is alive inside her that was once thought physiologically impossible?

* * * *

Gunnar Ivansey looked in the mirror. He looked down at the place where his penis used to sit. All that remained were his lonely testicles. His penis hadn't even started growing back.

Tillsley was going to pay. He had taken his best friend, he had taken his dignity, and now he had taken away his pecker. None of this would be easy as the Coalition had issued a warrant for his arrest and placed a bounty on his head.

The last couple of months had been really, really shit.

* * * *

The helicopter landed at Ricard's home in the North Yorkshire Moors. Bwogi had contacted the Coalition after the enormity of the situation had finally sunk in. The clean-up team had been on standby since the operation began and were on the scene within the hour.

The night had left so many questions unanswered. With Sparle's death, the night had finally brought relief to the vampire nation and to the human councillors. However, the method of Sparle's demise had sent shock waves across the world.

A human, a normal human, was able to kill the most powerful vampire born of the Firmamentum with a single blow.

The three vampires sat in Ricard's house. Ricard said nothing. It was time to mourn the loss of his sons and accept the guilt for the decisions he made, and the deaths he had caused. Bwogi and Viralli, however, talked intensely about the night's events.

"He exploded…exploded! We hit that thing with air-to-ground missiles and it didn't stop running. A punch from a human cannot cause that. He must have a secret weapon and Chambers must be involved." Viralli was thankful that he hadn't faced Tillsley in unarmed combat. His ego was not as large as his lust for life.

Bwogi shook his head. "If it was a secret weapon then Chambers would have used it himself. His self-love wouldn't allow another to use that sort of power. We will reconvene with the Coalition, and set immediate actions. The vampire faces a new enemy."

Viralli nodded. "You are right. With the death of Michael and the discovery of Tillsley, a new age is upon us."

"There are difficult times ahead." Bwogi addressed Ricard and placed one hand on his leg. "We will be in touch, old friend. I will give you time to grieve." Bwogi got up to leave and Viralli followed. "Back to London. We have much to do."

* * * *

Sid sat at the bar of the Miner's Arms with a pint in his hand. It was the day after he had given Sparle a slap for playing silly buggers and his first official day as a vampire hunter. He was fully dressed in his vampire-hunting regalia: blue jeans, horrifically tight in all the wrong places, a white T-shirt emblazoned with a mighty tiger face and "The Collection" written underneath it, and his cool leather jacket.

He was taking the next few days off to get drunk. Rich didn't know this yet, but he would be here in a few minutes and he'd get the good news then. He was drinking with friends, whilst the lads were watching Tarrant in the corner of the pub. Kevin Ackroyd was excitedly sticking up a poster for the forthcoming Ladies' Night. Arthur Peasley was telling some local red-hot lasses about Sid's new line of work, and possibly setting them up for some action later. Sid's good friend, Brian Garforth, sat next to him. Peter Rathbone was there.

"New career, hey?" asked Middlesbrough's ladies' man.

"Aye, forty-six years old and here I am, a working man," he said. He was surprised, himself, at the outcome of all that had befallen in the last few weeks. "I'm taking the next few days off as I want to get into this thing gently. I don't want to risk me hand either as it still knacks a bit after hitting that lad the other night—had a good jaw on him, like."

"Sensible stuff, Sidney, sensible stuff." Brian was pleased that the new working life hadn't changed his good chum.

Arthur left the women he was speaking to and rejoined his drinking buddies. "Hey man, we are on with them chicks tonight. I told them you are a vampire-hunter and they proper digged it!"

Sid turned to look at the two absolute lovelies who uncharacteristically waved back and—smiled! Things were really looking up for Sid Tillsley and he raised his glass to the rest of his drinking companions.

"Howay the lads!"

About the Author

Full name: Mark James Jackman
Pen name (if I had the balls to use one): Brock Steel
Nicknames: Jacko, Jackhammer, Joe Brand, Jockey Wilson, Little H, Pale Turk, Statto, Fatman, Bitch, White Noise,
Birthdate: 24th April 1980
Height: 6'2"
Weight: 16 stone
Fighting weight: 26 stone
Marital status: Long-term girlfriend (I've got one)
Hometown: Great Yarmouth
Current home: Loughborough
Profession: Research scientist, author, hunk
Education: Master of Chemistry at York University.
Interests: Writing, sports, weightlifting, cinema, Xbox; gamertag: Sid Tillsley
Ambitions: To write a successful series of books, The Sid Tillsley Chronicles.
To make it on to Dragon's Den and obtain funding for my big idea... wait and see, people, it's bloody brilliant.
To own and drive a Ford Capri 2.8i.
To punch a shark.

Mark Jackman started life as a normal boy, just like any other. Things went wrong when he decided to take on the life of a scientist. The chemicals that he ingested, throughout his career, and the accidental stabbing of a syringe full of drugs into his chest altered his DNA to that of a mutant. Unfortunately for Mark, the mutation was not the cool kind where he developed superhuman strength, or the ability to get a woman to sleep with him. Oh no, his DNA was altered so that his imagination became warped beyond comprehension (it was either that, or his childhood trip to the Neverland Ranch). Mark decided to plough his (legally)chemical-enhanced head into the writings of a novel and The Great Right Hope was born. Now he looks to write more books and try to rid the demons from inside his mind and hopefully get out of chemistry... because he's crap at it, and syringes in the chest really, really hurt.

Coming Soon

Book Two of the Sid Tillsley Chronicles

Sid Tillsley is back!

And this time he's not claiming benefits.

Sid *is* a vampire-hunter, but even the coolest job in the world can't nab him any red-hot Middlesbrough maidens, and after numerous unsuccessful dogging attempts, Sid Tillsley decides to take on Internet dating. Still, there are more important things to worry about than his pecker. The Miner's Arms has been shut by the vampire-bastards and he is forced to drink sub-standard ale!

His trusted friends aren't doing much better: Arthur Peasley is now well and truly under the thumb after getting the vampire, Lucia, up the duff; Brian Garforth has discovered that vampires are allergic to his "manmilk" which means he has no chance of a cheeky jump with one in the ladies; and then there's Rathbone, who is still a greasy, horrible, little bastard.

And even though Sid defeated the most dangerous, vicious animal in history with a big right hook, the world is still in danger. With Michael Vitrago's death at the hands of Sparle, the floodgates are open for any vampire to enter Britain, the heart of the vampire nation. Plus Gunnar Ivansey is really, *really* angry that Sid punched his cock off and the build up of testosterone is wreaking havoc with his body. He cannot control his rage and it is only a matter of time before his actions are witnessed by the press and the Agreement is shattered.

Can the Coalition bring order to the vampire world?

Can Sid get a jump with the use of the Internet?

Can the Coalition risk using Sid as a weapon?

Can Sid find a decent pint of best bitter?

Look out for Book Two in 2010!

Other books by LL-Publications

A Human Reaction by Peter Ashley

Earth is gripped in a devastating, post-apocalyptic final war that only one nation will be allowed to survive…

In his quest to bring a proud nation to its knees, Commander John Henson fails to destroy a seemingly insignificant enemy base, and in doing so is captured.

Lost

Commander John Henson, wanted for his lethal ability to obliterate the enemy compound of Fort Millawa, missing in action along with fellow soldier and lover, Salome.

Found

"Prisoner X" awakes to find himself a captive of Captain Rachel Dahan. He must now face what he has inadvertently found—a new perspective on the destructive conflict that has torn civilisation apart, and its impact on his very soul.

A Human Reaction finds a man suddenly no longer dedicated to his old life but struggling for a place in a new world.

BARK! – The hilarious tale of little Tonto, the dog who has to save the world from an accidental alien invasion, with a little help from his owners and some of the craziest characters you'll ever read about!

"Tonto, a cross-eyed, ADHD affected little Weenie Dog with only one testicle is suddenly called upon to save the world from an alien invasion! Can he do the job? Well, perhaps, if a compulsively cursing alcoholic super-genius and his co-ed groupies combine forces with a cigar-chomping Italian from the pentagon and his air headed secretary. And of course they have to have help from Tonto's owners, who think politicians aren't much smarter than lizards.

Get ready for a wild and crazy ride with Tonto and his friends, the most amazing characters Darrell Bain has created in his eclectic writing career.

This is a science fiction novel so insane it only begins to make sense when it's discovered that the aliens had a part in Tonto's conception to begin with!"

Included in **BARK!** is the autobiography of Darrell's own quirky little dog, Tonto, the inspiration behind **BARK!**

PIT-STOP
"EPPIE 2009 WINNER, Best Horror"

By Ben Larken

The focus of excellent reviews and **EPIC's 2009 EPPIE award winner for Best Horror**, PIT-STOP is an eerie tale of purgatory.

When ten people find themselves inside the eerie diner, unable to get out or remember how they arrived, all they know is what their waitress, Holly, tells them: a bus is coming. It will take them the rest of the way to a destination of unspeakable horrors.

Led by highway patrolman, Officer Scott Alders, the group of strangers unite with a common goal—escape. Each of them holds dark secrets, but personal demons are no match for the wraithlike bus driver who arrives bearing the nametag RAMSEY.

Driving an oily black bus with ghostly headlights and exhaust that smells of brimstone, Ramsey wastes no time picking them off one by one. As their number dwindles and the terror mounts, Scott Alders realizes it will take more than a police-issued sidearm to stop the evil that tracks them. But is there enough power in their battered spirits to combat a crimson-eyed driver with a schedule to keep?

One thing is clear: you'll think twice before you make your next Pit-Stop.

Buy PIT-STOP from LL-Publications, Amazon, Barnes & Noble, and all great retailers!

ORDINARY WORLD

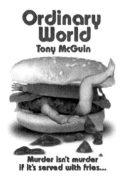

By Tony McGuin

"A modest proposal for the 21st century…"

This is the future.

Democratic institutions in the West have collapsed under the weight of the public's fear of terrorist attack. In uncertain times what people crave is the firm smack of fatherly dictatorship and the Church has stepped in to ensure a firm smack is exactly what the people get.

A world now betrothed to organized religion has nevertheless allowed big business to become even more debauched. GORDON A. GARGOYLE, owner of Recovered Unwanted Meat Deals, (RUM Deals) UK, a manufacturer of reprocessed meat run-off, has secured a concession to exploit the virgin market of producing burgers made from aborted babies. As far as Gargoyle is concerned, the only thing Jonathan Swift lacked was a slogan and a jingle.

TOHON SEHSA finds himself twisting in the financial clutches of his distressingly pregnant ex-girlfriend, MARY IRELAND. He risks prosecution under the Parental Irresponsibility Labour Law, (the PILL), and a life of indentured servitude to the Ministry of Sin unless he can persuade the intractable and obstinate hag to list their child as "an Act of God" on the birth certificate. Mary tells Tohon that doing this won't be easy … or cheap.

Tohon, with the help of his colourful friend BOATER, a man of complicated personal history, take jobs at the hellish foetus burger factory in an effort to pay her off.

Meanwhile, Gargoyle and Mary have quietly agreed to publicly sacrifice her new-born child, in a jaw-dropping marketing wheeze that might make the concept of Foetus Burgers seem marginally less shocking.

Can anybody stop this? Well, with the seemingly random interventions of our two desperate friends, a child-smitten romantic, the world's most feeble (and ginger) terrorist, a cancer-ridden devil dog, a curious little blue car and a mysteriously knowing Pub landlord, somebody may already have.

Mornings are hateful.

Afternoons are quite pleasant.

It's just another day in an Ordinary World.

No ordinary book, ORDINARY WORLD is a refined taste of exquisite satire which takes a stab at a near future world gone mad…

All are available from LL-Publications, Amazon, Barnes & Noble, and all good retailers!